Her Mother's Shadow

Diane Chamberlain

GETS TO THE **HEART** OF THE STORY

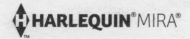

Published in Great Britain 2013
Harlequin MIRA, an imprint of Harlequin (UK) Limited,
Eton House, 18-24 Paradise Road,
Richmond, Surrey, TW9 1SR

© Diane Chamberlain 2004

ISBN 978 1 848 45233 6

58-0613

Also by Diane Chamberlain

Kiss River

Keeper of the Light

The Lost Daughter

The Bay at Midnight

Before the Storm

Secrets She Left Behind

The Lies We Told

Breaking the Silence

The Midwife's Confession

Brass Ring

The Shadow Wife

The Good Father

In memory of Nan Chamberlain Lopresti

HER MOTHER'S SHADOW

The girl in the kitchen
has her mother's eyes
the color of new jeans
and old sapphires.

She has her mother's hair,
scarlet and sienna.
Her mother's lips
and bird feather hands.

But…

When she turns her head
just so,
The indigo eyes are
flecked with amber.

The hair,
streaked with gold.
She is not her mother
at all.

—Paul Macelli

Prologue

Christmas 1990

THERE WAS CHEER IN THE HOUSE IN THE HEART of Manteo. From the outside, the large two-story frame building that served as the battered women's shelter was nondescript. There were no Christmas lights hanging from the eaves, not even a wreath on the door, as if the people who ran the house were afraid to draw attention to it, and Lacey supposed they were. Cruel men had put the women and children here, the sort of men she had no experience with and found hard to imagine. But she could see the fear in the women's faces and knew those men existed. More than that, she did not really want to know.

Although there was no sign of the season outside the house, inside was another story. Fresh garlands decorated the railing that led up to the bedrooms, and branches of holly were piled on top of the huge old mantel. The scent of pine was so strong it had seared Lacey's nostrils when she first walked inside. A huge tree stood in the corner of the living room, decorated with white lights and colored glass balls and topped by one of her mother's stained glass angels. The tree was alive, and Lacey did not need to ask if that was her mother's doing. Of course it was. Annie O'Neill always insisted on live trees. They had one at home, and Lacey knew both trees would be taken inland, away from the sandy soil of the Outer Banks, to be planted once the Christmas season was over.

She had not wanted to come to the battered women's shelter tonight. She'd wanted to stay home and listen to her new CDs and try on her new jeans with the rivets down the sides. She'd wanted to talk to her best friend, Jessica, on the phone to compare the gifts they'd received and decide what movie they would see the following afternoon. But her mother had insisted.

"You have so much," she'd said to Lacey the week before. "You will have already opened your presents and had Christmas dinner with me and Daddy and Clay. These women and their children will have nothing. *Less* than nothing. They'll have *fear* for Christmas, Lacey." Her mother spoke with great drama, the way she always did. "Their families will be torn apart," she continued. "Serving them dinner, singing a few carols with them—that's the least we can do, don't you think?"

Now, standing behind the long tables and dishing out Christmas dinner to the women and children, Lacey was glad she had come. At thirteen, she was certainly the youngest of the volunteers, and she felt proud of herself, proud of her kindness and generosity. She was just like her mother, whom all the other volunteers turned to for direction. Annie O'Neill was the most important person in the room. The tree in the corner probably wouldn't exist if it weren't for her mother. The buffet tables would probably hold half as much food. Maybe the entire shelter would not be here if it weren't for Annie. Lacey wasn't sure about that, but it seemed a real possibility to her.

She smiled at the women as she spooned green beans onto their plates. Six women, some of them still bearing the bruises that had sent them to the shelter, and more than a dozen children filed past the tables, balancing real china plates. Her mother had insisted that all the volunteers bring their good china for the women and their children to use. "They can't eat Christmas dinner off paper plates," Lacey had heard her say to one of the volunteers a few weeks before. At the time, she thought her mother was just being silly, but now she could see how much the beautiful plates and the cloth napkins and the glittery lights from the tree meant to these women. They needed every speck of beauty and warmth they could get right now.

Outside, a cold rain beat against the house's wood siding and thrummed steadily against the windows. It had rained all day, a cold and icy rain, and she and her mother had skidded a couple of times as they drove to Manteo.

"Remember how it snowed on Christmas last year?" her mother had said as Lacey complained about the rain. "Let's just pretend this is snow."

Her mother was an excellent pretender. She could make any situation fun by twisting it around so that it was better than it really was. Lacey was too old for that sort of pretending, but her mother could always charm her into just about anything. So, they'd talked about how beautiful the snow-covered scenery was as they passed it, how the housetops were thick with white batting and how the whitecaps on the ocean to their left were really an icy concoction of snow and froth. The dunes at Jockey's Ridge were barely visible through the rain, but her mother said they looked like smooth white mountains rising up from the earth. They pretended the rain falling against the windshield of the car was really snowflakes. Lacey had to put her fingers in her ears to block out the pounding of the rain in order to really imagine that, but then she could see it—the wipers collecting the snow and brushing it from the car. It fluttered past the passenger side window like puffs of white feathers.

"The first Noel..." Her mother began to sing now as she used salad tongs to set a small pile of greens on the plate of a young girl, and the other volunteers joined in the carol. It took Lacey a bashful minute or two to join in herself, and the beaten-looking women standing in line took even longer, but soon nearly everyone was singing. The smiles in the room, some of them self-conscious and timid, others overflowing with gratitude, caused Lacey to blink back tears that had filled her eyes so quickly she had not been prepared for them.

A tall woman smiled at Lacey from across the table, nudging her son to hold his plate out for some green beans. The woman was singing "Oh Christmas Tree" along with the group, but her doe-eyed son was silent, his lips pressed so tightly together that it looked as though no song would ever again emerge from between them. He was shorter than Lacey but probably around her age, and she smiled at him as she spooned the beans onto his plate. He looked at her briefly, but then his gaze was caught by something behind her, and his mouth suddenly popped open in surprise. Or maybe, she wondered later, in fear. His mother had stopped singing, too. She dropped the good china plate filled with turkey and mashed potatoes, and it clattered to the floor as she stared past the volunteers toward the door of the room. Lacey was afraid to turn around to see what had put such fear in the woman's eyes. One by one, though, the women and children and volunteers did turn, and the singing stopped. By the time Lacey could force herself to look toward the door, the only sound remaining in the room was the beating of the rain on the windows.

A huge man stood in the doorway of the room. He was not fat, but his bulk seemed to fill every inch of the doorway from jamb to jamb. His big green peacoat was sopping wet, his brown hair was plastered to his forehead and his eyes were glassy beneath heavy brows. Held between his two pale, thick, shivering hands was a gun.

No one screamed, as if the screams had already been beaten out of these women. But there were whispered gasps—"Oh, my God" and "Who is he?"—as the women quietly grabbed their children and pulled them beneath the tables or into the hallway. Lacey felt frozen in place, the spoonful of green beans suspended in the air. The tall woman who'd dropped her plate seemed paralyzed as well. The doe-eyed boy at her side said, "Daddy," and made a move toward the man, but the woman caught his shoulder and held him fast, her knuckles white against the navy blue of his sweatshirt.

Lacey's mother suddenly took the spoon from her hands and gave her a sharp shove. "Get into the hall," she said. Lacey started to back away from the table toward the hallway, but when she saw that her mother wasn't moving with her, she grabbed the sleeve of her blouse.

"You come, too," she said, trying to match the calmness in her mother's voice but failing miserably. Her mother caught her hand and freed it from her sleeve.

"Go!" she said, sharply now, and Lacey backed slowly toward the hallway, unable to move any faster or to take her eyes off the man.

In the hallway, a woman put an arm around her, pulling her close. Lacey could still see part of the room from where she stood. Her mother, the tall woman and her son remained near the tables, staring toward the doorway, which was out of Lacey's line of sight. Behind her, she could hear a woman's voice speaking with a quiet urgency into the phone. "Come quickly," she was saying. "He has a gun."

The man came into view as he moved forward into the

room. The woman grabbed the doe-eyed boy, pulling him behind her.

"Zachary," the woman said. She was trying to sound calm, Lacey thought, but there was a quiver in her voice. "Zachary. I'm sorry we left. Don't hurt us. Please."

"Whore!" the man yelled at his wife. His arms were stretched out in front of him and the gun bobbed and jerked in his trembling hands. "Slut!"

Lacey's mother moved in front of the woman and her child, facing the man, her arms out at her sides as though she could protect them more efficiently that way.

"Please put the gun away, sir," she said. "It's Christmas." She probably sounded very composed to everyone else in the room, but Lacey knew her well enough to hear the tremulous tone behind the words.

"Bitch!" the man said. He raised the gun quickly, squeezing his eyes together as he pulled back on the trigger. The blast was loud, splitting apart the hushed silence in the room, and the women finally started to scream. Lacey's eyes were on her mother, who looked simply surprised, her deep blue eyes wide, her mouth open as if she'd been about to speak. The tiniest fleck of red appeared in the white fabric of her blouse, just over her left breast. Then she fell to the floor, slowly, as if she were melting.

The man fell to the floor, too. He dropped the gun and lowered his face to his hands, sobbing. One of the volunteers ran into the room from the hallway. She grabbed the gun from the floor and held it on him, but the big man no longer looked like a threat, just weak and tired and wet.

Lacey broke free from the woman holding her and ran to her mother, dropping to her knees next to her. Her mother's eyes were closed. She was unconscious, but not dead. Surely not dead. The bullet must have only nicked her, since the amount of blood on her blouse was no more than the prick of a thorn would produce on a fingertip.

"Mom!" Lacey tried to wake her up. *"Mom!"* She turned her head toward the man, who still sat crumpled up on the floor. "Why did you *do* that?" she yelled, but he didn't lift his head to answer.

Women crowded around her and her mother. One of them knelt next to Lacey, holding her mother's wrist in her fingers.

"She's alive," the woman said.

"Of course she's alive," Lacey snapped, angry that the woman had implied anything else was possible. The sound of sirens mixed with the pounding of the rain. "Her body just needs rest from being so scared." She could hear her mother's voice in her own; that was just the sort of thing Annie O'Neill would say.

The woman the man had meant to kill was huddled in the corner, her arms around her son. Lacey could hear her speaking, saying over and over again into the pine-scented air of the room, "I'm so sorry. I'm so sorry," and another woman was telling her, "It's not your fault, dear. You were right to come here to get away from him." But it *was* her fault. If she and her son hadn't come here, this crazy man wouldn't have run in and shot her mother.

The room suddenly filled with men and women wearing uniforms. They blurred in front of Lacey's eyes, and their voices were loud and barking. Someone was trying to drag her away from her mother, but she remained on the floor, unwilling to be budged more than a few feet. She watched as a man tore open her mother's blouse and cut her bra, exposing her left breast for all the world to see. There was a dimple in that breast. Just a trace of blood and a small dimple, and that gave Lacey hope. She'd had far worse injuries falling off her bike.

She stood up to be able to see better, and the woman who

had tried to pull her away wrapped her arms around her from behind, crossing them over her chest and shoulders, as though afraid she might try to run to her mother's side again. That was exactly what she wanted to do, but she felt immobilized by shock as much as by the heavy arms across her chest. She watched as the people in uniform lifted her mother onto a stretcher and wheeled her from the room. The man was already gone, and she realized the police had taken him away and she hadn't even noticed.

Lacey tugged at the woman's arms. "I want to go with her," she said.

"I'll drive you," the woman said. "We can follow the ambulance. You don't want to be in there with her."

"Yes, I *do!*" Lacey said, but the woman held her fast.

Giving in, she let the woman lead her out the front door of the house, and she turned to watch them load her mother into the ambulance. Something cool touched her nose and her cheeks and her lips, and she turned her face toward the dark sky. Only then did she realize it was snowing.

1

June 2003

THE CHAIN AT THE END OF THE GRAVEL LANE hung loose from the post, and Lacey was grateful that Clay had remembered she'd gone out for dinner with Tom and had left the entrance open for them.

"Will you put the chain up after you drop me off?" she asked Tom.

"No problem." He drove between the posts and onto the forest-flanked lane, driving too quickly over the bumps and ruts.

Lacey pressed her palm against the dashboard for balance. Although it was only dusk, it was already dark along the tree-shrouded gravel lane leading to the Kiss River light station. "You'd better slow down," she said. "I nearly ran over an opossum on this road last night."

Obediently, Tom lifted his foot from the gas pedal. "I'm glad you don't live out here alone," he said in the paternal tone he occasionally used with her since learning he was her biological father a decade ago. "I'd be worried about you all the time."

"Well," Lacey sighed. "I won't be living out here too much longer." The Coast Guard had finally decided to turn the nearly restored keeper's house into a museum, a decision she had hoped would never come.

"You're upset about it, huh?"

"Oh, a bit." She was frankly scared, although of what, she couldn't say. The isolation the keeper's house had offered her had been more than welcome, it had been necessary, especially this last difficult year. "They've restored every inch of it except the living room and the sunroom." She shared a studio in Kill Devil Hills with Tom, but she'd turned the sunroom of the keeper's house into a small studio, as well, so she could work on her stained glass when she was at home. "They'll restore the sunroom after I leave, and the living room will be turned into a little shop and information area."

"When do they want you out?" he asked. They were nearing the end of the road. A bit of dusky daylight broke through the trees and she could clearly see the gray in Tom's wiry blond ponytail and the glint of light from the small gold hoop in his ear.

"Some time after the first of the year," she said.

"Where will you...holy shit." Tom had driven from the gravel road into the parking lot, and the keeper's house came into view in the evening light. The upper portions of nearly every window were aglow with her stained glass creations.

She followed his gaze to the house. "In the year and a half I've lived here, you haven't seen the keeper's house at night?" she asked.

Tom stopped the car in the middle of the lot and a smile came slowly to his lips. Shaking his head, he leaned over to pull Lacey toward him, wrapping her in the scent of tobacco as he kissed the top of her head. She had gotten him to stop drinking, but had failed at getting him to give up cigarettes.

"You're your mother, Lace," he said. "This is just the sort of thing she would do. Turn her home into a…I don't know. Someplace magical."

She felt defeated. She wanted to tell him that she was not her mother any longer, that she had worked hard this last year to rid herself of her mother's persona. Apparently she had not succeeded. It was hard to succeed when you had no identity of your own to take the place of the one you were trying to discard.

She was surprised to see her father's van parked in the lot next to Clay's Jeep. "Dad is here," she said. "Weird."

"He doesn't come to visit you much?" Tom asked, and she heard the competitive edge in his voice. Tom often displayed a quiet envy of Alec O'Neill for having had the honor of raising her.

"He's smitten with Rani," she said, not really answering the question. "He likes having a grandbaby."

Tom laughed. "You have one hell of a complicated family, you know that?"

"I do, indeed." Lacey unfastened her seat belt. The tight little nuclear family she'd grown up in had added and subtracted so many people that it sometimes seemed difficult to keep track of them all. To complicate her life even further, she worked with both her fathers, spending her mornings in the animal hospital run by the father who had raised her and her afternoons in the art studio with the father who had given her life.

"Is that a kennel?" Tom pointed toward the large fenced area near the edge of the woods. "Is Clay training dogs again?"

"Uh-huh," she said. "He's been back at it a few months now." With Gina and Rani in his life, her brother had undergone a metamorphosis. He was a devoted husband, and practically overnight, he'd developed parenting skills she had never expected to see in him. But it was the day she'd watched him roll chunks of wood and concrete into the forest—obstacles for the dogs he trained in search-and-rescue work—that she knew he was once again a man at peace with his world.

She realized that Tom had not moved his car from the center of the lot.

"Park your car and come in for a while," she said.

He shook his head. "No, I'll just head on home."

"You know you're welcome," she said.

"I know that, sugar. But...I just never feel comfortable around Alec. Your dad."

Lacey smiled. "I'm nearly twenty-six years old, Tom," she said. "What happened between you and my mother is ancient history and you know my father got over it a long time ago."

"Some other time," Tom said.

"Okay." She opened the car door and stepped out. "I'll see you tomorrow."

She waved as he turned the car around and drove back onto the gravel lane. Slipping off her sandals, she dangled them over her fingertips and started walking across the sand toward the house. The air was thick with salt, and the rhythmic pounding of the waves against the shore was nearly drowned out by the buzz of cicadas.

She often wondered if she should tell Tom the truth about her mother. It was clear that he thought he had been her only affair, as if he alone had been so irresistible that he could cause a woman as saintly as Annie O'Neill to stray. As far as Lacey knew, he did not date anyone, still so haunted by Annie's ghost that he thought it impossible to find a woman who could take her place. Yet Lacey couldn't bring herself to hurt him with the truth.

Inside the house, Clay's black lab, Sasha, ran into the kitchen to greet her, and she dropped her sandals on the floor and bent down to scratch the dog behind his ears. The room smelled of Gina's cooking—cardamom and turmeric, coconut and ginger. She could hear voices coming from the living room.

"Who's here, Sash?" she said, as if she didn't know. "Let's go see."

Sasha led the way through the kitchen to the living room, tail wagging, and Lacey stopped in the doorway of the room, not wanting to interrupt the scene in front of her. Gina was stretched out on the sofa, grinning, her arms folded behind her head as she watched Clay and Alec playing on the floor with Rani and her dolls. Clay was making the Indian Barbie, which was bedecked in a pink sari, walk across the rug toward the plastic dollhouse.

"Let's go to Rani's house!" he said in a high-pitched voice.

Alec was walking a brown-skinned baby doll—a big blob of a doll compared to the slender, shapely Barbie—around on the carpet. "No," he said. "I want to go fishing!"

Rani looked alarmed, reaching for the baby doll. "No, no, no!" she said, her enormous black eyes wide in her caramel-colored face. "Everyone comes to *my* house."

Lacey laughed. At nearly two and a half, Rani tried hard to control her world. She'd had so little opportunity to control it during her first two years that she was making up for lost time. The little girl looked up at the sound of Lacey's laughter, then jumped up from the floor.

"Lacey!" she said, running toward her. "I love you!"

Lacey bent down to pick her up. She was a little peanut of a child. So tiny. So full of joy. And so, so wanted.

"Hi, baby," Lacey said. "I love you, too."

Gina had struggled to adopt Rani, and once Clay had fallen in love with Gina, he had joined that struggle with his whole heart. They'd spent from July to September in India the year before, fighting the system to get the court's permission to adopt Rani. The little girl had desperately needed heart surgery, but so many obstacles stood in the way of the adoption that Gina had feared the toddler might die before she could bring her home. Once permission had been received, the three of them were quickly ushered out of the country, escaping before the foreign adoption antagonists could become involved. By that time, Rani was so weak from her heart condition that she could barely hold her head up, and Gina and Clay feared it might be too late to save her. Gina had already made contact with a surgeon in Seattle, so she flew there with Rani. The surgery was successful and the two of them remained in Seattle as Rani healed. Clay had moped around the keeper's house, unable to think of anything other than the woman and baby he had fallen in love with. He and Gina talked for hours on the phone—for so long, in fact, that Lacey had insisted he get a separate phone line installed in the keeper's house. In February, Gina and Rani traveled across the country to the Outer Banks. Gina and Clay were married the following day, and Rani, who had arrived shy and quiet and skinny as a twig, quickly blossomed into an insatiable chatterbox who fully recognized her role as the center of the universe. She was spoiled—if it was possible to spoil a child who had spent her first two years with little more than dirt and deprivation—and no one cared.

Lacey carried Rani over to the sofa and sat down next to Gina's bare feet. She looked at her father, who still sat on the floor, holding the fat baby doll on his lap. "What are you doing here, Dad?" she asked.

Alec set the doll down on the rug and leaned back on his hands. "I wanted to talk to you and Clay," he said. His serious tone was worrisome. She looked from her father to Clay, who shrugged, apparently as much in the dark as she was. The two men looked so much alike. Long, lanky bodies, translucent blue eyes. The only difference between them were the lines on her father's face and the gray in his hair. Clay could look at Alec O'Neill and know exactly how he, himself, would look in another twenty years.

Gina sat up and reached for Rani. "I'll put her to bed," she said, as if knowing this conversation was meant for Alec and his children and not necessarily for her.

"Good night, sweetie." Lacey planted a kiss on Rani's cheek before handing her over to Gina.

Her father stood up as Gina left the room. "Let's go outside," he said.

She and Clay followed him through the kitchen, down the porch steps and onto the sand, which felt cool now beneath her feet. In another few weeks the sand would be warm, even at night, never losing the heat from the day. As if on automatic pilot, the three of them started walking side by side toward the remains of the lighthouse. Illuminated by the half-moon, the white lighthouse glowed, its broken rim a ragged line across the night sky. A breeze had kicked up in the short time she'd been inside the house, and Lacey's long, wild hair blew across her face. If she'd known about the change in weather, she would have tied her hair back before stepping outside. People thought her hair was impossibly beautiful. She thought it was merely impossible.

"What's up, Dad?" Clay asked, and Lacey wondered if he, too, was remembering the last time their father had asked to speak to both of them, the day he told them that their mother had been unfaithful to him throughout their marriage.

"I received a letter today," their father said. "I forgot to bring it with me for you two to read it, but essentially it stated that a parole hearing is scheduled in September for Zachary Pointer."

Clay stopped walking and turned to face his father. *"Parole?"* He sounded as astonished as she felt. "He's only been in prison...what?...twelve years?"

"Apparently that's long enough to get him out on parole."

Lacey caught her hair in her hands and began to braid it down her back, concentrating hard on the task. She didn't want to think about Zachary Pointer or relive that night, although the memory was always so near the surface that just the mention of his name would bring it back. Nothing could prevent her from remembering his face, the crazed look in his wild eyes. She could still hear his angry and ugly words toward his wife and see her mother's noble—and successful—attempt to protect the woman.

Lacey had refused to attend the trial back then; in those days she could focus on nothing other than trying to survive the pain of losing her mother. But once and only once, before she realized what she was looking at and could turn away, she saw Pointer on television. The big man was leaving the courthouse with his lawyer. She'd been riveted by the sight of him. He wept when he spoke to the reporters. She'd been struck by the humanness in his face, by the unmistakable remorse and sorrow and shame she saw there. Now she pictured him in prison all this time, alone with the pain of that remorse. He'd been sick. Mentally ill. There'd been no doubt in her mind, but the jury had adamantly ruled against an insanity plea. Maybe she and Clay and their father *should* listen to the arguments for allowing him out on parole. Twelve years was a long time.

Stop it, she thought to herself. She had her mother's genes, whether she wanted them or not; she was doomed to feel compassion for everyone.

"He should have been fried," she said, the words so alien

coming from her mouth that her brother and father both turned to stare at her.

"Well, we're in agreement then," her father said after a moment. "We'll fight his parole. I'll hire an attorney to find out what our next step should be."

In her bedroom later that night, Lacey opened the windows wide and let the strong breeze whip the sheer seafoam-colored curtains into the room. Sitting on the edge of her bed, she could hear laughter coming from Clay and Gina's room. She loved them both and loved that they were together, but the sound of their laughter increased the feeling that often crept over her in the evenings: loneliness. The feeling would only intensify once she was under the covers. That was the most alone time in the world, being in bed at night, in the dark, when all you had for company was your thoughts. The emptiness she felt was not new. It had started when her mother died. She'd lost her father then, too, as he became absorbed in grief. Once he started seeing Olivia, the woman he'd eventually married, he'd shifted that absorption to her. Although Olivia had been very kind to Lacey, she'd been more parent than friend, wrapped up in her own pregnancy and her growing love for Lacey's father.

Sometime that year Lacey learned that she could fill the void with boys, however temporary that filling might be. She grew to be a woman, the boys grew to be men, but the void remained, yawning and insatiable, and she'd continued to fill it the only way she knew how. She hadn't had all that many lovers. Not as many as Clay seemed to think when he chastised her about her promiscuity. But all the men she selected seemed to fit the same mold: they were "bad boys," edgy and exciting, who wanted nothing more from her than a good night in bed. That was the one thing she'd excelled at. Maybe the only thing.

It had not been a conscious choice for Lacey to begin emulating her mother after her death. She'd tried only to be the sort of woman her mother would have wanted her to be, taking on volunteer activities, tutoring kids, reading to the seniors at the retirement home, donating blood as often as allowed. But the pull she'd felt to the wrong sort of men had always distressed her; surely her mother would have disapproved. Little did she know that she was emulating her mother in that regard, as well, and the revelation had shocked her. Annie O'Neill had been, quite simply, a fraud.

Since learning the truth about her mother and her adulterous behavior, Lacey had not had a single lover. Not a single date. She had avoided men altogether, distrustful of her own judgment. She felt like Tom, trying to fight his yearning for alcohol. Tom could not have a single drink or he would be right back where he started. It was the same with her and men.

She'd discarded other qualities she thought of as her mother's, as well, pulling back from the many volunteer activities she used to do, turning inward. At Clay and Gina's insistence, she'd seen a counselor, a woman who had been too damn insightful for Lacey's comfort level. Lacey had presented herself to the woman as a sex addict. The label comforted her somehow, a neat little package that could be addressed through a twelve-step program, the way Tom's alcoholism was being treated. But the counselor had not agreed. "Depression, yes," she'd said. "Some self-esteem issues, yes. Sex addiction, no. You don't fit the criteria." She'd forced Lacey to look at pieces of her behavior she could not bear to examine. "You're always doing things for other people," the counselor had said, "as though you don't feel you deserve anything for yourself.

Focusing on others keeps you from feeling your own pain. You need to let yourself feel it, Lacey, before you can fix it."

Well, she thought as she slipped beneath the covers on her bed, she was feeling it now.

2

FROM THE OUTSIDE, THE STAINED-GLASS STUDIO in Kill Devil Hills looked the same as when her mother had worked there. Set back just a few yards from Croatan Highway, its floor-to-ceiling windows were filled with stained-glass panels, but the trained eye would be able to detect a difference between then and now. Tom's glasswork had changed over the years and was now more geometric, and there was less of it since he had gradually shifted his focus to photography over the years. Lacey's stained-glass panels hung intermingled with his. She did not think her work was as beautiful as her mother's had been; she had never mastered some of Annie's special touches, which had seemed more of an infusion of feeling rather than the result of a specific technique. But Lacey's work was popular, nonetheless. She had her own style, and her subject matter leaned more toward animals and florals than the stunning gowned women her mother had been known for. Lacey's worktable was the same one her mother had used, placed next to Tom's, as it had always been. She used her mother's tools, as well. For a long time she used her mother's green safety glasses, in spite of the fact that they were scratched and worn. A year ago, though, she'd tossed them away and bought her own glasses, amazed at how clearly she could suddenly see her work and the world.

Two women—tourists—were in the studio, oohing and aahing over the artwork. Although Tom was out to lunch, a third woman stood next to his worktable, seemingly mesmerized by the work in progress resting on the tabletop. From the corner of her eye, Lacey saw one of the women run her fingers lightly over a stained-glass egret hanging in the window. She would buy it, Lacey knew. She could read the people who came into the studio. Those who were simply spending idle time held their arms folded across their chests as they walked around the room, looking without really seeing. Others, like the woman touching the egret, could not tear themselves away from a particular piece. They studied it from every angle. They reached out and touched. They imagined how the colors would look in their homes. They'd drag a friend over to see the piece. The friend would nod. Sold.

Sure enough, the woman walked toward Lacey, a smile on her lips.

"I'd like to buy the egret," she said. "Are you the artist?"

Lacey set down her glass cutter and slipped off her safety glasses. "That's me," she said, standing up. "I'm glad you're taking that one. It's one of my favorites." This was not a lie, not a ploy to make the woman feel good about her purchase. She loved the shades of green she'd found for the tall grasses surrounding the giant bird. She would make another piece similar to this one now that it was sold, but it would not be exactly the same. She liked the idea that each of her stained-glass panels was one-of-a-kind.

The woman and her friends were just leaving the studio with the carefully wrapped glass egret when a man walked through the front door. His eyes lit briefly on Lacey, then on the large black-and-white photograph hanging on the movable wall in the center of the room. The picture had been there for as long as Lacey could remember.

The man stopped walking. Slipping his hands into his pockets, he stared at the photograph, then at Lacey again. "What a beautiful shot of you," he said.

"That's not me," Lacey said. "That's my mother."

"Oh." The man winced as though embarrassed by his mistake. "Quite a resemblance."

"People always think it's me," she said. A year earlier she had wanted to take that picture down, but Tom was the photographer and she could never have explained to him why a photograph she had once loved had come to disturb her.

"Were you the photographer?" the man asked.

"No. I was only about ten when that was taken."

"Oh. Of course." He had wandered toward the display table near the window and carefully picked up one of her kaleidoscopes. "This is beautiful," he said, holding the heavy stained-glass tube in his hands.

"Look through it," she said.

He lifted the kaleidoscope to his left eye and faced the window. "It's beautiful," he said again, turning the disk, and she knew what he was seeing—triangles of design formed by intensely colored glass beads and slivers of mirror.

Lowering the kaleidoscope, he looked over at her. "Did you make this?"

"Uh-huh."

He looked like one of those preppy sort of guys you might see modeling clothes in a catalogue. His brown hair was cut short and his eyes were dark, with lashes she could see from across the room. He was hardly dressed for the beach, in his khaki-colored chinos and plaid sport shirt. Although she supposed most women would find him drop-dead gorgeous, he was not her type and that relieved her, because he was obviously interested in her. She would not be tempted. She went for the earthier types—a little disheveled, imperfect features, knowing grins and the sort of eyes that cut right through to her soul. She was grateful that this guy did not come close to fitting that bill.

"What's your name?" he asked.

"Lacey O'Neill."

"And is all this stained glass yours?" He motioned toward the windows.

"Most of it. Some of it was made by Tom Nestor." She nodded toward Tom's empty worktable. "He's at lunch. All the photographs are his."

The man glanced again at the huge black-and-white print of her mother.

"Including that one," she said.

He walked across the room to her worktable. He was still holding the kaleidoscope, and he shifted it to his left hand as he held his right out toward her.

"I'm Rick Tenley," he said.

She shook his hand. "You just here for the week?" she asked, making conversation. Most tourists visited the Outer Banks for a week.

"Actually, no." He lifted the kaleidoscope to his eye again and gently spun the wheel. "I'm staying in a buddy's cottage while I'm working on a book. He's in Europe, and I wanted the peace and quiet."

She had to laugh. "Not much peace and quiet around here during the summer."

He lowered the kaleidoscope with a smile. "Well, it's away from my regular life," he said. "None of the usual interruptions."

She spotted Tom walking up the front steps of the studio, and Rick followed her gaze to the door.

"This is the other artist," she said as Tom walked into the room. "Tom Nestor, this is Rick..."

"Tenley." Rick turned to shake Tom's hand. "You do beautiful work," he said.

"Thanks."

There was an awkward moment of silence between the three of them. Rick turned to face Lacey again, a question in his eyes she couldn't read, and in that instant, she knew he wanted something more from her than stained glass.

"Rick is here for the summer, working on a novel," she said, to break the silence.

"Not a novel," Rick said. "It's nonfiction. Dry stuff."

"Ah." Tom moved to the coffeepot at the side of the room. He poured himself a cup, then lifted it to his lips, looking at Rick over the rim. "Where are you from?" he asked.

"Chapel Hill," Rick said. "I teach at Duke."

She couldn't help but be impressed. He looked too young to teach in a high school, much less a university. "What do you teach?" she asked.

"Law."

"Wow," she said. "That's great."

Tom sat down at his table, slipped on his safety glasses and returned to his work, probably figuring that the stilted conversation was not worth his time.

"How long have you lived here?" Rick asked her.

"My whole life."

He held the kaleidoscope toward her. "I'd like to buy this," he said.

"Good choice." She wondered if he truly liked it or if he was simply trying to ingratiate himself with her. Taking the kaleidoscope from him, she began wrapping it in tissue paper. She could feel him appraising her.

Don't look at me that way, she thought to herself. From the corner of her eye, she saw him glance at Tom, then back at her, and she guessed he was trying to figure out if they might be a couple. A very odd couple. A twentysomething-year-old woman and a fiftysomething-year-old ponytailed ex-hippie. Apparently, he came to the correct conclusion.

"Any chance you'd have dinner with me tonight?" he asked her. "You probably know all the best places to eat."

"Oh, sorry, I can't," she answered quickly, prepared for the invitation. She thought of telling him she was going to the gym, which was the truth, but then he might ask if he could join her there. She slipped the wrapped kaleidoscope into a plastic bag and handed it to him. "I can recommend some places for you, though."

"Are you…attached?" He caught himself. "Sorry. That was blunt. None of my business."

She might have lied, but found she couldn't with Tom listening in on the conversation.

"Not really," she hedged. "I'm just…I'm busy tonight."

"Okay." He seemed to accept that. "Some other time, maybe." He held the bag in the air like a salute. "Thanks for the kaleidoscope."

"You're welcome."

She watched him leave the studio and walk across the small lot, where he got into a BMW the same color as his pants. She felt Tom's gaze on her and knew he was smiling.

"He'll be back," Tom said, standing up to pour himself another cup of coffee. "A guy like that isn't used to rejection."

3

THE COTTAGE WAS TUCKED DEEP IN THE WOODS on the sound side of the island, but when Rick sat on the small, rotting deck, he could see patches of sun-soaked water between the branches of the loblolly pines. He could hold the kaleidoscope to his eye, aim it toward those silvery patches of water, and watch the beads of glass form designs as he twirled the wheel.

The cottage did not belong to a friend, as he had told Lacey O'Neill. He wasn't even certain why he'd said that. Maybe he was simply practicing for the other lies he would have to tell. He was actually renting this place. It had two minuscule bedrooms, one more than he needed. No TV to distract him from his writing. No air-conditioning, but he could handle the heat. There was a phone line to connect him to e-mail and the Internet, and electricity for his computer. That was all he required. When he'd first entered the musty-smelling cottage four days earlier, he'd guessed it had not changed in the seventy years or so of its existence. He doubted a stick of furniture had been replaced. The tourists who usually came to the Outer Banks for the summer would disdain this sort of place. They wanted houses that slept ten, televisions in every room, hot tubs, pools, views. That's why he'd been able to get the run-down cottage for a song. And it was perfect.

There was a short, overgrown path that ran from the deck through the woods to a sliver of sand at the edge of the sound. Each day since his arrival, he'd taken a beach chair down to the water's edge and read or worked or just watched the boats from his nearly hidden vantage point. Last night, when it had been too hot to sleep, he took his flashlight and walked through the trees to the water's edge, then swam out into the bay, the quiet of the night surrounding him. He planned to make that nighttime swim a habit. There were grasses or something underwater that had given him the creeps as he swam away from the shore, but once he'd gotten past the grasping tendrils, the cool, dark water had buoyed him up and felt good against his skin. He'd floated on his back, and thought about Lacey O'Neill. That red hair. The warmth in her blue eyes. She was a kind person; you could tell that before she even opened her mouth. He would have to try again with her. He was not the type to give up. You didn't make it through law school by being a quitter.

He'd practiced law for only a year before going the teaching route. The university had overlooked his lack of experience for his excellent command of his material, and he'd been grateful. He preferred teaching law to practicing it. He'd never liked twisting the truth to fit the needs of his clients, and sometimes that had been not only necessary but expected. He could never tell a lie without remembering his father's advice. He'd been only eight or nine when he'd overheard his father tell an elderly aunt that she looked nice in a new outfit when in reality, she'd looked like a pruny old woman trying to appear far younger than her years. In private, he'd asked his father if he really believed the old woman looked nice. "Sometimes a lie can be a gift," his father had said. They were the words Rick tried to follow in his life. He would lie only when it was a gift.

He waited two days before returning to the stained glass studio, and he was glad to find Lacey there alone. The older man with the ponytail had made him uncomfortable. He'd seemed entirely too interested in his conversation with Lacey.

She was standing on a stepladder, hanging a stained-glass panel in the window, when he walked in.

"Hi, Lacey," he said.

She glanced down at him, and he was pleased to see her smile.

"Hi, Rick," she said, slipping the wire attached to the panel over a hook above the window.

"Do you need some help there?"

"I do this all the time," she said as she descended the ladder. Once on the floor, she started to fold the ladder, but he took it from her hands.

"I don't mean to badger you," he said, folding it for her. "But you've been on my mind. Every time I look through that kaleidoscope, I think about you and your red hair. I'd really like to buy you dinner. Any night. You can choose."

She sighed with a smile, and he knew he was making it difficult for her to offer a graceful rejection.

"I'm sorry," she said. "The truth is, I'm taking a break from dating these days."

"Oh. Oh, I understand." He had the feeling she was being honest, and that only increased his guilt. "I've done that a time or two myself. You're getting over a bad relationship, I guess, huh?"

"Something like that." She took the ladder from him and carried it over to the side of the studio, resting it against the wall.

"Well, how about if it's not a date?" he asked. "We won't dress up. I won't even pick you up. We can meet someplace very public. And we won't have any fun."

That made her laugh. "All right," she said, shaking her head. "You win."

They made arrangements for the following night, and he left the studio far happier than when he'd arrived. In the parking lot, he got into his car and buckled his seat belt.

Yes, he thought as he turned the key in the ignition. *I win.*

4

FAYE COLLIER WALKED INTO THE HOSPITAL GYM
and climbed onto her favorite elliptical trainer machine, the
one positioned in the middle of the wall of windows, so she
could have an uninterrupted view of the San Diego hills while
she worked out. Judy and Leda, the two physical therapists
in the chronic pain program and her workout buddies, took
the elliptical trainers on either side of her. Faye wondered
briefly how the three of them looked from the rear. She was
Judy and Leda's supervisor and had a master's degree in nursing. She was blond, while they were both brunettes, yet she
was twenty-five years older than either of them, and when it
came to the backs of their thighs, she had no illusion that the
physical therapists had her beat.

"What do you think of that new patient?" Judy pressed
some buttons on the console and started moving her legs and
arms in a long, smooth stride.

"The young guy with bone cancer?" Faye asked. "I think
he needs—"

"Hi, Faye." Jim Price was suddenly next to her, standing
between her elliptical trainer and Leda's. The sight of him put
an instant smile on her face. She hoped she wasn't blushing.

"Hi," she said, slowing her pace on the machine. "I didn't know you worked out during lunch."

"I don't," he said. "But I just finished the paper you gave me to read and wanted to compliment you on it. Excellent."

"I'm glad you liked it," she said. She could feel perspiration, the result of the workout and a poorly timed hot flash, running down her throat and between her breasts. She wiped her forehead with the back of her hand.

"I made a few comments on it," Jim said. "I'll show you tonight, okay?"

She *was* blushing now. Judy and Leda had grown very quiet. They both slowed their machines to soften the noise from the flywheels, and she knew they were hanging on every word of her conversation with Jim. "That'll be great," she said. In the light from the window, his eyes were a delicate bronze color. She had not noticed that about him before.

Jim motioned for her to lean down so he could whisper in her ear. "You look terrific," he said, his breath soft against her skin.

She straightened up again, smiling, and mouthed the word "thanks."

He left her side, and Faye was grateful that Judy and Leda had the presence of mind not to say anything until he was well out of hearing distance.

"So," Judy asked. "When's your next date with him?"

"Tonight," she said. Even though she had slowed her pace significantly, the monitor showed that her heart rate was the highest it had been since she'd climbed on the machine. She could not believe she was allowing a man to have that sort of effect on her.

"You are so lucky," Leda said.

Faye knew that many of the women—and some of the men—working in the hospital had a thing for Jim Price. Even the young women wanted him. A widower for two years, Jim had left his surgery practice to take care of his wife during the last few months of her life, and nearly everyone found that sort of love and sacrifice laudable. He had money, looks that were rare for a man of fifty-five, and he was kind to patients and staff alike. Faye had known him for years, since he often referred patients to the pain program she had created, but he had not truly seemed to notice her until a few weeks ago, when her book on treating chronic pain was published. Someone must have told him that she had also lost a spouse, and his interest in her had been doubly piqued. In their first real conversation, they'd discovered another commonality: they had both grown up in North Carolina. That fact seemed to seal their fate as two people who should get to know one another better.

"Is it getting serious?" Leda asked.

"Define serious."

"Have you slept with him?"

"Of course not. Not that it's any of your business."

"But this will be the third date, right?" Judy asked.

"Yes. So?"

Leda laughed. "So you'd better shave your legs."

"Why?" She felt dense. Old and dense. She was also a little breathless and couldn't help but notice that Leda and Judy seemed to be having no problem talking as they pedaled the machines.

"The third date is when you do it," Leda said.

Faye laughed. "Who says?"

"That's the rule these days, Faye."

Faye pulled her water bottle from the holder near the machine's console and took a drink. "Well, he probably doesn't know the rules any better than I do," she said. As their superior, she knew she was crossing a boundary by talking to Judy and Leda about her love life, but this was one area in which they were more knowledgeable than she was and she wanted their input. "We talked about that, actually," she said. "About dating being new to each of us." She hoped no one was filling Jim in on "the third-date rule."

"It really depends on what those first two dates were like, though." Judy let go of the handlebars to pull the scrunchie from her dark hair and stick it in the pocket of her shorts. "Where did you go?"

"Starbucks the first time, and out to eat the second." Their first date had been a casual, impromptu sort of thing. He'd bumped into her in the hospital corridor, told her he'd read her new book and been impressed by it, and asked her if she wanted to get a drink after work that evening. They'd ended up at a Starbucks instead of a bar, and the coffee date lasted four hours. He did most of the talking, and that had been fine with her. As a matter of fact, she'd asked him questions non-stop to keep him from asking any of her. She was not good at sharing her life story. He had opened up easily about his, though, telling her about his North Carolina childhood, his marriage, his two daughters. He was so open that she'd felt guilty for all she was keeping to herself. But he didn't seem to mind. He wanted someone's ear to bend, and she'd been very willing.

"Starbucks doesn't really count." Judy took a swig from her own water bottle.

"How long did you stay there?" Leda asked.

"Four hours." They probably would have stayed longer, but Starbucks had been closing.

"Oh," they both said at the same time, nodding.

"That counts, then," Leda said. "That's totally a first date."

"And do you talk on the phone a lot?" Judy asked.

"Not really." He had called her a couple of times and e-mailed a couple more, but nothing lengthy or deep.

"Because a lot of phone calls count as a date."

Faye laughed. "You two…"

"I would say that four hours on the phone equals one date," Judy said.

Faye rolled her eyes, nearly too winded to respond. Her thighs were burning.

"Where was the second date?" Leda asked.

"The Sky Room," she managed to say. Again, he had been the talkative one. By the end of the evening, she realized he had not asked her a single question about herself other than what she wanted to eat. Another woman might have found that annoying. She'd welcomed it.

"Very nice." Judy nodded her approval. "Did he pay for you?"

"Yes…but I wasn't sure how to handle that," she said. "Should I have paid for myself?"

"No. Always let the guy pay," Leda said.

"I don't agree," Judy countered. "You should at least offer to pay your share. Or pick up the check the next time you go out. So, you can pay tonight."

"I would never pay," Leda said. "Especially not with someone as wealthy as Dr. Price."

"Where is he taking you tonight?" Judy asked.

Faye hesitated. She really was saying far too much. She pushed the button to lower the machine's resistance. "We're going to a party," she said. "Some friends of his."

"And then back to your house for a nightcap?" Judy asked.

"I haven't thought that far ahead."

"Oh, girl," Leda laughed. "You are ending up in bed tonight. No doubt about it."

"I barely know him." Faye felt priggish. "Or rather, he barely knows me."

"Well, what did you talk about all those hours in Starbucks and at the restaurant?" Leda asked.

"He did most of the talking."

Leda groaned, shaking her head in disgust. "That is so typical. All they want is someone to listen to them."

"You make sure he gets to know you before you sleep with him," Judy said. "You know, you as a person." She let go of the handlebar to take another swallow of water. "Otherwise you'll feel used," she continued. "He can say to himself, I slept with that hot-looking nurse and I didn't even have to listen to her whine about her life."

Faye was quiet, enjoying the fact that Judy had called her hot-looking. She hoped she was not being patronized.

"How long has it been for you?" Leda asked.

"Hey!" Faye said with a shake of her head. "I'm your supervisor, remember?"

"This conversation is off the record," Leda said conspiratorially. "Okay? You need help."

She let out her breath, knowing she was going to tell them. She *did* need help. "My husband was my first and only," she admitted.

"Oh, my God." Judy stopped her machine altogether. "And he die...passed away, what? Ten years ago?"

Faye had to smile at the euphemism. They worked in a hospital, for heaven's sake, and Judy never used the term "passed away." But somehow, everyone had learned to treat Faye with kid gloves when it came to the subject of her late husband.

"Nearly thirteen years," she said.

"Wow, Faye," Leda said. "It must feel like being a virgin all over again."

She grew quiet. That was exactly how she felt, awkward

and scared by the thought of taking off her clothes in front of a man, by the uncertainty of what to do, what would be expected of her. No one would call her fat—at least she hoped not—but she had grown bulky the way women often did at middle age, despite working out and watching her diet. She had little waistline left, her thighs were well padded. When she lay on her side in bed, she was aware of the force of gravity on her belly and breasts and could hardly imagine a man wrapping his arm around her in that position. Yet she *had* been imagining it lately. She'd been wondering what it would be like to lie in bed with Jim Price.

Judy reached out to touch her arm in sympathy. "It will be fine. He's the type who'll use protection and make sure you're…you know, happy."

"He wouldn't need to use protection," she said. "He hasn't had anyone since his wife. And I'm menopausal."

"Oh, my God." Leda laughed. "You'd better take a tube of K-Y Jelly from the supply room."

"Okay, that's really enough!" Faye's cheeks burned, although she was laughing herself. She stopped the machine and stepped off it too quickly. The carpeted floor felt as if it was moving beneath her feet. "I'm done," she said. "See you downstairs."

Jim picked her up at 7:30 p.m., looking handsome, his salt-and-pepper hair in contrast to his black suit and tie. It was to be a fancy event, something for charity, and she hoped she was dressed appropriately. Semiformal, he'd said. She wore a short-sleeved, tea-length burgundy dress. She had good ankles—of that she was confident. His eyes lit up when she opened the door for him, and she guessed she was dressed just fine.

He was talkative, as usual, on the way to the party, but the conversation was geared to the article she had written on the use of meditation in the treatment of chronic pain. She'd wanted his feedback on it before she submitted it to a journal. His comments were excellent, right on target, and she could tell the subject matter was nearly as close to his heart as it was to her own. She wondered if he was thinking about the pain of his patients or of his wife as he made a few suggestions for changes in the article.

The party was held on the twelfth floor of a downtown hotel, in a huge penthouse that offered a spectacular view of the city lights and the Coronado bay bridge. The crowd, slightly stiff and overdressed, was made up of doctors and politicians and their spouses. The women glittered with jewelry, and she wondered how obvious it would be to them that her earrings were made of cubic zirconium and her dress had been purchased at JCPenney's.

Jim took her arm and held it locked through his own, as if to give her courage. She recognized many of the physicians and saw a few of them raise their eyebrows in what she gathered was surprise at seeing her so firmly tethered to Jim Price's side. A photographer from *San Diego Magazine* snapped pictures of the guests as they milled around the huge, open room, and Faye wondered if she would see her face in the society pages of the magazine. She'd never cared for glitter, for the trappings of wealth, but she could not help but be impressed with both the other guests and with herself for simply being there. She wondered how much Jim had paid to get them into this party. It was a cancer benefit, though, she reminded herself. Cancer had killed his wife. He probably welcomed any opportunity to donate to that cause. He had not asked her what had killed her husband, and for that, she was grateful.

Conversation with the other attendees was easier than she'd anticipated. Several people knew who she was; a few of the doctors even knew about her book. Jim was good at introductions, telling her a little something about each person she met and giving that person a tidbit or two about her. He was used to this sort of high-powered social event. That much was obvious.

Halfway through the evening, when Jim had been taken aside by someone to talk business, one of the women ushered Faye away from the crowd and into the women's lounge.

"I just wanted to tell you how thrilled we all are to see Jim with someone," the woman said. She was very attractive, her dark hair twisted into a knot at the back of her head. She had to be close to sixty, but her skin was flawless. "He grieved for so long."

Faye was touched by the woman's words, but she felt a need to defend Jim. "Thank you," she said. "I don't think there's a time line on grief, though."

"No, of course not," the woman said. There was a faint hint of an accent to her voice. Italian, perhaps. "It's just that he hasn't looked happy in years. He looks happy tonight, though." The woman smiled. "We were worried that if he finally did find someone, it would be one of the young nurses he works with. We're a little sick of watching the older guys leave the wives who've stuck by them all these years for some young babe."

"Well, I guess I'm glad for once that I look my age." Faye laughed. She knew a backhanded compliment when she received one.

"Oh, sorry." The woman laughed at her own faux pas and squeezed Faye's hand. "I didn't mean to imply that you look old. Just—"

"I know what you meant," Faye said, forgiving her with a smile.

"Just, someone with maturity," the woman continued. "It's

refreshing. My husband has an oncology practice in Escon-
dido and he read your book. He said you're the real deal."

"That's so nice to hear," Faye said, as sincere as she was
surprised.

"I'm Rosa Stein, by the way," the woman said.

"How do you do."

"So, is it serious between the two of you?" That question
again.

"Not yet."

"Well." Rosa touched her shoulder. "I hope it gets that
way."

"Me, too." Faye surprised herself with the words.

When they stepped out of the lounge, she spotted Jim across
the room, near the window. He was engaged in conversation
with a man and a woman, and the sight of him filled her chest
with warmth. God, she liked him.

"Thanks for going with me," he said later, as he drove her
back to her house. "I know those affairs can be stuffy, but
they're for a good cause."

"I enjoyed it," she said honestly. She was wondering how
to handle the next part of the evening. Leda and Judy's discussion of the third-date rule still rang in her head.

He pulled into the driveway of her modest, one-story
house, shut off the engine, and turned to her with a smile.
Reaching over, he gently touched the short hair at the back
of her neck. Her heartbeat kicked up a notch, both at his
touch and at her uncertainty about what to do next. She had
to say something.

"If I invite you in," she said, "does it sound like I'm asking
you for more than coffee and conversation?"

He laughed lightly, then took her hand. "That's what I like
about you," he said. "You're so straightforward. No games.

And though I'd love to come in for some coffee and conversation, I think maybe I'd better not. I'm not ready for...for..."

It was the first time she'd seen him at a loss for words, but she understood.

"Neither am I," she said.

He walked her to her door, where he leaned down and kissed her softly on the lips.

"I can't believe I used to work with you and never even noticed you," he said, drawing back to look at her.

"You were thinking about your patients," she said. "And your wife."

He nodded slowly. "I think that's one thing that drew me to you." He smoothed a strand of her hair away from her forehead. "You know, the fact that you were widowed. That you know what that's like."

"Yes," she said, although the truth was, she didn't know. She was only pretending.

5

LACEY DIDN'T EVEN CONSIDER TELLING CLAY
and Gina that she had a date. She left the keeper's house at
six-thirty, stating only that she was meeting a friend for dinner. They would assume it was a female friend; they knew
she wasn't up for dating. They were proud of her. Everyone
was, as though she'd successfully battled her demons and won.
For the most part, she had, although she knew she wasn't yet
ready for temptation.

A date with Rick Tenley, however, was no threat to the
pact she'd made with herself to end her promiscuous behavior. He was the sort of man that might make other women
swoon, but his preppy good looks did nothing for her. He was
simply a nice guy, and she would have dinner with him as
friends. She also had an ulterior motive in meeting with him:
he was a lawyer. She might be able to pick his brain about
how she and her family should approach Zachary Pointer's
parole hearing.

She'd had trouble deciding where to meet him, finally deciding on the Blue Point Grill in Duck. She would have preferred a restaurant less filled with tourists, but Shorty's Grill,
her favorite eatery, was not the sort of place she could pic-

ture a guy like Rick. Besides, everyone knew her at Shorty's, and tongues would start wagging. If people wondered why they never saw her with a man these days, they were keeping their curiosity to themselves, and for that she was grateful. She didn't need to stir the pot. It would be best if she and Rick simply blended in with the tourists.

He was already waiting for her when she pulled into the parking lot by the Blue Point. She could see him on the deck next to the little restaurant, leaning against the railing, looking into the water. He was dressed in a sports coat and crisply pressed trousers, and she wondered if her description of the restaurant had made it sound more formal than it was. Didn't he realize he was at the beach? No one dressed up here. Plus, it was hot. He had to be roasting in that jacket.

She pulled a wide barrette from her purse and clipped back as much of her hair as would fit inside the clasp, letting the rest of it fall free over her shoulders. Her long sundress skirted her sandaled feet as she got out of her car and started walking toward the deck. The dress was loose-fitting without being matronly. At least she hoped it was not matronly. Her wardrobe had changed dramatically. She'd tossed out her more provocative clothing, shocked at how little that left in her closet, and she'd taken herself on one of the most depressing shopping sprees of her life. She might as well let her belly button piercing close up for all the exposure it had gotten this year.

Rick turned just as she climbed the last step onto the deck, and he smiled broadly when he saw her. "Great choice," he said, motioning toward the restaurant. "The specials look fantastic."

"I thought you'd like it," she said. "Everything they serve is good."

They had a short wait for a table and they passed the time

standing on the deck, leaning against the railing and watching the sailboats on the sound.

"It's going to be a beautiful sunset," he said, noting the clouds on the horizon.

She nodded. "I grew up on the sound," she said.

"That must have been wonderful." He pointed south. "The cottage I'm staying in is just a mile or so in that direction. It's on the water, too, but it doesn't have a view like this. It's very small and so deep in the woods you can barely see it until you're on top of it. But there's a path leading to the sound."

"It must be perfect for someone working on a book," she said.

"You're right. It is."

The hostess stepped onto the deck to call them into the restaurant, and Rick rested his hand on her back as they walked into the welcome air-conditioning. They were lucky to get a table by the window, and he held the back of her chair as she took her seat.

"Did you write today?" she asked as he sat down across from her.

"Not as much as I should have," he said. "It was so beautiful out, I had to play a round of golf."

"Ah," she said. "Do you do that often? Play golf?"

"As often as I can." He smiled at the waitress who brought them their water, and Lacey saw the young woman nearly melt under the power of Rick's long dark eyelashes and white teeth.

They studied the menu for a few minutes, both of them selecting the shrimp and scallops. The waitress took their order, and once she had walked away, Rick returned his gaze to Lacey.

"So," he said, lowering the cloth napkin to his lap. "Do you want to tell me about your breakup?"

For a moment, she thought he had said "break*down*" and

was startled by the question. She would not have described what she went through after learning about her mother's infidelities as a breakdown, and how could he know about that, anyhow? With relief, she realized what he had actually said.

"What breakup?" she asked.

"You know, the breakup that's made you take a breather from dating."

"Oh, it's not that." She suddenly wished she were a more dishonest person. She could simply say, "Yes, it was painful, but I'm getting over it." Even as a kid, though, she'd been a lousy liar. "I've just sworn off men for a while," she said.

"Because you were hurt?"

"Only by myself." She offered a rueful smile. "By my choices. My actions. I have a tendency to move too fast. To not look out for myself. To pick the wrong kind of guy." That was enough. She didn't need to go into any more detail with him.

The waitress poured wine into their glasses and neither of them spoke until she had walked away again.

"What's the wrong kind of guy?" he asked.

"Oh, well." She squirmed uncomfortably, wanting to change the direction of the conversation. "Not a guy like you."

He raised his eyebrows, and she realized she might be giving him hope with that statement.

"All I mean is that you seem very safe to me," she said.

He laughed, his wineglass halfway to his lips. "Why does that feel like an insult?" he asked.

"It's not," she said. "At least I didn't mean it that way."

He took a sip of his wine and set the glass on the table again, then leaned forward. "You don't need to worry about me, Lacey," he said. "You've made it clear you don't want a romance. I'll honor that."

"Thank you," she said, grateful for that clear communication. He really had a lot of charm. She could think of a couple of friends she could fix him up with who would appreciate him far more than she would.

"So, now," he said. "Tell me everything there is to know about you."

"Everything?"

"You grew up on the sound, you said. A child of the sand and the sea."

She nodded. "Exactly."

"Is your family still in the area?"

"My father and stepmother live nearby, in Sanderling. My brother and his wife and their little girl live with me in the keeper's house at the Kiss River light station."

"You're kidding. You live in a keeper's house?"

She nodded.

"How did you manage that?"

"I got very lucky. My brother and I helped with the restoration of the house. It's going to be turned into a museum next year, though, and we'll have to leave then, unfortunately."

"Amazing." He sipped his wine again. "You didn't mention your mother," he said. "That beautiful woman in the photograph at your studio. You have her dimples. Does she live nearby, too?"

"No," Lacey said. "She died when I was thirteen."

"Oh, I'm so sorry." He looked a bit embarrassed and she wished she could say something to put him at ease.

"It was a long time ago," she said.

"It must be so hard to lose a mother, especially as a girl that age. Had she been sick long?"

"She wasn't sick. She was murdered."

"God, no. What happened?" He raised a hand to prevent

her from answering him. "I'm sorry. We don't have to talk
about this. I mean, I'd understand if you don't want to."

"Actually, I'd like to tell you about it since you're a lawyer.
I'd like to pick your brain a little, if you don't mind."

"What about?" He leaned back as the waitress set their
plates of shrimp and scallops in front of them, and Lacey
waited until the woman had walked away again.

She picked up a slice of bread from the basket on the table.
"Well," she said, spreading butter on the bread, "my family and I just learned that her murderer may be getting out
on parole and we want to prevent that from happening. My
dad's getting in touch with an attorney, but I wondered if
you might know what we should do to fight it." She took a
bite from the bread and watched him absorb the information.

He sighed. "That's not my area of expertise, I'm afraid,"
he said. "Not by a long shot. I'm a tax attorney. I could run
it by some of my friends, though, if that would help."

"Oh, no, you don't have to do that." She suddenly felt
guilty for asking.

"How did it happen exactly?" he asked. "Your mother."

Between bites of seafood, she told him about the battered
women's shelter and how her mother had saved the life of
Zachary Pointer's wife. Rick listened with rare attentiveness
for a man, barely touching his food as she spoke.

"It's heartbreaking," he said. "She sounded very special. I'm
so sorry." He reached across the table for her hand, and she let
him hold it. His touch felt friendly, brotherly. She thought he
actually had tears in his eyes, but she wasn't sure. One thing
she *was* certain of was that she really was safe with this guy.
Maybe he *could* be a friend. But she let her hand rest in his
only a moment before gently withdrawing it.

"What's your goal?" he asked. "I mean, with the legal
system. Do you want to punish him longer or do you want

to keep him off the streets because you think he might hurt someone else?"

"Well, we—my father and brother and I and all the people around here who loved my mother—we just feel that twelve years is not long enough. He'd be out, alive and healthy and free and getting on with his life, while my mother can never come back."

"I'm going to look into this for you," he said with sudden determination. "I can check with people who know that part of the law better than I do."

"That's so nice of you."

"I have one important question for you first," he said.

She set her fork on the edge of her plate, waiting for him to continue.

"I may be…I apologize, because this might not be fair of me to ask, but…have you thought about what pursuing this will cost you?"

She opened her mouth to reply, but he stopped her.

"I don't mean financially," he said. "I mean emotionally. It could be long and drawn out. You and your family need to really think this through. You need to be sure you're up for going through the whole thing again."

"I think we have to do it," she said.

He moved a scallop around on his plate. "I'm just playing devil's advocate here, all right?" he asked. "I can't possibly know how this feels to you, how it feels to lose your mother… but have you thought of…just letting it go? Putting it behind you? Maybe even taking it one step further by forgiving the guy who did it?"

He must have seen her stiffen, because he continued quickly.

"Maybe not forgive him, exactly, although I have to tell you, I believe strongly in the power of forgiveness," he said. "It brings peace to the person doing the forgiving. I understand that's probably too much to ask. But you might consider not fighting his release. Not wasting your energy on him. As long as the parole board decides he's not a danger to anyone else, as long as he's truly been rehabilitated, can you just let it go?"

She shook her head. "No," she said.

"Lacey, I'm not talking about letting it go for his sake, but for yours," he said, his dark eyes searching her face. "If you fight this, you'll have to relive everything that happened."

"I'll never stop reliving it," she said, but she was frankly touched by what he had said. He was a kind man, and she knew there was wisdom in his words. "You sound like you've been through something like this."

He shook his head. "No," he said. "Not really." He pressed his napkin to his lips, then smiled at her again. "I haven't known you long," he said, his voice soft, "but just seeing you with customers at the studio, seeing the sweet and gentle way you are with *me,* I can tell that you're a compassionate person. I bet you usually forgive people very easily."

"Well." She sighed, lifting her fork from the edge of her plate. "The irony is that my mother would have been the first to forgive him," she said, spearing a scallop. "Unfortunately, though, I'm nothing like her."

6

LACEY STOOD NEXT TO THE EXAMINING TABLE
at the animal hospital, her hands buried in the thick, black
shoulder fur of a Bernese mountain dog, while her father
snipped the stitches from several shaved areas on the dog's side.

"You're being such a good boy," Lacey cooed to the dog.
He was huge, a hundred and ten pounds, and panting up a
storm. His heavy coat was not designed for a North Carolina summer.

"He's healing very well," her father said.

From where she stood, she could see how the gray was rap-
idly invading her father's once dark hair, and for some reason,
that distressed her.

"Don't you try to escape again," Lacey said to the dog,
who appeared to be ignoring her. He stared straight ahead
at the wall, stoically tolerating the procedure until he could
return to the waiting room and his beloved owner. The dog
belonged to a family staying in a beachfront house, and he'd
run straight through a flimsy wooden fence on the day of
their arrival, anxious to cool off in the ocean.

Suzy, the receptionist, suddenly opened the door to the
examining room and poked her head inside.

"There's a gorgeous vase full of yellow roses out here for you, Lacey," she said. "They were just delivered."

"You're kidding." Lacey looked at Suzy. "Who are they from?" She knew there could only be one answer to that question.

Suzy held up a small envelope. "You've got your hands full," she said. "Want me to open it for you?"

Lacey nodded, and Suzy pulled out the card and held it toward her. One hand still deep in the dog's fur, Lacey took the card and read the handwritten message to herself. *You are the best thing about this summer. With affection, Rick.*

"Well?" Suzy asked with a grin, her curiosity clearly piqued.

"A friend." Lacey slipped the card into the pocket of her lab coat. "Thanks for letting me know."

Suzy left the room, and Lacey did not need to look at her father to know his eyes were on her.

"Roses, huh?" he asked. Two little words, but she knew all that was behind them. *What are you doing, Lacey? Are you being careful? Are you falling into your old ways?*

"Not from anyone special, Dad," she said.

He returned his attention to the stitches without another word, but she knew he wasn't finished. He wouldn't be able to help himself. She wasn't surprised when he spoke again. "None of them were ever special to you, though," he said. "That was the problem, wasn't it? That you were indiscriminate? That caring about a person wasn't really what mattered to—"

"Dad," she said. She loved him immensely, but he could be such a pain in the neck. "I don't want to talk about this, okay? The roses are from a nice guy I've been seeing recently. *Platonically.* They're *yellow* roses, not red. Please have a little faith in me." She was quiet a moment, then added, "Gina and Clay have met him, and they like him."

She and Rick had been out three times so far, and she'd finally allowed him to pick her up at the keeper's house the night before. She'd been nervous about introducing him to her brother and sister-in-law, but they'd instantly been able to tell that Rick was different from the other men she'd dated. The house had been full of people when he arrived, and she'd worried that Rick would be overwhelmed. Henry, the grandfather of Clay's first wife, and Walter, Gina's grandfather, were both there. The two elderly men were frequent visitors to the house, especially now that Rani had arrived. The men had lost their dear, longtime friend, Brian Cass, over the winter and some of the joy had gone out of them. Rani, though, had brought it back.

Rick had handled all the introductions easily, and this morning at breakfast, Clay and Gina had given him their stamp of approval.

Her father snipped the final stitch and straightened up. "I'm sorry, hon," he said, reaching for a dog treat from the bowl on the counter.

"I feel like a kid who gets an A-minus on a test and you yell at her for not getting an A," Lacey said, still wounded.

He smiled at that. "I know you've tried hard to change, Lace," he said. "I've admired that. And I do trust you. I just flipped out there for a sec."

He was backpedaling so fast she felt sorry for him. "It's okay," she said. She helped him lift the dog from the table and set him on the floor. The dog instantly ran to the door of the room, pawing to be let out. She reattached his leash to his collar.

"I'll take him out," Alec said, taking the leash from her hand. "Your shift's nearly over."

"Thanks," she said. "I'll see you tomorrow."

The roses, resting in a glass vase on the reception counter, were beautiful and just about to open fully. Ordinarily, she would stop at a restaurant, usually Sam and Omie's, for lunch between her morning at the animal hospital and her afternoon in her studio, but she wanted to take the roses home with her and they would bake in the car while she was eating. So, instead, she bought a sandwich from the Subway around the corner and settled into the small kitchen at the animal hospital to eat and read.

The book she was reading was titled *Making Good Choices: A Woman's Guide to Relationships,* and was one of a half dozen her therapist had recommended to her. Most of the books, filled with psychobabble, had not spoken to her, but this one did. She could see herself in the anecdotes the author used to illustrate her points. And this author was forward-looking rather than focusing on the past. Lacey appreciated that. She did not want to be analyzed. She didn't want to look at how, in some bizarre way, she had followed her mother's promiscuous footsteps without even knowing about them. She just wanted to stop. This author made sense. *It's so much easier to stop an old behavior when you have a new behavior to take its place,* she suggested. The author was big on relationships that started as friendships, that did not rush toward physical intimacy, that involved deep and open communication. The person selected for that relationship should be someone different from the type of person the reader was ordinarily drawn to, the author advised. Someone who would not trigger those old behaviors. Someone, Lacey knew, like Rick.

He had kissed her for the first time last night. She doubted she had ever been on three dates before without kissing. In truth, she had not been on three dates before without going to bed with the guy. Last night's kiss had been chaste, closed-mouthed, and that had been fine with her. She'd wanted nothing more than that. She was a bit worried she had permanently frightened the libido out of herself, but maybe that wasn't such a bad thing. She knew she should be thrilled that Rick had come along at this point in her life. Someone decent, who listened to her when she said she needed to move slowly, who made no demands on her. It felt like a gift, like some greater power was telling her, "You've been a good girl for a whole year, Lacey. Now you have earned this truly decent man." And yet, something was missing.

She was now reading a chapter she desperately needed: Discovering Attraction Where There Is None. *"Often,"* the author wrote, *"women are attracted to 'bad boys,' those men who are a challenge or who are in need of 'fixing.' The 'good boys' are uninteresting and unattractive to these women. But feelings follow behavior. If the man seems right, but the chemistry is lacking, stop focusing on that point. Instead, talk to yourself about his good qualities. I promise, if it was meant to be, loving feelings will follow."*

This was perfect timing, Lacey thought. She had the man. The good boy. And he was even attractive. *Feelings follow behavior.* Standing up from the table, she reached for the phone on the wall. She would call to thank him for the roses.

7

EVEN AS HE PULLED INTO THE PARKING LOT IN
front of Lacey's studio, Rick could see the roses through the
broad front windows. She had brought them with her from
the animal hospital. They meant something to her, and that
could either be good or bad.

He was not exactly sure how to proceed with Lacey. All he
knew was that he needed to move carefully. It was unusual
for a woman not to fawn all over him. He was undeniably
handsome. He was an attorney. He drove a BMW. But it was
clear that superficial trappings didn't matter to Lacey, and that
frankly intrigued him. She couldn't handle too much of him
at once, though. Of that he was certain.

He turned off the ignition and picked up a book from the
passenger seat, resting it on his lap. He wondered if stopping
in to see her after sending her roses and after speaking to her
on the phone only an hour before—and now bringing her
yet another gift—would qualify as too much. He was willing to take the risk, though. The roses in the window gave
him courage.

He'd learned to time his visits to the studio when Tom
Nestor wasn't present. He'd actually been relieved to learn

that Tom was Lacey's biological father, because it explained the extreme interest the man seemed to take in her affairs. Still, he would just as soon visit with her alone.

He walked into the studio, the book in his hand, and was surprised when Lacey stood up, walked over to him, and gave him a quick hug.

"It's good to see you," she said.

"You, too."

This was a rare welcome from Lacey. He must have turned a corner with her with those flowers. The vase rested on the table next to the kaleidoscopes, and the afternoon light shone through the fragile petals.

"What a perfect spot for the roses," he said. "They nearly look like they're made of stained glass sitting there."

"That's exactly what I was thinking," she said, taking her seat behind her worktable again. She was so pretty in her pale, freckled way. So delicate looking. He hoped he would not hurt her. "They're inspiring me, actually," she continued. "I think my next piece will be yellow roses."

He sat down on the chair adjacent to the table. "Glad I could tweak your artistic sense a bit," he said, then added, "You act like you don't receive flowers very often."

"I don't think I ever have," she admitted. "At least not from a man. Well, other than my father or Tom."

"Hard to believe," he said. "A woman like you deserves flowers."

She shrugged off the compliment, and he thought he might have taken things a bit too far with it.

Two customers, a man and a woman, walked into the studio and began wandering among the glass and photographs. Rick lowered his voice to avoid being heard by them.

"Listen," he said. "I wanted to tell you that I spoke with a friend of mine who's more familiar with criminal law than I am. He had some suggestions for you on how to protest that guy's parole."

She was suddenly all ears. "What did he say?"

"You'll need to contact the members of the parole commission," he said. "They're the people who decide whether this guy…what's his name again?"

"Zachary Pointer."

"Whether he should be paroled or not. They'll take into account his previous criminal record and his behavior in prison. Do you know anything about that?"

Lacey glanced over at the man and woman, who were standing in front of a glass panel, talking about its colors.

"I don't think he had a criminal record," she said, looking as though that fact disappointed her. "And I have no idea what he's been like in prison."

"Well, here's where you have some input," he said. "The commission has to take into account any information they get from you or from other people who knew your mother and were impacted by her death. You'll need to write what they call a victim impact statement. How his crime has impacted your life. Everyone in your family can submit one. You're in the best position to write one, though, since you were impacted both by the loss of your mother and by witnessing her…what happened."

She nodded slowly, her gaze somewhere in space as she thought over what he'd said. "Okay," she said. "I can do that."

The man and woman headed for the door, and the woman turned to Lacey, waving with a smile. "We'll be back later," she said. "I want to get my sister to see that stained-glass rooster."

"Okay," Lacey said. "See you then."

Rick waited for Lacey's attention to return to him. "You— or your attorney, at least—will want to look back at any statements the guy made after the arrest and during the trial," he continued. "Look for a lack of remorse, or that he's still protesting his innocence. Anything that shows he needs continued incarceration."

"All right," Lacey said.

He hesitated, a little nervous about the next item on his agenda. "On another note, though," he said, "I have something for you." He handed the book to her. She looked at the title. *Forgiveness*. Then she raised her eyes to him, her expression quizzical.

"Are you very religious or something?" she asked.

He smiled. "Nope. Just a run-of-the-mill, hardly-ever-goes-to-church Presbyterian. But I've just… Well, I've worked hard at figuring out my priorities," he said. "You know, what's most important in life. What's worth my effort and energy and time and—"

"He killed my mother, Rick," she said, a flash of fire in her deep blue eyes.

He nodded. "I understand. Or rather, I guess I *don't* understand what that must feel like. I'm sorry."

The jingling sound of glass against glass caught their attention, and Rick turned to see a woman push the studio door open with such force that the small, stained glass sun-catchers hanging on it were in danger of breaking. The woman was very tanned, her white-blond hair pinned up at the back of her head. She wore a navy blue suit with a small gold pin on the lapel, and she was not a customer, that much was clear. Her eyes were red and smudged with mascara.

"Nola!" Lacey was instantly on her feet, rushing toward the woman. "What's wrong?"

"Oh, Lacey, I'm beside myself!" The woman stood in the middle of the floor, looking as though she might burst into tears. Her hands were pressed to her cheeks and the heavy gold bracelets on her wrists clanged together. Her fingers sparkled with rings.

"I can see that." Lacey took her arm and drew her toward Tom Nestor's worktable. "Here, sit in Tom's chair. Are Jessica and Mackenzie all right?"

"I think so," the woman said. "I mean, I think they'll be all right. But I'm on my way to Arizona and wanted to stop in to let you know what was going on before I left." She looked at Lacey, her eyes wide and filled with pain. "Jessica and Mackenzie were in a car wreck," she said.

"Oh, my God." Lacey's hand flew to her mouth. She lowered herself to her haunches in front of the woman, her long skirt billowing around her on the floor, and rested one of her hands on Nola's. "How bad?"

"Mackenzie's fine, or at least that's what they're telling me. But Jessica has broken ribs and a collapsed lung and a broken pelvis—" the woman ticked the injuries off on her fingers "—and who knows what else."

"Oh, Nola, how awful." Lacey looked over at Rick. "Jessica—Nola's daughter—is an old friend of mine," she explained. "How did it happen?"

"A drunk driver," Nola said. "That's all I know. I'm going out there to take care of Mackenzie while Jessica is in the hospital. Right now, she's with a neighbor."

"You'll feel better once you see Jess and know she's in good hands," Lacey said, and Rick could see tears forming in her eyes as well. He felt intrusive.

Nola nodded, but she looked unconvinced. "My poor little girl."

Lacey stood up and leaned over to hug her. The woman was unresponsive, stiff as a stick. He wondered how old she was. There was not a wrinkle on her tanned face, and it was obvious she'd visited a plastic surgeon more than once.

"She's tried so hard to make it, Lacey," Nola said, a mix of anger and sorrow in her voice. "You know that. Raising Mackenzie by herself, holding down a stressful job, going to school at night."

"I know," Lacey agreed. "Maybe I should go with you."

"No, no." Nola opened her large brown leather purse and pulled a tissue from inside it. She stood up, dabbing at her eyes. "I'll call you when I see how she is."

"Please do," Lacey said, embracing the woman once again. "Please call me right away."

With a nod, Nola turned and walked out the door, the sun-catchers clanking against the glass once again.

Lacey sank into her chair behind the worktable. "I can't believe it," she said. "Poor Jessica."

"You're very close to her?" he asked.

"We grew up together." She was staring at the door, but he could tell she was not really seeing it. "She was my best friend from the time we were in kindergarten through junior high. She got pregnant when she was fifteen, though, and Nola shipped her off to Arizona to live with her cousins and she ended up staying out there. We've lost touch a bit since then, but we still have these long, wonderful phone conversations a few times a year. I haven't seen Mackenzie—her daughter— since the last time they visited the Outer Banks, which must have been three years ago." She stood up abruptly. "I've got to go home," she said. "I want to call her. I need to hear for myself how she is."

"Of course," he said, standing up.

Lacey looked at her watch. "I'll call Tom to come back to the studio to keep it open, but would you mind staying until he gets here? In case that couple comes back? Or I could just lock up and put a sign on the—"

"I'll stay," he said. "It'll make me feel like I'm helping somehow."

She smiled at him, a quick, distracted sort of smile. "Thanks," she said, gathering up her purse and day planner. "I'll talk to you later."

He watched her leave. She was gentle with the door; the sun-catchers barely clinked against the glass. Looking over at her worktable, he noticed she had left behind the book on forgiveness. He wanted to run after her, press it into her hands, but he didn't dare. She already thought him strange in that regard, a religious zealot, perhaps. And the last thing he wanted to do was to scare her away.

8

IF IT HAD NOT BEEN FOR THE BEACH TRAFFIC, Lacey would have ignored the speed limit and raced all the way to Kiss River from her studio. As it was, she was stuck in a sluggish trail of cars making their way north from Kill Devil Hills. She wanted to call the hospital and hear for herself that Jessica was all right. She wanted to talk to her old friend, hear her voice, reassure her that Mackenzie would be taken care of while she recovered. Again, she thought of packing a bag and flying to Arizona with Nola. They could spell each other while they took turns taking care of eleven-year-old Mackenzie and spending time with Jessica in the hospital. But even though she'd known Nola for as long as she could remember, she had never felt completely at ease with her. Nola could be difficult. She'd been divorced for many years and had never remarried or even dated, although at one time it had been clear that she had her eye on Lacey's father. Thank God Olivia had come along at that point, or Lacey might have ended up with Nola as a stepmother. Just talking to Nola on the phone could send a chill up her spine.

Nola had been a lax and permissive mother with Jessica. Lacey's mother had certainly been lenient and indulgent, as well, but Annie O'Neill's permissiveness had been balanced by her deep love for her children. Although Jessica had often been critical of Lacey's parents, she'd admitted just a few years ago that she had actually been envious of the close and loving relationships Lacey had enjoyed growing up in the O'Neill family.

The traffic was ridiculous! She was driving through Duck, her car creeping so slowly that she feared it might overheat. It had happened before. She turned off the air-conditioning and opened the windows to try to prevent it from happening again. She knew every alternate route available along the Outer Banks, but the island was so narrow here that there was only one road running south and north, and she was on it. She glanced at her cell phone lying on the passenger seat. She could try to call Jessica on the cell, but she didn't know what hospital she was in, and the thought of coping with cellular information and the iffy reception in the area was more than she could manage.

Her thoughts turned to Mackenzie. What had the accident been like? Mackenzie wasn't hurt, Nola had said, so maybe she had been conscious and had witnessed everything. Maybe she saw her mother's body pinned behind the wheel, or maybe the car had flipped over. Then she began wondering, as she always did when she thought about Mackenzie, what had become of the girl's father. That had been a sore spot between her and Jessica for years. Mackenzie's father was Bobby Asher. He'd been one of the many guys she and Jessica had hung around with the summer Lacey was fourteen. In her mind, Bobby would always be that seventeen-year-old chain-smoking, beer-drinking, pill-popping, sexy-as-hell guy, with the blond hair that touched his shoulders and the same light blue eyes she saw in every picture of Mackenzie. Lacey had lost her virginity to him, as had Jessica, the very next night. She'd been hurt that Bobby had ultimately picked Jessica over her. Jess had been less uptight, ready for anything. Lacey had been fairly wild that summer, too, but she knew the scared little kid inside her had been evident to anyone who looked hard enough. Nothing had seemed to frighten Jessica, however, and Bobby had been drawn to that quality in her.

At the end of that summer, Bobby returned to his home in Richmond, Virginia, and neither she nor Jessica ever saw him again. When Jessica realized she was pregnant, she adamantly refused to tell Nola or anyone else who the baby's father was. Only Lacey knew. Jessica had had other lovers, if you could call them that at age fourteen. They'd both had others. But the timing of her pregnancy fit perfectly with her time with Bobby.

At first Lacey thought that Jessica was right to keep the identity of the baby's father to herself. Bobby was crazy. Undoubtably, he would have talked her into an abortion so he could rid himself of the problem. Nola had tried to talk Jessica into an abortion herself, but Lacey had persuaded her not to do it. Lacey had only recently lost her mother, and the thought of yet another life being wiped off the planet, no matter how tiny and unformed that life might have been, was unbearable to her. Jessica agreed. She had turned fifteen by then, and there was no way any doctor would take that baby against her will. So Nola arranged for her to leave the Outer Banks, spiriting her away to an aunt in Phoenix so that her expanding belly would not be a source of gossip and shame for Nola, a prominent real estate agent.

When Lacey was sixteen, she learned that Tom was her biological father and her feelings about Jessica keeping the identity of Mackenzie's father to herself changed. A child needed to know who her father was, even if knowing the truth created more problems than it solved. And a man needed to know that he was responsible for a child. The subject of Mackenzie's paternity had nearly caused a falling-out between her and Jessica. As recently as Mackenzie's eleventh birthday this past April, Lacey had once again brought it up with her. "You really should tell Bobby Asher," she'd said. "Mackenzie's getting old enough to know the truth." As always, Jessica had adamantly refused to even consider it.

She knew Jessica had told Mackenzie that her father was someone she'd seen for a short time and that she didn't know where he was. That was true, but he was findable. Anyone was findable. Lacey tried to picture Bobby Asher now—he would be nearly thirty, Clay's age, but the only image that came to her mind was of a long-haired man in need of a bath, standing at a corner of a busy Richmond street, holding a bowl out to drivers passing by, the sign at his side reading: *Homeless. Please Help.* That was surely the direction in which he'd been heading.

When she finally reached Kiss River, she was glad to see that the chain across the driveway was already down and she wouldn't need to get out of the car to unhook it. She turned onto the shaded lane and sped over the ruts, spraying gravel behind her, not really caring about anything other than getting to the phone.

Clay's Jeep was next to Gina's van in the parking lot, and she knew he was either in the woods with one of his search-and-rescue trainees or in the house waiting for a client to arrive. She jumped out of her car and ran across the sand toward the house.

Clay and Gina were in the kitchen when she pulled open the screen door, and Gina lifted a finger to her lips.

"Shh," she said. "I just got her down for her nap."

Clay was sweeping the always-sandy kitchen floor and he

looked up from his task. "What's wrong?" he asked, and she knew her worry was showing in her face.

"Jessica and Mackenzie were in an accident," she said. "They're alive, but Jessica was hurt." She rattled off Jessica's injuries to the best of her memory. "I'm going to try to call her at the hospital."

"Whose fault was the accident?" Clay asked, as if it mattered.

"Drunk driver." Dropping her purse on the table, she reached for the cordless phone and dialed Information.

"Who's Jessica?" Gina asked Clay.

"An old friend of Lacey's," he said. "She was crazy. She got pregnant when she was fourteen, and I think she used every drug in the book that summer."

"She's completely different now." Lacey felt tears burn her eyes as she waited to get a human being on the line. She didn't know the name of a single hospital in Phoenix, much less which one Jessica was in. "Besides," she added, "you were not so staid yourself." She was annoyed at the speed with which her brother jumped to judge her friend.

"My guy?" Gina asked, putting her arm around Clay's shoulders and planting a kiss on his cheek. "Did you have a wild side back then?"

"Lacey was so wasted that summer that she wouldn't have known what I was doing," Clay said.

She *had* known, though. She'd been at parties where she'd watched her older brother drink himself into the adolescent oblivion that was typical of the other graduating seniors that year. True, he'd only used alcohol, at least to the best of her knowledge, while she and her friends had dabbled in marijuana and an occasional tab of LSD. Some of the rowdier kids had actually used crack. But Clay had been old enough to pass himself off as a responsible adult when he needed to. She—and Jessica—had simply been a mess.

Finally, a male voice came on the phone. He gave her the numbers for three different hospitals and she wrote them down on a piece of paper Gina slipped onto the counter in front of her.

"I'm going to call her from the studio," she said, clutching the paper in her hand as she headed out of the kitchen in the direction of the sunroom.

"Good luck," Gina called after her, and as Lacey walked through the living room, she could hear her sister-in-law chastising Clay for his insensitivity.

Sunlight poured into her small home studio, filling it with color from the panels of glass hanging in the windows. The room was at the back of the keeper's house, away from the ocean and the lighthouse. Her view was of the stretch of sand between the house and the scrubby maritime growth in the distance. There were two worktables, one where she drew her designs out on paper, the other where she cut glass. Sitting down at that second table, she reached for the phone and dialed one of the numbers on the list.

"She's in the ICU," the hospital operator told her after Lacey gave her Jessica's name. "No phones in the rooms up there."

The ICU. She pictured machines and tubes. Respirators and EKGs. Poor Jess.

"Can I find out how she's doing?" Lacey asked. "Maybe talk to a nurse?"

"Hold on." The operator sounded sick of her job. "I'll connect you to the ICU."

A woman answered quickly, her voice friendly and upbeat.

"Hello," Lacey said. "I'm calling to find out how one of your patients is doing. Jessica Dillard."

"Are you family?" the woman asked.

"Nearly," Lacey said. "A very close friend."

"Her condition's been upgraded from critical to serious," the woman said.

"Critical!" Lacey said. "I had no idea it was that bad."

"She's doing much better now," the woman reassured her. "We'll be moving her out of the ICU sometime this afternoon. Would you like to speak with her? I can carry the cordless into her room."

"Oh, yes, please," Lacey said. Jessica was well enough to talk. Thank God.

A few moments passed, and she could hear a rustling sound. The next voice she heard on the phone was weak but familiar.

"Hello?" Jessica said.

"Jess, it's Lacey."

"Lacey." She sounded tired. Maybe half-asleep. "You're so sweet to call."

"How do you feel? Are you in terrible pain?"

She was slow to answer. "I think I would be if they weren't pumping me with drugs," she said. "How did you know I was here? Did Mom call you?"

"She came into the studio to tell me about the accident and that she's going out there to help with Mackenzie."

"Poor Mackenzie," Jessica said. "I think it was worse for her than for me, since I was knocked out and don't remember a thing."

"Do you want me to come out, too?" Lacey asked. "I can, you know. I mean, Dad has enough help that he can get by for a few days without—"

"No," Jessica said. "I'll be fine. But you have to promise me that you'll come visit *after* I've recovered, okay? All these years I've been out here, and you've never visited."

Lacey had to smile. As terrible as Jessica must be feeling,

she was still able to push her guilt buttons. And she was right. Lacey always said she would visit Jessica "some day soon," but in the nearly twelve years Jessica had lived in Phoenix, that day had never come.

"I will," she said. "I promise."

Jessica sighed. "I was so lucky, Lace," she said. "This morning they told me how close I'd come to dying. I am going to really embrace every minute of my life from now on. You do the same, okay?"

"You sound so strong," Lacey marveled. "How did you get that way?"

Jessica laughed, though the sound was weak. "Motherhood," she said. "It either makes you strong or it kills you."

"I love you," Lacey said.

"Love you, too, Lace. Don't worry about me, okay?"

"Okay."

Lacey hung up the phone, relieved by the conversation and wondering what she could do to help from two thousand miles away. Sending flowers was one option, but Jessica would probably get plenty of those. She'd buy her books and magazines, things to help her pass the time as she healed. Yet even that idea didn't ease her powerless feeling, and she wished she could do more.

She had no idea just how much she would be asked to do.

9

LEDA AND JUDY HAD BEEN WRONG ABOUT THE
rules. It wasn't until Faye's sixth date with Jim that they finally made love. And by then she felt so comfortable with
him, so trusting and at home, that she was no longer anxious
about her body or her performance. He had shared so much
with her about himself and his life. He'd told her about his
own performance anxiety—he'd had some prostate problems
a few years ago—and she'd been able to share her own inse-
curities about her weight, her crepey skin, her wrinkles. He
had only laughed, as though her concerns had been the fur-
thest thing from his mind.

Of course, once the line had been crossed, they spent a lot
more time in bed than they did going to dinner or the movies. The third time they made love, they had not even bothered with the pretense of going out. She drove directly from
work to his house. She was exhausted, having taught an all-
day seminar for chronic pain clinicians, and although she'd
loved every minute of the training, it had taken a lot out of
her. She found new energy in the car, though, as she thought
about spending the evening with Jim.

It was the first time she'd been in his home, and he gave her a short tour before leading her up to the master suite. She'd known he had money, but she hadn't expected the absolute luxury that surrounded her when she walked into the grand foyer. It was obvious that every inch of the house had been professionally decorated, and she couldn't help but wonder if she was seeing Jim's taste in the elaborate window treatments and floral print upholstery or his late wife's.

The view from the bedroom—from nearly every room of the house, actually—was spectacular. The house stood on a hillside, and in the evening light La Jolla stretched out beneath it like a quilt. The sun was a vivid coral as it drifted toward the sea. Faye studied the scene before her with great attention, doing her best to ignore the fact that she would soon climb into Alice Price's antique bed. Was Jim thinking about that, too? Did it feel strange to him to have another woman in this room?

The thought slipped from her mind, though, as he began undressing her. Lovemaking with Jim was slow and sweet, and Judy had been right about him leaving her satisfied. Judy would have to speculate about that, though, since Faye had stopped sharing private information with her and Leda, much to their frustration.

After they made love and darkness had fallen in the room, Jim hugged her close and let out a long sigh. It sounded like contentment to her, and she nestled her head against his shoulder.

"I've been thinking about you a lot the past couple of days," he said, rubbing her bare shoulder.

"You have?"

"I want you to know how much I've appreciated all the listening you've done," he said. "I haven't been able to talk to anyone the way I've talked to you in a very long time. Maybe never."

She was touched. "I'm glad you've felt able to," she said, resting her palm flat against his chest.

"I realized, though, that you haven't really told me much about yourself," he continued. "You tell me how you feel about things, and I really like that. You're such a straight shooter. I don't have to guess with you. But..." His voice trailed off.

"But?"

"I don't know anything about your past."

"Ah," she said. She'd hoped to avoid talking to him about her past, but clearly that was going to be impossible.

"Here's what I know," he said. "You grew up in North Carolina, like I did. You were an only child. Your parents are dead. You have no children. You were married, but your husband died long ago and you haven't dated since. But I don't know what it was like for you growing up, or what your parents did for a living, and that's my fault for not asking questions. I know that. And I'm sorry."

"It's all right," she said.

"The biggest blank of all is your marriage." His hand toyed with her hair where it fell in wisps at the back of her neck. "Your husband," he said. "You never talk about him. You know all about Alice. I talk about her too much, I suppose." He laughed self-consciously and she felt a little sorry for him.

"No, you don't," she reassured him.

"I guess what I'm trying to say is that I'm sorry I haven't asked you about these things before now," he said. "That I haven't given you the chance to tell me about yourself. I hope you haven't misconstrued that as disinterest. It's really been..." He laughed. "It's been selfishness, pure and simple. I needed to dump my problems onto you. But I'm ready now."

She was quiet, and he nudged her.

"So go ahead," he said. "Tell me."

She let out her breath. "Oh," she said, "this is hard."

"Why is it hard?"

She could feel the blank slate he'd placed in front of her, waiting for her to fill it. "Some things are difficult to talk about," she said. "But I *do* want to tell you. I want a good relationship with you and I know I can't build one on lies."

"Have you been lying to me?" It sounded as though this was not a complete surprise to him.

"Yes," she said, "though mostly through omission."

"You can tell me anything," he said, and she wondered if he knew what he was getting himself into.

"I have to ask you to keep what I say just between us, okay?" she asked. "I mean, I'm ready to tell *you*...some things...but not the world."

"All right."

She was quiet a moment, forming her thoughts, and he spoke before she could get the first word out.

"You *have* had a child," he said.

The question surprised her. Of the things she was preparing to say, that was low on her list. "Yes, I have," she said. "But how did you know?"

"Your body gave it away."

"My stretch marks?"

He laughed. "You are so self-conscious about your body," he said. "I didn't notice any stretch marks. But the color of your nipples. The areolae are dark."

"That's what I get for dating a doctor," she said.

"Did you lose the child?"

She pressed her palm against his chest again, trying to formulate her response. "Yes," she said. "But not the way you mean." She squeezed her eyes shut. "My husband didn't die," she said. "I'm not really a widow." She hurried on as she felt the muscles in his chest tighten up beneath her hand. "And

I'm very, very sorry for having led you to believe that I am, because I know that's part of what drew you to me. Thinking we had that in common. I'm sorry."

"You're still married?" he asked.

"No. I'm divorced. But when I moved here—to California—eight years ago, I couldn't bring myself to tell complete strangers the truth. It was easier to just say he'd died. I didn't want to have to answer questions about my ex. He *was* dead to me, as far as I was concerned, so it wasn't a lie that was hard for me to stick with. Until now. until you."

"It was a nasty divorce, then." He was upset over her pretense of being a widow. She could hear it in his voice, and she didn't blame him.

"I want you to know that I'm an honest person," she said. "I mean, basically, I'm very honest. I do have this one big lie I've been living, but please don't think that it defines who I am. Because it doesn't."

"Tell me," he said.

"My ex-husband is in prison for murder." She had said those words to herself many times, but never, not once, had she said them out loud. They echoed in the huge room.

"God," he said. "What happened?"

She rolled away from him to turn on the Tiffany lamp on the night table. The old, nauseating images were filling her head and whenever that happened, she couldn't tolerate being in the dark.

"Are you okay?" he asked.

She rested her head on his shoulder, swallowing hard against the nausea.

"Could that be enough for now?" she asked. "Enough of the truth? I still get nightmares about it sometimes and don't really want to have any tonight." How could she tell him she had lived in a cramped little North Carolina trailer—and spent time in a battered women's shelter—when here she was, lying in a $3000 carved cherry bed in La Jolla, trying to fit in with the sort of people she hadn't even known existed back then?

"Just tell me one thing," Jim said. "He didn't kill your child, did he?"

"No," she said. "Nothing like that."

"Is it a boy or a girl?"

"A boy." A man by now. "His name is Freddy. Fred. We're estranged. He blamed me for what happened with his father. He thought I somehow drove him to kill someone. After it happened, Freddy and I left North Carolina and moved to L.A., where I had an old girlfriend from nursing school. We moved in with her and I got my master's degree there. My son was very hard to manage, though. He wasn't a bad kid. Just...so terribly angry with me. The day he turned eighteen, he moved out. I went to a counselor who said I should practice tough love. You know, let him go, let him make it on his own. So that's what I did." She recited the situation with little emotion. She couldn't let herself feel the pain behind the words or she might fall apart, and she wasn't ready to do that with Jim. With anyone.

"And you haven't been in touch with him since?"

"I don't know where he is, and he's never tried to find me."

Jim sighed, rubbing her shoulder again. "I actually had a similar problem with my daughters," he said.

"You did?" She had not yet met his adult twin daughters, but she'd seen pictures of them just that night during the house tour. Photographs of the blue-eyed blondes at various ages were on the bookshelf in the den. There were a few photographs of Alice on that bookshelf, too, and she looked just as Faye had expected: well-coifed, well-dressed and glittering with gold. The woman was her opposite, at least on the surface.

"They didn't talk to me for a year after Alice died," he said. "Why?"

It was his turn to hesitate. "They blamed me for their mother's death," he said. "I talked Alice into enrolling in an experimental treatment program. I didn't see that she had much of a chance otherwise, and I think—I hope—she understood that. The girls were furious with me, though. They said I turned Alice into a guinea pig, et cetera, et cetera." He sighed, and she knew he'd been through quite a battle with his girls. She could only imagine what it had been like for him to endure the loss of his wife and his daughters' antipathy at the same time.

"I think they were cruel to turn their backs on you," she said.

"They were in a lot of pain," he said, "but eventually, they realized that I'd truly had Alice's best interest in mind. So maybe, someday Fred will come around, too."

"God, I wish," she said, struggling not to feel the sorrow welling up inside her. "Every time I see a young man come into the pain clinic, I think of him. Even when they don't look a thing like him." Gunshot victims, especially, tugged at her emotions. If it hadn't been for Annie O'Neill, Freddy might have been one of them himself. She waved her hand in front of her face as if trying to bat away the thought. "I can't talk about it anymore," she said.

She lifted her head to study his face. In the light from the Tiffany lamp, she could see the arc of wrinkles at the corners of his eyes, the deep crevices that ran from his nose to his chin, and she knew he must be seeing similar flaws on her own face. She should turn off the light. But before she could roll over, he touched her cheek with his fingertip, tracing whatever lines he might be finding there, and smiled. "When you're ready to tell me more," he said, "I'll be here for you."

10

THE KEEPER'S HOUSE WAS QUIET AND CALM AS Lacey and Rick sat at the kitchen table, sipping iced tea and wrapping gifts for Jessica. Sasha slept by the screen door, occasionally opening his eyes to see if Clay or Gina or Rani might be walking through the sand toward the house. It was Clay's long day at work, and Gina had taken Rani to her toddler swim lessons.

"Isn't she a little young for swimming lessons?" Rick had asked when Lacey told him where they were.

"It's mostly to get her used to the water," Lacey said. "She was afraid of it when she first got here. She couldn't even look at a full bathtub or the toilet without crying." For reasons they were never to understand, Rani would scream even when approached with a damp washcloth. Gina's best guess was that her little daughter had been subjected to rough shampooing with harsh soaps, necessary to kill the lice and nits that every child in the orphanage seemed to have. But Rani's phobia was improving. She let Gina or Clay bathe her now in a large basin, and the previous week, Gina had finally coaxed her into the pool.

It was at moments like these, when the only sounds in the

house were from the ocean and the cicadas, that Lacey realized how much chatter and energy Rani produced. Just a few months ago, Gina had worried there was a problem with her development, because Rani never spoke. One morning, though, the child simply woke up a chatterbox. Not only did she seem to know the right words for nearly every object she encountered, but she also strung those words together in sentences. She may not have been speaking, but she'd certainly been listening. She ran into the kitchen that morning, looked up at Clay, and said, "Daddy, I want you play with me, *now!*" Gina and Lacey had looked at each other and laughed, but Clay had cried. He had changed so much since Rani came into his life. There was a softness to him Lacey had never expected to see.

"Should I wrap each of these separately?" Rick held up the three gel pens they had bought for Jessica.

"Sure," Lacey said. "It will be more fun for her to have a bunch of things to open, don't you think?"

She and Rick had shopped most of the afternoon, picking up small gifts to send to Jessica. Little things like pens and magazines, tiny jigsaw puzzles and one of Lacey's kaleidoscopes, gifts that could help her while away her time in the hospital. Lacey planned to put all the wrapped gifts into one big box and ship it to her. It had been kind of Rick to go shopping with her, and he'd seemed to get into it, picking up things on his own that he thought someone like Jessica might enjoy. Adding the kaleidoscope had been his idea.

A car door slammed shut in the parking lot, and Sasha was immediately on his feet, nose pressed against the screen and tail wagging. It was too soon for either Clay or Gina to be home, and Lacey got up to walk over to the door.

Her father was walking—strolling, really—toward the house. His head was down, his hands in his pockets. He was not a stroller. He always moved quickly, like Clay, and the sight of him like this scared her.

She pushed open the door and stepped onto the porch.

"Dad?" she called.

He looked up from his pensive staring at the sand and waved to her.

"What's wrong?" she asked, as he neared the house.

"Let's go inside." He reached past her for the handle of the screened door. "Go on in," he said.

He followed her into the kitchen, and Rick was quick to stand up.

"Dad, this is Rick Tenley," she said. "Rick, this is my father, Alec O'Neill."

"Hello, Dr. O'Neill." Rick held out his hand, and Alec shook it, frank curiosity on his face, but the expression disappeared quickly as his somber look returned.

"What's wrong?" she asked again. Her heart was beating hard, and she thought of Rani's little heart, so newly repaired and delicate. "Please tell me Rani's okay."

"Rani's fine." Her father touched her shoulder. "Sit down," he said, and she dropped into the chair Rick pulled out for her.

"Nola just called me," her father said. "She was trying to reach you, but didn't have your number out here."

All of a sudden, she knew. "It's Jessica," she said.

Her father leaned against the kitchen counter and nodded. "She died this morning, honey. I'm sorry."

Lacey leaped to her feet so quickly that Sasha started barking at her. "Oh, Dad, no!" she said. "How could that happen? She sounded so good when I talked to her yesterday."

"They think it was a blood clot from the surgery," her father said. "It was fast. She probably didn't even know what hit her."

That's what they had said about her mother, but her mother

had known. Lacey would never forget the look of surprise on her face.

"Oh, God, I don't believe it." She sat down again, one elbow on the table, her fist pressed to her mouth. She was not aware of crying until she felt the tears falling over her clenched fingers. Rick rested his hand on her back. She knew he was trying to console her, but his touch felt like more of an intrusion than comfort.

"Nola said they weren't sure about arrangements for a service yet," her father said, "but that it would probably be Monday."

"I'll go," Lacey said into her fist. "I have to go." She turned toward her father and saw that he looked tired and drained. The O'Neill family had become all too accustomed to coping with unexpected loss. "How's Nola taking it?" she asked.

"She's in a lot of pain, as you can imagine. I had trouble understanding her, she was crying so hard. Oh." He reached into his pocket and drew out a piece of paper, handing it to her. "She left this number in case you wanted to call her," he said.

Lacey took the piece of paper from his hand and stared at it numbly.

"I have to get back to the office, hon," her father said. "I still have some appointments today, but I didn't want to tell you over the phone."

"Thank you." She knew he had done some major shuffling of his patients to be able to make the trip to Kiss River.

Her father turned his attention to Rick. "How do you know Lacey, Rick?" he asked.

"We met at her studio," Rick said.

"Well, I'm glad you're here." Her father surprised her with the words. "I'm glad Lacey's not alone right now."

After Alec left, Rick began unwrapping the items they had bought. "I'll return these things for you," he said.

She glanced at the puzzles and pens without seeing them. "You don't have to do that," she said.

"I want to. I know there's not a lot else I can do to help out right now." He stood up and began digging through the trash can beneath the sink for the receipts. "I'd like to go with you to Arizona," he said as he pawed through the trash.

"Thank you, but no." She didn't want him there. He would feel like more of a liability than an asset. She stood up, the piece of paper her father had given her in her hand. "I'm going up to my room to call Nola," she said. "You don't have to stay."

He looked up from his work in the trash can. "Your father didn't want you to be alone," he said.

"I'll be okay. Gina and Clay will be home soon. And I really just want to crawl into bed and pull the covers over my head."

He put his hands in his pockets, worry on his face. "It's not even four-thirty," he said.

She shut her eyes, drained of energy to explain her need for time to herself. "I just want to go to bed," she said, and it came out like a plea.

He nodded. "All right." He slid the trash can back under the sink, then walked over to her and hugged her tightly, and all she could think about was having him leave so that she could fall apart in peace.

Once he was gone, she carried the cordless phone upstairs and crawled, still dressed in her blue T-shirt and striped capris, into her bed. A breeze billowed the sheer curtains into the room, but it was still too hot for more than a sheet. She pulled the box of tissues from the night table to her bed. Hugging her arms across her chest, she thought, *Should I let myself break down before or after I talk to Nola?*

Without making a decision, she dialed the number on the piece of paper. A woman with a quiet voice answered.

"I'm trying to reach Nola Dillard," Lacey said. "This is Lacey O'Neill."

Her name seemed to mean nothing to the woman. "Nola's lying down," she nearly whispered. "Can I have her call you when she gets up?"

"Yes, I'm calling from the east coast, but please tell her to call me any time," Lacey said. "No matter what time it is here, all right?" She gave the woman her phone number and made her repeat it back to her. For once in her life, she wanted to talk to Nola Dillard. She needed to talk to someone else who loved Jessica.

Once she hung up the phone, her tears started. They lasted for five or six minutes, then faded away, and just when she thought she was done with them, she pictured Jessica's smile and thought about the fear and disbelief Mackenzie was enduring, and her sobbing started again.

She'd long ago given up asking why things like this happened. Her mother had died from a bullet meant for someone else. Her sister-in-law, Terri—Clay's first wife—had died while doing search-and-rescue work. The losses seemed so random, so meaningless—although once this past year, she'd wondered if her mother's death had been fitting punishment for all the cheating she'd done during her marriage. If God existed, though, she refused to believe he worked that way.

She longed for the escape of sleep, but her nose was stuffy from crying and she could not prevent memories of Jessica from slipping into her consciousness. When they'd been very young, she and Jessica had been in Brownies together, with Lacey's mother as their much-adored troop leader. Lacey could not count all the milk shakes and French fries they'd shared at McDonald's over the years, or all the times she and Jessica had slept at one another's houses. Jessica had changed dramatically during their time in middle school, when she'd become one of the "cool crowd," leaving Lacey confused and envious, but after Mackenzie was born, she'd reverted quickly to the sweet person she'd once been.

She heard Gina and Rani come home, followed by Clay a half hour later, but she didn't want to get up to talk to them. The only person she truly wanted to talk to was the person she could never talk to again: Jessica. Why hadn't she gone to Arizona to visit her sometime in the past twelve years? She had taken their friendship for granted. She should have known better than that. Now she was finally going to Phoenix, just a little bit too late.

Someone knocked lightly on her bedroom door.

"You awake, Lace?" Clay asked.

"Yes."

"Dad called to tell me," he said. "Can I come in?"

"I want to be alone," she said.

He hesitated a moment. "I'm sorry, sis," he said, finally. "And I'm sorry for the things I said about Jessica yesterday."

"It's all right." She pressed a damp, overused tissue to her eyes. "Clay?"

"Yes?"

"I love you. Please don't die."

She heard his soft laughter through the door. "I love you, too, Lacey," he said. But he didn't promise her anything. He knew better than that.

She did not sleep, did not even doze, the entire night. She lay with the box of tissues on the pillow next to her and the phone clutched in her hands, waiting for the return call from Nola. But the call never came, and it would be nearly noon the following day before she understood why.

11

LACEY DIDN'T GO INTO WORK AT THE ANIMAL hospital the next morning. It was Saturday, and the hospital would be packed with patients, but she knew her father would understand. Instead, she sat in her home studio trying to reach Nola and getting no answer to her calls, not even an outgoing message on an answering machine. She studied the piece of paper on which her father had written the phone number. Whose number was it, anyway? A friend of Jessica's probably. She knew Jessica had several good friends in Phoenix, since she'd talked about them over the years. Lacey had always felt an uncomfortable mixture of happiness and envy during those conversations, glad that Jessica had those friends, yet jealous that they had taken her place.

Between phone calls, she tried cutting glass for a panel she was making, but her heart wasn't in it. She knew better than to cut glass when she could not give it her full attention. Finally, she took off her safety glasses and settled on staring out the window. She could see Clay working with one of his search-and-rescue clients, a tall man with a skinny golden retriever. She could not make out what they were doing, but the golden could barely contain his excitement. Lacey couldn't help but smile at the happy, anticipatory dance the dog was performing in the sand near his owner.

She wanted to call a travel agent to make plane reservations for her trip to Phoenix, but hated to tie up the phone line in case Nola tried to reach her. Finally, though, she took the risk and contacted one of Olivia's friends who was a travel agent. The fare to Phoenix was exorbitant at this late date, and although she wondered if she would qualify for a discount based on the fact that she was flying there for a friend's funeral, she didn't feel like going into the subject with the agent. Instead, she gave the woman her credit card number, wrote down the flight numbers and hung up.

The instant she got off the line, the phone rang, and she picked it up quickly.

"Nola?" she asked.

There was hesitation on the line. "No, this is Charles Rodriguez," a male voice said. "Am I speaking with Lacey O'Neill?"

A telemarketer? "Yes," she said, "but I'm waiting for an important call, so—"

"Ms. O'Neill, I was Jessica Dillard's attorney," the man said.

Lacey frowned. "Her attorney?"

"Yes," he said, "and first let me express my sympathy over your loss."

"Thank you."

"I was the attorney who drew up Jessica's will and her other legal papers. She was a very responsible young woman. Amazing for her age, the way she took care of everything. She even had an advance medical directive, although that turned out to be unnecessary. It's still always good to have—"

"Excuse me, Mr....Rodriguez? Can you tell me why you're calling? I'm waiting to hear from Jessica's mother, and I don't want to tie up the line."

That hesitation again. "Did Jessica talk to you about this?"

"About what?"

"Her daughter Mackenzie's guardianship."

Lacey searched her memory. As far as she could recall, it was a topic she and Jessica had never discussed. Why would they? Jessica was only twenty-seven.

"No," she said. "Not that I remember."

The attorney sighed. "I'd hoped she discussed it with you long ago. She said she would. She wanted you to be Mackenzie's guardian if she were to die."

"Her guardian? You mean…to make decisions about—"

"She wanted you to raise her."

"I… *Me?*" She felt a moment of panic. "I live in North Carolina and I'm not even related to her. Mackenzie has a grandmother. And Jessica had some very close friends out there. And I haven't even *seen* Mackenzie in three years. I've only seen her three or four times in her entire life."

"I understand," the attorney said. "And Mrs. Dillard, Jessica's mother, was very upset when I told her about this last night. She may try to fight it, but I doubt very much she will win, because Jessica was adamant that she wanted you to be her daughter's guardian. She stated clearly in the document that she did not want her mother to have guardianship of Mackenzie."

Lacey winced, thinking about how hurtful it must have been for Nola to hear those words. No wonder she hadn't returned her calls.

"But when did she make out this will?" she asked. "I mean, was it years ago? We were much closer friends years ago, so maybe—"

"She did initially file all these papers several years ago. That's what I mean about her being so responsible. What twentysomething-year-old takes care of things like that? But she also updated all the documents only last year. She just made a few minor changes, and she was still clear that she wanted you to be Mackenzie's guardian."

"It doesn't make sense," Lacey said. "I'm sure she never thought she'd die this young. Maybe she just wasn't thinking."

"Ms. O'Neill, she and I talked about it at length," the attorney said patiently. "I suggested her mother might be a better and more logical choice, or failing that, the parents of one of Mackenzie's friends, perhaps, but she said she trusted you to be the same sort of mother she had been."

Lacey started to cry, moved by the sentiment and yet frightened by its meaning. Jessica had been a good mother. A superlative mother. She wanted to tell this stranger how motherhood had forced her to grow up quickly, how beautifully Jessica had risen to that challenge. But she would never be able to get out all those words.

"Ms. O'Neill? Are you still there?"

"Yes." She reached for a tissue from the box on her worktable and pressed it to her nose. "I'm here."

"I suggest you plan to stay out here a few extra days when you come for the funeral so that you and I can take care of the necessary paperwork. And more importantly, so you can get to know Mackenzie better before taking her back with you."

Bring her back? To Kiss River? The sense of panic was so strong that she could barely breathe. She didn't want to do this; she had never wanted a child and certainly didn't want one thrust on her when she was so totally unprepared. Her thoughts shamed her, yet if someone could tell her how she could get out of this new and unexpected responsibility, she would jump at the chance.

"I don't know if I'm suited to be anyone's mother," she said, more to herself than to the lawyer.

"Do you think Jessica was more suited at the age of fifteen?" he asked.

"That's not the point."

"This can't be forced on you," the attorney said. "If you can't take on the guardianship of this girl, we'll have to work out some other arrangements."

Jessica had wanted her to do it, to be Mackenzie's mother. She'd been adamant about it, the lawyer had said. She knew the other options open to her and she'd chosen her. Lacey thought of the little trinkets she'd wrapped the previous day to send to her friend. The gel pens and jigsaw puzzles suddenly seemed as insignificant as a grain of sand on the beach, silly gifts for a woman who would trust her with the life of her daughter. She had the ability to give Jessica a far greater gift—her life, her dreams for the future, her freedom.

"I'll do it," she said. "I'll bring Mackenzie home with me."

12

ONE OF JESSICA'S FRIENDS, A VERY YOUNG-LOOK-
ing woman named Amelia, met Lacey in the baggage area of
the Phoenix airport. She was holding a sign that read "Lacey"
in huge red block letters. Once Lacey introduced herself,
Amelia hugged her tightly, and Lacey let herself remain in the
embrace for a long time, breathing in the scent of the woman's dark hair, knowing she was finally connected to someone who felt her loss as deeply as she did.

"I'm so glad to meet you," Amelia said as she let go of her.
"I've heard a lot about you." Her voice was sweet and high-
pitched. She looked about twenty-two and sounded fifteen.
Her nearly black hair was long and swung free around her
shoulders, and freckles were spattered across the bridge of
her nose.

Lacey had to rack her brain to remember if she'd ever heard
Jessica talk about this particular friend. She supposed she had.
Jessica had been one to say "my friend this" and "my friend
that," rather than speak of them by name.

"Same here," she said. "I'm sorry we couldn't have met
under better circumstances, though." The trite words slipped

out of her mouth and she was relieved at having found them without a struggle.

The day before, she had finally been able to reach someone at the number she had for Nola, and although Nola was purportedly "still sleeping," the woman on the phone told her she would be picked up at the airport and she would have a place to stay. The woman had sounded frazzled, as though she was trying to organize too many things at once and Lacey was just one more ball for her to juggle.

"I could get a hotel," Lacey had told her.

"No, no," the woman said. "We've got it all worked out."

"You're going to stay with me," Amelia told her now as she started rolling Lacey's suitcase toward the exit.

"Thank you," Lacey said. "That's great."

Amelia didn't say another word until they were in her car in the parking lot. It was a convertible, but the top was up and the air-conditioning on, and Lacey was glad of that because the temperature had to be at least a hundred degrees.

"I've never been to North Carolina," Amelia said. "How's the weather there now?"

"Just really starting to heat up," Lacey said. She knew they were about to get into a conversation about the difference between Arizona heat and North Carolina heat. Jessica used to talk about it all the time. "It's 115 degrees here today," Jessica would tell her over the phone, "but it's a *dry* heat. Not like the Outer Banks." Sure enough, Amelia started down the same path, and Lacey played along. Why did every conversation between strangers always begin with the weather?

"How did you know Jessica?" Lacey asked when they'd exhausted the topic of the heat.

"We worked together," Amelia said, then shook her head. "I don't know how I'm going to be able to go back to work without her. She made it bearable."

Lacey knew that Jessica had worked in an office doing something with computers, but she'd never understood precisely what.

After quite a long drive, Amelia turned into the parking lot of a large complex of cute and well-maintained Spanish-style condominiums. "You can stay with me just as long as you need to," she said, swinging the car wide to pull into a marked parking space.

"I'm expecting to be here three or four days," Lacey said. "Are you sure that's not too much of an imposition?"

"Actually, I don't think three or four days will be long enough," Amelia said.

"No?"

"You might be underestimating the time it's going to take to get Mackenzie ready for the trip back with you."

They got out of the car, and Lacey pulled her suitcase from the trunk.

"How is she doing?" she asked as they walked toward the building.

"Terrible," Amelia said. "You can imagine what it's been like for her. She only had her mother. She's lost her world."

Lacey thought back to her own mother's death. "Is she able to sleep?" she asked. "Is she having nightmares?"

"I don't know." Without asking, Amelia took the suitcase from Lacey and began lugging it up the stairs to the second story of condominiums. Lacey didn't protest. It was too damn hot. "She's staying with Mary," Amelia said, "another friend of Jessica's who has a daughter Mackenzie's age. Mary could tell you how she's doing. All I've heard is that she's gotten very quiet and has lost about five pounds in the past two days."

Lacey could barely picture Mackenzie. She'd been a skinny kid the last time she saw her. If she'd lost five pounds back then, she would have been skeletal.

Amelia stopped at one of the second-story doors. She slipped her key into the lock and pushed the door open, and Lacey felt the welcome rush of cool air hit her face.

The condominium was small and neat and tastefully decorated with furniture and accessories that looked as though they'd come from Pier One.

"Your place is so cute," Lacey said, touching the arm of the squat gold sofa. "And it's so nice of you to put me up."

Amelia rolled the suitcase into the guest bedroom, which was filled with white wicker furniture. "Not a problem," she said. "Why don't you get unpacked and then come into the kitchen and have a glass of iced tea or something."

"Okay." What Lacey really wanted was a shower. She felt grimy from the flight and the heat.

"Mary—the woman Mackenzie's staying with—and another friend are coming over in a little while," Amelia said. "We're going to try to plan the memorial service tonight. I hope that's okay with you. We thought you'd probably want to be in on the planning."

"Sure." Lacey nodded, although she had not even thought of that. "Will Nola be here, too?"

Amelia opened the closet door and pulled some empty hangers from among the items of clothing. "I don't think Nola's up to it," she said, her back to Lacey. She turned, handed her the empty hangers, and sat down on the edge of the bed. "The truth is, Nola's really upset about you being named guardian," she said. "And we're all…well, we're a little confused about it. Not that you wouldn't be the right person to do it," she added quickly. "It's just that…" She looked at the wall instead of Lacey. "Well, we didn't think you've had any special connection to Mackenzie."

"Who is 'we'?" Lacey hoisted the suitcase onto the bed and started to unzip it.

"All Jessie's friends," Amelia said. "And, of course, Nola. Nola has seen Mackenzie at least once a year, and well, I don't have kids, but Jessica has lots of friends who do and who would take Mackenzie in a heartbeat. And who are married, so Mackenzie would have two parents raising her." Amelia lifted her hands in a helpless gesture, then dropped them to her lap. She had tears in her eyes. "I'm sorry," she said. "I know this is coming out all wrong. I don't seem to have the energy right now to make it come out right."

"Are you one of the friends who would be a better choice?" Lacey asked, and Amelia's eyes widened.

"No!" she said. "I'm only twenty-three, I'm not married, and I don't have any kids of my own."

"Well." Lacey tried to smile. "Except for the twenty-three part, you just described me." She pushed the suitcase toward the center of the bed so that she could sit down, herself. "I'm just as confused about this as you are, so you don't need to feel awkward about it," she said. "But Jessica's attorney told me that she was very firm about wanting me to take Mackenzie. She obviously had her reasons, and I want to do what she wanted. I think it would be horrible to put a lot of thought and care into making a huge decision like that, and then have the people left behind not follow through on my wishes."

Amelia nodded. "I know Jessica really cared about you," she said. "Some of her friends don't remember her talking about you, but I do. I was probably closest to her. She said that, even though you didn't see each other much, she still considered you her best friend. Or maybe she didn't say *best*, but she said that when you saw each other, you could just pick up where you left off without any problem."

"That's true." It seemed like a slim reason to leave her child to her, though, Lacey thought. She pulled her thick hair up and held it against the back of her head to let the air-conditioning reach her neck. "I had a lot of time to think on the plane," she added. "I came up with a few reasons she might have wanted me to take care of Mackenzie."

"What are they?" Amelia asked.

"Maybe she wants Mackenzie to be raised in the place she was raised," Lacey said, dropping her hair to her shoulders again. "In the Outer Banks."

"That's possible," Amelia said. "She always talked about how she loved it there and she complained about how dry it was here. But she stayed here, didn't she? I mean, she could have gone back. And if that was the reason, she could have left Mackenzie to her mother."

"True. But I think Jessica really liked my family. She felt comfortable with us. Maybe she wanted Mackenzie to be part of that."

Amelia nodded. "Well, maybe. Was she very close to your family? Is it big? I know she was always sad she had no brothers or sisters."

"Well, she was close to us when we were kids, though not since she moved out here," Lacey said. "I have a brother and a niece and a father and stepmother and half siblings. And my mother also died—"

"Yes, I remember Jessica saying something about that," Amelia interrupted her. "Do you think that could be her reason? That she knew you would understand how Mackenzie felt, losing her mother?"

"I thought of that," Lacey agreed. She'd also thought of another reason: Nola's wanting Jessica to have an abortion and Lacey's dissuading her from that decision, but she didn't want to mention that to Amelia with Nola in town. "And there's one other possibility I can think of," Lacey added.

"What's that?"

"I was always after Jessica to let Mackenzie's father know

that he had a daughter. To let the two of them at least *know* about each other's existence, if not actually be in each other's lives. Maybe she really wants that for Mackenzie and thinks I'll do it."

"Oh, I don't think so." Amelia shook her head, almost violently. "She never talked about him. What was his name? Bobby?"

Lacey nodded.

"The only thing she ever said about him was that he was no good—her very words—and that she didn't want Mackenzie to have any part of him."

"But she knows—" she caught herself "—she knew that I didn't feel that way." Lacey pleaded her case. "I don't care what a person is like, unless he's an abuser or something. Children still have a right to know who their parents are. Jessica knew that was the way I feel and she still chose to leave Mackenzie to me."

Tears of frustration filled Amelia's eyes. "God, I wish we could talk to her and find out what she was really thinking!" she said.

"Me, too." Lacey stood up, suddenly anxious to have her hostess out of the room so that she could cry herself. She reached for her suitcase. "I'll unpack and be out in a minute."

Two other women arrived at the condominium shortly after she and Amelia had eaten chicken salad sandwiches for dinner. At least, they'd tried to eat the sandwiches. Neither of them had much of an appetite.

The women, Mary and Veronica, were the mothers of Mackenzie's closest friends. It was Mary's family with whom Mackenzie was staying. The women were in their middle to late thirties, blond, well dressed and with an air of casual sophistication that accompanied them into the condo. Lacey felt them appraising her shorts and T-shirt, her unruly red hair and her youth, and finding her lacking. She felt instantly on edge. She had not expected to come to Arizona and face such scrutiny. Or maybe she was reading too much into the cool greetings the women gave her.

Amelia, clearly nervous and out of her league with the two older women, ushered them into the little living room. She poured them iced tea and set a plate of Pepperidge Farm cookies on the glass-and-wrought-iron coffee table, next to a stack of books Mary had carried with her into the room.

"When can I see Mackenzie?" Lacey asked Mary, as she reached for a cookie she had no interest in eating.

"We haven't told her about you, yet," Mary said. "She's been through so much. We thought we'd wait to tell her until after the memorial service. I guess we were hoping that it was a mistake and didn't want to tell her until we were absolutely sure she'd be going with you." Mary didn't even attempt to spare Lacey's feelings as she spoke. "But the lawyer said it's valid, so…" She shrugged her shoulders. "I just hope Jessica wasn't out of her mind when she drew up those papers."

"Me, too." Lacey tried to smile, to join in the subtle attacks against her competence with good humor, but the attempt fell flat and all three women simply stared at her, expressionless. "So," she said awkwardly, "I guess I won't see Mackenzie until the funeral, then?"

"It's a memorial service," Veronica said. "Not a funeral."

"I have it mostly worked out." Mary pulled a small notebook from her purse and opened it on her lap. "I'll do a reading, and Amelia, you wanted to say something, right?"

Amelia nodded.

"And Jessica's boss will speak," Mary continued. "And how about you, Lacey? Would you like to do a reading?"

"I…" It had never occurred to her to participate in the

funeral. The memorial service. "I wouldn't know what to read," she said.

"We can find something for you," Veronica said in a voice meant to reassure, although Lacey did not feel reassured in the least.

Mary studied her notes. "Oh," she said suddenly, her gaze returning to Lacey, "to answer your question, I don't think you'll be seeing Mackenzie until after the service, back at my house. She refuses to go to the service itself."

"Oh, she has to go!" Veronica said. "She'll regret it for the rest of her life if she doesn't."

"She shouldn't go if she doesn't want to," Lacey said. The words surprised her as much as they did the women. All of a sudden, she was the one who knew what was best for Mackenzie, at least in this regard, and the feeling was alien to her. "My mother died when I was thirteen," she explained, "and I didn't go to her funeral. I just couldn't. I wish I could have, but I don't regret it. I know I wasn't capable of handling it at the time. Don't make her go."

"Oh!" Veronica said. "You lost your mother, too." She turned to Mary. "Maybe that's why Jessica decided Mackenzie should go to Lacey."

Mary shrugged again. "Who knows," she said. Picking up one of the books from the coffee table, she leaned forward to hand it to Lacey.

"I know Jessica liked this book," she said. "It's about living simply and that sort of the thing. I haven't read it myself, but maybe you can find something in it to read."

Lacey took the book from her, wondering how she would ever be able to get up in front of a group of people she didn't know, all of whom loved Jessica and most of whom would forever wonder why this childless, unmarried woman was taking Mackenzie away from them, and read the words of an author who meant nothing to her.

"Thanks," she said. "I'll look through it tonight."

13

LACEY FOUND NOTHING IN THE BOOK SHE
wanted to read at the service. She leafed through the pages,
studying a phrase here and there, unable to truly absorb what
she was reading. Then she lay awake much of the night, putting her own words together. She was no speaker and had
never spoken in public, unless you counted the occasional
stained glass class, and she was afraid she would freeze at the
last minute. But she was not going to read an essay that had
no meaning for her.

It wasn't until she awakened from a fitful sleep the morning of the memorial service that she remembered the date:
July third. Her birthday. So she was twenty-six. She would
be without her friends and family today, but she would have
more birthdays. Jessica would have none. She vowed to tell
no one the significance of the date.

She'd had so little sleep in the past few days that by the
time she and Amelia arrived at the small, crowded chapel, she
was in a strange, dreamlike state. It felt as if she were moving
through someone else's life rather than her own. She followed
Amelia to the front pew of the church where the participants
were all seated. And there was Nola. The woman's eyes were

red, her mouth a tight, down-turned arc, and although her face was unlined thanks to way too much plastic surgery, she looked very old. Lacey separated from Amelia and walked over to Nola, knowing she had to do this. She could not allow the tension to exist between them any longer.

"Nola," she said, sitting next to her on the pew. She reached for her hand and was forced to hold on to just the bony tops of her fingers, since Nola would not turn her hand or lift it toward Lacey's.

"I'm heartbroken, Nola," Lacey said. "And I know it must be so much worse for you. I'm so sorry."

Nola turned her head away from her, staring in the direction of the chapel's stained-glass windows. Lacey lightly squeezed the lifeless hand, then stood up, and as she walked back to her seat next to Amelia, she was mortified to see all eyes on her. Everyone in the front pews had surely witnessed the rebuff.

She'd met with the attorney the day before and signed the necessary paperwork to take Mackenzie back to Kiss River with her. The placement would be temporary, the lawyer explained, because "several people" had come forward, concerned that Lacey's guardianship would not be "in the best interest of the child." They would have to make their case to have her removed from Lacey's custody, he said. For now, though, Jessica's wish would be granted.

Lacey floated through the service in a daze, her brain not truly in sync with her body. A woman with a stunning voice sang a couple of Sarah McLachlin songs—*Angel* and *I Will Remember You*—and although Lacey could hear sniffling all around her, she felt cried out. People stepped up to the podium to speak or to read, and when it was her turn, she welcomed the foggy state she was in because it dulled her nerves.

She walked up to the podium and turned around, stunned

for a moment at the sight of so many people crammed into the tiny chapel. They filled all the pews and lined the walls.

"I'm Lacey O'Neill." She spoke into a microphone for the first time in her life and jumped a little as she heard her voice echo in the air of the church. "I was Jessica's best friend when we were children, up until the time she moved to Arizona. Some of you might think you know her better than I do because you knew her as an adult, but I knew all those things you get to know about a person when they're young. Those things people learn to hide from other people when they get older. I knew her secrets and her longings and her dreams. And I knew what she wanted to be when she grew up: a cowgirl."

People chuckled at that. Lacey clearly remembered the conversation with Jessica. They'd been eight or nine years old, lying on the beach and finding shapes in the clouds, and Jessica thought one looked like a bull. "I want to do what those cowboys get to do," she'd said. "You know, ride wild horses and throw ropes around the cows or calves or whatever they are. I want to be a *cowgirl*." From time to time over the years, Jessica had mentioned that aspiration and it had become a running joke between them.

"It's true," Lacey said. "There are only two things she ever told me she wanted to be—a cowgirl and a mom." The crowd was beginning to blur in front of her and she blinked hard. "She got to be the most important one of those two," she continued, "and I'm really, really glad she did."

It seemed an awkward place to stop speaking, but she stepped down from the podium before she could say more. She wanted to talk about how today was her birthday, and how Jessica had told her to embrace every minute of her life, and how she planned to do that, always, in Jessica's name. But she knew if she tried to say another word, she was going to simply fall apart.

After the funeral, many of the people from the chapel drove to Mary's house. The one-story house, with its spacious rooms and vaulted ceilings, was like Mary herself—elegant, sparely decorated, with every corner and window ledge filled with prickly cacti.

In the backyard, children played in a huge, meandering pool, and Lacey guessed Mackenzie was among them. Mary poked her head out the sliding glass doors to tell the children she was home from the church, but she did not invite them in. Several women, probably caterers, placed platters of hors d'oeuvres on the massive dining room table, and the guests filled their plates. Lacey stayed close to Amelia's side, the one place she felt safe. Funny how one of the youngest women in the room was also the warmest, as though age had sapped the warmth right out of the older women.

Two nights before, after Mary and Veronica had left the condominium and before she and Amelia had gone to bed, Amelia had apologized for them. "They were rude to you," she said. "They're not always like that."

"It's hard for me to picture Jessica being friends with them," Lacey had felt brave enough to say.

"They were friends because of their children," Amelia said, and that seemed to explain everything. Lacey wondered if having Mackenzie would force her to be friends with women she couldn't stand. "They truly care about Mackenzie, though, and just want what's best for her," Amelia added.

She and Amelia now sat next to each other on dining room chairs pushed against the walls of the room. "Well," Lacey said, after nibbling some sort of egg roll and knowing that was all she would be able to eat, "there are two people here I really need to talk with."

"Mackenzie and Nola," Amelia said, and Lacey nodded. Nola was keeping her distance from her, but Lacey thought she looked as uncomfortable as she was feeling. Nola was chatting with a group of people, talking quickly as she always did when she was anxious, and focusing on the features of the house. Lacey saw her point out the tall windows and ceramic floors and the open kitchen with its decorative tile. She had on her Realtor hat; houses were a safe topic for her. Watching Nola's own discomfort gave Lacey courage.

She stood up. "Here goes," she said to Amelia. "Will you excuse me?"

"Go for it." Amelia smiled at her. She reached for Lacey's empty plate. "Let me ditch that for you."

She gave Amelia her plate, then walked toward the massive arched window, where Nola was talking to a man, waving her arm in the air as if describing something. Lacey touched her elbow, and Nola turned to look at her.

"Could I speak with you for a few minutes, please?" Lacey asked.

Nola hesitated, but only for a second. "Yes," she said. She smiled at her companion. "It was nice talking to you. Please excuse us."

Lacey looked behind her at the vast open space that contained the living room, kitchen and dining room. People were everywhere. Privacy would be hard to come by.

"Should we go out front to talk?" she suggested.

"In this heat? We'll melt." Nola pointed toward a hallway. "Let's just find one of the bedrooms. No one will mind."

Lacey wasn't sure about that, but she followed Nola down the hall and into a large bedroom with French doors leading out to the pool. This had to be the palm tree room, Lacey thought. Palm trees graced the bedspread and the curtains and the art on the wall, and a potted palm stood in one corner.

Nola sat down on the platform bed and Lacey took the up-holstered chair next to the dresser.

"How are you doing?" Lacey asked.

"How do you think I'm doing?" Nola snapped back, but there was so little energy in her voice that the question lacked punch. She rested one hand on her chest. "There's a big empty, aching void in my heart," she said. "First, I lose my only daughter. Then…" She shook her head and looked up at the ceiling, and Lacey waited for her to continue. Nola finally lowered her gaze to Lacey again. "Knowing that Jessica wouldn't immediately think of me when she considered who should take care of Mackenzie… I just don't understand that. She's *my granddaughter.* I'm her only relative."

"If it was up to me, I'd agree with you, Nola," Lacey said. "That's what would make the most logical sense. But it wasn't up to either of us, and we have to make the best of this. Please. I have to do what Jessica wanted, but I'll make sure you have all the time you want with Mackenzie. I promise that."

Tears filled Nola's eyes and she stood up to pull a tissue from the box on the dresser, then sat down again. "I'm think-ing of fighting for custody of her, Lacey," she said, and there was a warning in her voice. "My attorney says I could get her if I did. You need to know that. A court would take into ac-count the best interest of the child, and any judge worth his salt would know that it's not in her best interest to be with you. You're so irresponsible and—"

"I'm not irresponsible." Lacey felt wounded.

"Jessica would never have gotten pregnant if she hadn't been hanging around with you."

She had to bite her tongue to keep from telling Nola she had it backward, that her dear daughter had been far more reckless and irresponsible than she had been that summer.

"That's history, Nola," she said. "I'll do my best with Mackenzie. That's all I can do."

"You know, Lacey." Nola sighed and her features suddenly softened. "I also want to carry out Jessica's wishes. I truly do. And the only thing I can think of is that she wanted Mackenzie to have a mother your age. Just please…" Nola's lower lip trembled so terribly that Lacey wanted to wrap her arms around her. "Just please don't cut me out," she said.

Lacey nodded and stood up. "I won't," she said, then leaned over to hug her. "I want to see Mackenzie now," she said. "Could you take me to her?"

"She doesn't know yet." Nola looked a bit alarmed. "You won't tell her, will you? I think it should really come from me and Mary."

"I won't tell her," Lacey promised. "But I want to at least say hi to her and give her my condolences."

Nola got to her feet and walked toward the French doors. Her hand on the doorknob, she turned back to Lacey, a small smile on her lips.

"I'd completely forgotten that Jessica wanted to be a cowgirl," she said.

Lacey followed Nola across the patio toward the pool. The yard was filled with the giggles of preteen girls and the sound of splashing water. Five slender, tanned bodies in various stages of prepubescent development sat on the edge of the pool, their backs to the house, their legs idly kicking the water. Nola walked toward the skinniest of the girls.

"Mackenzie?" she said.

The girl turned to look up at her grandmother. Lacey was not certain she would have recognized Mackenzie, she'd changed so much in the few years since she'd last seen her. Her hair was long, a dark blond bleached paler by the sun. The beginning of breasts sprouted beneath her hot pink bikini top.

Her eyes, reddened from crying, reminded Lacey of Bobby Asher's blue eyes, but her face was Jessica's, pure and simple.

"What?" Mackenzie asked her grandmother.

"Do you remember Lacey O'Neill?" Nola asked her. "Your mother's old friend?"

"Oh, yeah. Hi."

"Mackenzie—" Lacey had to shade her eyes from the sun "—I'm so sorry about your mom."

"That's okay," the girl answered, as if Lacey had apologized for bumping into her in the hallway.

"Could I talk with you for a few minutes?" Lacey asked.

Mackenzie hesitated. It was obvious she wanted to stay with her friends, but good manners seemed to win out. She stood up. She was long-waisted, like her mother. Lacey was going to have an everyday reminder of Jessica in her home and that thought brought a smile to her lips. Mackenzie smiled back at her.

"Why don't you go into that bedroom we just came out of," Nola suggested. "And I'll go back into the house through the living room door."

Lacey was grateful to Nola for giving her time alone with Mackenzie. She touched the girl's shoulder, pointing her in the direction of the French doors. Walking in silence next to her, she wondered what she would say to her once they were inside the bedroom.

She took her seat on the upholstered chair again, while Mackenzie climbed onto the platform bed on all fours, like a little kid, then sat cross-legged near the pillows. Her hands rested on her knees and chipped pink nail polish graced her stubby fingernails.

"You look so much like your mother." Lacey smiled at her.

"That's not news," Mackenzie said, her voice tinged with annoyance. She seemed a little hard, not at all like the child

Lacey'd been expecting to encounter, the child who had suffered the loss of the most important person in her world. Puffy, dark half circles beneath her eyes, though, gave her grief away.

"Do you remember me from your visits to your grandmother's?" Lacey asked.

"Sort of," Mackenzie said. "Were you the lady with those triplets?"

Lacey shook her head. She had no idea who Mackenzie was talking about. "No," she said. "I don't have any children. I guess when your mother visited your grandmother, you and I didn't get to spend much time together. Your grandmother would baby-sit for you while your mom and I went out."

Mackenzie looked at her blankly.

"It's a shame," Lacey said. "I would have liked to get to know you better."

"Why?" Mackenzie sounded perplexed by the thought.

"Just… You're the daughter of my best friend."

"I guess." Mackenzie glanced toward the French doors, leaning back on the bed so she could see her friends at the pool. She wanted out of the conversation, and Lacey couldn't blame her. She knew she wasn't handling this well.

"You'd like to go back to your friends, huh?" Lacey said, smiling a smile that felt plastered to her face.

Mackenzie nodded.

"Go on, then. It was good to see you."

Mackenzie scooted off the bed. "TTYL," she said, as she headed for the French doors.

Lacey sat alone in the bedroom for another minute, her smile gone now as she replayed her pathetic attempt to engage Mackenzie in conversation. That little girl didn't belong with her. She belonged here with her friends.

"Jessica," she said aloud, "what the hell were you thinking?"

★ ★ ★

The following day, Mary called Amelia to say she had finally told Mackenzie about the custody arrangements. Sitting in the living room of the condominium, Lacey listened to Amelia's end of the conversation, and it was apparent that Mackenzie had been anything but pleased by the news. Lacey didn't blame her a bit.

That night, she took Mackenzie out to dinner, just the two of them. Mackenzie refused to talk to her in the car Lacey had borrowed from Amelia, and as soon as they sat down in the restaurant, she knew this had been a stupid plan. Mackenzie wasn't hungry. There was nothing on the menu she was willing to order, and she wouldn't even look Lacey in the eye.

"Let's leave," Lacey said, after the waiter had come back a third time to attempt to take their order.

Mackenzie raised her eyebrows at her. "Just leave?"

Lacey nodded. "You're not hungry. I'm not really hungry. Let's get out of here."

Mackenzie hopped up from the seat and walked ahead of Lacey out of the restaurant.

In the car, Lacey turned on the air-conditioning and pressed the lever to move her seat back a few inches. "We'll just talk here for a while," she said.

Mackenzie rolled her eyes. "I don't have anything to talk about with you," she said.

"I want to change that," Lacey said. "I want to get to know you. You're going to be living with me, after all."

The eye roll again. "That is so totally stupid," she said. "I can't believe my mother did that."

"Well, maybe that just shows you how close your mom and I were. That she would leave me her prize possession to take care of."

Mackenzie shut her eyes instead of rolling them this time.

"You and I have one very important thing in common, Mackenzie," Lacey said.

"My mother?" Mackenzie ventured, eyes open now.

"Besides your mom."

"Stop calling her my *mom*," Mackenzie said. "She's my *mother*."

"Okay," Lacey said. "Besides your mother."

"So what's the big thing we have in common?"

"My mother died, too," Lacey said. "I was a couple of years older than you. I think maybe your mom...your mother knew that I would understand how terrible it is to go through what you're going through."

"If you understand so much then you should know I need to stay here. I want to stay in Phoenix."

"I know you do, honey."

"Don't call me honey."

Lacey was perspiring in spite of the air-conditioning, and she worried that Amelia's car might overheat. Hers certainly would if she let it idle like this with the AC on.

"Mackenzie," she said, "I know this is hard, but we have to trust your mother's judgment, okay? Neither of us understands her reasoning right now, but we have to do what she wanted."

Mackenzie shut her eyes again, and when she spoke, she bit the words off one by one, her nostrils flaring. "I don't get why I can't just stay here."

Lacey was not getting it either. She didn't see how Jessica's plan could possibly work out.

She pressed the lever to move her seat forward again. "Let me take you back to Mary's," she said.

"Good idea."

They drove in silence, Lacey annoyed with herself for her naiveté. She'd pictured this evening so differently. She knew Mackenzie would be upset, but she'd planned to ask her questions about herself and her interests and her friends and her hobbies. She'd planned to *connect*. If anything, she'd driven a wedge between herself and the girl.

The next afternoon, Mary, Veronica and a third woman whose name Lacey did not catch showed up on Amelia's doorstep. They marched into the little living room of the condominium, filling it with an angry presence.

"This is not going to work," Mary announced as she sat down on the sofa.

"What are you talking about?" Amelia asked.

"We've tried to understand and honor Jessica's wishes," Mary said, "but Mackenzie is going to pieces about this. She cried all night long. It's bad enough she had her mother die, but ripping her from the place and people she loves is just nonsense."

Lacey was growing weary of defending a decision she, too, thought was ridiculous. "I know it seems—"

"It's just crazy that Jessica left her to you," the third woman said. "She was so young. She probably had some romanticized notion about leaving her child to an old friend. But Lacey—" she leaned in Lacey's direction "—you don't *know* Mackenzie, and you don't know us. Our group of friends. You don't know how close we all are."

"She didn't ask for this," Amelia said in Lacey's defense.

"She doesn't like you," Mary snapped at Lacey.

"She doesn't know me, yet," Lacey said. "And you're right. I don't know her, yet, either. But I will. And I owe it to Jessica to try."

"But Mackenzie doesn't owe anything to anyone," Veronica said. "And this is her *life* we're talking about."

"And you don't 'try' to raise a child," Mary said. "Either you do it or you don't." She folded her arms across her chest. "Nola told us about you, Lacey."

"What do you mean?"

"She said you run around with the wrong crowd. That you sleep with every guy in town."

Something inside Lacey broke apart at that, and she started to cry. She couldn't handle one more bit of criticism. She thought of saying, "I used to be that way, but I've changed," yet she knew any defense at this point was useless.

She stood up, wiping her cheek with the back of her hand. "I want to say something to all of you," she said. "This has been hard for me and hard for Mackenzie, and all of you are only making it so much harder."

Mary stiffened her spine at that. "You have no idea how—"

"This is the way it is." Lacey cut her off. "I am Mackenzie's guardian. I know you don't like that. And for some reason, you don't seem to like me, and I think Nola's told you some lies that just add to your feelings. But you care about Mackenzie, and so do I. What Mackenzie and I need from you is *support*. She needs you to stay in touch with her, to let her know you're still there for her, no matter where she's living. That you'll never forget her or discard her. So, *please* give Mackenzie and me your support and stop making it sound like I'm kidnapping her."

She walked away from them, into the guest room, sick of them all except for Amelia. She knew she was leaving Amelia to deal with their wrath alone, but she could not tolerate another second of it.

She crawled into bed with her cell phone and called Rick, who she knew would listen to her ramble on as long as she needed to about the situation. She'd spoken to him a few times this week; his had been one of the many "happy birthday" messages on her cell phone the night after the memorial service. And he was, she mused as she dialed his number, exactly the type of man that the women in Amelia's living room would approve of.

★ ★ ★

If Mackenzie had had the energy, Lacey felt certain she would have resisted physically as they boarded the plane for the trip to North Carolina. Her relationship with the girl had not improved much, if at all, over the past couple of days, but now she would have her undivided attention for hours as they flew east. Maybe she could finally get her talking.

She'd helped her pack the night before. It was the first time she'd been inside Jessica's little condominium, and seeing her old friend's surprising decorative touches—her use of pastel colors and her penchant for hanging mirrors in unexpected places—made her feel she had not really known the adult Jessica at all.

The walls of Mackenzie's room were covered with posters of singers and musical groups Lacey had never heard of. God, she was getting old! Mackenzie wanted to take everything from her room with her. Lacey helped her pack it all in boxes, only a few of which they'd take with them on the plane. The rest would be shipped to Kiss River at a later date.

They were lucky to have three seats to themselves on the plane, and Mackenzie took the window seat. Lacey could tell the girl was an uneasy flyer. Her tan faded several shades as the plane ascended and her hands gripped the armrests. She was wearing hip-hugging shorts and a tank top, leaving her skinny preadolescent tummy bare, and once the plane had leveled off, she broke open the plastic-wrapped blanket and covered herself with it from toes to shoulders.

"Did your mother die in an accident?" she asked, the question so out of the blue that it took Lacey a minute to respond.

"No," she said. "My mother was killed." Somehow the word *killed* sounded better than murdered. "A man shot her."

Mackenzie had no response to what had to be an alarming revelation, but it was clear she was lost in her own thoughts.

"We were arguing when we got hit," she said. "I was yelling at her. I don't think she was paying attention to her driving."

Lacey instantly understood; she'd suffered from survivor's guilt herself after her own mother's death. "Oh, Mackenzie," she said, "it wasn't your fault. The man who hit your car was drunk. He is totally responsible for what happened."

Mackenzie grew quiet again, and Lacey wasn't sure what more to say. An announcement came over the loudspeaker. Lunch would be served shortly, the male voice said, followed by the second *Lord of the Rings* movie.

"Awesome," Mackenzie said, with the first genuine smile Lacey had seen on her face.

"You're a *Lord of the Rings* fan?" she asked.

"I've seen the first one four times and the second one three times."

"And you want to see it again?"

Mackenzie looked at her. "Elijah Wood," she said, as if that explained everything.

They sat through the movie and as soon as it was over, the plane began to bounce a bit, ever so slightly, not even enough to make the captain turn on the seat-belt sign. Mackenzie paled again, though, her hands once more clutching the armrests. Lacey tried to talk to her to take her mind off her discomfort.

"What kinds of things do you like to do?" Lacey asked.

"What do you mean?"

"I mean, do you have any hobbies or anything?"

"I don't want to talk right now."

Lacey wondered if she was feeling sick. She felt a little queasy herself.

"Well," she said, "you don't have to talk. Just listen, instead. I'm going to tell you about who's picking us up at the airport and who you'll be living with." It did not seem the time to tell her that they would be booted out of Kiss River in less than a year, when the museum opened. Mackenzie couldn't think past the next moment, much less the next year. Let her get used to one uprooting at a time.

"My brother Clay will pick us up," she continued. "He knew your mother, too. He was a few years older than your mom—mother—and me, but we hung around together sometimes." That was certainly an exaggeration. The year Jessica got pregnant, Lacey and Clay had not gotten along at all. There had been a deep love between them, certainly, but it had not been reflected in their adolescent banter with one another. And although she and Jessica would sometimes show up at the older kids' parties where Clay was in attendance, he would have a fit when he saw her there and tell their father about it to get her into trouble.

"Clay recently got married to a woman named Gina, and they adopted a little girl from India. Her name is Rani. So you'll have a cousin."

Mackenzie rolled her eyes. "No, I won't," she said with a nasty edge to her voice. "She's not related to me."

Take it slower, Lacey warned herself.

"And we have a dog named Sasha."

She thought she saw a spark of interest at that piece of information.

"I wasn't allowed to have a dog," Mackenzie said. "Mom was allergic."

Lacey remembered that Jessica had never been comfortable around animals. She had not been allergic, though, or at least not to Lacey's knowledge.

"Well, you have one now," she said. "He's a black lab, and we all live together in this wonderful old house where the lighthouse keeper used to live."

"Weird," Mackenzie said.

"And your grandmother only lives a short distance away," Lacey said. "I go right past her street on my way to work at the animal hospital my father owns. He's a vet. Your grandmother should have gotten home yesterday, so tomorrow we can go and visit her."

"I don't want to," Mackenzie said, and Lacey was surprised.

"You don't want to see your grandmother?"

She shook her head and unbuckled her seat belt. "I need to get out to go to the ladies' room," she said.

Lacey got out of her own seat to let Mackenzie pass by her.

"Do you feel all right?" she asked, but the girl didn't answer her.

Lacey sat down again and stared at the phone that was built into the seat back in front of her. When she first got on the plane and saw that phone, she'd wondered who in their right mind would make a phone call that probably cost several dollars a minute. Now she knew: desperate people. She read the instructions, then dialed the emergency room in Kill Devil Hills and asked the receptionist if she could speak to Dr. Simon. "This is her stepdaughter," she said.

It took a few minutes, but she finally got Olivia on the phone.

"How's it going?" Olivia asked.

"Terrible," she said. "We're on the plane and she's in the rest room and I'm about to tear my hair out. She doesn't want to be with me. She hates me. She's… I think she might be getting sick in the rest room. I am not cut out for this, Olivia."

"If you think she's sick, you should be with her."

Lacey pictured trying to work her way into the tiny rest room, holding back Mackenzie's hair as she got sick. Oh, God. She was relieved to see Mackenzie in the aisle, walking toward her.

"Oh, she's coming back," she said. "I'll get in touch when we're home and settled in a little, Olivia."

"Yes. Bring her over to meet Jack and Maggie."

"Olivia?"

"Uh-huh?"

"I'm sorry if I was difficult when you first met me."

Olivia laughed. "You were pretty easy, Lace, but then you weren't being uprooted like Mackenzie is."

"True," she said. "I've got to go."

Mackenzie was very pale. There were dark rings around her eyes, and as she pushed past Lacey to return to the window seat, Lacey thought she could detect the faint smell of vomit.

"Did you get sick?" she asked.

"I'm okay," Mackenzie said, cutting off the conversation with the curt tone of her voice.

Lacey patted her arm. "Only another forty minutes," she said. "Then we'll be in Norfolk and you can meet your new family."

Mackenzie turned her head toward the window, eyes glistening.

"I don't want a new family," she said. "I just want my mother."

14

AS SOON AS THEY STEPPED OFF THE PLANE, Mackenzie was on her cell phone. Veronica and Mary had chipped in to give it to her, along with unlimited minutes of talking time, so that she could stay in touch with her Phoenix friends. At the time, Lacey had thought it was a thoughtful gift and criticized herself because she never would have thought of it. Now, though, as Mackenzie walked several paces in front of her, jabbering away on the phone, using more words in ten seconds than she had used with Lacey in the past five days, she was not so sure.

She followed the girl to the baggage area to begin watching for their suitcases and Mackenzie's boxes. They had not brought her computer, and Mackenzie had been upset about that. Lacey promised that Mary would ship it to her quickly, but the truth was, they would not need it. That had been Clay's kindness. He'd bought a computer Mackenzie could use and had reinstalled the second phone line to the house so she could have her own access to e-mail and the Internet. Yet another one of Mackenzie's needs that Lacey had not thought of.

Standing next to the girl at the baggage area, she felt alone and helpless, much as she had on the plane. Mackenzie was talking in hushed tones into the phone, and Lacey figured the conversation was about her—how she had forced Mackenzie to go away with her, how the only good thing about the trip had been getting to see Elijah Wood in *Lord of the Rings* again. Lacey bit her lip and studied the bags, which were thumping along on the conveyor belt. Either Jessica had lost her mind, or she knew something about Lacey's strength and resilience of which she, herself, was unaware.

With great relief, she spotted Gina walking toward the baggage area. Rani was with her, pushing her stroller instead of riding in it, and the brown baby doll was sitting in the seat.

"There's Gina," Lacey said, although she knew Mackenzie was too involved in her phone conversation to hear her. She tapped the girl on her shoulder. "Could you please tell your friend you'll call her back later?" she asked. "Clay and Gina are here and they'll want to meet you."

"It's a him, not a her," Mackenzie said. Then in a voice tinged with annoyance, she spoke into the phone. "I have to go," she said. "TTYL."

"What does that mean?" Lacey asked, trying to sound interested rather than nosey. "TTYL?"

"Talk to you later," Mackenzie said, her tone flat. She stood on her toes to look for her suitcase and boxes.

"Hello!" Gina called cheerily as she neared them. Clay was right behind her, pushing an empty baggage cart.

"Hi." Lacey wanted to grab Gina, hug her and scream into her ear, "Help me!" Instead, she motioned toward Mackenzie. "This is Mackenzie," she said, her hand light enough on the girl's shoulder that she hoped it would not be felt and shrugged off. "Mackenzie, this is Gina and Clay and their daughter, Rani."

Mackenzie muttered her hello, then turned her attention back to the conveyor belt. Lacey gave her brother and sister-in-law a pained look and they smiled at her with sympathy. She bent over to pick up Rani, who molded her little body easily into her arms with a pliability so welcome it nearly brought tears to Lacey's eyes. "Hi, baby girl," she said to her niece. "I missed you."

Rani pointed to the conveyor belt. "Boxes come fast," she said.

"That's right," she said. "They do."

Clay pushed the baggage cart forward.

"Point out your stuff," he said to Mackenzie, "and I'll load it onto the cart."

"How was your flight, Mackenzie?" Gina asked the girl.

"It sucked." Mackenzie didn't shift her gaze from the conveyor belt.

"I'm sorry to hear that." Gina gave Lacey a sympathetic smile. "Nothing worse than a flight that sucks."

Mackenzie glanced at her then, but only for a second.

"It was a little bumpy," Lacey said. "But they showed *Lord of the Rings,* which is one of Mackenzie's favorite movies."

Mackenzie uttered an exasperated sound, as though Lacey had revealed some secret information about her. When the girl turned away again, Lacey mouthed *I can't win* to her sister-in-law. Gina leaned forward to kiss her cheek in sympathy.

When all the suitcases and boxes had been accounted for and piled onto the cart, the entire entourage started walking toward the exit. Rani insisted on getting down from Lacey's arms to push the "baby" in the stroller again, and Lacey let go of her reluctantly. Mackenzie walked ahead of them all, pulling her phone from her waistband again and lifting it to her ear.

"Whew," Clay said, as he walked next to Lacey. "She's a tough one. Is she at least crate-trained?"

Lacey laughed, and it felt as though it had been months

since that sound had left her mouth. Although Clay had quickly become a loving father to Rani, his skill in fostering creatures truly lay with dogs. And "Is the dog crate-trained?" was always his first question about any animal he took on.

In the parking lot, Lacey was glad to see that Gina and Clay had brought the van. They would need the space for Mackenzie's luggage.

"Why don't you ride in the front seat so you'll be able to see the area better?" Lacey suggested.

"My mother never lets me ride in the front seat," Mackenzie said.

"Well, you can now." Lacey enjoyed the feeling of being a permissive parent, but it lasted only a second.

"I guess you don't care if the air bag takes my head off," Mackenzie said.

"They really suggest children ride in the back until they're twelve," Gina said quietly.

"I didn't know that," Lacey said. "Okay, you and I can sit in the back with Rani."

Mackenzie watched Gina buckle the little girl into her car seat. "She sure doesn't look like any of you," she said. Apparently she had not been listening when Lacey told her Rani was adopted.

"That's because she's Indian," Gina explained. "We adopted her last year."

"What's her name again?"

"Rani. *R-A-N-I.*"

"She's so cute." Mackenzie actually smiled and the expression made her look exactly like her mother.

"Thanks," Gina said.

"She doesn't look anything like the Indians on the reservations in Arizona, though," Mackenzie said.

Gina straightened up, her task with the car seat completed.

"She's from India," she explained. "She's not a Native American."

"Oh, I get it," Mackenzie said, and she walked around the car to climb into the middle seat so she'd be next to Rani.

Lacey had never appreciated Rani more than she did on the trip from Norfolk to Kiss River. The little girl was impossible to ignore. Mackenzie chatted with her about her baby doll and actually taught her a song about a rabbit and a fox. For the first time Lacey saw a softness, a goodness in the girl that gave her hope for the future.

Still, the drive was a long one, and when Rani dozed off, the car grew quiet. They stopped briefly at a Wendy's for some dinner, but Mackenzie only ate the top part of her hamburger bun, nothing more, and Lacey felt a little twinge of empathy, remembering how her own appetite had disappeared after her mother's death. Gina tried asking a few questions of Mackenzie, the same questions Lacey had already asked her—what did she like to do, what were her hobbies—but Mackenzie's monosyllabic answers made the conversation too exhausting and most of the ride was spent in silence.

When they pulled into the Kiss River parking lot, the world had taken on the pink-gold tint of sunset. Clay turned to look at Lacey. "Why don't you and Mackenzie get out and stretch your legs and I'll cart this stuff into the house," he said. "You can give her a tour."

"Thanks." She was grateful for the offer. "Come on, Mackenzie. Let's walk over to the lighthouse."

Mackenzie shrugged her way out of the car and stretched, looking around her. "This is where I'm supposed to live?" She sounded incredulous. "This is the middle of nowhere."

"We're not all that far from things," Lacey said, although she knew that after Mackenzie's heart-of-Phoenix home, Kiss River would be a major adjustment. "And there are some great advantages to living out here. First of all—" she kicked off her sandals "—you don't ever have to wear shoes. Come on. Really. Take 'em off."

Mackenzie slipped out of her tennis shoes and stood on the sand-covered macadam of the parking lot. Lacey took the girl's shoes from her and set them next to her own at the edge of the lot.

"You were about eight the last time you visited the Outer Banks, right?" Lacey asked, one hand resting briefly on the girl's back to turn her in the direction of the lighthouse.

"Yeah."

"Did you like the ocean?"

Mackenzie shrugged. "It was full of jellyfish," she said.

"You must have been here during the red tide," Lacey said. "That's when all the jellyfish wash in. Not too pleasant, I admit. But I haven't seen any yet this summer." Not that she'd looked. "Do you like to swim?"

Mackenzie turned to look back toward the house. "Where's the pool?" she asked.

Lacey laughed. "Out there." She motioned toward the sea.

"You don't have a pool? Everyone in Phoenix has a pool."

"You and your mom—mother—didn't have one."

"But all my friends did."

"We don't need one here," Lacey said. "The ocean's a lot more fun. And if that's too rough for you, there's always the bay. There's so much to do here, Mackenzie. You'll be amazed."

"I don't want to do anything," she said, more to herself than to Lacey. "What's the matter with that lighthouse, anyway? What happened to it?"

They were getting close to the lighthouse, which was surrounded by a pool of nearly motionless ocean water. The sea was quiet this evening, the waves small and smooth. "The top broke off in a storm years ago," Lacey said. "But you can still sit up there. You can see forever and get a real feel for where we are. Come on."

Lacey started walking through the water toward the steps leading into the lighthouse.

"Ugh, the water's cold!" Mackenzie said, as she waded into the pool of seawater.

Lacey chose to ignore the complaint. She climbed the stairs to the interior of the lighthouse, and the marble tiles felt cool beneath her feet as she walked into the octagon.

Mackenzie stood next to her in the middle of the octagon and looked up. The black stairs, backlit by the pink evening sky, formed an ever-tightening corkscrew above them.

"Let's go up," Lacey said, grasping the railing and starting up the winding staircase. Mackenzie was moving far more slowly than she was. She took a few steps up the stairs, then hesitated.

"This is stupid," she said. "Why'd they leave it here if it's broken? It can't be used." She looked up at the dizzying, circular stairway above them, and Lacey picked up the chill in the girl's voice. She was afraid. Many people felt disoriented on these stairs.

Lacey turned and began to descend the stairs. "You can come up here some other time," she said. "We don't have to do everything today." She walked out of the building and down the steps, Mackenzie close behind.

Once back on the dry sand, Mackenzie slapped her shoulder, then her knee.

"You have mosquitoes here." She sounded accusatory.

"Afraid so, especially around now, when the sun's going down," Lacey said.

"There aren't any stupid mosquitoes in Phoenix," Mackenzie said.

"I'll give you your own personal bottle of repellent," Lacey offered. "But for now, let's go into the house. You can see the rest of the outdoors tomorrow in the daylight." They stopped to pick up their shoes at the edge of the parking lot, then walked toward the house.

Lacey pointed to one of the upstairs windows. "That will be your room," she said.

Mackenzie looked up and shook her head slowly, and Lacey didn't bother to ask what was bothering her now. She really didn't want to hear.

"How am I supposed to meet other kids, living out here?"

"It will be hard during the summer, I admit that. Maybe I can arrange something, though." Mackenzie could at least meet Jack and Maggie, although Jack, who was eleven himself, did not think much of girls. "Once school starts, you'll meet lots of kids. And we can actually only live in this house until sometime early next year, when it's being turned into a museum. Then we'll move someplace closer to civilization. I promise."

"Wait till I tell my friends I'm going to live in a museum," Mackenzie said, and the tone of her voice let Lacey know this was not a good thing.

"What's that fence there for?" Mackenzie pointed to the large dog pen near the woods. "Is that where your dog lives?"

"No, Sasha lives in the house. But Clay trains dogs for search-and-rescue work. That's a holding pen for them."

"What's search-and-rescue work mean?"

"You know, let's say a kid gets lost in the woods. They send specially trained dogs out to find them."

"Or there's an earthquake or a building caves in?"

"Right."

"Awesome." The word was said under her breath, but it sounded sincere.

Lacey led Mackenzie through the kitchen and living room, up the stairs and across the hallway. She could hear Clay and Gina's murmuring voices as they read to Rani in their bedroom. They had turned the smallest of the bedrooms into a nursery for their daughter. Although they couldn't truly alter the room, since it would be part of the museum, they were still able to fill it with baby furnishings: a crib, a changing table, cute lamps and mobiles. But Rani refused to sleep there; she had never slept alone in a bed, much less alone in a room. Clay and Gina gave up the battle and put a toddler bed on the floor of their own bedroom, and the nursery remained mostly unused.

Lacey reached the door of the room that would be Mackenzie's and motioned her inside. Mackenzie's suitcases and boxes were piled in one corner, but otherwise, the room held only a lovely old sleigh bed and an ancient dresser. "You can decorate this room any way you like," she said. It would not be fair to ask Mackenzie to live in the room as it was. Lacey had already decided she would pay to have the room restored before they moved out.

The view of the lighthouse was dead center from the windows. It was a beautiful sight as the gold of the sunset cast a flame against the white brick. She wanted to point it out to Mackenzie, to tell her how lucky she was to have this view, but by now, she knew better than to bother.

The new computer sat on a table near the door, and Lacey could see that the phone line already ran between it and the jack on the wall.

"Can I use this?" Mackenzie touched the keys.

"It's yours," Lacey said, loving her brother more than ever at that moment. "Clay bought it for you and set it up. And you have your own phone line in here to connect to the Internet."

"Why would he do that for me?" Mackenzie asked. "He doesn't even know me."

"I told you," she said. "He knew your mother. And he knows how hard it must be for you to be here, suddenly cut off from all your friends, and so he wanted to get this for you."

"Weird," she said.

"You know," Lacey said, sitting down on the edge of the bed, "a long time ago, the lighthouse keeper's daughter lived in this room. Her name was Bess and Gina is related to her."

Mackenzie touched the corner of the computer monitor. "He got me such a big screen," she said, and Lacey could not tell if she was happy about that fact or not.

"How about something to eat," she offered. "Or at least to drink. I know you don't have much of an appetite, but—"

"I'm fine."

"This has been a long day for you, Mackenzie." She wanted to touch her, to smooth the blond hair back from her cheek. "I understand everything that's happened is so hard and—"

"Don't make such a big deal out of it."

Lacey stood up, weary of having every attempt at connection with this child thwarted. "I'll leave the bathroom light on for you," she said.

"I don't need a night-light," Mackenzie said. "What time is it in Phoenix?"

"Two hours difference." Lacey looked at her watch. "Only eight."

"Good." Mackenzie lifted her cell phone from her shorts and began to dial.

15

"I WANT IT TO WORK OUT," LACEY SAID, "BUT
the truth is, I can barely stand her." She was lying on a raft,
floating on the dark water of the sound behind Rick's tiny
cottage. She'd thought he was crazy when he led her out here
in the darkness, and although she was used to the weedy entry
into the water in the daylight, the unseen tendrils wrapping
around her legs had given her chills. She'd been relieved to
get into the deeper water. Now she and Rick lay on their
stomachs on separate rafts, face-to-face, moving their hands
through the water only enough to keep their rafts from drift-
ing too far apart.

"I really feel for you," Rick said. She liked the way he
looked out here at night, his hair a bit mussed and his eyes
huge and dark in the faint light from the sliver of moon. "Is
there any way to get her involved with other kids before
school starts?"

Lacey ran her hands through the water. She was dressed in
a pair of his baggy swimming trunks and her T-shirt, having
been unprepared for this nighttime journey into the sound. "I
contacted the middle school to find out about summer activities for kids her age," she said. "There's plenty she could be

doing. Swim teams, nature clubs, field trips. I told her about them, but she doesn't want to do any of them. I really understand, though. It's too soon for her; she's still completely wrapped up in grieving. But understanding all that doesn't make it any easier for me to tolerate her."

The past four days had been some of the most trying in her life. She was suddenly responsible for a child who wouldn't talk to her, who, at times, actually seemed to hate her, and who certainly hated Kiss River. Lying in bed at night, Lacey would think of the living, breathing child who was in her care, not only now but for the rest of that child's life, and utter panic would set in. If she couldn't talk to Mackenzie now, if she couldn't summon up a modicum of caring for her when the child was eleven, what would it be like when she was a rebellious fifteen-year-old?

Tonight, Mackenzie was staying with Nola. It was a blessed reprieve. When she'd dropped her off at Nola's house, though, Lacey had noted that there were no hugs, no warm exchanges, and Mackenzie didn't seem any happier to see Nola than she had been to see her. She'd felt a little guilty leaving her there, but she was in desperate need of some time away from her.

"You know who she gets along best with?" Lacey asked Rick.

"Who?"

"Rani and Sasha," she said. "A toddler and a dog." Mackenzie would finger paint with Rani or read her one of her picture books or sing songs with her, displaying a gentleness that touched Lacey and that made her see, however briefly, another side to the girl. When Rani was not available, Mackenzie would spend time with Sasha, grooming the dog or just lying with her head on his flank as she watched television.

"She was extremely annoyed to discover we don't have cable." Lacey laughed. She'd told Mackenzie that cable didn't reach out to Kiss River, and the girl had replied, "I guess I should be grateful you have plumbing." She was both smart and smart-mouthed.

"I'm glad you finally have a night off," Rick said. "I've really missed seeing you."

"You've been great," she said, honestly. "You've let me complain on the phone to you nearly every night. I really owe you."

He smiled. "No, you don't. And I wish I could help you more, but I know zilch about kids."

She didn't need his advice on dealing with Mackenzie. What she'd needed had been his absolutely amazing listening skills. She'd never known a man quite like him. Good-looking, attentive listener, never pressuring her for more physical intimacy than she wanted to give. Every woman's dream guy, and he might as well have been a plate of mashed potatoes for all the attraction she felt to him.

"All I've done this week is kid stuff," she said. "Talking to the school. Taking her to a counselor who seems to be having as much trouble talking to her as I am. The counselor said I should tell her things about her mother that I know but that she might not." She laughed. "There are plenty of things I could tell her about Jessica, but most of them need to be censored."

"Jessica sounds like she was quite a kid."

"And I worry Mackenzie's going to be just like her." Lacey ran her hand through the cool water. "So, anyway, I tried telling her about her mother. I got my old photograph albums from my father's house and brought them back. She couldn't have cared less." She'd shown Mackenzie the old pictures of her mother from both the albums and their exceedingly slim middle school yearbook, but Mackenzie barely glanced at them. When Lacey talked about her experiences with Jessica,

Mackenzie would tell her to stop. "You were just a teeny, tiny part of her life," she said. "I have my whole lifetime full of experiences with my mother. I don't need to hear about yours."

"This must be very hard," Rick said. "I admire you for even trying to deal with her."

"She spends all her time on the phone and sending e-mail. I know she's terribly homesick, but she's just so hard to feel sympathy for."

Rick was quiet for a moment. "I don't understand why Mackenzie didn't automatically go to her father," he said finally.

"Because Jessica never acknowledged him as Mackenzie's father. Not even on the birth certificate. She didn't want him to have anything to do with her." She swirled her hand through the water again, making little ripples in the dark surface. "And that brings up a dilemma."

"What's that?"

"I always thought Bobby—Mackenzie's father—should know about her, but Jessica disagreed. Yet she left her to me knowing that was how I felt. So, did she want me to get in touch with Bobby or not? I just don't know."

"Do you know this guy?"

She wasn't about to tell Rick the exact nature of her adolescent relationship with Bobby. "Jessica and I hung around with him the summer she got pregnant," she said. "He used drugs and was…irresponsible and…just a mess."

"Where is he?"

"I don't know. He lived in Richmond back then. But I could probably track him down."

"I think you should do it," Rick said. "If I had a kid wandering around, I would certainly want to know."

"Yes, but you're a responsible and upstanding type of guy."

His look turned dark. "I'm not a Boy Scout, Lacey," he said. "It's just that I think every kid needs a father figure."

"I agree." She folded her hands together on the raft and rested her cheek on the backs of her fingers.

"On another note," Rick said, "how's the legal situation going?"

"With Mackenzie?"

"No, with that parole hearing. Have you had time to meet with a lawyer with everything else you have going on?"

She couldn't blame him for turning the conversation from child care to a legal issue, something he would feel on solid ground discussing.

"Actually, my brother and father and I have an appointment with one tomorrow morning to talk about it."

"Ah, that's good," he said, although she was not certain of the sincerity behind the words. She knew he thought it was a poor use of her time and energy.

She raised her head to look at him. "You'll be pleased to know, though, that it's about the last thing on my mind."

"And it should be," he said. "You're going to make yourself sick if you take one more thing onto your plate."

She felt suddenly very tired and wondered if he was right. "Well." She sighed. "As usual, I've been doing all the talking. Tell me how your book is going."

"I made a lot of progress while you were tied up," he said. "I went home for a few days—"

"To Chapel Hill?"

"Right. I needed to do some research in the law library at Duke. Got a lot done."

He reached for her hand and drew her raft toward him. Raising himself to his elbows, he leaned toward her for a kiss, his lips light on hers.

"How come you are so willing to settle for just a kiss?" she asked him once he drew away from her.

"Because I know you don't want more than that. At least not yet."

"Are you going out with other women?" she asked. "I mean, I don't mind. I'm just...curious."

"Nope." He smiled.

"Maybe you should." She felt guilty for taking up his dating time when her feelings for him were so conflicted.

"I didn't come to the Outer Banks to date," he said. "Meeting you was just a bonus."

She was never sure how to respond to him when he said things like that. She did not want to encourage him. Instead of speaking, she rolled onto her back, sloshing cool water over herself in the process, and looked up at the stars.

"I wish I could bottle this," she said. "Lying out here under the stars, I mean. I'm dreading tomorrow morning when I have to pick Mackenzie up again."

"You said that her grandmother might fight to get custody of her, didn't you?" Rick asked.

"Yes."

"Maybe it makes sense to let her take her."

She turned her head to look at him. "Do you think that's what I should do?" The thought was both enticing and guilt-inducing.

"What I think doesn't really matter."

Lacey looked up at the sky again, then closed her eyes. "Could we just stay here all night?" she asked. "I could fall asleep out here."

He laughed. "You go right ahead," he said, as if he really meant it. "I'll hold on to your raft so you don't float away."

16

LATE THE FOLLOWING MORNING, LACEY SAT IN the waiting room of the attorney's office, waiting for her father and Clay. She hadn't yet returned to work at the animal hospital, and she hadn't cut a piece of glass since the trip to Arizona, but that would change the following week. She and Nola had come up with a plan, however temporary it might be. Weekdays, she would drop Mackenzie off at Nola's on her way to work at the animal hospital and pick her up on her way home from the studio, although occasionally Mackenzie would spend the night at her grandmother's house. Mackenzie would spend her weekends, when Nola was busiest with her real estate company, at the keeper's house. In theory, it sounded like a good plan. They would have to see how it worked out in practice. She wondered how Nola had made out with Mackenzie's overnight visit, and hoped it was going well. Although she was not prepared to let Nola take Mackenzie away from her—at least not yet—she wanted the girl to be comfortable enough at her grandmother's to spend the night now and then so that Lacey would have some respite.

She'd slept better the night before than she had since learning of Jessica's death. Tempting though it had been to fall asleep floating on the sound, she'd craved a good night's sleep in her own bed, without the worry of Mackenzie in the room down the hall.

Clay and her father walked into the waiting room the same moment Diana Guest, the attorney, stepped out of her office to call them inside. In spite of her carefully cut light brown hair, her dark suit and her sophisticated plastic eyeglass frames, she could not have been more than Lacey's age.

"Wow," Diana spoke to the two men. "There's no doubt that you two are father and son, is there?"

Her father and Clay smiled the same smile at the attorney, their identical sets of ice-blue eyes acknowledging the truth in her statement. Lacey had long ago accepted the fact that, without her mother's presence, she did not look as though she fit into the little family unit at all.

Diana Guest ushered them into her office, and Lacey and Clay took seats on either side of their father.

"Okay." Diana sat down, and picked up some papers from her desk. "Let's see." She read a few lines to herself, then looked up at them. "The first thing you need to know is that, unfortunately, Zachary Pointer has a strong case for parole, so our task won't be easy."

"Why?" Clay asked. "What gives him a strong case?"

Diana tapped her closed fountain pen on the leather desk blotter as she checked her notes. "To begin with, he received psychiatric treatment when he first went into prison," she said. "The psychiatrist he saw said he'd had a stress-induced psychotic breakdown and—"

"Yes, all that came out at the hearing," her father said. "It's not news, and he was found to be sane at the time of the in-cident."

Diana nodded. "That's true, but it really isn't an issue at this point. He was treated for the psychosis and is stable on medication. According to prison records, he's been a model prisoner. And to make matters worse—for our case, at least—he studied theology while in prison and if he's released, he plans to attend seminary and become a minister."

"Convenient," her father said with a cynicism Lacey rarely heard him use. "Maybe every prisoner up for parole should try that line. 'Let me out and I'll become a minister.'"

"The prison records indicate that it's not a passing fancy with him." Diana lifted one of the sheets of paper from her desk. "This is dated 1993," she said, then began reading from the paper. "'Pointer is repentant for what happened and is involved in the Bible study program run by the prison chaplain.' Then in 1995—'Pointer is helping Chaplain Luce lead the Bible study classes.' And in 1997—'Pointer is studying theology in a correspondence course as well as with Chaplain Luce.'"

Saint Zachary, Lacey thought to herself.

"I'm delighted he found some solace in God," her father said in a flat voice. "I wish my wife had had that chance."

"I'm not saying it's impossible to keep him in prison," Diana said. "You just need to know what we're up against."

"So what do we need to do?" Clay asked.

"I wasn't in this area when your wife was killed," Diana spoke directly to Lacey's father, "but I've heard about all the good she did for the community. I suggest you come up with a carefully formulated letter-writing campaign. First, since you three are the direct victims, you should each write a compelling victim's impact statement."

Rick had been on the right track, Lacey thought.

"The statements should describe how the loss of your mother and wife affected you. Still affects you." She looked at Lacey. "This will be most important coming from you, Lacey, since you were there with her when she was murdered.

Even if no one else gets around to writing a statement, you absolutely must."

"I'm really not a good writer," Lacey said truthfully. She thought of Rick's warning that she would have to relive her mother's death if she pursued legal action to keep Pointer in prison. He'd been right, and she wondered if she'd be able to handle it. Revisiting her mother's death was not something she had the energy to do right now.

"You don't need to win a Pulitzer," Diana said. "Just write about the lasting impact that losing your mother—and being there when it happened—has had on you, and do it in a compelling but not overly emotional way. Too much emotionalism can be off-putting for the parole board. You have to strike the right tone, and I'll help you. All three of you. Write your statements and then I'll go over them with you."

"Is that all we can do?" Clay asked. "Write these statements?"

"Don't minimize their importance," Diana said. "And the statements won't just come from you. I need you all to think about who else should write one. The directors of the places she volunteered. That sort of thing. We want to demonstrate the magnitude of her loss on the entire community, not just on your family."

"When do you need them by?" her father asked.

"The hearing's in September," Diana said. "But to give me time to go over them with you, you'll probably want to finish them by mid-August. Here's some information I've put together to help you see what you should include." She handed a sheet of paper to each of them. "I suggest you make copies of it and give it to anyone you hope to have write a statement."

"We could have one hundred statements for you," her father said. "Is that overkill?"

"I would say it's more important to choose carefully. Qual-

ity over quantity." She stood up, obviously through with the
meeting. "Ten great letters would do more good than inun-
dating the parole board with a hundred overemotional dia-
tribes."

Her father stood up and reached out to shake Diana's hand.
"All right," he said. "You'll keep us posted?"

"I will." She smiled at Clay, then Lacey. "It was very nice
meeting all of you," she said.

They walked out of the office in silence, and once in the
parking lot, her father put an arm around each of them. "You
guys okay?"

"Fine," Clay said. "I wish there was something more we
could do, though. I didn't expect his staying in prison to boil
down to how well we write."

"Why don't we grab something to eat?" Alec pulled his
keys from his pocket and hit the remote button to unlock his
car. "Then we can talk about who we should ask to write the
other statements."

Lacey looked at her watch. "I can't, Dad," she said. "I have
to pick Mackenzie up at Nola's in a few minutes."

"How's it going, hon?" Her father had met Mackenzie a
few days earlier, when Lacey'd brought her over to intro-
duce her to Jack and Maggie, a visit which had not been a
success. No surprise there. Although she and Jack were the
same age, Mackenzie was a couple of inches taller than him
and looked a year or two older, and nine-year-old Maggie
had looked like a little girl next to the newcomer. While Jack
and Maggie swam in the sound behind their house, Mackenzie basked in the sun on their deck wearing her pink bikini.
She wanted nothing to do with the weedy, brackish-looking
water close to the beach. "In Arizona," Mackenzie had told
them with a haughty style she was quickly perfecting, "everyone has a pool."

"Let's just say that I've decided if Nola wants her, she can have her," Lacey said, not really sure if she was joking or not.

"Ouch," Alec said, and Clay laughed.

"She *is* a challenge," Clay said.

"Are you serious?" Alec asked her. "Is it that bad?"

"I don't know, Dad," she said. "I'm so crazed right now, I can't think straight."

Clay put his arm around her shoulders. "Well, I personally hope you keep her around," he said. "She'll make a great baby-sitter in another year or so."

Nola greeted her on the front porch of her three-story house in Southern Shores. "She's upstairs on my computer," she said. "She's been on my computer nearly her entire visit."

"I know." Lacey climbed the stairs to the porch and leaned against the railing. "She misses her friends."

"Has she talked to you?" Nola asked.

"About?"

"Her mother? Or…well, about anything." She looked exhausted. "I really haven't been able to get her to talk."

"Don't blame yourself, Nola," Lacey said. "She's not talking to me, either. Has she always been reserved like this?"

"Not when she was younger." Nola fanned herself with her hand. "But the truth is, she doesn't know me very well. I saw her once a year, if that. It was just not enough. I regret that now."

"I feel the same way," Lacey said.

Nola slipped a wayward lock of her white-blond hair back into her French twist. "Tell me something, Lacey," she said. "And please be truthful."

Lacey nodded, waiting.

"Why do you really think Jessica left her with you and not with me?" Nola asked.

"I simply have no idea," Lacey answered honestly.

"Was I a bad mother?" It was rare to see Nola look and sound so vulnerable, and Lacey felt sympathy for her. "Jessica told me that I could sometimes be cold."

"Of course you weren't a bad mother," Lacey said, letting honesty fly out the window. "I doubt that has anything to do with why she asked me to take Mackenzie. I think what we talked about in Phoenix is right. Jessica probably wanted a peer, someone her age, to raise her daughter. Maybe she thought she'd come up with a brilliant idea by having it be me, since she knew I lived close to you." She looked in the direction of the ocean. Although she couldn't see it from the front porch, she could tell the water was rough today; she could hear the waves smacking against the beach. "But—" she looked back at Nola "—if we mutually decide at some point that she would be better off with you, or if she says that's what she wants, I won't fight you on it."

"Well—" Nola let out a long breath "—I certainly expected to fight you for her," she said. "But the truth is, I don't know that I could handle her on an everyday basis. Maybe Jessica knew that, that I'm not cut out to have an eleven-year-old child in my life. Though I do love her. She's all I have left of Jessie." Nola sighed. "I just want whatever is best for her."

"I think I'm going to contact her father," Lacey said suddenly.

Nola's eyes widened. "She has no father," she said, a warning in her eyes.

"I know Jessica listed the father's identity as 'unknown' on the birth certificate, but you and I both know who her father is."

"She didn't want him involved," Nola said. "That boy was a complete and utter loser."

"Then why did she leave Mackenzie with me, when she knew I would want to let Bobby Asher know about her?"

"He corrupted Jessica."

"I thought *I* corrupted her." Lacey couldn't resist throwing that statement back in Nola's face.

"I was angry when I said that, Lacey. Angry and hurt. I'm sorry."

Lacey had never seen Nola as soft and wounded as she seemed today. Twenty-four hours with Mackenzie had humbled her.

"That's all right." Her head was starting to ache and she rubbed her temples. "I'm not exactly sure what I'm going to do about Bobby, Nola, but I'll keep you in the loop. Okay?"

Mackenzie was quiet on the drive back to Kiss River, giving her usual one-word answers to Lacey's questions about the time spent with her grandmother. When they arrived at the light station parking lot, she jumped out of the car and ran ahead of Lacey into the house. By the time Lacey got inside, Mackenzie was sitting on the floor of the living room, watching a soap opera on TV and cuddling with Sasha, the one creature whose love was unconditional, who didn't care if she talked or sulked. Mackenzie looked like a little child at that moment. Not like the girl who dressed like Britney Spears, who made scornful comparisons between life in Phoenix and life in this godforsaken place. She was, Lacey had to remind herself, just a hurt little kid.

When everyone was in bed that night, Lacey got up and rummaged through her top desk drawer for a notepad and a pen. Sitting down at her desk, she stared out at the moonlit lighthouse, thinking. Composing.

I was with my mother when she was killed, she wrote. *I still have nightmares about it. My mother had taken me to the battered women's shelter to give a little something to people who had less than we did. She was always like that. She would help anyone who needed it. She even donated her bone marrow to save the life of a child she didn't know. She was the kindest woman in the world.*

And she was also a self-centered whore who slept with half the men in the Outer Banks, and she hurt my father more than words can say.

"Shit." Lacey balled the paper up in her hands and tossed it across the room into her trash can. This would not be an easy thing to write.

17

TWENTY DOLLARS WAS MISSING FROM HER WAL-let, and Lacey was afraid she knew who had taken it. She and Nola were putting their new schedule of sharing time with Mackenzie into place, and Lacey had made a couple of stops with the girl in the car on her way to the Realtor's house. She'd gone to the bank, where she cashed a check for one hundred dollars, and she'd stopped at a 7-Eleven to pick up a cup of coffee for herself and a doughnut for Mackenzie. She'd taken one of the twenties into the 7-Eleven with her, leaving Mackenzie and her purse in the car, and she'd stuck the change from the twenty in her pocket. It wasn't until she stopped for lunch later in the day that she noticed only three twenties remained in her wallet. Her heart sank as she rummaged through her purse, hoping to find the missing twenty. She had no proof that Mackenzie had taken the money, though, and she didn't have a clue how to deal with the situation.

Driving home from Nola's that afternoon with Mackenzie, sullen and uncommunicative, in the backseat, she thought of ways she could broach the subject. She could simply make a declarative statement: "I got five twenties from the bank, took one into the store with me, and at lunch discovered there were only three twenties left in my wallet." Or she could make a bargain with Mackenzie: "A twenty disappeared from my wallet. If it reappears within the next day, all will be forgiven." The fact was, she was afraid to say anything to Mackenzie. *Chicken,* she chided herself. Their relationship was already rocky enough, and she feared making it worse. She would warn Gina and Clay to watch their money. She would keep her own wallet on her at all times. And she would give Mackenzie an allowance. She had not even thought about that. Of course. The girl needed money of her own.

She knew how her own mother would have handled the situation. She would have said something like, "Twenty dollars is missing from my wallet, and I guess someone needed it more than I did. I hope that someone will simply ask me for it in the future instead of taking it." That would have been so typical of Annie O'Neill's gentle and slightly goofy parenting style. But Lacey was not her mother. She would have to come up with her own approach, and right now, that appeared to be doing nothing.

Bobby Asher had been a thief. He'd stolen money from her and from Jessica. He'd stolen a Danish from a little corner store in Nag's Head nearly every day, and Lacey had felt sorry for the elderly clerk behind the counter, who was half-blind and who had no idea he was being ripped off. She'd seen Bobby steal something as small as a cigarette from a pack lying on a table in a restaurant, and as large as boogie board from a store window. He had been a master thief, and just as Lacey seemed to have inherited her mother's gene for promiscuity, perhaps Mackenzie had inherited her father's gene for stealing.

Why on earth had Lacey been so attracted to him? She'd dreamt about him at night and fantasized about him during the daytime. She would have done anything he asked her to, and she'd felt a deep ache in her chest every time she saw him with Jessica. Maybe Jessica had been wise to keep Bobby out of Mackenzie's life. Yet he was the girl's father. Even Rick, Mr. Conservative himself, thought that he should be told. And she was going to tell him. At best, he would understand Mackenzie better than she did. At worst, he would have graduated to more sophisticated forms of running outside the law. Either way, though, she'd decided that he needed to know he had a child.

The evening after discovering her twenty was missing, Lacey sat in her bedroom, the phone in her lap, and dialed information. There were several Robert Ashers in the Richmond area, the operator told her, and Lacey wrote down all the numbers. The first one she reached turned out to be Bobby's cousin. "He lives down the street," the cousin said, and he gave her Bobby's number, just like that. She wanted to ask the cousin, "What is he like? Does he still do drugs?" but the only question that came out of her mouth was, "Does he still go by 'Bobby'?"

The cousin laughed. "He sure does, " he said. "Just about all us Ashers go by Bobby."

Lacey chewed her lip now as she looked at the number he'd given her. Mackenzie was in her room exchanging e-mail with her Phoenix friends. Rani was asleep, and Gina and Clay were downstairs watching a movie on the VCR. She had the time and privacy she needed for the call. All she needed now was courage and the ability to find the words.

She dialed the number. It rang seven times, and she was trying to formulate a message for his voice mail when he suddenly picked up.

"Hey." He sounded winded.

"Is this Bobby?" she asked.

"Speaking. Who's this?" She would not have recognized his voice. It was the voice of a man, not the boy she had known.

"I don't know if you remember me or not," she said. "I'm Lacey O'Neill and I—"

"Lacey!" he said. "What a flash from the past! How are you doing, girl?"

She felt relief that he remembered her, that she would not have to add that explanation to this conversation. He'd been so wasted much of that summer that she'd not been sure he would be able to recall any of it.

"I'm fine," she said. "And how about you?"

"I'm doing good." He sounded boisterous and upbeat. She did not remember him that way. "So, how come I'm hearing from you after all these years?"

"Well," she said, "this is a little complicated, and I'm not quite sure where to start so bear with me, okay?"

"No problem."

"You remember Jessica Dillard?"

"Sure. I practically spent one summer of my life with her. How's she doing?"

"She recently…she passed away recently."

There was a beat of silence before he responded. "Jesus, you're kidding. She was only…what?…twenty-six?"

"Twenty-seven. She was a year older than me even though we were in the same grade. She started school a little later than—"

"What the hell happened?" He interrupted her.

"She was in a car accident. She was hit by a drunk driver, but she survived and had to have a lot of surgery. They thought she'd recover, but she got a blood clot in her lung and it killed her."

"A drunk driver?" he asked.

"Yes."

"Son of a bitch. How fair is that?"

"Not at all fair."

"The two of you stayed close, Lacey?"

She liked the way he used her name, the way it sounded in his new, grown-up voice. "Yes and no," she said. "She'd been living in Arizona since she was fifteen, and we didn't get to see each other much. And…here's the real reason I'm calling you. Jessica had a child. A little girl. She…that's why Jessica moved to Arizona, because she got pregnant and her mother really thought it was best that she not stay here. She—"

"Lacey." He stopped her frantic rambling. "What are you trying to tell me?"

"You're the girl's father."

That silence again, this time stretching for long, agonizing seconds, and Lacey squeezed her eyes shut as she waited for his response.

"I…uh…" He let out a short laugh. "What makes you think that?"

"Jessica knew you were the baby's father," she said. "There was never any doubt. But she also knew you were young and that it was just a summer fling and that you were…well, you weren't exactly the responsible father type back then, and she figured it was best just to put 'unknown' on the birth certificate where it asked for the father's name."

"Hold on," he said. "I've got to sit down for this." She heard some rustling of papers and then he was back on the line. "You don't plan to dump this kid on me, do you?" Now, *that* sounded like the Bobby she remembered.

"Jessica left her in my care," she said. "But I thought you should know."

"Why didn't *she* tell me?" he said. "I mean, she could have tried to get child support out of me, if nothing more."

"She figured you were…" What could she say? "The two of you didn't have a serious, adult relationship, Bobby. You know that."

He didn't respond, and she continued.

"I only picked up Mackenzie—that's Jessica's daughter—a week and a half ago," she said. "And the thing is, I always told Jessica I thought she should get in touch with you about her. That you should know. I didn't find out who my father was until I was sixteen, and—"

"Your father was that vet, wasn't he?"

"Yes, but my *birth* father was someone else altogether," she said. "I didn't know that, and I think I had a right to know. And so did he." She was rambling, talking fast. "Anyway, Jessica disagreed with me, but I think deep down, she really wanted you to know, or else she wouldn't have left her to me. So, that's why I'm calling. Just to let you know that Mackenzie exists. That you have a daughter."

Again, the silence, followed by a low chuckle. "I'm feeling something like…I think I'm having a panic attack."

His vulnerability softened her. "I guess I can't blame you for that," she said.

"You know, Lacey, Jessica was…well, she was pretty loose."

Her sympathy for him quickly evaporated, although she could understand his doubt. "Jessica talked a lot looser than she actually was," she said. "You were the only guy she was… intimate with around that time. And she was sure."

"A drunk driver," he said, suddenly returning to the previous topic. "Damn."

"Yes," she said.

"So, what's she like? The girl? What did you say her name is?"

"Mackenzie." Lacey pondered how to describe her. "She's going through a difficult time right now, losing her mother and moving here. Frankly, she's a handful."

He laughed. "Then maybe she *is* my kid."

Lacey had to smile. "She's sullen and sulky and obstinate

and negative and I'm pretty sure she stole some money from me, and she's demanding and bad-natured and thinks the world owes her for taking her mother. And she's impossible to talk to. And she hates me and everything else in the entire universe."

The laughter again, but this time much softer. "Yeah, but tell me what you *really* think about her," he said.

She sighed. "Sorry. I'm not in a good place right now."

"Well, I hope you never take a job in sales, because you're lousy at it. If you're trying to sell me on this kid, you're not doing the greatest job."

"I'm being honest."

"I get that," he said.

"Bobby, I have to ask you something straight-out, okay?"

"Please do."

"Sorry if this isn't diplomatic. But you were so crazy when I knew you. What are you like now?"

"Different," he said. "I'm not your button-down work-in-an-office-cubicle type, but I'm responsible. I own a little house. I pay my bills on time. I'm clean."

She closed her eyes. That was what she needed to hear. "I don't think there was a drug you hadn't tried when I knew you."

"I wasn't nearly the druggie I pretended to be. And I haven't used anything in five years. I'm in AA, Lace."

The use of the nickname touched her, the meaning behind the words even more so. She knew the change AA had made in Tom. Like magic, Tom turned into a different man, and yet she knew the change had been gradual and had involved hard work. It had been anything but magic.

"That's great, Bobby," she said. "Are you working?"

"No, Lace, I stand on a street corner and panhandle."

The image was so close to what she had imagined that it

took her a minute to realize he was joking. "Well, what sort of work do you do?"

"I went back to college and changed my major to art, although I never did finish. I got into scrimshaw. I'm a scrimshander."

She frowned into the phone, picturing the few pieces of scrimshaw she had seen; drawings of tall ships etched in black on ancient whale teeth. "That's what you do for a living?"

He laughed at the tone of her voice. "Actually, yes," he said. "I'm not living in the lap of luxury, but I love what I do. I work mostly on commission. And how about you?"

"Stained glass," she said. "And I work part-time as a vet tech in my father's practice."

"Didn't your mother used to do stained glass?"

"Yes."

"Like mother like daughter, huh?"

The thought irritated her. "Not quite," she said.

"I also teach drawing at the adult schools around here," he said. "Supplements my income a bit."

"Are you married?" She hadn't considered what this news might do to any relationship he was in.

"Uh-uh," he said. "I lived with a woman for a few years. She's the silversmith who does the work on the jewelry pieces I make. We split a year ago, but stayed friends. How about you?"

"Unattached," she said. "And although I'm happy with that status, it makes the idea of raising someone else's child even more daunting."

"Yeah, I bet." He was quiet, and she could almost hear him thinking through the next step of this conversation. "So look, Lace," he said. "I don't have much money, but if she's really mine—"

"She's yours."

"If she's mine," he said again, "I'll help. Can I meet her?"

"I think I should talk to her about it first," she said. "I'm really not sure what the best course of action is. If she wants to meet you, and you're willing, then I'll call you and we can figure out what to do next."

"Fair enough," he said.

"I'll talk to her tomorrow," she said. "That is, if she's in a decent mood."

"Sounds like you might have to settle for half-decent," he said.

Lacey laughed. "You're right," she said. "And thanks for... for being so easy about this."

He hesitated. "You don't think much of me, do you?" he asked.

It was her turn to be silent. "I don't know what to think, Bobby," she said.

"Right."

"I'll call you after I talk to her," Lacey said.

"Okay. And Lacey?"

"Yes?"

"I'm sorry if I hurt you in any way that summer."

She got off the phone, and to her surprise, began to cry.

18

BOBBY SAT WITH THE PHONE IN HIS LAP FOR A long time after hanging up with Lacey, a numbness settling over him as he replayed the conversation in his mind. He reached for the pack of Marlboros on the broad worktable, set up in what was supposed to be his dining room, and shook one of the cigarettes into his hand. He lit it, inhaled deeply and let the smoke out of his mouth in a long, slow stream.

Lacey O'Neill. He remembered how she had chopped off her beautiful, if out-of-control, red hair that summer. Chopped it off to within an inch of her scalp and then dyed it jet black. Yet every time he'd looked at her with that short, dark mop on her head, his mind had painted in the missing red hair. That's how much that long hair had been part of her: he could see it even when it wasn't there. He should have asked her what she looked like now. Was her hair long, or did she still try to hide who she was with dye and scissors?

And Jessica Dillard. Very young. A petite blond seductress. How easily a seventeen-year-old boy could be seduced. Although he'd always found Lacey's personality and big blue eyes and deep dimples more engaging than Jessica's sultry looks and provocative nature, Lacey's quiet fragility had scared him off. He'd made love to her once, if you could call deflowering a virgin on the beach making love. It had hurt her, that much he remembered. She'd yelped in pain and he'd stopped, but she told him to keep on going. He knew she wasn't having any fun, that she just wanted him to get it over with, but he was too far gone to get into a long discussion about the matter. He'd finished what he started and the very next night, turned to her best friend, who didn't seem to have a fear in the world, who did not yelp, who liked to wrap her body around his, her blond hair splayed out on the sand. Jessica had been an animal, bucking beneath him. They'd done it every which way. Most of the time with a condom. Some of the time without. What a goddamned asshole he'd been.

Sometimes you looked back at the person you once were and wanted to throw up. He'd tried so hard to hide from the past, but every now and then, a reminder would pop up that he just couldn't shake. Like Lacey's phone call. Like a child she said was his.

With a sigh, he set the phone back on the corner of the table, then reached for the piece of mammoth ivory he'd been working on when the call had come. The ancient piece of ivory, now plain and smooth and off-white, would become a belt buckle decorated with a delicate color portrait of three beloved dogs, a gift from one of his customers to her husband. It was going to be beautiful, and it would take him weeks to complete. It would also cost the woman a pretty penny.

He couldn't get into working on the ivory, though. He would mess it up if he tried now. He took another drag on his cigarette and looked through the dining room window. His view was of the alley behind his small house, and beyond the alley, the garage of one of his neighbors, the one with the dog that barked and snarled at him every time he took his garbage out.

A year ago he'd wanted a kid so badly he just about cried every time Claudia got her period. They'd been trying for nearly three years, and if they'd succeeded he would have married her and they would have made a go of it. He tried not to let his disappointment show, but she knew how much he longed for a child. Someone to pour his love into. Someone to raise better than he had been raised. He would correct all the mistakes his parents had made. *Mackenzie*. Funny name for a girl. It made him smile. So, she was belligerent and obstinate and all those other negative adjectives Lacey had used to describe her. She was still a real, living, breathing child in need of a father.

But he was as sure as he could be that she was not his.

19

MACKENZIE WAS EYEING THE CDS IN THE WINDOW
of the music store when Lacey came up behind her. She'd just
tossed three bags of new clothes for the girl into the car but
knew they weren't done shopping yet.

"Would you like to get a couple of CDs?" she asked.

"Where's the CD player?" Mackenzie kept her gaze on the
store window.

"There's one in the living room, but maybe you should
have a boom box for your room. What do you think?"

"I think yes," Mackenzie said. "Could we go in here and
get one?"

"Go on in and get a few CDs, and then we can go to
Kmart. The boom boxes will be cheaper there."

"How many can I get?" Mackenzie asked.

"Four," Lacey said. "I'll sit out here and you can come get
me when you're ready to pay, okay?"

"'Kay." Mackenzie walked into the store, and Lacey sat
down on a bench. She was wiped out. Her legs ached and
when she looked down at her pale, freckled arms, they looked
flabby to her. She hadn't made it to the gym since Mackenzie's arrival, and she wasn't sure when she would be able to

go again. Until a year ago, she'd liked to go to the gym in the afternoon or evening, when it was filled with young singles and she could easily meet guys. These days, though, she liked to go very early in the morning, when only the truly serious exercisers were present and she was safe from temptation. Now she would have to figure out when the mothers went to the gym and join their ranks.

She and Mackenzie had spent the entire morning shopping in the outlet stores. Lacey was handing over her credit card with abandon, but that could not continue. This was a special shopping trip, she told herself. Mackenzie's boxes of clothing and other paraphernalia had not yet arrived from Phoenix, and she needed new clothes and a few other things to help her begin to feel at home.

Money was going to be a problem. Nola had given Lacey two hundred dollars to use on this shopping spree, but she would have to ask her for more. She would need a regular infusion of money if she was going to be able to take care of Mackenzie above the poverty line. But she couldn't talk to Nola about this yet. Despite her ambivalence about wanting custody of Mackenzie, Nola was still smarting over Jessica's guardianship decision, and Lacey thought it politic to wait a while longer before broaching the subject of a monthly stipend for the girl. There was Bobby, of course, but even if he was willing to help, it didn't sound like he would have much to offer monetarily.

Living in the keeper's house had been a blessing, Lacey thought, since there had been no rent involved—only the responsibility of helping with the restoration. Next year, though, she would have to find a rental and go back to the real world. Her income was sufficient to meet her own modest needs, but not those of a child. Mackenzie had inherited the few thousand dollars that had been in Jessica's savings account and she would inherit about ten thousand dollars when the condo sold, but that money should go into a college savings account.

They had spent much of the morning in the GAP outlet, with Mackenzie wanting every belly-button-exposing outfit she tried on. "I need to get my navel pierced," she said, as if she was talking about her need for water or sunshine, and Lacey almost told her that she had a pierced navel herself. She longed to make Mackenzie see that she was not a pathetic old spinster, but the time didn't seem right.

After the GAP, they visited most of the stores on the strip, and Mackenzie's conflicted, preadolescent needs and desires were much in evidence. She wanted stuffed animals, and Lacey let her pick out a teddy bear and a dog for her room. She wanted a small glass horse. She wanted games for her computer. And she wanted nail polish and necklaces. Lacey bought her nearly everything she asked for, as if she could make up for the loss of a mother by giving her material possessions.

Mackenzie opened the door of the record store and poked her head outside. "Ready," she said, and Lacey walked inside to hand over her credit card once again.

"Let's get something to eat and then we'll stop at Kmart on the way home," she said, as they left the store and walked toward the car. Her plan for the morning had been to take Mackenzie shopping, then, over lunch, tell her about her conversation with Bobby. She had no idea how Mackenzie would respond to the fact that she'd spoken with her father.

It took them a while to decide where to have lunch, but Mackenzie finally agreed that Taco Bell would be all right. "In Phoenix, though, I would *never* go to Taco Bell," she said as they pulled into the restaurant's parking lot. "But since there's hardly any other Mexican food here, I guess it's the only choice."

"Maybe we can make some Mexican food at home one of

these nights," Lacey suggested, but Mackenzie was already out of the car and hearing range.

Inside the restaurant, they carried their trays of food to a table near the front window. As soon as they'd sat down, Mackenzie reached into her purse for her cell phone.

"No," Lacey said, for what seemed like the first time that day. She shook her head at the cell phone. "Please put that away," she said. "I want to talk to you."

"I don't want to talk," Mackenzie said. "I mean, I want to talk to my friends on the phone, but—"

"Not now," Lacey said. "I have something important to discuss with you."

"What?" She lowered the phone to her lap and began unwrapping her taco.

"I've spoken with your father."

"What?" Mackenzie's hands froze on the taco. Her eyes were huge.

Lacey nodded. "I contacted him. He'd like to meet you."

"No *way*." Mackenzie shook her head violently.

"Why not?"

"Because he's a jerk."

She wondered what, if anything, Jessica had told her daughter about Bobby. "Why do you say that?" she asked.

Mackenzie lifted the taco toward her mouth, but set it down again without taking a bite. "My mother said he was not the least bit interested in me," she said.

"He didn't know about you. She never let him know."

"He knew and he didn't care."

"No, Mackenzie, he had no idea. I'm sorry, but if your mother told you that she'd told him about you, she was…" She could hardly say that Jessica had lied to her. "She was probably trying to protect you, because she was afraid that if she *did* tell him, he might not care."

"She said he was a big loser, that it was probably good that he didn't want to see me."

"You know what?" Lacey said with a nod. "She's right that he was a big loser when she knew him. And I was a big loser back then, too."

Mackenzie looked unsurprised by that revelation and Lacey rushed on, wanting to avoid the girl's inevitable retort: *You're still a big loser.* "And so was your mother," she added.

"Don't you dare say that." There was fire in Mackenzie's eyes.

"We were *all* young and stupid and just trying to figure out how to get by in life," Lacey said. "Just like you're doing. Eventually, we grew up and got our acts together."

"I totally know how to get by," Mackenzie said. "And my mother was never a loser."

"Define loser, then," Lacey said.

"Someone who has no life."

"And what does that mean, exactly?" Lacey pressed her.

"You know, they don't have anything going for them. They use drugs or drink or do stupid things."

Maybe she was overstepping herself here, but she didn't bother to stop. "That defines me and your mother and Bobby. But it was a phase we were going through."

Mackenzie frowned. "My mother never used drugs."

"Maybe not," Lacey lied. "But she did make some stupid choices. Just like I did. And like all our friends did."

"That's his name? Bobby?"

Lacey nodded.

"What a dork."

"You know." Lacey looked down at her untouched burrito. "Ultimately it doesn't matter what you think. You can't change who your father is, so maybe you could try being grateful that he'd like to get to know you."

"Where does he live?"

"In Richmond, Virginia. That's about four hours away. He could come here to meet you. You wouldn't have to go there."

Mackenzie played with her taco, picking up shreds of cheese that had fallen onto her tray and sticking them back in the shell as a silence stretched between them. "I don't want him to come," she said.

"It's your choice," Lacey said. "You don't have to meet him if you don't want to."

"Good." Mackenzie wrapped up the taco and left it on the tray. "Can I talk on my phone now?"

Lacey acquiesced, exhausted from the simple conversation. She guessed Bobby would be relieved to hear that Mackenzie was not up for a visit from him. Maybe someday he and his daughter could meet, but not now. Mackenzie had been poisoned against him, and perhaps that was just as well. But she felt the sting of disappointment, not over losing any possible financial or moral support from Bobby, but over the lost chance to see him once again.

They stopped at Kmart, where Mackenzie found a boom box. Lacey picked up some paper goods, while Mackenzie disappeared into some other part of the store. Her cart filled with boom box, paper towels and toilet paper, Lacey walked through the store looking for her. She turned the corner of the cosmetic aisle just in time to see Mackenzie slip something into the pocket of her shorts. *Damn.* She pushed the cart down the aisle toward her, and Mackenzie glanced up, quickly covering a look of surprise with a false smile. "I'm ready to go," she said, turning away from the cosmetics and heading away from Lacey.

Lacey stopped pushing the cart right where Mackenzie had been standing. "Put it back, Mackenzie," she said.

Mackenzie turned to look at her. "What?" All innocence. Jessica had mastered that same look at an even earlier age.

"Whatever you just slipped into your pocket," Lacey said. "Put it back."

"You were *spying* on me?" Mackenzie looked indignant.

"You were pretty obvious," she said. "You're a crappy thief."

With a sound of disgust, Mackenzie pulled the small plastic box from her pocket and hung it back on the rack. Lacey looked at the purloined item and had to laugh.

"False *eyelashes?*" she asked.

"Leave me alone." Mackenzie turned her back on her and walked away. "Can we go now? It's almost time for *The Young and the Restless*."

They drove home, Lacey quiet at the wheel while Mackenzie talked softly on the phone in the backseat. Lacey caught snippets of conversation. Some giggling, a sound she only heard from Mackenzie when she was on the phone. It irked her that she might be laughing about her. Overnight, Lacey had turned into someone kids made fun of.

When she pulled into the parking lot, Lacey spotted Clay standing by the dog kennel, explaining something to a woman whose two dogs stood on either side of her.

Mackenzie clicked her phone shut and sat up straight. "Golden retrievers," she said, more to herself than to Lacey. "Is he doing that search-and-rescue training thing with them?"

Lacey nodded.

"Could I go watch?"

Mackenzie was willing to give up *The Young and the Restless* to watch Clay train dogs? In the rearview mirror, Lacey saw genuine excitement in her eyes. Although it pleased her to see Mackenzie show interest in something other than clothes and makeup and music, it was not a good idea.

She turned in her seat to look at Mackenzie. "That woman is probably paying for her lesson by the hour," she said, "so if you went over there right now, you'd be distracting the dogs and costing her money. But why don't you talk to Clay about it tonight? Maybe he'd let you sit in on some of the lessons, since you like dogs so much."

Mackenzie didn't answer her. She got out of the car and helped Lacey unload the trunk, then started walking toward the house with her arms full and her eyes on the dogs. Lacey followed close behind her, bags hanging from her fingertips.

When she was halfway to the house, Mackenzie turned to face her.

"I'll meet him," she said. "That Bobby guy. I mean, if he wants to come all the way out here, I might as well."

20

RICK BOWLED HIS THIRD STRIKE IN A ROW, AND he guessed that Lacey had figured out he was a ringer by now. In the lane next to them, Mackenzie, Jack and Maggie were bowling, all three of them for the first time, and while they weren't actually talking to one another, they *were* letting out sounds of joy or lament as their balls hit or missed their targets. Mackenzie had sulked a bit at first, but he had the feeling she simply couldn't let anyone know this was an activity she might enjoy. On the other hand, Jack, with his Harry Potter glasses and placid demeanor, and Maggie, with her frenetic chatter and energy, were delightful kids. But then, they hadn't just lost their mother.

Lacey had told him she'd practically had to drag Mackenzie out of the house. It was the first time the girl was to meet Rick, and she'd seemed less than taken with his choice of activities. As he was teaching her how to let go of the ball, she'd muttered under her breath, "Bowling. Who bowls? I am like *so glad* I don't know anybody around here who could see me."

Rick knew that Lacey had felt nervous having to entertain Mackenzie for an entire rainy Saturday, and he was pleased with himself for suggesting bowling. It gave the kids a chance to get to know each other better, and gave him a chance to be with Lacey in a setting where they could talk easily, without the children overhearing.

"I get the feeling you bowl often," Lacey said, as she stood at the end of the lane waiting for her ball to return to her. She glanced over at the kids and he followed her gaze. Jack was standing at the end of the lane, his ball poised close to his chest, concentrating hard on the pins.

"I'm in a league," Rick admitted. The guys he bowled with were blue-collar types, and he felt a certain comfort with them that he'd never experienced with his legal colleagues. His father had taught him to bowl. He'd grown up with the echoey sounds of the bowling alley, the smoke, the scent of hot dogs and the smell of men. And although this bowling alley was filled with children, smoke-free—at least this afternoon—and pizza-scented, he felt that old familiar comfort here.

"You're not too bad for a beginner," he said as Lacey rolled her ball down the lane. She wasn't. He liked watching her. She wore loose navy blue shorts that exposed the tight muscles in her calves. Her long hair was full and curly from the rain, and there was a gracefulness about her when she stepped forward to let go of the ball.

"Well," Lacey said, as he got up to take his turn. "I called Mackenzie's father again last night, and he's coming to the Outer Banks sometime this week. He plans to stay awhile."

"Are you glad?"

"I think it's the right thing to do."

"So do I." He was quiet for a moment as he concentrated on the pins at the end of the lane. He moved forward, swinging the ball back, controlling it carefully as he brought it forward and let it go. He watched it curve too sharply to the right, missing three pins.

"I just hope he's a decent guy and that I'm not making a huge mistake," Lacey said.

Rick cooled his hand over the fan as he waited for his ball to return. "How does he sound on the phone?" he asked.

"Decent." She smiled. "Like he's been through a lot and learned from it."

"Can't ask for more than that."

"Guess not, Mr. Forgiveness."

He laughed. "Speaking of which, how's your victim's impact statement coming along?"

She groaned. "Not too well. I'm not much of a writer."

"You can do it."

"The attorney said not to be overly emotional," she said. "But it's my *mother,* and when I start remembering what happened, I want to stab the paper with my pen."

"Hmm." He slipped his fingers into his ball and lifted it toward his chest. "I don't know if I agree about keeping your emotions out of it. I think you should play them up. Let out all the pain and fury."

"That's not what she said, and she's the one who'll be passing judgment on it." Lacey lifted her legs straight out in front of her and studied the ugly bowling shoes. "I think it might be hopeless," she said. "The lawyer says Pointer's been a model prisoner. That he plans to become a minister when he gets out."

Rick focused on the pins, moved forward and let go of the ball. It rolled down the alley and caught one of the pins, but left the other two standing. His concentration was off.

"Is he remorseful?" he asked, turning around to look at her.

"So he says."

He cooled his hand over the fan again. "I have a radical idea," he said.

"What's that?" She stood up to take her turn.

"What if you went to visit him?" he asked. "See him for yourself. Listen to what he has to say. Ask him your questions. Then you can make your own judgment as to what sort of man he's become."

He watched her face harden. "Frankly, Rick, that idea makes me feel nauseous." She lifted her ball from the rack. "I don't *ever* want to see him again. I saw him once—the day he shot my mother—and believe me, that was enough." She turned toward the pins and let the ball go with a vengeance. It practically flew into the gutter and she groaned. Then she turned to look at him, her hands on her hips.

"You know," she said, "it's a good thing you didn't go into criminal law. You are way too soft."

"You're soft, too, Lacey," he said. "You try to hide that part of yourself, but you're not very good at it."

She walked over to where he was sitting and plunked herself down on the bench. "I don't want to talk about this anymore," she said. "I have too much else on my mind. Like finding a place for Bobby to stay."

He motioned toward the lane. "You still have another ball," he said.

"I'll get to it." She lifted her pale legs to frown at the shoes again. "There are no cheap rooms in the Outer Banks in the summer."

"Could he stay at the keeper's house?" he suggested.

She wrinkled her nose. "Too close for comfort. I mean, what if he's still a scummy guy? And it just seems like that would be forcing him down Mackenzie's throat."

"Would Mackenzie's grandmother take him?"

Lacey laughed. "No way. She's furious at me for even contacting him. I'm thinking of asking Tom. My biological father. He's in AA, too, and he's pretty easygoing." She got up again and walked toward the balls.

Rick thought of the spare room in his cottage. "He can stay with me," he said.

She whirled around to look at him. "What?"

"I have that extra bedroom. It's just sitting there. He wouldn't have to pay me anything."

She looked doubtful. "I can't really vouch for what sort of person he is," she said.

Rick shrugged. "I'm not worried."

"And I don't know how long he'll want to stay. Wouldn't you feel cramped?"

"All I need is that little corner of the living room where my computer's set up. I haven't even walked in that extra bedroom once since I've been there. It's not a four-star hotel but—"

"God, you are so nice." She smiled at him, her dimples showing.

He returned the smile and shrugged. "I'd like to help," he said.

"Thank you. That would be fabulous." She turned and stood at attention, concentrating on the pins, and he could feel his heart pounding hard against his rib cage.

He did want to help her. To repay her. Because she was going to help him, too, whether she knew it or not.

21

LACEY HEARD THE VEHICLE BEFORE SHE SAW IT. She and Rick were sitting on the broad porch of the keeper's house when they heard the crackling of gravel, and the rough sound of an engine growled above the ocean's whisper. Lacey looked toward the woods and spotted a patch of powder blue through the trees.

"I don't believe it," she said, getting to her feet.

"What?" Rick followed her gaze toward the trees.

"He's still driving that van," she said. "It was already ancient in 1991." The battered-looking, faded-blue-to-white Volkswagen bus bounced from the trees into the parking lot, and Lacey felt a nearly forgotten visceral pull. How she had longed to see that van during the summer she was fourteen. She used to watch for it, eyeing the stream of cars along the beach road, searching for the distinctive blue bus. It had meant excitement. Forbidden danger.

Rick stood up, too, a grin on his face. "I haven't seen one of those since I was a kid," he said.

"I'll be right back." Lacey trotted down the porch steps and started walking across the sand toward the parking lot. Bobby got out of the van, and she had to mask her surprise at the sight of him. She wasn't sure she would have recognized him if she'd passed him on the street. He was completely bald! He wore old jeans and a pale blue T-shirt, the bottom edge of a tattoo visible beneath the sleeve. His shoulders were broader than they'd been when he was a kid and his arms more muscular. Still, the blue eyes and the cockeyed grin she used to fantasize about were the same, and if she hadn't already known it, she knew it now—having Bobby Asher in the area was going to be the ultimate test of her will.

"Lacey!" He reached out and pulled her into a bear hug, and she caught the scent of both soap and tobacco. He stood back to hold her at arm's length. "I'm sure glad you let your hair grow out again. That red-and-black checkerboard look just wasn't you."

She laughed, trying to gracefully extract herself from his embrace. "It's good to see you," she said. "I can't believe you're still driving this VW." She found it difficult to look him straight in the eye, as if he might be able to see right through to the melting core inside her.

He ran one hand over his bald head. "So, what do you think?" he asked.

"You look great," she said, and she wasn't lying.

"My older brothers both have the same hair gene, so I knew what was coming," he said. "I shaved it off before it fell out completely. Gave me the illusion of having some control over the process."

He was self-conscious about it, and that made her feel some tenderness toward him.

"Well," she said, waving for him to follow her, "come on up to the house."

He started walking next to her. "It's so cool you live out here," he said.

"I know," she said. "I lucked out." She wondered how she

really looked to him. She'd dressed with care that morning, annoyed with herself that what he thought mattered to her, as she tried to strike the right balance between the conservative young woman she was struggling to be these days and the little tart she had once been. She was wearing blue-striped capri-length pants and a sleeveless white shirt cut high on her shoulders, and when she'd looked in the mirror, she thought she'd managed to pull it off. Not too sexy, but not exactly puritanical, either.

They were nearing the house, and Bobby shaded his eyes to look toward the porch. "Is that your brother?" he asked.

"No, it's a friend." She wondered what he would read into that description of Rick. "Did you know my brother?"

"No, but I remember you have one," he said. "And where's Mackenzie?"

"Up in her room. She's nervous about meeting you." She laughed. "Not that she's *told* me she's nervous. She doesn't tell me anything. But when I asked her if she wanted to wait on the porch with us, she declined the invitation."

"Can't blame her for that," Bobby said. "This has to be hard for her."

They'd reached the porch and Lacey introduced Bobby to Rick as they climbed the steps. "Rick's going to let you stay at his place in Duck while you're here," she said. She hoped Rick didn't regret the invitation now that he saw the man in the flesh. The two of them shook hands, looking almost like separate species. Rick was squeaky clean, from his thick dark hair to his spotless BMW parked next to the old van in the parking lot. Bobby certainly was not grubby or even unkempt, but there was an earthiness about him that no amount of soap and water could ever remove.

"That's really nice of you," Bobby said to Rick. "I'll be happy to pay you something for—"

"No." Rick shook his head. "Trust me. The accommodations aren't worth much, but I think you'll be comfortable there."

"Have a seat." Lacey motioned to one of the chairs. "I'll get Mackenzie."

Bobby sat down, but Rick remained standing, leaning against the porch railing. "I'm going to give Bob directions to my house and then take off," he said to Lacey.

She moved forward to kiss his cheek, grateful that he seemed to know his presence could only complicate matters once Mackenzie came downstairs. "Thanks for being such a help," she said.

Upstairs, she discovered that Mackenzie was not in her room. Her old possessions had not yet arrived, so she had few things to strew around the room, yet she'd managed to make the space look sloppy, nonetheless. Her new clothes were tossed on the unmade bed and the chair, along with the jewel cases for the CDs. Only the stuffed dog and the teddy bear looked like they were in place, sitting neatly on her pillow.

"Mackenzie?" she called, stepping back into the hallway. She checked the bathroom, then the other rooms, then retraced her steps, this time peeking in closets and underneath the beds. She gave up on the second story and walked downstairs, hunting through the rooms there as well, calling her name.

She stepped back onto the porch, the screen door thudding shut behind her. "I can't find her," she said to the two men, wondering if her voice betrayed her worry. "She's not in the house." She scanned the open, sandy area around the keeper's house, then looked toward the woods, the only place that could offer the girl any cover. Cupping her hands around her mouth, she called in that direction. "Mackenzie!" There was no response, only the subdued sound of the waves on the beach and the ever-present buzz of cicadas.

"Do you think she's hiding?" Rick asked.

"She must be," she said. She looked at Bobby. "I guess she's more nervous about meeting you than I thought."

"Would she run away?" Bobby asked.

Lacey shrugged. "Anything's possible with that kid," she said, "but where would she go? It's not like we're near anything out here, and she's on foot."

"Why don't we spread out and look for her?" Rick suggested.

"Okay," Lacey said. "I'll cover the house again. Maybe she's up in the attic."

Lacey opened the screen door and walked inside. She stood still in the living room for a moment, her heart thudding in her chest, as she tried to imagine where Mackenzie might be. Crazy thoughts ran through her head. *Hitchhiking. Suicide.* She remembered stupidly leaving her purse on the kitchen table that morning. Mackenzie could have taken all her money and her credit cards. She could have gotten a cab to come out here and pick her up. She could be on her way back to Phoenix by now. She felt as though she'd been entrusted with someone's priceless jewels and, ignorant of their value, had let them slip from her bungling grasp.

She walked into the kitchen and checked her purse. Her wallet was there, along with all the cash she remembered having and her two credit cards. Scratch the running home to Phoenix theory.

She walked back through the living room, climbed the stairs to the second story, and headed for the door leading to the attic.

22

BOBBY WATCHED RICK WALK THROUGH THE sand toward the woods in his Docker pants and Rockport shoes, then slipped his hands into the pockets of his jeans and tried to put himself in Mackenzie's place. Poor kid. He could imagine what this was like for her. Her mother had died suddenly. She'd never known her father and had been told nothing good about him. She'd been thrust into a new world here in the comparative isolation of Kiss River with a woman she barely knew. He would have been able to handle it better than she would at eleven, because even at that age, he was already well into marijuana and beer, and he'd learned how to cope with just about anything that came his way by numbing his mind to the situation. His brothers had trained him well. Five years ago, when he'd finally gotten sober, he'd had to learn how to cope without those mind-numbing aids, and it had not been an easy task. He'd had to learn all those skills he should have perfected as a teenager.

This girl, Mackenzie, should be developing those skills now, when she was supposed to. If there was anything he wanted to do for her, it was to keep her from numbing herself to life's problems. His daughter or not, he could make that his gift to her.

So, where would he hide if he were an eleven-year-old female? Maybe the beach? His gaze went instantly to the lighthouse, and for the first time he noticed that the top was missing. He'd forgotten. There was a certain beauty to the tower now, in the way the late afternoon sunlight was reflected off the jagged bricks near the top. He began walking toward it, realizing quickly there would be little beach in Kiss River for Mackenzie to escape to, since the water was up so high that it actually surrounded the base of the lighthouse. He kicked off his sandals and rolled his jeans halfway up his calves, as high as they would go, to wade through it. There had been beach here twelve years ago, he remembered, a sliver of white sand, hidden away from much of the world. A great place to get high or have sex.

He climbed the three steps leading into the building and walked into the cool, octagonal foyer. "Mackenzie?" he called, craning his neck to look up at the narrowing brick cylinder. His voice echoed back at him, and he heard the twittering of birds, the flapping of their wings, and could see patches of the blue sky high above him. "Mackenzie, if you're up there, please answer me. We're worried about you."

"I can't move." The voice was soft, but loud enough for him to hear.

He started up the stairs. "Why can't you move?" he asked as he climbed. He pictured her with a foot stuck between the metal steps. Or maybe she'd fallen and broken an ankle.

It was a moment before the voice came again. "I just can't," she said.

"I'm on my way up," he said. "How high up are you?"

"I can't think about it."

He found her on the third landing, sitting on the floor,

her back against the bricks and her arms wrapped around her skinny bent legs. He stopped on the top step and looked at her. "Are you all right? Are you hurt or something?"

"I freaked out. It's so high. I can't make myself go up higher and I can't even go down. It's like I'm paralyzed or something."

"Oh." He nodded in sympathy, leaning against the brick wall near the top step. "That happened to me once. I was mountain climbing. You know, trying to scale a mountain that went straight up. I got halfway up and froze. Had to be rescued." The tale was a complete fabrication. He had never even been mountain climbing, but it seemed like a good time for a lie.

"Are you my father?" she asked.

He hadn't expected the question so soon, and he knew *this* was nothing to lie about. Sighing, he walked across the landing and sat down as she was, on the floor, his back against the wall and a few feet away from her. He didn't want to frighten her.

"The honest-to-God truth is, I don't know," he said. He had to pick his words carefully, knowing that his own rationale for being here was muddy at best. "But your mother thought I was, and that's good enough for me."

She was quiet, and he wondered if she was disappointed or pleased by his uncertainty. "What if you don't like me, though?" she said. "You might not."

"Hey, there isn't a kid alive who's likable all the time," he said. "Not a normal kid, anyway." He studied her face. She was beautiful. Jessica's daughter, without a doubt, but he could see none of his features in her. None at all. Her neediness, though, her vulnerability, was a palpable force here on the cool landing. It pulsed in the air between them, pulling his heart in her direction. "Let's go down, Mackenzie. What do you think?"

"I can't even stand up."

"Hold on to me." He stood and reached his hand out to her. She took it and got stiffly to her feet, as though her legs were made of wood. He could feel the quivering of her body through her hand. He walked her slowly toward the stairs. "Do you want me to hold on to you or you to hold on to me?" he asked.

She leaned forward gingerly to grab the railing as if it were a life preserver. "I'll keep one hand on the railing and one on you," she said. "But I have to close my eyes."

He laughed. "Okay," he said. "Whatever works."

They made their way down the stairs in that fashion, Mackenzie clutching his forearm hard enough to cause one of his fingers to go numb, and him repeating, "Step, step, step, step, okay, now we're on a landing, walk, walk, walk, now we're at the steps again. We'll be down soon."

When they reached the foyer, Mackenzie let go of his arm and ran ahead of him. She jumped over the three steps into the water, finally free. "I am *never* going into that stupid light-house again," she said, shaking her arms up and down, as if she could rid herself of the experience that way.

He walked with her through the sand toward the keeper's house. "Were you up there to avoid meeting me?" he asked.

"Of course not," she said, with a bit too much defensiveness. She grew quiet, then—she no longer needed him—and he didn't push her to talk.

He looked at his watch as they walked across the sand. It was nearly six o'clock. He should have timed his arrival better. He would be getting a call at six sharp and he'd need to take it in private. The thought made him anxious. He was trying to juggle too many balls at once.

Rick was returning from his fruitless search of the woods when Bobby and Mackenzie neared the house, and Lacey rushed onto the porch.

"You found her!" she said, running down the steps toward them. She tried to hug Mackenzie, but Bobby could tell it was like hugging the trunk of a rough-barked tree. "I was worried about you," Lacey said to the girl. "Where were you?"

"She was in the lighthouse," Bobby said.

"In the lighthouse?" Lacey looked amazed.

"I'm going upstairs," Mackenzie said, pushing past them.

"No," Lacey said. "Stay down here and talk to Bobby for a while."

He put his hand on Lacey's arm and mouthed the words, "Let her go."

"All right," Lacey said. "You can go up if you want."

"Thank you." The words were sarcastic, and the three adults watched the girl walk up the porch steps and into the house.

"I can't believe she was in the lighthouse," Lacey said. "I thought she was terrified of it."

"She is." Bobby looked at the screen door through which Mackenzie had disappeared. "But apparently not as much as she was of meeting me."

23

ONCE RICK HAD GONE HOME, LACEY LEFT BOBBY on the porch and went upstairs to check on Mackenzie. She found her sitting at her computer, madly typing an e-mail to her friends.

"You're making a big deal out of *nothing!*" Mackenzie shouted when Lacey asked if she was all right.

"I just wanted to be sure you weren't—"

"I am *fine,*" Mackenzie insisted. "I just decided it was time to see what it was like from the top of the lighthouse, but I got hydrophobia up there. That's *all.*"

Lacey struggled not to laugh out loud. "All right," she said. "I'm glad you're fine."

She went downstairs again and, as she walked through the kitchen, she could hear Bobby talking to someone on the porch. Maybe Clay or Gina had arrived home. It wasn't until she pushed open the screen door that she realized he was talking on his cell phone. He was sitting in one of the Adirondack chairs, his bare feet propped up on the railing and Sasha by his side, and he glanced at Lacey when she stepped onto the porch.

"Gotta go," he said into the phone. "I'll try to call you later."

She felt intrusive as she sat down in the other chair, but he quickly slipped his phone into his shirt pocket and looked over at her.

"How is she?" he asked quietly, and she wondered if he'd heard any of her conversation with the girl through Mackenzie's open window, which was right above the porch.

"Embarrassed, I think." Lacey kept her voice low. "She says she had an attack of hydrophobia in the lighthouse."

Bobby laughed. "Better keep her away from the ocean, then."

"Well," Lacey said, "this has been a really rocky start to your visit. Can I get you something to drink? Iced tea or soda?"

"What I would *really* like is to go all the way to the top of the lighthouse," he said, pointing toward the tower. "It's so cool, the way the stairs jut up in the air. Is it safe? Can we climb it?"

"Sure." She stood up, and Sasha leaped joyfully to his feet.

"You stay here, Sasha," she said, and the dog lay down again with a great sigh.

She and Bobby descended the porch steps, and they were quiet as they walked toward the lighthouse. The tide was high, and Lacey rolled her capris above her knees before wading through the swirling, knee-high water to get to the steps. Bobby's jeans were so tight that he could only roll them partway up his calves, and they were already wet from his earlier foray into the lighthouse. He didn't seem to care, though, and he plowed right into the water.

Once they were climbing the interior stairs, Lacey told him about the Fresnel lens. "It was salvaged from the ocean bottom last summer," she said, "and they're going to display it next to the keeper's house in a little building that will look like the old lantern room."

"Just last summer?" he asked. "I thought the storm was a long time ago."

"It was, but no one had the motivation to salvage it until Gina—my sister-in-law—moved here. It's a long story, but she was the one really responsible for raising it."

"You work out, huh?" he asked suddenly. Apparently his mind was not on the lighthouse at all. She was a few steps above him and suddenly grew self-conscious about her body. What part of her had given away the fact that she worked out?

"I have for years," she said, "although having Mackenzie here has put a dent in my schedule. What made you ask?"

"You're not the least bit breathless climbing these stairs," he said.

"Neither are you." She'd noticed that. Most people needed to stop at least once to catch their breath on the circular stairway.

"I try to stay fit," he said, as if his cut and corded arms had not already given him away. "Is there a Y around here?"

"I can get you a guest pass to my gym," she said.

"That would be great," he said. They had reached the landing closest to the top of the lighthouse. "This is where I found Mackenzie," he said, as they crossed the landing to start the next flight of stairs.

"Wow." Lacey was impressed. "I can't believe she made it up this high."

In another minute, they reached the top of the stairs. "Careful here," she said to him. "Hold on to the railing when you turn around."

"Whoa," he said, reaching quickly for the railing. "I guess I have a touch of hydrophobia myself." He turned carefully and sat down next to her on the top step, several feet above the jagged edge of the tower. "Oh, man," he said. "It's like being suspended in the air up here."

"I know."

He twisted his neck to the right, then the left to take in the three-hundred-and-sixty-degree view. "Do you ever see the horses from up here?" he asked.

"Oh, I hate to tell you, but the horses are gone." She explained how the wild mustangs had been moved farther north to protect them from the ever-increasing traffic. "You can only see them now by paying for an all-terrain-vehicle tour."

"You've got to be kidding." He shook his head. "Pave paradise and put up a parking lot."

"Right."

"Would it bother you if I smoked?"

She shook her head. "Not outside. Just please not in the keeper's house." Rick would not want smoke in his cottage, either, but she would leave it to him to set his own rules.

He reached into the rear pocket of his jeans and pulled out a crushed pack of Marlboros and a book of matches. He had to walk down a few steps to light the cigarette so that the breeze wouldn't blow out the match. Sitting next to her again, he exhaled a stream of smoke.

"I've been trying to quit," he said, then laughed. "But I've been trying to quit for five years, so I guess that's a load of bullshit, huh?"

"Yeah." She nodded. "I'd say so." She wanted to lift the sleeve of his T-shirt to see his tattoo. The part that showed beneath the hem of the sleeve looked like small blue squares.

"Thanks for arranging a place for me to stay," he said. "I figured I'd have to sleep in the bus. It wouldn't be the first time."

She remembered the mattress in the back of the bus. He used to park the VW in the lot at Jockey's Ridge and four or five of them would sit on that mattress and get high in the hot, smoky air. Bobby would eventually kick everyone out except Jessica, and Lacey would try to block from her mind what was happening inside the bus while she and her other friends sat on the sand, waiting. If Bobby still had a mattress in the van, she at least hoped it was not the same one he'd had in 1991.

"Well," she said, "I hope it works out okay. Rick's pretty easygoing, but his cottage is tiny."

"He seems like a nice guy." Bobby took a drag on his cigarette. "How long have you been seeing him?"

"Just a month, and it's not serious," she said. "I'm avoiding seriousness these days."

"How come?"

She shrugged. "He…the feelings just aren't there, at least not yet." She laughed, stretching her arms out in front of her. "I guess I still have this romantic notion that I could find a man I'd love enough that nothing else would matter. A till-death-do-us-part kind of guy. Someone I'd lay down my life for."

"Have you ever felt that way about anyone?" he asked.

"Not even close," she said. Her relationships with men had involved too little emotional intimacy and way too much sex. She squirmed at having revealed so much to him. "So, how about you? Have you ever felt that way about anyone?"

He nodded. "I felt that way about my ex-girlfriend, Claudia," he said. "I still do."

"You're still in love with her?"

"Not *in* love. I just love her. She's a special friend."

"You're lucky," she said.

"Well, who knows." He watched as the ash fell from his cigarette into the depths of the lighthouse. "Maybe it will work out for you with Rick."

"Maybe," she said, although she doubted it.

"What's the light like at his place?" Bobby asked.

"The light?"

"Right. Is there good natural light to work by? I brought my work with me since I didn't know how long I'd be staying."

"Oh," she said. "The light might not be great. The cottage is pretty deep in the woods."

"I'll work it out," he said.

"I'd love to see your scrimshaw." The image of three-masted schooners etched into whale teeth came back to her.

"I brought most of my stuff, actually." He took another drag on his cigarette and exhaled, and the breeze stole the smoke away before she could even see it. "This is the season when I usually exhibit at craft fairs and I'm going to miss a few. So I thought I'd bring my wares with me in case I could sell at any of the venues around here."

"There's a craft fair next weekend in Manteo," she said. "You were supposed to sign up months ago, but I'm sure I can get you a booth."

"That'd be great, Lacey. Will you be exhibiting there?"

"Yes."

"I want to see your work, too," he said. "I remember your mother's. I always thought it was so sad she'd died, you know, with all those ideas and creativity and talent inside of her. I'm glad you carried on the tradition."

"I'm not as good as she was," she said, annoyed at her self-deprecation the moment the words left her mouth. "Or at least, I'm different. I work mostly in her old studio in Kill Devil Hills, but I use the sunroom here, sometimes. Do you remember the studio?"

He took another pull on the cigarette. "I do," he said. "The guy with the ponytail, right?"

"Tom Nestor." She wasn't ready to tell him that Tom was the man who'd turned out to be her father.

"I think it's very cool that we both ended up being artists," Bobby said. He was smiling to himself, his gaze on the horizon. He held his cigarette in his mouth while he reached down to reroll one wet leg of his jeans, and removed the cigarette without taking another drag. "So, how's it been, having Mackenzie here?" he asked.

"I don't like her." The words slipped out before she could think. "God. That sounds terrible, doesn't it?"

"It sounds honest," he said.

"It's so strange." Lacey watched a speedboat as it bounced across the water in the distance. "I usually like everyone," she said, "but she really is a little twit. I'm honestly thinking about letting Nola have her. She wanted her at first. Planned to fight for custody and everything. But I don't think Nola's having much more luck with her than I am."

"Nola, ugh." Bobby shivered with what was—perhaps—mock horror, and Lacey had to laugh. "I'd tried to forget about Jessica's mommy dearest," he said.

"She's not that bad." Lacey felt strange defending Nola, but she was coming to feel sorry for the older woman. They were both in the same bind.

"What makes Mackenzie a little twit?" he asked. His cigarette had reached the point of needing to be crushed out, but he held it between his fingers, letting it burn itself out instead of crushing it on the lighthouse stairs. "You said on the phone that she was obstinate and that she stole from you. What else?"

"Like that's not enough?" she asked.

He shrugged. "Is there more?"

"Well, if I say black, she says white. She's very negative." She would not tell him about Mackenzie's most recent escapade: just that morning she'd found her vibrator in the center of the kitchen table, pointing up toward the ceiling, and knew that the girl had gone through her night table. She was glad she'd been the one to find it and not Clay or Gina. "I caught her lifting false eyelashes at the Kmart, and who knows what else she's stolen that I haven't discovered."

"False eyelashes?" Bobby laughed. "At least she's original."

"You think it's funny now, but just wait till you have to deal with her yourself."

"You never shoplifted when you were a kid?"

"No, I didn't," she said with some indignation. "I know you did, though."

He smiled at her, that crooked smile that she simply could not look at for more than a second without her legs turning to jelly.

"You were a good kid, weren't you?" he asked. "I mean, deep down. You really were. That's why—"

"That's why what?"

He rubbed his hands over his thighs. "I liked you a lot back then," he said. "More than I liked Jessica, at first. But there was something so vulnerable about you. So trusting. I just felt like you were too young and innocent for me to corrupt."

He'd liked her more than Jessica? She wanted to ask him for details about his attraction to her, but stopped herself. What did it matter now?

"You were right about me," she said. "I was trying to act tough, but I was actually a pile of mush inside."

He looked suddenly serious, turning his head from her slightly, and she saw a tightness in his jaw.

"What?" she asked him, knowing something dark had come into his mind.

He gave her a quick, apologetic smile. "I have to tell you

the truth, Lace," he said. "I'm not convinced I'm Mackenzie's father."

She felt him backing out. She could hardly blame him. She would back out herself if she could.

"Jessica said you were," she said.

"I understand," he said. "But…my girlfriend—my ex-girlfriend—Claudia and I wanted to have a child. We tried hard for a couple of years and were tested and everything. I have lazy sperm. That's what the doctor said. It upset me more than it did her, I think. I really wanted a kid."

"Well, maybe your sperm wasn't so lazy when you were seventeen."

"A possibility," he acknowledged.

His phone suddenly rang, the sound a simple, quiet *brrring* coming from his shirt pocket. He made no move to answer it. "They can leave a message," he said.

She waited for the ringing to come to an end, then spoke again. "So what are you saying?" she asked. "Do you want a DNA test?"

"No. Not unless you insist on it."

"I don't get it," she said. "Why not?"

"I'm afraid if I have the DNA test that I'll discover she's not really mine, and I don't want to know that. Is that crazy?"

"Uh…yeah." She smiled. "She's so difficult. You only talked to her for a few minutes. You don't know. Why would you take on a problem kid if you didn't have to?"

"You know who she reminds me of?" he asked, without answering her question.

"Who?"

"You. The way you were back when I knew you."

Lacey frowned. "She's *nothing* like me," she said.

His smile looked secretive now, as if he knew something she did not, and it annoyed her a little.

"Why do you think she is the way she is?" he asked her. "Belligerent, as you say. Obstinate and oppositional."

"I think that Jessica was not the best mother." Lacey was sorry for maligning her friend, but she was beginning to believe it was the truth. "She always sounded like a good mom when she'd tell me about the things she was doing with Mackenzie, but now that I know Mackenzie—" she shook her head "—I think Jessica spoiled her. She let her get away with too much."

He sighed, squinting at the horizon as if the early evening light was too bright for him. "I think you're smarter than that, Lacey," he said.

"What do you mean?"

She felt him turn to look at her, but she did not meet his eyes. He was too close; his eyes would be too blue. "Do you remember what it was like when your mother died?" he asked.

"All too well," she said.

"So, how'd you feel back then."

"Alone. Unbelievably sad. Scared."

"What were you afraid of?"

She hesitated, remembering. "How uncertain and unsafe the world was," she said. "What was going to happen to my family. What would happen to me, now that I was the responsibility of my father, who seemed to barely notice I existed."

"And if someone who didn't know you—know the *real* Lacey—was witnessing your behavior back then, how would they have described you?"

"Like I said, I pretended to be tough and rebellious, so no one could see the scared kid inside me." Suddenly, she understood. It was so simple, and the realization brought tears of sympathy to her eyes. "Mackenzie's just scared," she said, daring to look at him.

His face was serious and sad, and he nodded. "She's got

to be terrified," he said. "And it's even worse for her than it was for you. You still had your father and brother and friends and house and neighborhood and school, and she has nothing familiar around her at all. Just this stranger—practically a stranger, anyway—who came and took her away."

"So what do I do?" she asked.

"I'm not great at this, either, Lace," he said, shaking his head. "I'm still a work in progress myself. But whenever I find myself disliking the way someone acts, I try to think about their motivation and I can usually see that it boils down to fear. That helps me feel a little more sympathetic towards them."

"Well, I can try to do that," she said, but she thought of her vibrator standing at attention on the kitchen table and knew it was going to be a challenge for her to equate Mackenzie's incendiary behavior with fear.

The cigarette was cold and dead now, and Bobby pulled out the pack of Marlboros again, this time slipping the butt beneath the plastic wrapper before returning the pack to his pocket.

"There's something else I have to tell you," he said.

"What?" The breeze kicked up and she caught her hair in her hand and held it against her shoulder.

"When I was twenty-four," he said, "I was in a car accident myself. It was my fault. I was drunk on my ass, and I killed the parents of two little kids."

"Oh, God, Bobby." She felt disgust and sympathy, in equal measures.

"I spent some time locked up, which was the best thing for me because it forced me to get sober and it gave me time to think. When I got out, I tried to contact the grandparents of those kids to see how I could help, but they didn't want any part of me. So, when you called and told me Jessica was killed by a drunk driver, I just felt like…like this is my chance. Do you get it? I don't really care if Mackenzie's mine or not. I don't care if she's a little bitch. I just want to help."

She nodded slowly, letting herself truly look at him for the first time since climbing to the top of the lighthouse. He was not the same person he'd been years ago, and it wasn't just his lack of hair and his muscular frame that were different. "You've changed so much," she said.

"Not really," he said. "I've just grown up. Haven't you?"

"Sometimes I wonder," she said.

He looked at his watch. "The sun's going down," he said. During the time they'd been sitting on top of the lighthouse, afternoon had shifted to evening.

"I love watching the sunset from up here." She let go of her hair to circle her knees with her arms. Although the sun was actually setting behind them, from this vantage point, it colored the entire world.

He looked toward the horizon again, where the clouds were beginning to turn a deep purple. "I'd better get going," he said. "I've got the directions from Rick, but it doesn't sound like an easy place to find after dark."

"It's not," she said, standing up. She felt her hair blow wild in the breeze and caught it in her hands again.

"Sit," he said, giving her shoulder a little nudge as he got to his feet. "Stay up here and enjoy your sunset. I can find my way down."

"All right," she said, taking her seat again. "Thanks for coming, Bobby."

He looked down at her, the fiery light of the setting sun in his eyes. "You *have* grown up, Lace, whether you know it or not," he said. He bent down and brushed his lips across her cheek. "You're a beautiful woman, you know that?"

24

BOBBY'S HEAD AND GUT—HIS ENTIRE BEING, really—ached with the need for caffeine. Sitting across from his host at the little table in Rick's kitchen, he poured himself a second bowl of cornflakes, his eyes on the coffeemaker on the counter. He'd checked for coffee earlier, but had found none in any of the four old knotty pine cabinets in the kitchen. Plenty of wine in the refrigerator, though. Wine no longer tempted him, but it still gave him a jolt to see it. He'd had no alcohol in his own house for years.

"You're not a coffee drinker, huh?" he asked Rick as he poured himself a glass of orange juice.

"No, sorry," Rick said, swallowing a spoonful of cereal. "I take it you are?"

Bobby nodded. "I'll buy some today, and replenish the OJ. Anything else you need while I'm at the store?"

"Nothing I can think of."

So far, their breakfast table conversation had been comfortable, if mundane. They'd talked about where they grew up, where they'd traveled, what their families were like. Bobby tamed some of his answers, not wanting to get into anything too heavy. What he really wanted was to get a sense of Rick's relationship with Lacey. Lacey had downplayed their connection, but still, she was obviously involved with him, and Bobby didn't want to complicate her life any more than it already was. The truth was, he hadn't expected to feel such a pull toward her the day before. Yes, he'd been drawn to her once upon a time, but he'd been a different person then, attracted to anyone with breasts and a sense of abandon. The connection he'd felt with her this time, up on the lighthouse stairs, was something else. He had certainly taken stock of her beauty and the way her body had blossomed into something far more inviting than it had been at fourteen, but it was her goodness that touched him, her struggle to do what was right for a child she did not even like.

She'd been right about the lighting in Rick's cottage; it was going to be very poor to work by. Earlier that morning, he'd walked out on the rickety back deck for a cigarette. Through the gaps in the trees, he could see that the sun was shining on the water of the sound, although the inside of the cottage was still dark. Just sitting here at the tiny kitchen table necessitated having the overhead light on. He would have to buy a good halogen lamp, at the very least.

The run-down cottage appealed to him, though. It was funky and rustic, so different from all the new construction on the Outer Banks. In spite of the lighting problem, he liked how the woods had grown up around the house, concealing it from the world. His bedroom was fine. He didn't care that the double bed barely fit inside it or that the mattress smelled musty. He had slept in far worse places.

Best of all, he was not that far from Elise. The opportunity to come to the Outer Banks had seemed like a small miracle to him, and Elise had hungrily agreed to his plan. She would stay with old friends in Kitty Hawk, he'd suggested, and he would find a place somewhere near Kiss River. Rick's cottage in Duck put him even closer to her. It was perfect. The only problem was that he could not call her, and he knew already that waiting for her calls was going to drive him crazy.

"I like your house," Bobby said to Rick, returning his attention to his surroundings. "It has character."

Rick laughed, looking around him at the grimy cupboard doors and the old linoleum floor that ran through every room in the cottage. "I guess that's one word for it," he said. "Your room okay?"

"It's a palace compared to some places I've been."

He'd expected Rick to be a tight-assed conservative lawyer, but—except for the fact that he kept no coffee in the house—the guy was really okay. Rick had even told him he could smoke in the cottage if he liked, but Bobby'd declined. Even at home he only smoked outside, his theory being that if he had to go out to smoke, it would keep the cigarettes to a minimum.

It had surprised him that someone like Rick would spend a summer in a cottage like this, but since it belonged to a friend it probably cost him very little in rent. Maybe nothing at all. Rick was there for the whole summer, and even a lawyer didn't make enough to afford a decent place in the Banks for that long. He wasn't sure if Rick was fastidious or if the neatness of the place—especially the bathroom they were sharing—was merely a product of preparing the house for a guest. At any rate, Bobby would have to remember to pick up after himself. He wasn't a slob, but he could let things pile up without really noticing what was happening. If it was a choice between working on a piece of scrimshaw or putting away the cereal box after breakfast, there was no contest.

"Lacey said you knew her when you were kids," Rick said, and Bobby saw his opening.

"Yeah," he said. "I hadn't seen her in years." He moved the

cereal around in his bowl, deciding to test the waters. "She's great, isn't she?" he asked.

"She is," Rick agreed, and Bobby tried to quantify the light in his eyes to determine the level of his attraction. Rick poured more cornflakes into his bowl. "You might pick up another box of these, if you don't mind," he said.

"I will," Bobby said, hoping that was not the end of the conversation about Lacey. It was not.

"She's got a lot on her plate this summer, though," Rick said, dipping his spoon into his bowl.

"Yeah," Bobby shook his head in sympathy. "Having a kid suddenly dumped in your lap has to be rough."

"Well, she's getting dumped in yours, too," Rick said.

"Not to the same degree," Bobby said. "I could walk away if I chose to. Lacey can't."

Rick raised his eyebrows at that response. "I hope you won't," he said.

"I have no intention of walking away," Bobby assured him. He thought of going into his doubts about Mackenzie being his, but it was just too much for breakfast conversation with a man he barely knew.

"It's not just the whole Mackenzie thing," Rick said. "Do you know about the parole hearing?"

"Parole hearing?" Bobby lifted the last spoonful of cereal to his mouth.

"The guy who killed Lacey's mother is up for parole. Lacey and her brother and father are fighting it, and I think it's tearing her up. Opening old wounds and that sort of thing."

"Are you representing her?"

"Oh, no," Rick said. "I'm a tax attorney. I'm just trying to provide her with a sympathetic ear."

Finished with his cereal, Bobby leaned back and the legs of his chair creaked beneath his weight. "I didn't know her

mother," he said. The whole murder issue had gone over his
fuzzy-brained head, for the most part. "I met Lacey the summer after it happened. She was pretty screwed up, although
I don't think I knew the depth of it at the time, since I was
pretty screwed up myself."

"Well, I'm only telling you about the parole hearing so
you're aware of everything she's dealing with," Rick said. He
looked like the type of guy who'd never been screwed up a
day in his life. "It's my personal—and professional—opinion
that she needs to let the whole parole thing go," he continued.
"According to the prison documents, the guy's been a model
prisoner who presents absolutely no danger to anyone if he's
released. I think Lacey's beating her head against a brick wall,
but she still seems to feel a need to fight it. I hate to see her
suffer through all of this only to lose in the end."

"You can't really blame her for trying." Bobby thought he
would feel the same way in her shoes.

"I don't," Rick said. "But I think...when someone lets their
emotions take over, they can lose sight of reason."

"I suppose you're right." Bobby stood up and carried his
cereal bowl and orange juice glass over to the sink and started
to wash them.

"So." Rick was finished eating, but he remained seated at
the table. "What are your plans for this morning?"

"I'm going up to Kiss River in a few minutes," he said. "I'd
like to spend some time with Mackenzie and get to know her
better, as well as give Lacey a break." He dried the bowl, glass
and utensils and put them away. "I don't remember where
any of the amusement areas are," he said. "Do you know?"

"I've seen a big water park in Kill Devil Hills, if you want
to go down that far."

"Great idea, thanks," he said, walking into the living room.
He picked up his keys from the end table, wished Rick a pro-

ductive writing day, and walked outside with one thing on his mind: coffee.

Two cups of 7-Eleven coffee and one cigarette later, he pulled into the parking lot near the keeper's house, where he said a little prayer that Mackenzie would agree to go with him without a fight. He thought back to his conversation with Lacey the day before on the lighthouse stairs. He'd sounded so sure of himself, so confident, as though he knew how to handle a kid and it was no big deal. But it *was* a big deal and the reality was, he was nervous.

As he walked toward the house, he could see Lacey through the screen door, sweeping the kitchen floor, and he called out his hello. She opened the door for him, her smile so wide, so sexy and so sweet, that he couldn't help but smile back. The kitchen smelled like coffee.

She saw him eye the pot. "Want a cup?" she asked.

He nodded. "I've had two, but could use a third," he said. "Rick doesn't drink it and I nearly passed out over breakfast."

She laughed. "Still have a little monkey on your back, huh?" she asked as she poured the coffee into a mug.

"A kinder, gentler monkey, I hope." He took the mug from her hand and swallowed a mouthful of the coffee, and only then noticed the stained-glass panels in the windows of the kitchen. They sent a blue wash over Lacey's skin and her ethereal halo of hair.

"Are these yours?" he asked, pointing to the panels. The glass was cut to form delicate stalks of sea grass against a vivid blue sky.

"Uh-huh," she said.

"So beautiful. I'm going to have to buy something of yours to take back with me."

"Maybe we can make a trade," she said. Then she leaned against the kitchen counter, her arms folded across her chest.

"Some of Mackenzie's boxes arrived this morning, so she's unpacking. I'm not sure you'll be able to tear her away." She looked apologetic.

"I was hoping to take her to a water park. What do you think?"

"It's a great idea, Bobby, but I just don't know." She shook her head. "She's so…" She shrugged. "You know."

"I'll give it a try," he said.

"And Nola called," Lacey added. "She wants Mackenzie for the night, so if you can actually get her to go out with you, would you mind dropping her off there after your outing?"

He cringed. He knew he would have to see Nola at some point but was not looking forward to it. Even when he'd been with Jessica that long ago summer, he had done his best to avoid her mother. "Is she going to bite my head off?" he asked.

Lacey smiled. "Possibly."

"Great."

Lacey led him through the kitchen to the living room, then pointed toward the stairs. "Her room's a couple doors to the right in the hallway up there," she said quietly. "Good luck."

He climbed the stairs and walked down the hallway, noticing the intricate stained-glass panels adorning every window he passed.

Mackenzie did not seem to hear his approach, and he felt like a voyeur as he watched her from the doorway of her room. She sat on the floor, two large cardboard boxes on her left side, and the black lab, Sasha, on her right. She was talking softly to the dog, an arm around his back, nuzzling his neck.

"Mackenzie?" he said.

She quickly let go of the dog and turned to face him, looking embarrassed at being caught in a tender moment. Reaching into the box at her side, she pulled out the figurine of a horse.

"May I come in?" he asked.

She shrugged, and he walked in and sat on the edge of her unmade bed.

"Lacey said you got some of your things today," he said.

She shrugged again. "There's still a lot more." She pulled another horse from the box and unwrapped it carefully from a ream of paper towels. "I don't have anything of my own here. My whole life is missing."

He nodded. It was a great phrase. *My whole life is missing.*

"I can only imagine how strange that feels," he said.

"It pisses me off," she said, and the hesitancy in her words made him think she was trying that phrase out for the first time—or at least the first time in front of an adult—waiting to see what response she would get.

"I bet it does," he said.

He motioned toward the box. "Is that whole box full of plastic horses?"

"No," she said, a truly nasty and impatient edge to her voice as though he were the stupidest man alive. "It's full of *ceramic* horses. And *resin* horses. None of them are just plain old plastic."

"Do you collect them?" he asked.

"I have twenty-two."

"Do you like to ride?" He was trying to remember if there were any stables in the area. He hadn't ridden since the summer he'd spent on a Wyoming dude ranch, years ago. That week was a blur in his mind; he'd been wasted the entire time.

"I've never been on a horse," she said.

"Never? Not even one of those rides where they lead you around?"

She shook her head.

"Well, maybe we can find a place to do that. Last time I spent a summer here, wild horses roamed the area around

Kiss River. It was very cool. They've moved them up north and Lacey says there's a tour you can take to see them." To hell with his water park idea. The tour would probably be four times as expensive, but it was a much better plan. "How about we do that today?" he asked. "You and me?"

"I have to stay here and unpack and fix up my room," she said, reaching into the box again without looking at him. "I have to go to my grandmother's tonight, so this is the only chance I have."

"It won't take us all day," he said, "and I'd really like to see them. Please come with me." He made it sound like she'd be doing him a favor. She rolled her eyes at his insistence.

"Okay," she said, shoulders sagging. "You win."

He wanted to argue the win/lose point, but decided to let her save face if that's what she needed to do.

"Let me ask Lacey where the place is, okay?" He got to his feet. "And you can continue unpacking."

She went back to her horses, and he left the room, feeling pretty damn smug about his success with her.

Lacey was no longer in the kitchen and he called out her name.

"In here," she said.

He followed the sound of her voice through the living room and dining room to a sunroom filled with light. Stained-glass panels hung from a multitude of window panes, and Lacey sat at a broad worktable wearing green safety glasses and holding a cutting tool above a piece of amber glass. Bobby was awed by the sunlit space and instantly filled with envy.

"This is perfect!" he said. "Look at the natural light you have."

"It's not great at Rick's, is it," she said. It was a statement, not a question.

"The cottage is fine. The lighting is not. But I'm going to get a good lamp and—"

"Work here," she said. She motioned to a second, smaller worktable. "Would that give you enough space?"

"It would be perfect," he said. "Are you sure?"

She nodded. "Of course. I don't need both tables at once."

"Well, I may take you up on it." He sat down at the second table, liking that the chair swiveled. "Right now, though, I need to get directions from you to that all-terrain tour place you told me about. Mackenzie and I are going to go look at the horses."

Her jaw dropped open, and when she spoke, she was nearly whispering. "She said she'd go with you?"

He nodded. "Not with any great enthusiasm, but yes, she said she would."

"Well." Lacey grimaced. "There's a problem, though. You need reservations in advance." She reached into a wooden box beneath the table, pulled out a phone book and began leafing through it. "I doubt you can go today."

"Hmm. I didn't think of that," he said, disappointed. It was unlikely that he could get Mackenzie to agree to an alternate plan. "This place is crawling with tourists, isn't it?" he asked. "I thought it was crowded when I was seventeen, but when I drove up here and saw all the houses along the way, I—"

"I know, I know." Lacey started dialing the phone. "That's why I've loved living in Kiss River. It feels like it used to out here."

He turned the chair back and forth while Lacey pushed a couple of extra buttons on the receiver, obviously waiting to talk to a human being.

"Yes," she said finally. "Hi. I was wondering how soon I could get a reservation for an ATV tour to see the horses?"

He watched her face light up as she heard the answer. She had some major dimples. The sight of them made him smile.

"Great," she said. "Two people at two. That's perfect. Okay, I'll tell them."

She hung up the phone. "You are a lucky man," she said. "They had a cancellation at two o'clock today. But it's hugely expensive." She wrinkled her nose. "It's forty-four dollars for you and half price for kids twelve and under."

"And time with Mackenzie—priceless," he said, and she laughed. "That's excellent, Lace," he added. "Thanks."

Upstairs, he told Mackenzie she was free to fix up her room until one o'clock. Then he carried his scrimshaw case from his bus into the sunroom. He opened it on the second work-table and watched Lacey's eyes widen at the sight of the engraved and incised pendants and pins, belt buckles and knife handles, all spread out on black velvet.

"I've never seen anything like this before," she said, touching one of his favorite pieces, a pendant bearing a picture of a calico cat curled in a ball on a fireplace hearth. The colors were vibrant, the design intricate, the cat realistic. She looked at him. "I thought you meant the kind of scrimshaw…you know, the usual kind…the ships on whales' teeth and that sort of thing."

He laughed. "I started out that way and got bored very quickly."

"Oh, my God, Bobby." She lifted one of the pins and held it close to her eyes. "You're so talented. I just weld bits of glass together."

"Don't put your own work down, Lacey," he said. "It's exceptional."

"Even if you just drew these designs on paper, they'd be beautiful," she said. "But you've etched them into—"

"Engraved," he corrected her. Everyone made that mistake.

"What's the material?"

He pointed to the pin she was holding. "That piece is ten-thousand-year-old wooly mammoth tusk," he said.

She laughed. "You're kidding? Is that legal?"

"It's legal," he said. "And expensive."

He spent the next couple of hours telling her about scrimshaw, trying to keep his mind off the fact that Elise had not called. Twice during his conversation with Lacey, he pulled his cell phone from his pocket to check that it was on and the battery charged.

Lacey studied every piece he'd made, looking at many of them under a magnifying glass to see the delicate stippling, shaking her head in awe, asking him questions about technique. She was fascinated. If he stuck around Kiss River long enough, he thought, he was quite certain he'd be giving her lessons.

At one o'clock he and Mackenzie were sitting in the bus, pulling onto the gravel lane leading away from the keeper's house. Her small overnight bag was in the backseat and her grumpy mood had accompanied her into the front, where she'd insisted it was not safe for her to ride until he informed her that the bus had no airbag. It did, however, have seat belts, which he'd installed himself years ago. She'd been annoyed to discover the bus was not air-conditioned, and although he'd opened every window that was capable of opening, the interior of the vehicle was undeniably steamy.

"I hope no one sees me in this tin can," she said as they jostled over the ruts in the gravel road.

"A lot of people think it's pretty cool," he said.

"Like who?"

"Your mother did, although that was a long time ago."

"My mother wouldn't be caught dead in a car like this."

She turned her head away from him quickly, and he knew

her words had jolted her. He didn't know what to say to ease
her pain.

After an awkward moment, she turned to look at him
again. "You are, like, totally bald," she said.

"You're kidding." He looked in the rearview mirror, feigning alarm. "When did that happen?"

She rolled her eyes.

"I'm a little sensitive about it," he admitted.

"I didn't say it was *bad*," she said. "Just a fact." It seemed
as close to an apology as he was likely to get from her. He
longed for a change of subject.

"You really love animals, don't you?" he asked.

She shrugged. "They're okay."

"Did you have any pets in Arizona?"

"My mother was allergic."

"Oh," he said. "I'm sorry to hear that." He turned on the
radio. "Have you found any stations here that you like?"

She reached toward the console. "Where's the scan button?"

He laughed. "I'm afraid it's a *manual* scan," he said. "You
have to use the dial."

She turned the dial until she found a song he'd never heard
before, sung by a boy who sounded as though his voice had
not yet changed.

They listened to music all the way to the tour location, and
he was relieved for the distraction. At some point he knew
he should have a serious talk with her, but it didn't need to
happen now.

The tour was not half-bad. They piled into a Chevy Sub-
urban with six other people, a couple of them close to Mackenzie's age, and bounced along the beach. The female guide,
dressed in safari gear, described the ecosystem of the maritime forest, which clearly bored the kids. Once the horses
appeared, though, Mackenzie came to life.

"Can we get out and pet them?" she asked the guide, who shook her head.

"They're wild," the young woman said. "They look gentle, but looks are deceiving."

The horses appeared to be healthy. Fat and happy and safe from traffic, and he supposed moving them up here to no-man's-land had been the only solution.

Once they'd returned to the overheated air of his bus, Mackenzie immediately pulled her cell phone from the waistband of her shorts and flipped it open.

"Mackenzie," he said, "could you not talk on the phone right now?" He doubted the signal would be strong enough for her to use her phone this far north, anyway. His was not. He had checked his phone several times in the past hour.

Mackenzie looked at him, then let out her breath in exasperation, lowering the phone to her knees. She turned her head toward the window again. "I haven't talked to my friends all day," she said under her breath.

"Well, *I* want to talk to you," he said.

"Everyone wants to talk to me," she said. "Aren't I lucky."

He ignored the comment, although he was starting to understand Lacey's annoyance with the girl. "I keep trying to imagine what it's like to go through all that you have," he said. "How it feels. But I *can't* imagine it. I just can't. I wish you'd tell me what it's like."

For a long time, she didn't speak. Finally, she turned to look at him. "Was my mother a slut?" she asked.

Yikes. The question was not what he'd expected. "Why do you ask that?" he asked.

She turned her head away again without responding.

"No, your mother wasn't a slut, or anything close to it," he said. "When you're young, you sometimes make mistakes.

That's part of growing up." He knew instantly that he'd chosen the wrong words.

"I was her biggest mistake," she said.

"I bet that she never thought that for even a minute," he
said.

She didn't answer.

"Did she ever act like you were a mistake?" he asked.

She shook her head, and he noticed tears on her cheek. Shit.

"I just want my mom back," she said.

He didn't know what to say. He thought he should pull off
the road, but then what? Hugging her seemed inappropriate
and, he was sure, would not be welcomed by her. He kept
his foot steady on the accelerator.

"It's hard," he said. "It's unfair. She was too young to die,
and you're too young to be without her. I'm sorry."

She didn't answer, but her crying turned to sniffling and
after another minute, she reached for the power button of the
radio and turned it on.

It was a long drive to Kitty Hawk, and once they reached
the outskirts, he struggled to remember which street Jessica's
old house was on. Everything looked different to him. More
houses, many more stores. He slowed as he neared the inter-
section of a street he thought might be the right one, steeling
himself to see Nola Dillard for the first time in twelve years.
He'd been in Jessica's house plenty of times. Nola had always
been working and her bed had been big.

"Where are you going?" Mackenzie asked as he started to
make the turn.

"Taking you to your grandmother's," he said.

"She lives in *Nag's Head*," Mackenzie said.

"Oh." Nola had moved. He hadn't even considered that
possibility. He made a quick U-turn and was back on Croatan Highway.

Mackenzie directed him to the house. It was bigger and newer than Jessica's old house, and it was on a lagoon in the middle of a development of similar homes. He walked Mackenzie to the door, feeling profoundly uncomfortable.

Nola opened the door, and without a word, Mackenzie walked past her into the living room. He could see her flip open her phone.

"Hi, Mrs. Dillard," he said. She looked nearly the same as she had the last time he'd seen her. White hair. Navy blue suit. A little less tanned than she used to be, and she had that windblown look some women got when they'd had too much plastic surgery. She also looked a bit stunned at the sight of him.

"I never would have recognized you," she said.

He smiled, fighting the urge to apologize to her for everything he'd ever done wrong in his life.

Nola did not plan to invite him in, that much was clear. She kept one hand on the doorknob. "Lacey said you took Mackenzie on a tour to see the horses," she said.

"That's right." He could feel the sun burning the skin on his head. "I think she had a good time. She has a thing for animals."

Nola glanced behind her. "I'm frankly disappointed in Lacey for letting you spend time with Mackenzie alone," she said. "This early, I mean. You just met her."

"I wanted to get to know her better, and—"

"And did you?" Nola interrupted him. "Get to know her better?"

"A bit, I think."

She tightened her lips.

"I understand how you must feel about me," he said. "I was an..." He started to say "asshole," but caught himself. "I was a jerk when I knew Jessica. I'm not a jerk any longer. Okay?"

"I just didn't see the point of bringing you into her life," Nola said. "Mackenzie has enough to deal with right now."

He nodded, trying to look empathetic. "Lacey felt it was the right thing to do."

"Lacey's a child herself."

This was going nowhere and never would. "Well," he said, "I'm going to take off. I hope you two have a good visit together."

He turned and walked back toward the bus, feeling sorry for Mackenzie that she had to spend the next twenty-four hours with her grandmother, the ice queen.

25

FAYE WALKED INTO THE ENORMOUS CLOSET—
really a small room—on the lower level of Jim's house and
wasn't certain whether to laugh or cry. He had sent her down
there to find the rafts and other pool paraphernalia, but that
was not going to be easy. The walls were piled high with
boxes and tools and cookware and every other thing imag-
inable. She did not know where to begin looking for the
rafts. She walked back through the lower level and called up
the stairs.

"Jim?" She knew he was in the kitchen pouring them
glasses of wine. He'd had the pool and the hot tub filled the
day before, and this evening would be their first venture
into the water. He hadn't felt like using the pool since before
Alice's death. "She loved it," he'd said. "I just couldn't make
myself go in alone." Faye thought it was a good sign that he
felt up to using the pool again.

"Did you find the rafts?" he called down to her.

"I'm sorry, Jim, but I don't know where to start," she said.
"Can you give me a clue?"

She could hear him laugh. "I'll come down and help you,"
he said. "Give me a minute."

She went back into the closet and sat down on a trunk. This was one of the strangest parts of being in a relationship, she thought: starting to feel at home in someone else's house. To cook there, as she had several times in the past couple of weeks. To have her toothbrush and toothpaste, her shampoo and her robe in the guest bathroom. To sit in a huge closet, filled with personal items, that had not been cleaned out in twenty years. To see the history of your lover's life stacked up against the walls and piled on shelves.

It was too soon to be in love with Jim, she told herself, yet there were moments when she had to bite her tongue to keep from saying those words to him. They were truly in sync with one another. Intellectually, professionally, physically. She had never expected to have this sort of partnership with a man, and she was not quite over the surprise of it yet.

Jim walked into the room and handed her a glass of Chardonnay. "This closet is a mess," he apologized, standing in the center of the room and looking around him. "I'm embarrassed for you to see it. I just threw all the pool equipment in here when Alice died without thinking that I might want to find it again some day."

"You were grieving," she said, looking up at him from her seat on the trunk.

He took a sip of his wine. "I think it had more to do with… I don't know. Laziness," he said. "Lack of caring."

"Depression."

"I guess that's what it was," he said, as if he'd never thought about it before. "I just didn't feel like doing anything for the longest time." He walked across the room to her and tapped his glass lightly against hers. "Thanks for changing that."

She stood up and put her arms around his neck, balancing the wineglass carefully in her fingers as she kissed him. She would have loved to forget about the pool and go up to his bedroom with him. She had rediscovered sex. In some ways, it felt as though she was actually discovering it for the first time.

He knew what she wanted. "Can you wait?" he asked her with a smile. "I couldn't relax right now, with all I want to get done today. And it would be so nice to sleep with you tonight after we've had a swim and some time in the hot tub."

Besides letting the pool go, Jim hadn't filed a single piece of paper since before Alice's death. All the bills and receipts and other important papers he'd received during that time were piled on the desk in the study across the hall, and Faye knew that he finally had the energy to put his life back in order. She would not stand in his way.

"I have an idea," she said, lowering her arms from his neck. "You go into your study and file your papers, and I'll organize this closet."

He stared at her as though she'd lost her mind. "I can't let you do that," he said.

"I *like* organizing." Her husband had called her anal retentive, and she had not been able to argue with him about the label. She liked having everything in its place. In a trailer that had been barely twice the size of this closet, that had been a challenge.

"Do you really mean it?" he asked.

She nodded.

"I'll leave the door open so we can talk across the hallway," he said.

"I need some big garbage bags."

He looked around the room and set down his wine to pull a dusty box of black bags from one of the top shelves. "Just promise you'll ask me before you toss out anything that looks important," he said, setting the box on the floor for her.

"Of course," she said. "Now, go." She handed him his wineglass and gave him a gentle shove.

She started in one corner of the room, emptying shelves of an eclectic assortment of items, from men's boots to old Tupperware. Across the hall she could hear him shuffling papers in the large study, and she wondered what his mood would be like after he'd gone through them. Almost certainly, many of them would be reminders of Alice. Old medical records, perhaps. Death certificates. Bills for her care. Most of the time, he was good-natured and good spirited, but grief occasionally still tugged at him. He let her see him in those moments, and she knew that was an honor.

She tried to organize the things she was finding, piling kitchenware in one place, clothing in another, magazines and books in a third. There were old tools and car parts, two irons, an ancient food processor and a silver tea service, thick with tarnish. What a mess. She carefully pulled the tea service from the shelf, and what she saw behind it made her scream. A *gun*.

"What's wrong?" Jim called from the study.

She couldn't speak, couldn't make her mouth form the word. After a moment, he appeared in the doorway.

"Why do you have a gun?" she asked. She was standing in the middle of the closet, fist pressed to her mouth.

"A gun?" He followed her gaze to the shelf. "Oh." He laughed. "I haven't seen that in years. Alice insisted we have a gun when we first moved here. There'd been some serious burglaries in the neighborhood." He reached toward the gun.

"Don't pick it up!" she said.

"It's not loaded."

"I don't care. I hate guns."

"I'm not crazy about them, either," he said. "I'll get rid of it. Toss it in the trash." He reached for it again and she sprang forward to grab his arm.

"Don't!"

"Faye." He looked perplexed by her irrational response,

and she wished she could prevent her nearly phobic reaction. It could only lead to a long conversation she did not want to have. It had been two weeks since she'd told him her husband had murdered someone. He had not pressed her, and she'd hoped—irrationally—that the subject could rest there. She wanted to move forward. She had hoped never to look back at her past.

She let go of his arm. "Are you sure it's not loaded?" she asked.

He hesitated. "I'm sure. Or at least, I don't remember it being loaded…it's so long ago. We *did* have it loaded at one time. But I—"

"Please don't touch it then. If you're not sure."

"How am I going to get rid of it if I don't touch it?"

"I'll do it," she said. "You go away and I'll check it and make sure it's not loaded, or if it is, I'll take the bullets out and throw it away."

"You don't trust me?" he asked, and she knew that must be how it sounded. Men could snap.

"I trust you," she said. "Just…please. Let me do it. Let me have control over this."

"Do you know how to handle a gun?"

"No, but I don't think it would be that hard to figure out how to unload it."

He stared at her for a long moment, then reached for her hand.

"Come on," he said, leading her out of the closet. She let him walk her out the back door, their wineglasses forgotten. They crossed the patio surrounding the pool to a wrought-iron bench at the edge of Jim's property, where they had a view of all of La Jolla and the Pacific. It was a bit overcast, as it often was in La Jolla, but that kept the air cooler, and the view of expensive homes and greenery and blue sea were muted in a way that appealed to her. The gun suddenly seemed very far away, and her reaction to it overblown enough to embarrass her. Still, she was trembling as she sat down on the bench.

"So." Jim sat down, too, leaning forward, his elbows on his knees, hands together. He turned his head to look at her. "Does this have to do with your husband?" he asked. "With the murder he committed? He used a gun?"

She nodded. Her mouth felt too dry to speak.

"I think it's time you told me everything," he said. "Okay?"

"I overreacted," she said. "It was silly." But she knew she wasn't getting out of it this time.

"What was his name?" Jim asked. "Your husband?"

"Zach," she said. "He was…" She shook her head in frustration. In spite of more than a decade of trying to analyze the situation, she had never understood what had happened to her husband. "We had a pretty good marriage," she said. "He was…you know…a decent man. He was a terrific father to Freddy, our son. Freddy was fifteen when…everything happened, and he was going through a rebellious phase, but Zach was still good with him. He'd tell me how Freddy was behaving like a normal kid, that he'd been the same way at his age and not to get on his case so much. They were close." She remembered the earlier years, the happier times before Freddy's adolescent hormones had kicked in. "Freddy was my baby," she said. "My little sweetie when he was little, but he and Zach definitely bonded as he got older." She'd felt peripheral to the two of them at times. The two men. They'd filled the trailer with talk of sports and fishing. She had loved that they had a strong bond but had felt lost outside them at times.

"How was he as a husband?" Jim asked.

It took her a moment to answer. "The only thing we ever argued about was money," she said. "I had my nursing degree and was a school nurse, but I always wanted to get my master's and work in a hospital. There was no hope of doing that, living where we were. It was just a little coastal village. Zach loved it there, though, and he was really against moving to a larger town, although he told me that when Freddy got out of school, we could live wherever I wanted. He just thought it was best for Freddy to grow up in Manteo, like he did."

"You had to put your dreams on hold, huh?"

"Yes, but it was okay," she said. "I knew I'd get my chance eventually."

"What kind of work did your husband—did Zach—do?"

"Well, he'd gone to college," she said, wrapping her hands around her knees. "That's where we met. He had a bachelor's degree in sociology. But he loved Manteo so much that we moved back there after we got married, and of course there was no work for anyone with a B.A. in sociology, so he took a job in one of the little shops." Zachary had been a sales clerk, selling flip-flops and sunscreen to the tourists. "He was completely content with that, even though he barely made enough to pay the phone bill."

"You know, though," Jim said, "there's something to be said for someone who can be content with so little."

"Yes, I agree," she said. "And I knew that even back then. I thought I was lucky to have such an easygoing husband."

"He couldn't have been that easygoing, though, if he killed someone."

She shook her head. "He snapped." She snapped her fingers. "He...I still haven't really figured out what happened. We started...just not getting along. Things I said seemed to irritate him. He was drinking too much. He always drank a fair amount, but he was getting inebriated from time to time. And he picked fights with me. That's how it felt, anyway, that he'd turn everything into a fight. He never hit me or anything, but he would scream at me. He'd *curse* at me." She shuddered at the memory. "I'd never heard him use that kind of language before, and we'd been married sixteen years. It seemed like, if he wasn't yelling, he just wouldn't talk to me at all."

"Was he depressed?" Jim asked. "It sounds like he sank into a clinical depression and needed help."

"He *was* depressed, I have no doubt about it in retrospect," Faye said. "But I couldn't see it then. I just knew he was different and that I was getting…well, I felt afraid of him sometimes. Like I said, he never hit me, but I thought it was only a matter of time. I do blame myself for not pushing him to get help. I was a nurse, after all. I should have realized how desperately he needed it. But it seemed more like anger and frustration than depression, and I just didn't recognize it for what it was."

Jim said nothing, waiting for her to continue. In the distance, the clouds lifted a bit and the rooftops grew clear and sharp in the sun.

"He had a couple of guns," she said. "That wasn't unusual where we lived. He kept them locked up from Freddy—I insisted on that." She still berated herself for not insisting he get rid of the guns altogether. Would that have made a difference in the way things had unfolded? "We lived very close to our neighbors." She still couldn't make herself say the words "we lived in a trailer park" out loud to Jim. "They could hear us when we fought. Zach had a loud, booming voice, and I guess it carried all over the neighborhood. On Christmas Eve in 1990, I got a phone call from a woman who worked at a battered women's shelter. She said that she'd received two calls from people who were worried about Freddy and me. One was from a neighbor. The woman wouldn't identify who it was. The other call was from some friend of Zach's who was also afraid Zach might hurt me. I still to this day don't know who those callers were. The woman from the shelter—

her name was Annie O'Neill—said she thought we should come there right away." The story sounded so ludicrous, so sordid, from the vantage point of a bench high above mani-cured landscapes and blue, kidney-shaped pools. "I thought the whole thing was ridiculous, at first," she continued. "I told her my husband was just very loud and that he'd never laid a hand on us. But Annie went on about how stressful the holidays could be for people who were already troubled, and how Zach's friend was worried that he was mentally ill and knew there were guns in the house. It was like I couldn't deny it any longer, when she said that. Someone outside the family had noticed he was different. It wasn't just me." She was barely aware of Jim sitting next to her now. The story was taking on a life of its own as she told it aloud for the first time in more than a decade. "Zach's friend said that he—that Zach—had said something about using his guns soon. He didn't know if that meant Zach planned to kill me or Freddy or himself or maybe all three of us. That's when I started get-ting afraid. I felt as though I didn't even know my own hus-band, and the truth was, I didn't. Whoever he'd turned into wasn't the man I used to know. Then Annie said that, even if I didn't care about protecting myself, I owed it to Freddy to protect him. She was very persuasive and I finally agreed to go. Even though I just couldn't picture Zach actually hurt-ing us, she let me know I couldn't take the chance. And she was right. I got Freddy from one of his friend's houses and told him we needed to go to the shelter." She shook her head, remembering her son's reaction. "He was furious!" she said. "He didn't understand at all and kept saying we couldn't just leave and not tell his father where we were going, especially not on Christmas Eve. He was crying when we drove away from the house. I felt terrible. I was afraid that Freddy was right, that what we were doing was crazy and I was overre-acting, but as it turned out, Annie O'Neill saved our lives."

"Zach went on a rampage?"

She shook her head. "No. When we got to the shelter, we were…*distraught,* is the best word for it, I guess. Annie was there, though, and she was…" Faye shook her head, remem-bering the natural beauty of the red-haired woman, the open smile, the warmth in her touch, the husky voice. Annie would still be alive now if she hadn't reached out to help her and Freddy. "She was one of those people who instantly made you feel like a friend," she said. "Taken care of. Like you could turn all your worries over to her and she would carry them for you." She turned to look at Jim. "Do you know what I mean?"

He nodded. "I think so."

"She got us settled in a room we would share with another woman and her two sons. It was cramped in the house, really a sad place to be on Christmas Eve, but Annie and the rest of the women running the shelter were wonderful. They did their best to make it cheery. There was a Christmas tree and Christmas music. Still, away from home, it was hard to feel much joy. Plus, Freddy wouldn't speak to me. He just kept crying." Her son's crying had been full of anger, not sorrow. He'd been furious with her for bringing him there.

"We stayed there overnight," she said. "I couldn't sleep at all. I kept wondering what Zach thought when he came home and found us gone. I'd left him a note saying we were safe but that we needed to give him some time alone to get help for himself. I really didn't know what to write. I kept remember-ing what he was like in the old days, the good Christmases the three of us had had together. I wanted to call him, to be sure he was all right, but of course, that was against the rules."

Jim had grown quiet and she wished he would say some-thing. He still sat with his elbows on his knees, looking out at the nice clean view from his nice clean property, perhaps wondering how he had allowed this woman into his nice clean life.

"The next day was Christmas," she said. "Annie was gone, but some other women brought gifts for the children who were there. Fred wanted no part of it. He sat sulking in a corner. I tried to help the other women—there were five others and a bunch of children—because I thought if I could help them get through that day, it would make it easier on me." It had. The stories the other women told were so much worse than hers. Some of them were bruised. One had a broken arm. Talking with them had made Faye wonder once again if she'd overreacted by leaving Zach and dragging Freddy to the shelter.

"Sometime in the afternoon, Annie came back," she continued. "She had her thirteen-year-old daughter with her." The girl had been a miniature version of her mother, and Faye often wondered what had become of her. "Some of the staff had cooked a really nice dinner for all of us, and we were in sort of a buffet line, filling our plates. All of a sudden, Zach showed up in the room. I don't think anyone ever figured out how he knew where the shelter was. It was supposed to be a safe house. They kept the door locked, but he busted right through it with his shoulder. He was a big guy. And there he was, standing in the doorway, cursing me up and down and holding a gun straight at me."

Jim sat back then and put his arm around her. "How terrifying," he said.

"It was." She nodded. "Then all of a sudden, Annie jumped in front of me and told him to put the gun down, and he ended up shooting her instead of me." The memory was unbearable, and Faye began to cry. "I...I didn't know who he was anymore. He'd just gone crazy. And Annie died."

"Oh, God."

"She died trying to save Freddy and me. If she hadn't cared enough about us—about total strangers—to get us to the shelter to protect us from him, we would be dead. I have no doubt about it. Instead, *she* was the one to die."

Jim pulled her closer. "I'm sorry she died," he said, "but I'm very grateful that you and your son were spared."

Faye rested her head on his shoulder, closing her eyes to the sunlight that now filled the sky. She sat quietly for a moment, her mind still in the Outer Banks. "People used to call her Saint Anne, and that was *before* all of this happened," she said. "You can imagine how people felt about her afterward."

"What happened to Zach?"

"He went to prison, and I filed for divorce right away," she said. "Freddy and I moved to California as soon as we could, and I did what I'd always wanted to do—got my master's in nursing. I tried to forget about the past. Fred never forgave me, though. He said his dad only went crazy because we deserted him on Christmas. He never understood that Zach had gone crazy long before that day."

Jim drew in a long, slow breath. "What a lot you've been through," he said.

"I hate that you know this about me," she said. "That I had a crazy husband. That I spent time in a women's shelter. That my son hates me. That I—"

"Hey," he said quietly. "That's the past. And it only makes me feel even more positively about you. About what a strong person you are. I admire you."

"You do?"

"Look at what you've overcome," he said. "Look how much you accomplished. And have you ever thought about the fact that you've paid it forward?"

"What do you mean?"

"Annie saved your life and you went on to do good things for other people. Think of all the people you've helped through your pain program."

He made her sound far nobler than she felt, but his words touched her deeply.

"Thank you for saying that," she said. "I'd really never looked at it that way."

He took his arm from around her shoulders and turned to face her, taking both her hands in his. "I want you to go home now," he said. "I'll find the pool stuff, and you can come back this evening and we'll go for a swim. And by the time you get here, the gun will be gone."

Relief washed over her. She felt so cleansed. So free. "Thank you," she said, starting to stand up, but he held her hands to keep her seated.

"And one more thing," he said.

"What?"

He smiled at her, the sun catching the silver in his hair. "I love you," he said.

26

WEARING BATHING SUITS AND WIDE-BRIMMED
hats, Lacey and Gina sat on the sliver of beach just south of
the lighthouse, slathering sunscreen on their legs and watching Mackenzie play with Rani and Sasha. Mackenzie, in her
pink bikini, held Rani's hand as the little girl stomped her
feet in the waves, and Sasha ran around them in joyful circles,
splashing water into the air. What a threesome they were! A
gentle threesome, at least in this configuration. In two and
a half weeks' time, the bond between the dog, the toddler
and the preteen had been woven and the threads pulled tight.

"Do you believe this?" Gina was grinning at the sight of
the three playmates.

Lacey guessed Gina was referring to the way Mackenzie
could turn from a moody little brat into a nurturing, loving girl when she was around Rani. Her tone of voice would
change in an instant when the little girl entered the room.

"I know," she said. "She has a good side to her."

For a moment, Gina looked confused. Then she laughed. "I
was talking about Rani," she said. "A month ago she couldn't
even look at the ocean without crying."

It was Lacey's turn to laugh. "You're right," she said, curious to realize how each of them had a different child at the center of her universe. "She's come a long way." Mackenzie flopped down on the wet sand, sitting where the waves would wash over her when they rushed onto the shore. She patted the sand next to her, but Rani was not quite that brave. Shaking her head no, the toddler remained standing, her eyes on her braver, older friend. She moved forward until she was right behind Mackenzie, and she patted her hands softly on the older girl's blond head, as if she needed to be touching her to feel safe with all that water around. Watching their interaction brought tears to Lacey's eyes. Rani was a gentle child; she always would be. Whether it was from being so sick early in her life, or being in an orphanage where noise was not only discouraged but ignored, or whether it was simply part of her nature, Lacey didn't know. But it always touched her to see Rani's struggle to find safety in her world.

"She loves having Mackenzie around," Gina said. "I know you still have some issues with her, but I'm glad she's here. She's so good to Rani, and so good for her."

Lacey nodded. "It's just me she hates."

"I wouldn't go that far," Gina said, but Lacey knew her sister-in-law could not be much more encouraging than that.

"There was money missing from my wallet again this morning," Lacey admitted.

"Did you ask her about it?"

Lacey shook her head. "I can't prove anything, so what could I say?" She had not been as careful about keeping her wallet out of Mackenzie's reach as she should have been. "At least she's starting to get along with Bobby," she said. "It's funny, isn't it? I mean she's never really had a man in her life and yet she seems more comfortable with him than with anyone." The day before, Bobby had taken Mackenzie all the way to Hatteras for her first ride on a horse. She didn't have much to say to him, Bobby had told Lacey later, but she'd stopped giving snotty retorts to everything he said, and that was certainly more than Lacey could claim.

"I bet she really missed having a father," Gina said. "She seems to like Clay, too."

"Because he works with dogs," Lacey said.

"Go ahead, Rani!" Gina called to her daughter. "You can sit down next to Mackenzie. She'll hold your hand."

Rani turned to shake her head at her mother, then dug her fingers deeper into Mackenzie's hair and kept her eyes on the waves. She wore a tiny, blue, one-piece bathing suit that hid the long scar from her surgery. Her skin was a nut-brown color, her hair now down to her shoulders and jet black.

"Bobby suggested I give Mackenzie some work to do around the house," Lacey said. They'd talked about it the day before, at the gym. She'd gotten him a guest membership and had started going with him in the late afternoon. She was talking to him more than she was Rick these days. Bobby was not the sort of unselfish, completely attentive listener Rick was, but there was an intensity to their conversations that was lacking when she talked to Rick. "He said it would do her good to have some responsibility," she added.

"I think he's right," Gina said. "It would make her feel more like she's part of the family."

"What should I have her do?"

"Vacuum?" Gina suggested. "Dust? Sweep the kitchen? You know how much sand gets in that room, and we don't sweep it nearly enough. They're going to have to refinish those floors again before they can open the museum."

"Okay," Lacey said, already dreading the conversation with Mackenzie. "We'll start with sweeping the kitchen every evening."

"Bobby showed me some of his scrimshaw yesterday," Gina said. "It's incredible."

"I know," Lacey agreed. "He sold a lot of it at the craft fair, which was great because he doesn't have his usual following here." She'd had no problem getting him a booth at the craft fair in Manteo. He'd been on the other side of the fairground from her, but she could see the crowd of people milling around the tables displaying his work.

"You know," Gina said, "it's okay with Clay and me if you want to ask Bobby to move into the house while he's in the Outer Banks. He's around so much of the time, anyway, working in your sunroom or hanging out with Mackenzie, and then he wouldn't have to drive back and forth between here and Rick's."

Lacey had been thinking about exactly that. There were two free bedrooms in the house, and he was there a good deal of the time, as Gina had said. But she knew it would be a mistake.

"I can't, Gina," she said.

"Why not?"

She hesitated, looking toward the water. Mackenzie had moved up to slightly higher ground and Rani was now bravely sitting at her side, letting the tail end of the waves run over her legs. Sasha was lying down next to the little girl, cooling his belly in the water. "Because I'm way too attracted to him," she said finally. "If he lived here, it would be too easy for me to slip into bed with him."

"Wow, Lacey." Gina sat up straight, one hand on her hat to keep the breeze from stealing it off her head. "I hadn't even thought about that. I've been thinking of you with Rick."

"With nice, safe Rick, right?" Lacey smiled at her.

"Yes," Gina said. "But now that you mention it, Bobby *is* your type, isn't he? Your old type?"

"I'm afraid so."

"Good for you, then, to know it would be a mistake to have him here," Gina said. "Rick doesn't put any pressure on you for…you know, to get closer, does he?"

Lacey laughed. "I don't even think Rick has a libido," she said. "He's perfect for me."

"I think he's great," Gina said. "He's good-looking, he treats you well, he's comfortable to be around, he's intelligent and educated and probably makes boatloads of money as a lawyer. And he seems to really like you."

She was right, on all counts, and Lacey didn't care. With Mackenzie's arrival, she'd forgotten her resolution to behave as though she was truly interested in him and wait for the "feelings to follow."

"I am so screwed up, Gina," she said, admitting her fears out loud for the first time.

Gina moved closer to put an arm around her. "No, you're not," she said. "Why do you say that?"

Lacey drew a line in the sand with her finger. On one side she drew an *R,* on the other a *B.* "Here's Rick," she said, pointing to the *R* side of the line. "He's handsome. Looks like a model or something, right? And here's Bobby." She poked at the *B* with her fingertip. "He wears an earring, has a tattoo on his arm—"

"I noticed that," Gina said. "What is it? I've only seen that part that hangs down below his sleeve."

"It's a wooly mammoth," Lacey said. She'd finally asked him to show her the tattoo a week ago.

"A wooly mammoth?" Gina laughed.

"Right. He uses wooly mammoth tusks for his scrimshaw, so it seemed appropriate." Lacey laughed. "And don't worry, he only has one." She knew Gina was remembering a man they had known the summer before who'd been covered with tattoos and who had hurt them both.

Gina leaned forward and drew an *L* above the chart Lacey was making in the sand. "And here's Lacey," she said. "And she's perfectly fine without any man."

"I know that, Gina," she said, only a bit annoyed by her sister-in-law's inference. It was easy for Gina to say; she'd found her soul mate in Clay. "If I've learned anything this year, I've learned that I can manage without a man. That doesn't mean that's what I want for the rest of my life, though."

"Okay." Gina seemed to sense that she'd stepped on some sensitive toes.

Lacey returned to her chart, pointing to the *R*. "And Rick drives a BMW," she said, "while Bobby's been driving the same old rusty van since the beginning of time. And Bobby has a history as a drug addict, and Rick has one little glass of wine with dinner. And Rick was at the top of his law class, and Bobby didn't even finish his art degree. And Rick has money. And Bobby has very little. And do you know which one of them I want to spend my time with? Go to bed with? Bear the children of?" She was exaggerating on that last point, but Gina got the message.

"Bobby," Gina said quietly.

"What is *wrong* with me?" Lacey wailed, and Sasha lifted his big head to look over at her. "Why do I always gravitate toward the guy who is bad for me? I am just like my mother. Just as self-destructive and—"

"Stop it, Lace," Gina said quietly. "You're not like your mother at all. You've looked at what you were doing wrong and you've stopped doing it. Your mother never did that. And you know what else?"

"What?"

"I think you've got infatuation mixed up with love."

"Possibly," she admitted. "I was infatuated with Bobby when I was fourteen and the feelings I get around him now are almost exactly the same. I know that in my mind. But my heart and body don't care."

"I think Rick's the sort of guy who could grow on you if you give him a chance," Gina said. "Do you remember how I couldn't care less about Clay when I first met him? How I gradually fell in love with him?"

Lacey nodded, although she knew Gina's indifference to Clay had had more to do with her desperate need to adopt Rani than her feelings about Clay himself.

"Just keep yourself open to Rick," Gina said. "See him more than you do. You haven't gone out with him much since Bobby arrived."

Gina was right. She needed to see more of Rick, as she'd planned to do before learning about Jessica's death. She needed to remind herself how marginal Bobby's existence was, how her attraction to him was more physical than cerebral. She needed to reread that book about making good choices. She needed to remember how good Rick had been to her, how attentively he listened to her each time she called.

She studied the *R* in the sand. But how did you make yourself feel something when there was simply nothing there?

27

ON THE DRIVE TO NOLA'S THE FOLLOWING morning, Mackenzie tuned Lacey's car radio to a particular station she'd discovered and started mouthing the words to the songs. It distressed Lacey that the songs, obviously so familiar to Mackenzie, were completely unknown to her. She loved music, owned several dozen CDs, and listened regularly to the radio. But it was clear that she was out of it when it came to knowing what a preteen would like.

She glanced at Mackenzie, who was clutching her cell phone in her hand like a lifesaver. When it came to cell phones, though, Bobby was really no better than Mackenzie. He was always checking for messages. A few times he even went outside to take a call, claiming that the signal seemed stronger out there than in the house, but it was obvious to Lacey that he simply wanted privacy. She wondered who he wanted to speak to without being overheard. It was none of her business. She had to remind herself of that.

With Mackenzie unable to call her Phoenix friends due to the early hour, Lacey knew this was the best time to talk to Mackenzie about chores.

"Could we turn the radio down for a sec?" Lacey asked her. "I wanted to talk to you about helping around the house."

Mackenzie didn't touch the volume button. "What do you mean?" She sounded suspicious.

"I mean that we all have certain chores we do in the house," Lacey said, turning the volume down herself. "I thought you might like to have some, too. You know, so you'll feel like part of the family." It had sounded good when Gina had said those words the day before, but she instantly knew that her awkward presentation wasn't going to produce the result she was after.

"I'll *never* be part of this stupid family," Mackenzie said. "I don't even want to be."

Lacey tightened her grip on the steering wheel. "Well, I still think it's important for you to do your share, don't you?" she asked.

"What exactly do you want me to do?"

"You can pick," Lacey said. "The bathrooms—"

"No way."

"You can sweep the sand out of the kitchen. Or dust. You can vacuum if you want, but I know I always hated doing that when I was your age."

Mackenzie rested her head against the headrest and looked up at the ceiling of the car. She let out a huge sigh.

"We haven't even asked you to help with the dishes." Lacey glanced at the girl again. In profile, Mackenzie had Jessica's nose, right down to the indignant little flare of her nostrils.

"Why don't you have a dishwasher?" Mackenzie asked.

"Because the house is supposed to be historically accurate back to the early twentieth century," she explained for the hundredth time. "There were no dishwashers then." It was her turn to sigh. "Don't you think it's even a little bit cool to live in an old lighthouse keeper's house?" She always felt personally offended by Mackenzie's negativity about the house. Even as an eleven-year-old, she'd had an appreciation of Kiss River's history.

"There is nothing cool about it," Mackenzie said. "It doesn't even have air-conditioning."

Lacey laughed at the small joke, but Mackenzie didn't seem to notice that she'd made one. Perhaps she hadn't meant to. God, she could be a sour kid. *It's fear.* Lacey reminded herself of Bobby's words. *Remember that. She's scared.*

"So, how about you wash or dry the dishes?"

"Every meal?" Mackenzie sounded incredulous.

"No, just dinner."

"Sometimes I eat at my grandmother's."

"Well, of course you wouldn't have to do them at home when you eat over there."

"And what about tonight?" Mackenzie asked. "Bobby's taking me to a movie."

"You'll have plenty of time between dinner and the movie to dry the dishes." She was grateful that Bobby was taking Mackenzie out; she wanted the evening with Rick, determined to make the effort to reconnect with him.

"Mom doesn't dry the dishes," Mackenzie said, not even seeming to notice that she spoke of her mother in the present tense. "She says it's better to let them air-dry."

"Well, there probably weren't as many, since she used the dishwasher most of the time, right?" Lacey asked. "And there were just the two of you in the house. When there are as many dishes as we have, you have to dry them or there's no room in the rack. And since you'll be working in the kitchen, how about you sweep up after the dishes are done. You'll be in there, anyway."

Mackenzie let out her breath in a shocked little puff. "What am I," she asked, "your maid?"

"No, you—"

"You're probably happy my mom died so you could have someone come clean up your house."

Lacey wanted to smack her. Pull the car to the side of the road and just let her have it, but she kept her hands tight on the wheel, her eyes straight ahead.

"That's not true, Mackenzie," she said. "And I think you know that."

A silence stretched between them and Lacey could practically hear the wheels turning in Mackenzie's brain.

"All right," the girl said finally. "I'll dry the dishes and sweep the kitchen. But I won't vacuum or dust or any of that other stuff."

"That's fine," Lacey said. "That's fair. Thank you. The broom is in the pantry."

"An actual *broom?*" Mackenzie said, as if she'd never seen one. "Do you even have to be historically accurate when you sweep? Mom always uses a Swiffer."

"A Swiffer wouldn't get up the sand in the kitchen," Lacey said.

"You are *so* not like my mother," Mackenzie said, turning up the volume on the radio again. "It's hard to believe you were ever friends."

After dinner that night, Lacey washed the dishes and Mackenzie dried. Or at least, she pretended to. The dishes were put away half-wet, and Lacey didn't feel up to arguing with her over it. She wiped down the table and countertops as Mackenzie ineffectively swept the kitchen floor, as if the broom was too heavy for her to use properly. Was she being intentionally sloppy in her work or was she simply a lousy housekeeper? Whichever the case, Lacey kept her mouth shut.

They'd had enough animosity between them that morning.
She didn't think she could handle any more that night.

Mackenzie was in her room when Bobby arrived to pick
her up for the movie, and Lacey called up the stairs to let her
know he was there.

"She has chores now," she said, returning to the kitchen.
"Drying the dishes and sweeping the floor."

"Excellent," Bobby said. "How'd she react to them?"

"She said I wanted her to be my maid. And if you notice—" she ran one bare foot across the floor "—she didn't
do such a great job."

Smiling, he tugged at a strand of her hair, and he might
have been touching her breasts for the shock it sent through
her. His smile changed quickly to a grin, as if he knew how
he was affecting her. He *had* to know. She turned away from
the crooked grin, relieved to see Mackenzie walk into the
room, grunting her hello to her father.

"You two better get going," Lacey said, feigning a look at
her watch to avoid Bobby's eyes. She ushered them toward
the door with a maternal sweeping of her hands. "Go on,"
she said. "Have a good time."

Once they were out the door, she leaned against the counter, arms folded tightly across her chest, eyes squeezed shut.
Get a grip, she told herself. Since when had her hair become
an erogenous zone?

Clay walked into the room. "Whoa," he said, feeling the
grit on the floor beneath his bare feet. "I thought Mackenzie
was going to sweep?"

"She did."

He looked at her quizzically. "You all right? What's the
matter?"

"Nothing." She tried to look surprised by the question,
wondering what he'd seen in her face.

Clay opened the pantry door and took out the broom. "Well, I have another idea for a job for her," he said as he started to sweep.

"You've got to be kidding," Lacey said. "She'll run away if we ask her to do anything else."

"This one I think she'll like." Clay was smiling as he swept. "She can be the victim with the dogs."

Lacey knew exactly what he meant. Clay needed people to hide in the woods for the search-and-rescue trainees to find. "That's actually not a bad idea," she said. She reached into the pantry for the dustpan and handed it to him. "But you'd better be the one to ask her," she said. "She turns up her nose at anything I suggest."

Upstairs she took a quick shower and changed into long pants and a T-shirt, then walked out to her car for the drive to Rick's house. Although it was still light outside by the time she turned onto the road leading to his cottage, the trees quickly engulfed her car and it might as well have been ten o'clock instead of eight. She parked behind his BMW, got out and walked along the wooded path to his house.

The trees created a nest here, she thought. A dark little nest. No wonder Bobby had trouble working in Rick's cottage, and no wonder he loved working in her sunroom. A few times in the evenings, after Bobby had left, she'd walk into the sunroom to stare at the piece he was creating: a mammoth tusk belt buckle adorned with the intricate image of three dogs. Every day there was more detail in the portrait. Still no color, but the precision of the stippling and engraving was simply astonishing. She could smell Bobby in that room. He wasn't one for aftershave, but the scent of his shampoo or his deodorant or maybe the laundry detergent he used on his clothes lingered in the room, mixing with the faint tobacco smell that was so much a part of him, and she liked to simply sit there and breathe it in.

Damn it. Here she was, about to knock on Rick's door, and she was still fixated on Bobby. Her counselor—whom she was thinking she might need to revisit sometime soon— had warned her that her resolve would be tested occasionally. She'd thought her test had been the men at the gym, those hard-muscled guys who cut their eyes at her when they thought she wasn't looking, who left the gym in tight jeans and climbed onto their Harleys. She knew now that her real test had arrived in an old VW bus.

Rick opened the cottage door with a smile, his hair damp from a shower, his teeth perfect and very, very white, even in the dim light of the woods. She smiled back, as warmly as she could. Gina had thought nothing of Clay in the beginning, she reminded herself, and then he'd grown into someone she treasured.

"I made dessert," he said.

"You *made* it?" That was the premise for their getting together tonight: dessert. She'd expected something store-bought. Ice cream, perhaps, or cookies. She followed him into the kitchen, where he'd been slicing strawberries to put on top of a freshly baked angel food cake.

"I'm impressed!" she said. "How can I help?"

"You can just stand there and talk to me," he said, slicing a fat strawberry into a bowl.

"How is it, having Bobby live with you?" she asked before she could stop herself. "He's been here over a week now. You've got to promise you'll let me know if his welcome starts wearing thin."

"It's no problem at all," Rick said. "We get along fine."

She wondered what conversation would be like between them, two men with absolutely nothing in common.

Rick glanced at her as he picked up another strawberry. "He's in AA. Did you know that?"

"Yes, and I think it's great," she said. "Tom's in AA and it turned him around."

"He goes to a lot of meetings," Rick said, and she could not quite tell if he thought that was a good thing or not.

She glanced toward the corner of the living room, where his computer monitor sat on a table, next to two tall stacks of papers.

"How about you tell me about your book," she said. "We've never really talked about it." They had discussed his work so little. Always talking about her, about Mackenzie, about Zachary Pointer's parole hearing. Maybe the reason she felt so little for him was because she hadn't allowed herself to get to know him.

"That's because I don't want to bore you," he said, the smile still on his face as he pulled a bowl of whipped cream from the refrigerator.

"I want to hear about it, though." She picked up one of the strawberry slices and popped it into her mouth.

"Let's construct our desserts and eat out on the deck," he said, handing her a serrated knife to use on the angel food cake. "And then I'll tell you all about my book until your eyes glaze over."

They piled berries onto their slices of cake and topped the desserts with whipped cream, and then she followed him outside. The deck tipped a bit to the south, and Lacey felt as though the rotting wood might cave in under her weight. She sat down on a creaky old porch swing, while he lit a couple of citronella candles. It had grown dark out, and the only other light came from the cottage windows.

Lacey swallowed her first mouthful of cake. "It's delicious," she said with sincerity. "You would make a good wife."

He sat down next to her on the swing, laughing as though he found that very funny. "Glad you like it," he said.

"So—" she stuck her fork in a slice of berry "—you were going to tell me about your book."

"Ah, yes." He took a bite of cake and chewed it slowly, his gaze focused in the direction of the sound. He swallowed, then rested his plate on his thighs. "Well, it's titled *Cases and Concepts of Federal Income Taxation* and it's geared toward the law student," he said.

"Uh-huh." She injected all the interest she could into the tone of her voice.

He told her about a couple of the more interesting—to him, at least—cases, and although she fought the boredom, her face apparently could not mask it.

"Your eyes *are* glazing over," he said after he'd been talking for a few minutes. He leaned toward her for a better look. "Literally. I can see the candles reflected in a thick layer of glossy, dewy tears."

"Sorry," she said with an apologetic smile. "I tried, but it's hard for me to get a handle on."

"And you don't need to." He lowered his empty plate to the floor of the deck and slipped his arm around her shoulders. He smelled good, and this *was* the scent of expensive aftershave, no doubt about it. She turned her head to him and it was she who started the kiss. His lips were light on hers at first, and then she felt his tongue gently slip into her mouth. She wanted to pull away, but held her ground. *Feelings will follow behavior.* Wasn't that what it said in the book? *Fake it till you make it.* Her mind was working overtime as she tried to return the ardor of his kisses. If she behaved as though she wanted this, she might truly start to want it. Or maybe it was a good sign that she didn't want to simply take this man to bed. Maybe that meant he was the right guy for her. But when Rick lifted his hand to touch her breast through her T-shirt, she caught his fingers in hers.

"Sorry," he said.

"Don't be," she said. "I'm being ridiculous."

"No, you're not."

"You must think I'm a huge prude," she said.

He shook his head. "I'm in no rush," he said. "Should we stop? Play cards? I found a checkerboard in one of the kitchen cupboards."

He was so patient with her. So sweet. She suddenly realized that she felt genuine affection for him, and the feeling both surprised and comforted her. She leaned back to get a good look at him. "You're really amazing," she said.

"So are you."

"Okay," she said, standing up from the porch swing. "So where are the cards?"

28

LACEY SAT NEXT TO RICK ON A BENCH AT THE far side of the house, the area away from the ocean, where Clay did his "box training." Eight large wooden crates were spread out across the sand, varying distances between them. A young woman held a nearly white golden retriever on a leash, while Clay explained to Mackenzie what she was to do. Mackenzie held a glove in her hand, wadding it up over and over again as she listened intently to Clay's words. Lacey leaned forward, her straw hat shading her face, trying unsuccessfully to hear what her brother was saying. She was aware of Rick's hand resting lightly on her back. It felt like nothing to her, and that frustrated her. His hand might as well have been a dish towel lying against her back. She laid her own hand on his thigh, struggling to feel, if not a jolt of electricity at touching him, at least some small itch of desire, but there was nothing. How long was she supposed to wait for the feelings to follow her behavior? She felt safe and comfortable with Rick, and that was the most important thing, she told herself. She'd never—not once—experienced that sense of security with a guy she'd dated. Rick was interested in more than her body. They were creating the sort of foundation they could build a relationship on. What other man would play cards with her until late at night, when he'd obviously had something a bit more carnal in mind?

Bobby had returned to Rick's house around eleven, after his movie-and-ice-cream date with Mackenzie. If he'd thought it strange to find Lacey and his housemate in the middle of a game of gin rummy, he'd said nothing about it. Lacey wondered if Bobby was watching her and Rick right now. The bench they were sitting on would be in clear view from the sunroom where he was working, and ever since taking her seat next to Rick, she'd been aware of his presence somewhere behind her.

Clay told the woman to walk around the side of the house so that her dog would be unable to see what was happening in the yard. Then he took the glove from Mackenzie and sent her out to one of the boxes. She skittered across the sand, a happiness in her gait that Lacey had not seen before—although Bobby's description of her enthusiastic response to horseback riding sounded as though it might have been similar. The boxes had doors hinged on one side, and Mackenzie pulled open the door and slipped inside. Once she was safely hidden away, Clay called the woman and her dog back.

"Is he going to sniff the glove and then find Mackenzie by following her scent?" Rick asked.

"Uh-huh." Lacey had seen Clay's box training before, and apparently, the golden retriever had, too. The dog sniffed hungrily at the glove, his whole body quivering with excitement. When the woman unfastened the leash from his collar, he took off, running directly for the crate in which Mackenzie was hiding. He sat down next to it, his tail beating the sand, and let out one bark. Mackenzie hopped out of the crate, laughing, letting the dog knock her to the ground. The woman jogged over to the box to give the dog a treat, although it was clear that Mackenzie's affection had been all the reward he'd needed.

The sequence was repeated several times, with Mackenzie hiding in a different box each time. Clay had her run around the area before hiding, so that the dog would not simply follow her scent to the correct crate. Mackenzie was perfect for this. Lacey had occasionally served as the "victim" for her brother's training, and she'd found it boring, but the girl seemed to have plenty of energy for the process and it was apparent she adored dogs. Maybe they should consider getting her one of her own.

"He's going to the wrong crate," Rick said quietly. The dog sniffed around the box in which Mackenzie had hidden the last time.

"He still smells her there," Lacey said.

The dog looked back at his owner uncertainly.

Clay whispered something to the woman. "Go find!" the woman called, and the dog continued his hunt, barking when he found the right crate, struggling to sit still as he waited for his playmate to come out of the box.

Rick tilted his head back and sniffed the air. "Speaking of scents," he said, "what did you say Gina's fixing for dinner?"

The exotic scent of Gina's cooking had made its way out into the yard.

"*Aloo gobi* and *biryani*," Lacey said. "She's a fabulous Indian cook." She and Clay had never eaten Indian food before Gina's arrival, but she'd gotten them hooked on it.

"It smells incredible," he said. His hand crept up her back to her neck and he kneaded the muscles there, and she did her best to prevent them from tightening under his touch.

Over dinner Mackenzie was full of questions about training dogs for search-and-rescue work. There was an electric charge in the air that everyone except Mackenzie seemed to be aware of. She was talking. She was *engaged*. She was even eating *aloo gobi* without protest. Bobby caught Lacey's eyes across the table and raised his eyebrows at her, smiling, nodding his head in Mackenzie's direction. She smiled back, holding his gaze as long as she dared.

She shifted her eyes to Rick. Rani sat in her high chair between Gina and Rick and had somehow managed to stick some rice onto Rick's hair when Gina wasn't looking. Rani giggled, and Rick played along, asking her what she was giggling at, which only made her giggle harder.

"I have a dog coming tomorrow afternoon that's just starting her wilderness training," Clay said to Mackenzie. "Would you be comfortable going into the woods to hide?"

"Sure," she said, a forkful of *biryani* halfway to her mouth. "As long as it's not dark. Would I be standing behind a tree or what?"

"There are plenty of places to hide in the woods," Clay said. "I dragged in huge boards and some chunks of concrete, and there are fallen trees to hide behind. But you might want to take a book or something with you. It can get pretty boring while you wait for the dog to find you."

"I'll take my cell phone."

"Well, that won't work," Clay said.

"Oh, yeah. The dog would hear me." Mackenzie slipped the *biryani* into her mouth and swallowed. "I can text message, though, right?" she asked.

"As long as the phone doesn't beep or make any sounds, that would be fine."

"Sweet," Mackenzie said, then she set down her fork. "Can I be excused, please?" She looked at Lacey, who suddenly felt like her keeper. "I want to check my e-mail. I can dry the dishes and sweep the floor after, all right?"

"Sure," Lacey said.

Mackenzie got up from her seat and had nearly left the kitchen when she remembered her plate. Coming back to the table, she picked it up, along with her milk glass, and carried them both to the sink. "That was good, Gina," she said as she headed for the stairs.

"Wow," Lacey said to Clay when Mackenzie was out of earshot. "I guess you found the key to her heart."

Clay shrugged. "She's a natural. She has good instincts with dogs, and the dogs pick that up."

"It was obvious how much she loved working with that retriever," Rick said.

"I was watching from the sunroom," Bobby said. "She was having a blast out there."

So he *had* been watching. Had he noticed Rick's hand on her back, and hers on his thigh? And so what if he had?

"You know—" Rick patted his lips with his napkin and shifted in his seat "—I've mentioned this to Lacey, but I'll tell you, too, Clay. If you or your father want any help preparing for the parole hearing, let me know. I'd be happy to take a look at your victim's impact statements for you."

Lacey wanted to groan. She supposed Rick saw this topic as his one inroad with not only her, but her family, as well.

"Thanks," Clay said, "but my dad and I have already turned ours in to the attorney we're working with. We're waiting for a few more statements from people in the community. But the main holdout is Slowpoke O'Neill, here." He kicked Lacey lightly under the table. "Maybe you can influence her to speed it up."

Lacey sighed, pushing her empty plate a few inches toward the center of the table. "I'm trying," she said, annoyed with both Rick and her brother. "I'm just a bad writer."

"I doubt the quality of the writing matters," Gina said.

She'd gotten to her feet and was wiping Rani's grimy little face with a washcloth.

"Yours counts the most, kiddo," Clay added. "You know that."

"Maybe with all the other statements you're getting, hers won't be necessary," Rick said. Surprised, she looked across the table at him and thought she saw sympathy in his eyes. He may not be doing much to increase her physical desire for him, but he was certainly working his way into her heart.

"Wishful thinking, Rick," Clay said. "Our attorney said we could forget all the rest of them if we had a good one from Lacey. Hers is critical."

Rick looked directly at her. "Maybe you're having trouble writing it because you have ambivalent feelings about keeping a guy in prison when he's made amends," he said.

"I'm not ambivalent," she said, wanting to put an end to the conversation. "I'm just a pathetic writer. Maybe I'll work on it tonight."

After Rick and Bobby left the house, Lacey went upstairs and knocked on Mackenzie's closed bedroom door.

"Come in," the girl said. She was sitting at her computer, as usual, both hands on the keyboard.

Lacey leaned against the doorjamb. "I didn't know how to type until I was in high school," she said.

"Mom taught me when I was little." Mackenzie's fingers tapped quickly on the keys.

"You had a great time with Clay and the dog today, huh?"

"It was okay." Mackenzie kept her eyes on the screen. She wasn't going to give Lacey an inch. The enthusiasm she'd shown at the dinner table seemed to disintegrate now that Lacey was her only audience.

"Well, have a good night," Lacey said, giving up. She

backed out of the room, and then, because she could think of nothing else to say, added, "Don't stay up too late."

She closed the door, imagining Mackenzie's fingers flying across the keyboard as she typed the e-mail to her friends: *My jailer just told me not to stay up too late. She's such a loser.*

In her room, she pulled a notepad from her desk and sat on her bed, her back propped up against the pillows.

I miss my mother very much, she wrote. Was that the truth? She missed the Annie O'Neill she had once known, but not the Annie who had lived a secret, shameful life. She should focus on the mother she had known her to be. Before the revelation. She set her pen to the paper again. *She was the sort of mother that was a friend to all my friends. Everyone loved coming to my house. She baked and sang and was a very creative artist. She was good to everyone. Good to sailors and fishermen and tourists and—*

What was wrong with her? Why couldn't she stay on track? Why couldn't she get this stupid thing written?

She got up and pulled out the photograph album from her bookshelf. She turned to the picture of her mother, a miniature of the one in her studio.

"How could you?" she asked in a whisper. "I thought you were so wonderful. I loved it when they called you Saint Anne. How could you do that to Dad? How could you do that to *us?*" She took the picture and tore it end to end, then side to side. Then she tore the pieces again. "I don't want to be like you, Mom," she said. "I don't ever want to be like you."

29

MACKENZIE COULD NOT POSSIBLY BE HIS DAUGH-
ter. If Bobby had had any doubts, they were erased now as
she sat in the sunroom with him, trying to draw a picture of
a dog from a photograph in a magazine. Artistic talent ran
in his family as surely as alcoholism did, and this child had
absolutely none.

She'd wanted an art lesson, and he loved that she'd asked
him to give her one. But her dog looked more like a rabbit. It was hard for him not to laugh. She was only eleven.
Maybe he'd been as clumsy with a pencil at that age, but he
didn't think so.

"I'm not too good at this," she said sullenly. She sat at
the other worktable in the sunroom, which he had carefully
cleared of the glass Lacey was cutting for her work in progress. Mackenzie's stubby nails were painted an almost nauseating fuchsia, and at her request, he had added a small, delicate
sunflower to the nail of her ring finger. Every few minutes
he'd catch her lifting her hand to admire his artwork.

"I think you're trying too hard," he said, looking up from
the scrimshaw belt buckle. He was using a fine blade to cut
fur lines onto one of the dogs in the illustration, a task that

would have been impossible without the sunlight that filled the room. The light came with a price, though: heat. He'd opened all the windows, but the thick, clammy air worked its way into every corner of the room, putting waves of dampness into Mackenzie's drawing paper. "Loosen up a little," he said to her. "You don't need all the details. Start with just getting the basic shape down."

She shook her head, leaning away from the table. "I think I'm giving up," she said.

He smiled. "You can't be good at everything." He ran a hand over his scalp, a habit he'd developed when he'd had hair to run his fingers through. It still surprised him sometimes to feel nothing there. "Look at how much skill you have with animals," he said. "With dogs. They love you. Clay said you could be a trainer yourself someday." He hadn't seen much of Clay and Gina since his arrival in the Outer Banks; dinner the night before had been the first quality time he'd spent with them. Clay had looked familiar to him. Bobby couldn't recall meeting him during the summer of '91, but perhaps he had. He was grateful for the way Clay had taken Mackenzie under his wing.

"I'd like to be a vet," Mackenzie said, holding her ring finger up to study the sunflower. "Clay's father is a vet."

And so is Lacey's, he thought. He knew how much it bothered Lacey that Mackenzie simply would not connect with her, and he felt sorry for her. The harder Lacey tried, the more she failed.

"He's Lacey's father, too," he said. "Maybe she could take you to his office for a visit sometime."

Mackenzie shrugged, tapping her fuchsia fingertips on the photograph of the dog.

"I could see you as a vet," he said, not wanting to lose the momentum of the conversation. "How are you in math?"

"Pretty good," she said. "I'm even better in science." Then she let out a great, dramatic groan and flopped her head and arms down on the worktable. "I can't *believe* I have to start school in three weeks. August eighteenth! That is so crazy. In Phoenix I wouldn't have to start until after Labor Day."

He set down the blade he was using. It was always dangerous to try to make exacting cuts in the ivory when he could not give it his full concentration. "Are you scared about going to a new school?" he asked.

"No. Just pissed."

Of course she was scared. Who wouldn't be?

"The kids around here are really nice," he said.

"How would you know? You're not from here, either."

"But that's just the way it is here," he said. "People are friendly."

"All the kids are going to know each other, though."

"I bet there'll be other new kids." He swiveled his chair to face her directly. "People move here all the time. And even if you're the only one, you'll fit in fine. Just one warning."

She looked a bit alarmed. "What?"

"You have to stop saying 'in Phoenix this' and 'in Phoenix that.' It drives people crazy and they'll talk about you behind your back."

"I can't help it if Phoenix is so much better than this place."

"When I was a kid," Bobby said, "my family moved from Norfolk to Richmond, and I fell into that trap. I was always saying, 'in Norfolk our school was newer,' 'in Norfolk we had pizza in the cafeteria,' and pretty soon people starting answering me with 'so go back to Norfolk then.'"

Mackenzie laughed. "Okay," she said. "I'll try not to say it."

"Bite your tongue when the word 'Phoenix' comes into your mind."

"Okay."

He heard the back screen door slam shut and knew that Lacey was home. So did Mackenzie, apparently, because she suddenly became engrossed in the drawing of the dog once again.

Lacey walked into the sunroom, instantly filling the room with her presence, at least in his mind if not in Mackenzie's. Her hair was pulled back by a black scrunchie and her fair, freckled skin glistened from the heat. She had on a long, light blue wraparound skirt that hugged her hips and a cropped navy blue top that suggested, but did not flaunt, the curve of her breasts. Since the moment he'd arrived in Kiss River, he'd wanted to kiss her, to take off whatever clothing she had on and make love to her. He wanted to undo the sloppy way he'd taken her virginity from her. It would be so much better now, when his desire for her body was both tamed and heightened by his affection for her. He liked her gentle way with people, he admired her artistic talent and the sympathy he felt over her struggle with Mackenzie ran deep.

"Hi, you two," Lacey said. "How's the art lesson going?"

"Great," Bobby said quickly before Mackenzie could deny it. She was leaning over her drawing, moving her pencil around on the page as though she were focussing on the work. "I hope you don't mind that we appropriated your table."

"No problem at all." Lacey looked at Mackenzie. "Can I see what you're working on?" she asked.

Mackenzie answered her by turning her drawing face-side down on the table. "I think Bobby should live here instead of at Rick's," she said out of the blue. "He's here all the time, anyway."

He was both surprised and touched by the suggestion. "I have a perfectly good room at Rick's," he said. It would be harder for him to see Elise if he lived in the keeper's house, yet the idea was seductive.

"Actually, I've been thinking about that." Lacey leaned against the wall and folded her arms across her chest. "It really would make sense for you to be here," she said to him. "Your work is here. Mackenzie's here. We have a big pot of coffee brewing every morning." She smiled, as if that would be the one enticement sure to win him over. "Why don't you consider it?"

"I'd love it," he said, forgetting about Elise for the moment. He liked the idea of being closer to Mackenzie. And, if he was being honest with himself, he liked the idea of being closer to Lacey, as well. "How soon can I move in?"

30

FAYE LAY NESTLED IN JIM'S ARMS. HE'D BEEN IN a wonderful, generous mood tonight, and the lovemaking had been so tender it had made her cry. Now she felt content. Her body was heavy from the warmth of the hot tub and there was an undeniable bliss inside her she had never expected to feel. In her chronic pain program, one of the tenets she emphasized was that peace and happiness could only be found inside oneself, that perfect health or a million dollars or another person could never have the power to make someone happy or unhappy. She was beginning to wonder if her theory might be wrong about the "other person" part of that equation. Having someone special in your life certainly didn't hurt.

She felt Jim press his lips to her temple. "I know something you don't know," he said, sounding like a little boy with a secret.

The childish taunt intrigued her. "What?" she asked.

"Can't tell."

Gently, she pounded her fist against his chest. "That is so mean of you."

"Yes, you're right. But I'm still not going to tell you."

"Well," she said, "can I assume it's something good?"

"You can assume anything you like."

"When will you tell me?"

"Tomorrow."

"First thing in the morning?"

"I don't think so." If she were not in love with him, she would be getting angry. Instead, she laughed.

"*When* then?" she asked.

"I'm not sure."

"Jim!"

He laughed. "I really am sorry. I shouldn't have said anything."

She wanted to press him for more information, but he stopped her questioning with a kiss.

The following morning, she was sitting in on a pain management class, evaluating the young nurse who was teaching it, when Judy poked her head in the door and motioned for her to come into the hallway. Quietly, Faye left the classroom.

"You have a call," Judy said.

"It couldn't wait?" Faye was surprised that Judy would drag her out of the classroom, since the physical therapist certainly knew how critical a thorough evaluation could be for the nurse's advancement.

"They said it was important," Judy said. "Sorry."

Faye walked down the hallway to her office and lifted the phone from her desk. "Faye Collier." She hoped her annoyance wasn't evident in her voice.

"Hello, Ms. Collier," a woman said. "My name is Sharon Casey and I'm president of the San Diego County Nurses Association."

The woman's name was familiar. "Yes," she said, "I recognize your name. What can I do for you?"

"Not a thing," the woman said. "I'm calling to tell you that you are the recipient of the Nurse of the Year award for San Diego County."

Faye was quiet as the news sank in. "I am?" she asked, incredulous.

"Many doctors and several nurses submitted your name for your work with chronic pain. I've read your new book. It's rare to read something that can speak to both the professional and the lay person so beautifully. Congratulations."

"Thank you." She lowered herself to the chair behind her desk, smiling now. "I don't know what to say. I'm just amazed and…and thrilled." She knew this had to be what Jim had teased her about the night before. Somehow, he'd been privy to the information.

"We'll be presenting your award along with others at the annual awards ceremony in September, so mark the twentieth on your calendar."

"I will," she said. "Thank you so much for letting me know."

She paged Jim the minute she hung up the phone, and he called her back almost instantly.

"How did you know?" she said, without even saying hello.

Jim laughed. "I'm a longtime friend of Sharon Casey's, and she knows I'm seeing you and couldn't stop herself from spilling the beans."

"You didn't influence the outcome, though, I hope." For a moment she felt the wind leave her sails.

"Honey," Jim said, "you've earned this all on your own."

She spent that night at his house. They'd both had to work late, but Jim had still been determined to take her out for a celebratory dinner, and now the lobster she'd devoured far too close to bedtime rested heavily in her stomach. Unable to sleep, she got up and put on her robe. She walked through the house and out the sliding glass door, skirting the pool and hot tub, until she reached the bench overlooking the city. The night was clear and cool, and La Jolla was a blanket of twinkling lights below her.

Nurse of the year. It was still so hard to believe.

"Hey."

She turned to see Jim walking toward her in his satin robe, and she smiled at him. "Hi," she said.

"Too excited to sleep?" He sat next to her on the bench, putting his arm around her.

She rested her head on his shoulder. "I used to live in a trailer park," she said. "I never told you that. It was too embarrassing. I lived there when I was married to Zach. I lived in a trailer park, and I had a husband who murdered someone, and I got fired from my job as a school nurse because I was such a mess I couldn't concentrate, and my son essentially divorced me as his mother." She shook her head. "And now, by some miracle, I'm nurse of the year."

Jim took her free hand in his. "Not by some miracle," he said. "Can't you get it through your head that you've earned this? That you're worthy? No, you didn't have an easy time of things. You didn't have money. You didn't have stability. That's all the more reason why you need to give yourself credit for what you've achieved."

She shut her eyes. He was right. She'd worked hard. She'd set goals for herself and exceeded them. But none of that erased her one failure: her son.

"I want to talk to you about Freddy," Jim said, reading her mind.

"What about him?"

"It's time, don't you think?" he asked. "Time to find him? Wouldn't you love to have him at the awards ceremony?"

She laughed, though the sound was bitter. "I can just imagine," she said. "He hates me, and I get in touch with him and say, 'Hey, come look what I did. I deserted you and then went on to make a name for myself. Come see me get my award.'"

"You didn't desert him."

"I'm sure he felt like I did."

Jim was quiet for a moment. "I know you want him in your life," he said. "You don't even know if he's still angry with you, and you've made it very hard for him to find you. You've moved a couple of times. You took back your maiden name. I'm willing to bet that Freddy grew up and realized you did the right thing by taking him to the shelter that night."

"I doubt it," she said.

"Do you think about him?"

La Jolla and its display of lights blurred in front of her. "Only every day," she said. "I pray for him. I pray that the scars from that night have healed. That he's doing okay. What's the chance of that, though, given the start he had in his life?"

"If he inherited your fighting genes, he will have turned out just fine," Jim said.

God, she wanted to see her son! Hold him. Beg him to forgive her for trying to do what she thought was right. "If I wanted to find him, how would I do it?" she asked. "Hire a detective or what?"

Jim stood up. "Come with me," he said, holding his hand out to her.

She took his hand and walked with him into the house. He led her downstairs to the small study and told her to take a seat next to the desk.

"We'll Google him," he said, seating himself in front of the computer.

Faye leaned sideways to see the screen. "You mean, put his name in a search engine?" she asked.

"Have you ever tried it?" Jim logged on to the Internet.

"I never thought of trying it." She'd spent hours research-ing chronic pain information on the Internet, but it had never occurred to her to research her son.

Jim typed in the name "Fred." Then he glanced over at her. "What's his last name again?" he asked.

"Pointer." She moved her chair behind his to be able to see better, and she watched him type in the surname that had once been her own and which she had come to loathe. He clicked on "search," and scrolled through the many references that appeared on the screen. Several of them contained both the words "Fred" and "Pointer," but never together as a name.

"Try 'Frederick Pointer,'" she suggested.

This time, several Frederick Pointers appeared, but they all seemed to be part of someone's genealogical research, and the men had died long before her Freddy had even been born. There was one reference to a runner in a 10K race, and Faye sucked in her breath as Jim clicked on the link to read more about the race and its participants. Sure enough, a Frederick Pointer had been in the race—he'd even placed fifth—but he was thirty-five years old. She shook her head.

"Freddy would only be twenty-seven, now," she said, dis-couraged.

"Don't give up," Jim said. "Let's see if we can find him in one of the address locators."

Jim's fingers flew across the keyboard as though he did this all the time. In a moment, the name, Frederick L. Pointer, was on the screen along with an address in Princeton, New Jersey. Faye lifted her hand to her mouth. "Oh, my God," she said.

"Does the middle initial fit?" Jim asked.

She nodded. "Leonard," she said. She searched the address for more information, for something that would tell her if this was her son. There was a phone number, but no other clue to his identity. She straightened up again. "It doesn't make sense that he'd live in Princeton," she said.

"We could call the number and find out."

She shook her head. The thought was terrifying to her. If the number *did* belong to Freddy, and he hung up on her, she would lose any chance she had of ever talking to him. She would rather simply imagine that it was him, imagine the call, imagine the warm reception. Better to imagine it than to know a sad reality.

Jim had returned to Google. "Just on a whim, let's see if there's a picture of him on the Web," he said. He typed in the words "Pointer" and "Princeton." Several pictures, none of them containing a human being but rather mechanical drawings of one sort or another, appeared on the screen. Jim scrolled down the display, though, and the image of three young men suddenly appeared. Faye drew in her breath.

"That's him!" she said, pointing past Jim toward the screen. "Oh, my God, Jim, I think it's really him."

Jim stood up and let her have his seat directly in front of the monitor, and she realized that her hands were shaking as she sat down. She clasped them together in her lap as she studied the picture. Freddy was the man in the middle. "His hair's darker," she said. "He was nearly blond when he was a child. But look at those eyes! Oh, he's beautiful." She hadn't thought about loving this boy in many years, but now her chest swelled with her love for him. She touched the screen, touched his hair, the shoulder of his dark suit, and tears ran down her cheeks.

"You know what?" Jim leaned over her shoulder and squinted at the screen. "I think that's the chapel at Princeton in the background."

For the first time, she noticed that Fred and the other two

men stood in front of a church. "That's too big to be a chapel," she said.

Jim laughed. "I think it's one of the biggest in the country,
if my memory serves me well. I've attended more than one
conference in Princeton."

So had she. Was it possible that she'd been in the same town
at the same time as her son?

Jim reached around her shoulders to type on the keyboard,
and she leaned her head back against the warmth of his belly.

A Web site for the Princeton campus appeared, and in an
instant, Jim had found a picture of the chapel. Sure enough,
it was the same church.

"He *does* live in Princeton," she said. Her eyes still on the
monitor, she reached behind her to grab a fistful of Jim's robe.
"Oh, Jim, I want to know everything!" she said. "Did he go
to school in Princeton? Are the two guys in the picture his
closest friends? What's happened in his life since the last time
I saw him? Can we get back to that picture of him?" She was
nowhere near done studying the grown-up face of her son.

Jim tapped a few keys to return Freddy's picture to the
screen, then stood up straight and rested his hands on Faye's
shoulders. "Do you want to call him?" he asked. "Or do you
want to write to him?"

She shook her head, thinking. Planning. "I need to go
in person," she said. "This is something I can't do over the
phone." She sat back in the chair and grasped Jim's hands in
her own. "All I want is a second chance to know my son."

She felt Jim kiss the top of her head. "Of course you do,"
he said. "And you're going to get one."

31

LACEY LAY IN BED, STARING AT THE CEILING, aware of Bobby's presence in the room at the end of the hall. She could feel his nearness in her bones. It had been a mistake to ask him to move in. She'd been caught up in the moment, wanting to please Mackenzie, and maybe wanting to test herself. She'd felt strong when Mackenzie had brought up the idea in the sunroom. After all, she was involved with Rick, spending time with him, focusing on him, waiting for those feelings of love and desire to magically emerge. But the truth was, her body yearned for the man at the end of the hall.

At one in the morning, she gave up trying to fall asleep and got out of bed. She was wearing the boxers and tank top she often slept in, and she padded quietly down the stairs in her bare feet. In the kitchen, she reached into the cabinet next to the sink for the bottle of insect repellent and the flashlight. Then she walked outside, softly shutting the door behind her.

She never felt afraid out here. Even though she had witnessed her mother being gunned down in front of her, she never feared such a thing would happen to her. It had been an aberration, a rarity of enormous proportions in the Outer Banks. And in Kiss River, where only an occasional tourist ever ventured, she never felt endangered. God, she was going to miss living here!

The night was hot, but breezy. A half-moon lit the sky as she walked toward the lighthouse and the sea. She could still feel the heat of the sun in the sand beneath her feet, and she dug her toes into the fine powder as she walked. The ocean was gentle tonight; she could tell by the way it whispered instead of roared, and as she neared the lighthouse, she could see that the water was lapping at the steps instead of devouring them. She walked through the calf-high water and up the steps into the dark octagon of the tower. The tiled floor was always cool. Sometimes she would come into the octagon just to cool off. Tonight, though, she wanted to climb.

She didn't bother with the flashlight, even though it was quite dark in the interior of the lighthouse. Instead, she climbed the stairs in the pale wash of light from the sky. When she reached the top step, she turned and sat down to face the ocean. There were no lights on the water except for those reflected from the sky, and the moon lit the jagged edges of the bricks that surrounded her.

She often wondered what would have happened if the Kiss River lighthouse had remained intact. Like the Corolla light farther north, it probably would have been refurbished and opened to the public. The keeper's house might already be a museum, and the gravel road leading to the parking lot would have been paved. With a jolt, she realized that, once the keeper's house *was* turned into a museum and open to tourists, the Coast Guard would have to find a way to block the lighthouse off from public access. Then even she would not be allowed up here. The thought was unbearable. Funny how something she had once hated had become something she loved.

She remembered how Bobby—the Bobby she'd known

in the summer of 1991—had found her hatred of the lighthouse strange.

"What's it ever done to you?" he'd asked her once, after she'd unleashed a ten-minute tirade against Kiss River and its light. They'd been standing in line at one of the amusement parks, waiting to ride the roller coaster for the fourth time. Jessica was there, of course, and Bobby had his arm possessively around her, his hand on her neck. Jessica's long blond hair fell over his forearm, making Lacey regret chopping her own hair off. She could have just dyed her hair black or blond and left it long, but she'd gone a little crazy with the scissors in her hand, furious with her father for calling her "Annie" over and over again, as though he'd forgotten her own name. She'd wanted to look as little like her mother as possible.

Some other guy, whose name she couldn't even remember now but whom she slept with on the beach later that night, had been with them as they waited in line for the roller coaster. His breath stank of alcohol and she remembered wanting the sex, the physical closeness, the human touch, but not the kissing.

"It's taken my father away," she'd said in answer to Bobby's question. "First, my mother gets killed. Then my father gets, like, totally obsessed with the stupid Kiss River lighthouse."

"What do you mean, obsessed?" Bobby had asked.

"It reminds him of my mother, so he takes pictures of it practically every day. He's head of the committee that's trying to save it from falling into the ocean. He knows every fact about it. I mean, *everything*. He knows more than anyone else and he still tries to learn more. It's sick."

"He forgot her birthday because of it," Jessica said, adding fuel to Lacey's fire.

"He's so busy thinking about the lighthouse, he can't think about anything else," Lacey said.

"He sounds wacko," the other boy said, and she'd felt just the tiniest edge of guilt at her portrayal of her grieving father.

"He *is* wacko," she agreed. "I really, really wish that stupid lighthouse would just fall into the ocean. Get it over with. Make him come back to the real world again."

Bobby let go of Jessica to rest his hand on Lacey's arm. "You need a little something to relax you," he said, sounding like a doctor. His hand was warm and smooth against her skin, and she remembered how it had felt on her small breasts and the inside of her thighs only a few weeks earlier, the night she'd lost her virginity to him.

He pulled a few pills from his shirt pocket and held them out so that only she could see them. "Take a couple of these," he said quietly. "They'll make you feel better."

She shook her head. She drank, but she couldn't make herself take drugs, although she'd faked it a couple of times so she didn't look like a complete dork, taking the pill and pretending to place it in her mouth while she really pocketed it in her very short shorts.

"Sounds like her father's the one who needs some of those," the other boy said. "You could, like, slip them in his OJ or something."

The slamming of a car door jerked Lacey from her memories. She turned to look toward the parking lot. Bobby's van was there, along with a strange car that did not belong to anyone in the house. The parking lot was dark, but not too dark for her to see Bobby get out of his van and pull a slender, blond-haired woman into his arms. She'd thought he'd been asleep in his room. Had he actually been out with this woman? This stranger? Were they kissing? From this distance, she couldn't tell. The only thing she was sure of was that the old jealous feeling was back, the same feeling she used to have when she'd see Bobby and Jessica together. It spread out from the center of her chest and tightened itself around her throat.

The woman took a step away from Bobby and opened the car door. In the light spilling from the car, Lacey could clearly see Bobby hand her a thick wad of green-tinged bills. Her first thought was that the woman was a prostitute. Her second, even worse, was that he was buying drugs from her. Either way, she knew then that she'd made a mistake inviting Bobby Asher into the keeper's house. Was it Mackenzie's needs she'd been thinking of or her own?

The woman got into her car and drove out of the parking lot, and Bobby walked toward the house, his hands deep in the pockets of his jeans, under what he probably assumed was the cover of darkness. Lacey stayed rooted to her seat on the top of the lighthouse, unable to move. Maybe she had witnessed a completely innocent exchange. Maybe Bobby owed the woman money for a carton of cigarettes.

Or maybe Jessica had been right when she said it would be a mistake to bring Bobby into Mackenzie's life. Maybe, despite his protestations to the contrary, he was the same man he used to be, after all.

32

AT BREAKFAST THAT MORNING, LACEY WATCHED Bobby pour his third cup of coffee and eat his second bowl of cereal and wondered if she was being used. She was feeding him, giving him a roof over his head, letting him work in her sunroom and providing him with a pass to her gym, and all he had to do was hang out with an eleven-year-old kid he would not even acknowledge was his. Before inviting him into their lives, she should have had a session or two with her counselor to examine her real motives.

It was a rare breakfast at the keeper's house, because everyone was present. Usually one of them would have eaten alone or skipped breakfast altogether and taken off for work. This morning, though, it was raining, the sky so dark that they had the kitchen light on, and no one seemed in a rush to go anywhere. It was a strong and steamy rain, and through the screen door they could hear it pummeling the sand outside. They'd shut all the windows on the east side of the house, but it was just too hot to shut the kitchen door, as well.

Rani was fussy. She'd finished her breakfast and was kicking her doll-like brown feet, ready to get down from her high chair.

"Can I take her out and hold her on my lap?" Mackenzie asked Gina, who nodded her assent. Rani went to Mackenzie easily and sat comfortably in the girl's lap, and Mackenzie played a little game with her using Cheerios on the tabletop.

Bobby was watching the two children with a smile on his face, and Lacey felt guilty for her negative thoughts about him. She was making something out of nothing. There was no doubt that he was good to Mackenzie, and no doubt that Mackenzie felt a bond with him. Lacey reminded herself that Tom had been an alcoholic at the time she'd learned he was her father. She still would have wanted to know the truth about her relationship to him. As troubled and screwed up as Tom had been, he had welcomed her as his daughter. Bobby was doing no less for Mackenzie. No matter what sort of person he was, Lacey wouldn't harm the relationship between father and child.

Despite his smile, though, Bobby seemed pensive this morning, and Lacey couldn't help but wonder if his mood had something to do with the woman in the parking lot. Was she the one he'd been having those secretive cell phone conversations with? Her brain hurt from trying to figure him out, and she knew she needed to shift gears and focus on the day ahead. If she didn't leave the house soon, she would be late for work at the animal hospital. She turned her attention to Mackenzie.

"Do you have the book you're reading to take to your grandmother's with you?" Lacey asked her.

"I don't need it today," Mackenzie said, moving the Cheerios around on the table in the game only she and Rani seemed to understand. "Grandmother's taking me shopping." Nola had discovered the one activity that Mackenzie would embrace. "But I was wondering if I could come home early?" she asked, glancing at Lacey. "I mean, could you pick me up

after you get off work at the animal hospital? I want to help
Clay with the training." She looked across the table at Clay.
"You're training this afternoon, aren't you?"

He nodded. "I'm working with Boomer," he said.

"Oh, I love Boomer!" Mackenzie said. "So, can I come
home early?"

"I want *finger paint!*" Rani insisted, apparently growing
tired of the Cheerios game.

"Do you want me to take her?" Gina asked Mackenzie.

"I've got her," Clay said, getting to his feet.

"I'll finger paint with you tonight," Mackenzie said to the
little girl as she transferred her to Clay's arms. "I have to leave
in a few minutes, so I can't do it now."

Rani pouted, pressing her head against Clay's shoulder.

"Let's get you cleaned up." Clay carried her to the sink,
where he washed her hands and face, a procedure Rani had
only recently been able to tolerate. Then he set her down on
the floor. "Why don't you go look at one of your books?" he
said to her, and she ran into the living room, Sasha at her side.

Mackenzie looked at Lacey. "So, can I?" she asked again,
as Clay poured himself another cup of coffee. Lacey had to
hand it to Bobby; at least he'd had the courtesy to make a
second pot when he realized he was going to be drinking
most of the first.

"It's okay with me," she said. "But it's really up to your
grandmother. Call me at the animal hospital after you talk to
her." She felt certain that Nola would be delighted to have
less time with her granddaughter. A couple of days ago, she'd
actually thanked Lacey for taking her in, although she'd also
made it clear that she was still angry at her for contacting
Bobby. Oh, God. Maybe Nola had good reason to be angry.

"Speaking of calls," Clay said as he took his seat again, "I
got one yesterday from a woman whose dog I trained years

ago." He leaned back in his chair, fingering his napkin on the table. "The dog's name is Wolf," he said, "and he was one of the best I'd ever worked with. He and his owner, Susan, were a great team, but a few months ago, they were involved in a search-and-rescue operation looking for a little girl. She'd been camping with her family and disappeared, and they thought she'd wandered off, but she'd actually been snatched by some guy. Wolf was the dog that found her. She was safe and unhurt, but the guy who'd taken her kicked Wolf around a bit and then shot him."

"Oh, no!" Mackenzie's hand flew to her mouth and a pained expression came over her face. "Did he die?" she asked.

Clay shook his head. "Susan said that he recovered from the gunshot wound, and for a while, he seemed fine. Then, all of a sudden, he changed. He would growl at people on the street, and he attacked Susan's friend when she came over to the house."

"Like, what do you mean, he attacked her?" Mackenzie asked.

"He lunged at her and took a chunk out of her arm."

"Man," Bobby said. "Did they put him down?"

Clay shook his head. "The friend he attacked was, fortunately, a dog person, and she and Susan both realized that something was radically wrong. Wolf had always been very gentle. Susan's afraid that he's not only been ruined as a search-and-rescue dog, but that he's not trustworthy around anyone besides herself anymore."

Lacey knew from the moment Clay started talking about the dog that he wanted to attempt to rehabilitate him, but Gina only seemed to be catching on now. "You're not thinking of working with the dog again, are you?" she asked him.

Clay turned to his wife. "I'm telling you, Gina, this is one of the best dogs I've ever worked with. He has some kind of…post-traumatic stress disorder."

"Oh, Clay, please," Gina pleaded. "Don't bring a dog like that here."

"It'll be fine," Clay said. "He'll be locked up in the kennel."

Gina looked as though she wanted to say more, but wisely decided to save it for a private conversation.

"You should have Dad look at the dog," Lacey suggested, "Maybe there's something physical going on with him."

Clay nodded. "That's first on my agenda."

Bobby looked at his watch, then reached for the box of raisin bran and poured himself another bowlful.

Lacey turned to him. "You're quiet this morning," she said. She heard the suspicious edge to her voice and wondered if anyone else noticed it.

He smiled at her, that smile she still could feel down to her toes regardless of any negative thoughts she might have about him. "All the dog talk made me think about the piece I'm working on," he said. "The belt buckle. I start adding the colors today."

"Can I watch?" Mackenzie asked.

Bobby laughed. "You've got a lot you want to do today, don't you?" he asked. "Shop with your grandmother. Help Clay train a dog. Finger paint with Rani. Watch me work."

Mackenzie shrugged, drawing in a little, as if afraid to let her housemates know that she was enjoying life in any way, shape or form.

"I'll show you how I do it tonight, okay?" Bobby asked, and she nodded.

It was midmorning when Rick stopped by the animal hospital with flowers for Lacey. Everyone made a fuss over them, and Lacey felt embarrassed by the public display of his affection for her. She would have to answer her co-workers' questions about him later. Still, it was kind of him. He was a sweet man.

"You're spoiling me," she said across the reception counter as she slipped the mixed bouquet of flowers into a vase.

"You deserve to be spoiled," he said.

She arranged the flowers so that they appeared to spring from the vase like fireworks. "I have a question for you," she said, the words slipping from her mouth before she could stop them. She turned to one of the vet techs. "Could you cover for me for a few minutes?" she asked.

The tech agreed, and she walked through the waiting area and its community of dogs and cats as she led Rick outside. The rain had stopped, leaving thick steamy air in its wake, and they walked to the curb at the edge of the parking lot. She turned to face him, her arms folded across her chest.

"When Bobby was staying with you," she began, "did you notice any…druggie behavior or anything?"

He shook his head with a frown. "Why? Have you?"

"Did you ever see him with a blond woman?"

"A woman did come around once," Rick said. "Tall. Thin. Pretty. Bobby went outside with her for a while. I didn't think much of it."

"I saw him give her money."

Rick raised his eyebrows. "For what?" he asked.

"I have no idea, but it worries me."

Rick pursed his lips and looked in the direction of the ocean. They couldn't see the water from where they stood, but they could hear the waves pounding the beach behind the line of cottages. "Maybe you should just come out and ask him," he suggested.

She knew he was right. She should ask Bobby about the woman instead of wearing herself out with guesswork, but she didn't think she had the right to poke around in his private affairs without stronger evidence that he was doing something wrong. Besides, she was not certain she wanted to know the answers to her questions.

"I'm torn," she said. "He's so good with Mackenzie."

Two SUVs pulled into the parking lot, and she watched a Great Dane jump out of one of them, a yellow lab out of the other. She would be needed inside.

"I'd better get back to work," she said. She stood on tiptoe to kiss his cheek. "Thank you for the flowers," she said. "You really are too good to me."

Lacey sat with Bobby in the sunroom that evening, both of them working by lamplight. She was creating a pattern for a stained-glass panel, drawing the same lines over and over again with her pencil, unable to concentrate. If she didn't ask him now, she would never get any work done.

Bobby was bent over the second table, working on the belt buckle under the circle of light from a halogen lamp.

With a sigh of resignation, she set down her pencil. "Last night," she began, "I couldn't sleep and I went up to the top of the lighthouse."

"Uh-huh," he said, still engrossed in his work. Unsuspecting. Innocent?

"I was up there when you met a woman in the parking lot." She saw his hands pause and watched him slowly set down the tool he was using. He swiveled his chair to look at her, and he wore the expression of a kid caught with his hand in the cookie jar.

"And you're wondering who she is?" he asked.

She nodded. "It's none of my business, I know that, but it just…"

"She's someone I met at an AA meeting," he said. "Just a

friend. She called me last night because she was about to have
a drink. She picked me up here and we drove around a bit
while I...you know, talked her down. I'm sorry if I weirded
you out."

"I just..." Lacey looked past him to avoid his eyes. "You
don't owe me any explanations," she said. "It was just unexpected. I thought you were asleep upstairs and so it came as
kind of a shock to see you out there."

"In AA," he said, "if someone needs you to keep them from
taking that drink...well, you've got to do it."

She nodded, not truly believing him. She wanted to ask
him more questions. Was this the person he spoke with on
the phone all the time? Why did he give her money? But her
worry and her jealousy felt like a combustible mixture in her
chest, and it was far easier to simply retreat.

"I'm sorry to be so nosy," she said.

"That's okay," he said. "I understand. It's your house. You
have a right to know who's coming and going."

She watched him turn his chair to face the table again, apparently satisfied that he'd sufficiently answered her question,
and she knew she would have to be satisfied, as well.

In spite of all the thoughts churning in her mind, she fell
asleep quickly that night. The hot, oppressive air had finally
given way to a cool breeze that blew the heat from her room
and made it the perfect temperature for sleeping.

In the middle of the night, though, she awakened. She'd
been dreaming that a cat was howling on the beach, the sound
so horrible that it pulled her quickly from her sleep. She sat
up, her head groggy. *It's only Rani,* she thought. But the sound
came again, and now that she was awake, she recognized it
for what it was: a scream. *Mackenzie.*

She jumped out of bed and rushed into the hallway. Bobby

was walking out of his bedroom, zipping up his jeans, and she was surprised by the relief she felt at seeing him there. He could go to Mackenzie; the girl would be more at ease with him. He'd know what to say.

But he stopped walking when he saw her. "Go," he said quietly, nearly mouthing the word, as he motioned toward Mackenzie's room.

She wanted to ask him to go to Mackenzie himself, but something in his face told her that she should be the one to do it. The screams had stopped, but the unmistakable sound of sobbing came from the bedroom. Nodding to Bobby, she opened the door.

Mackenzie was huddled close to the sleigh bed's head-board, arms around her legs and her head buried on her knees. Lacey sat down on the edge of the bed, and to her amazement, Mackenzie reached for her, arms outstretched, the way Rani reached out when she wanted to be picked up. Lacey moved closer and pulled the girl to her. Still crying, Mackenzie curled up against her, and Lacey held her tight, resting her cheek against her head. Mackenzie's skin was damp and hot, her hair soft beneath Lacey's cheek. She had to be in a bad way to want such intimate contact with her.

"Bad dream?" she asked into Mackenzie's hair.

Mackenzie's body jerked with a sob. "I *dreamt* it," she said, "but it wasn't really a *dream,* because it really happened." She cried as she spoke, her shoulders shaking beneath Lacey's arms. "It was the accident. It was like it was happening all over again."

Lacey closed her eyes, but instead of picturing the drunk driver ramming his car into Jessica's, she found herself back at the battered women's shelter, Zachary Pointer bursting into the room, his gun aimed at his wife.

"It's going to be okay," she said to Mackenzie, although

she knew that the girl's life would never truly be okay again. Not the way it had once been.

"She was looking at me when it happened," Mackenzie said. "If I hadn't been there, maybe she could've gotten out of the way of that drunk...that drunk shithead." Lacey wondered how Mackenzie would feel if she knew that Bobby had taken the lives of two people with his own drunk driving. Someday, she would probably have to know.

"Life is full of 'what ifs' and 'if onlys,'" Lacey said. *If only she and her mother had not gone to the battered women's shelter on that particular day. If only she had been the one to leap in front of Zachary Pointer's wife instead of her mother. Maybe Pointer would not have shot a child.* "We can't change what's already happened," she said.

"Well then, life sucks," Mackenzie said.

"Uh-huh," Lacey agreed. "It truly does sometimes."

"How did you stand it when your mother was killed?" Mackenzie kept her head locked to Lacey's shoulder. It was the first time Mackenzie had asked her anything about her own loss.

"Not very well," Lacey said. "I rebelled, just like you're doing."

"I'm not rebelling."

"No?" Lacey smiled. "You're surly sometimes. You shoplift. You steal money from my purse. You leave my vibrator on the kitchen table for all the world to see."

Mackenzie let out a sound that sounded more like a giggle than a sob. "What does surly mean?" she asked.

"Grouchy. Ornery."

The girl sighed. "I don't know why I get like that," she said. "I never used to be that way."

"I think you just don't know which way is up anymore," Lacey said. "Your life has changed way too much way too fast for you and that's scary. When people are afraid, they can act out in all different ways." *Thank you, Bobby.*

"Did you get surly, too?"

"Worse than surly," Lacey said. "And then my father started dating Olivia—you know, Jack and Maggie's mother—and that was terrible. I didn't like her at first, not only because I was afraid she was trying to take my mother's place, but because if I liked her, I felt like I'd be betraying my mother somehow."

"Yeah." Mackenzie spoke with such conviction that Lacey knew the idea had real meaning for her.

"Then I realized I had enough love inside me that I could leave a ton of it with my mother and still have plenty left over for other people."

Mackenzie sniffled against Lacey's shoulder. "Do you love Olivia?" she asked.

"A lot. In a different way from the way I loved my mother. Olivia wasn't a replacement. Just a new person for me to care about."

Neither of them spoke for a moment, and Mackenzie's body began to shake with a new set of tears. Instinctively, Lacey rubbed her back. "It's going to be all right," she said, wishing she had the power to make it so. Each sob, each shiver that passed through Mackenzie's body sent a fresh surge of emotion—something like love, but it couldn't possibly be that—through Lacey's heart, and she held her tighter. She could feel the protective shell she had built around herself, a shell she had not even known existed, slip from her shoulders and fall to the floor. What had she been protecting herself from? *Feeling this,* she thought. *Feeling this pain all over again.* And from the crime of being the compassionate sort of nurturer her own mother had been.

Finally, Mackenzie spoke again.

"Do you think things happen for a reason?" she asked. "That's what Amelia said to me. Other people said it, too. 'This happened for a reason, Mackenzie. We don't know what it is, but you can be sure it was supposed to happen.' But I can't think of a single solitary reason why Mom should have died."

"Well, a lot of people do say that," Lacey said. "I guess it gives them comfort to think there's a reason for everything."

"Is that what you think?"

She hesitated, not wanting to tamper with the girl's beliefs if they were giving her comfort. Yet she thought she should be honest. "I guess I don't believe it myself. But, honey—" the endearment left her mouth with amazing ease, and if it surprised Mackenzie, it surprised her even more "—I think people who have something terrible happen to them have to try to make the best of things. That's our task. That's harder to do than just thinking that things happen for a reason and letting it go at that, don't you think? Much harder. I used to think, 'What would Mom want me to do?' when I was faced with a decision." She no longer thought that. She no longer trusted her mother's judgment. But maybe the concept would work for Mackenzie. "That helped me so much," she said. "It made me feel as though my mother was still with me." The good mom. The mom who had not yet fallen from grace.

"Sometimes I think it was all a mistake," Mackenzie said. "That my mother's still alive and will come back."

"I know." Lacey remembered that fantasy very well.

Mackenzie suddenly let go of her and sat back, wiping her wet face with her fuchsia-tipped fingers. "God, I'm so embarrassed," she said.

"What about?" Lacey still had her hand on Mackenzie's arm. She didn't seem to want to let go.

"That I woke up screaming. I'm such a loser."

"Don't feel bad. Dreams can be very frightening."

"Did you ever do that?" Mackenzie asked. "Wake up screaming?"

It wasn't difficult to remember those months after her mother had been killed. She didn't think she'd been able to sleep long enough to dream. "I don't think I screamed out loud," she said. "But I screamed a lot in my head. And that wasn't very helpful, because that meant that no one ever heard it, so no one came running to be with me."

Mackenzie leaned away to look at her. Slowly, she raised her hand, reaching out to touch Lacey's cheek, touching tears Lacey had not even realized she was crying.

"I love you, Mackenzie," Lacey said. She pulled the girl close again as the remarkable words filled the room, and she knew all at once that they were the truth.

33

"I WANT TO MEET THE NEW DOG," MACKENZIE said, peering through the sunroom windows. She'd spent the past half hour watching Bobby's meticulous application of paint on the belt buckle, but although she'd kindly pretended to be interested, he knew that her heart had not really been in it.

He looked up from his work to see Clay and a woman standing in the rear yard. The woman had long gray hair plaited in a braid down her back, and at her side sat a huge, handsome German shepherd. The sun was so bright, it cast sharp shadows of man, woman and dog in the sand.

"Is that the dog Clay was talking about?" Bobby asked. "The one with post-traumatic stress or whatever it is?"

Mackenzie nodded, her gaze glued to the yard. "He said they were coming today," she said. "Poor dog."

It was Saturday, so Mackenzie was home all day, giving Nola the weekend for her real estate business. She had e-mailed her friends, talked to them on her cell phone and read books to Rani, who was now out running errands with Gina, leaving Mackenzie restless and bored.

"I'm not sure meeting that dog is such a good idea," Bobby said. "Remember, he attacked someone."

"I'll call Clay and ask him." Mackenzie whipped out her cell phone and dialed a number. Bobby thought of stopping her, telling her not to interrupt him while he was working, but he knew Clay wouldn't mind. Clay had done a great job of involving Mackenzie in his dog training, and it seemed as though she was a true help to him.

They both watched Clay unclip his cell phone from his belt and raise it to his ear.

"It's me, Clay," Mackenzie said. "I'm in the sunroom."

Clay turned toward the house, and Mackenzie waved at him through the window.

"Can I come out and meet Wolf?" she asked. She waited for his answer, then broke into a pretty smile. "Sweet!" She flipped her phone shut and turned to Bobby. "He said it's fine."

"I'll go with you, okay?" Bobby said, feigning curiosity about the dog, but his real reason for wanting to accompany her was that he didn't like the idea of her approaching the dog alone. He had little experience with dogs and had never been truly comfortable around them. Surely, though, Clay would not have said it was okay if there was a problem.

Together, they walked out onto the rear porch of the keeper's house and down the steps to the sand. Wolf stood up as they approached, and Bobby was surprised to see the dog's tail wagging. Nevertheless, he was glad that the animal was on a leash.

"Avert your eyes," Mackenzie said to him under her breath.

"What?"

"Don't look him right in the eyes. It feels like a challenge to dogs when you do that. Like a threat."

"Got it. Thanks." Despite his lack of knowledge about

dogs, that was one thing he did know, but he wanted to let Mackenzie feel like she knew more than he did. He smiled at Clay and the woman, keeping his eyes on their faces and away from Wolf.

The woman was stunning. She had to be close to sixty, but her hair was thick in the braid running down her back and her smile was very wide, displaying a mouthful of white teeth.

"This is Bobby and his daughter, Mackenzie," Clay said to the woman.

Bobby and his daughter, Mackenzie. My God. It was the first time he'd heard those words spoken, and although he was certain they were not the truth, they filled him with an undeniable sense of joy and pride. He couldn't resist resting a fatherly hand on Mackenzie's shoulder.

"And this is Susan," Clay said to them.

Susan reached out her hand. Bobby hesitated a moment before shaking it in case Wolf might misinterpret his contact with the woman. Wolf, though, seemed perfectly placid. Almost drugged.

"Mackenzie's my assistant," Clay said.

"Can I pet him?" Mackenzie asked.

"Let him sniff your hand," Susan said. "Then pet his chest. Don't go for the top of his head."

Mackenzie nodded, approaching the dog and letting him sniff the back of her hand. She reached low to scratch his chest, and Wolf leaned into her, obviously enjoying the physical contact. Bobby began to relax.

"Clay said he helped you train Wolf years ago," he said to Susan.

Susan nodded. "He was a great search-and-rescue dog, but he's become untrustworthy since about two months ago." She described the terrifying incident Clay had told them about in which Wolf had been shot by the kidnapper. "After he attacked my friend, I considered having him euthanized, but I just can't do that if there's a chance of rehabilitating him."

"He's so sweet." Mackenzie was now sitting in the sand and Wolf had rolled onto his back for a belly rub.

"He's unpredictable," Susan said. "I wish I knew what was going on in his head."

"I'd like to have my dad look him over before I start working with him," Clay said. "Give him a good physical so we can rule out any medical problems."

"You'll take him on, then?" Susan asked.

"Yes. Are you willing to leave him here so I can work with him every day? He'll stay in the kennel." Clay pointed in the direction of the fenced-in area near the parking lot.

"Of course," Susan said, "although I'll miss him terribly." She sat down in the sand next to Mackenzie and rubbed Wolf's chest while Mackenzie concentrated on his midregion. It was clear that Wolf was in doggy heaven. Susan looked up at Clay. "How long do you think he'll have to be here?"

"That depends on the progress he makes," Clay said. "I'll work with him every day, and of course, I'll only use positive reinforcement with him."

Susan nodded. "That's why I wanted you to be the one to work with him," she said.

Bobby heard the sound of a vehicle on the gravel lane and turned to see Lacey's car pull into the parking lot. Mackenzie waved to her as she got out of the car. It seemed that a small miracle had taken place the night before, and that the time Lacey had spent in Mackenzie's bedroom had been a turning point for the two of them. Lacey hadn't said much about it, but she thanked him for encouraging her to go to the girl. When he came downstairs that morning, he found the two of them making French toast together, an easy camaraderie between them.

He'd felt awkward around Lacey the last couple of days, still reeling from the fact that she'd seen him with Elise in the parking lot. The middle of the night had seemed a safe time to meet, but it was obvious that he would have to be far more careful. Lacey had not bought his lies—of that he was certain—but she seemed willing to let the topic go and he was not going to bring it up again on his own.

Now he watched Lacey pull a scrunchie from the pocket of her capris and use both her hands to gather up her hair and secure it in a ponytail. Then she started walking across the sand toward them.

In an instant, everything changed. Wolf leaped to his feet, a growl forming deep in his throat. Bobby saw Susan tighten her hand on the leash, and Mackenzie quickly stood up.

"Hi," Lacey called out with a smile, obviously unable to hear the dog's warning. She was ten feet away when Wolf lunged for her. Susan held the leash with both hands, calling out futile commands to the dog—"Come! Sit! Down!"—all of which Wolf ignored as though suddenly deaf. Lacey froze in her tracks, and Clay grabbed on to the leash, as well. Bobby's heart kicked into overdrive, and he gripped Mackenzie's shoulder and pulled her toward him and away from the dog.

"Uh." Lacey's smile was nervous now. "This must be the infamous Wolf."

Susan looked at Clay. "See what I mean?" she asked, bobbing around as she tried to hang on to the leash while Wolf snarled, baring his huge, pointed teeth. Even though Bobby's hand was on Mackenzie's shoulder, he could feel her heart pounding beneath his fingers.

Clay nodded. "It's very interesting," he said, scratching his chin with his free hand as if trying to solve a puzzle.

"I think I'll go inside," Lacey said, taking a slow step backward.

"You look like my friend he attacked," Susan said. "She had red hair, too."

"Dogs can't see color," Lacey said.

"Well, they can't differentiate between red and other colors," Clay said, "but it's obvious that Wolf feels threatened by you, for whatever reason. It's great we'll have a threatening person right here to help me desensitize him when I get to that point."

"Oh, wonderful." Lacey's sarcasm was unmasked. "So pleased I can help."

Wolf was settling down again. He looked worn-out from his explosion of aggression, but a low growl still rumbled deep in his throat.

They all turned at the slamming of a car door and saw Gina reach into the the van to release Rani from her car seat.

"Tell her not to come out here, okay, Lacey?" Clay asked.

Lacey nodded. With one final glance at the dog, she walked slowly toward the house, catching up with Gina near the side porch, talking with her a moment as she took a bag of groceries from her arms. Bobby saw Gina quickly grab Rani's hand and look in their direction.

Clay turned to wave at his wife and daughter. The sunlight caught him full in the eyes, which looked like the palest blue glass. Like clear, seawater marbles. Bobby stared at his eyes, transfixed. Suddenly he realized why Clay had looked familiar to him. He knew those eyes, and he knew exactly where he'd seen them before. You did not forget eyes like those.

34

THE WOODS SURROUNDING RICK'S COTTAGE were thick with the sound of cicadas as Lacey opened her car door. She slipped on her sandals before getting out of the car; she had learned the hard way that walking through these woods barefoot could be painful. The last time she'd tried it, she'd stepped on a sandspur.

She could smell the onions on the sandwiches she'd brought with her, even though they were wrapped in paper and inside a brown bag. She carried them the short distance to the cottage, climbed the two steps to the deck and peered through the screen door. Rick was working at the computer in the corner of the minuscule living room, and she hoped he wouldn't mind being interrupted.

"Hello!" she called through the screen.

He twisted in his chair to look at her, breaking into a smile, and she knew right then that he would never mind being interrupted by her.

"Surprise!" she said, pulling open the door. "I hope you haven't had lunch yet." When he was working, he sometimes forgot to eat.

He hit a couple of buttons on his keyboard and stood up.

"No, and I'm starving, now that you mention it." He looked freshly scrubbed, as he always did. "This is so sweet of you." He moved forward and kissed her on the lips.

It *was* sweet of her. She was still not certain she believed Bobby's explanation of his liaison with the woman in the parking lot, but nevertheless, witnessing that event reinforced her belief that she should focus her attention on Rick.

"You sit, and I'll wait on you." She pulled out a chair for him at the doll-size kitchen table. He sat down, grinning at her as she opened one of the kitchen cabinets, then another, in search of plates.

"I forgot to get us something to drink," she said. "Do you have anything?"

"Root beer," he said. "Wine. OJ. Water. Take your pick."

She took two plates from the cupboard, then opened the refrigerator to find a six-pack of root beer, three bottles of wine, a carton of orange juice and two large bottles of water. There was little else on the shelves. "Which would you like?" she asked.

"I'll take a root beer," he said.

She poured one for him and another for herself. "Was it weird having wine in the house when Bobby was here?" she asked as she set the glasses on the table.

"What do you mean?" His big eyes and long lashes made him look completely guileless.

"You know," she said, shrugging. "A recovering alcoholic."

"If you mean, did I find wine missing while he was here, the answer is no. Not that I paid attention, but I think I would have noticed."

She sat down at the table, the plates in her hands. "I'm a bit paranoid about him," she said.

"Well, I can understand that, but I think he's okay."

"He told me the blond woman is from AA."

"She probably is," Rick said.

Lacey unwrapped the sandwiches and transferred them to the plates.

"Onions," he said, breathing in the scent of the sub on his plate. "I hope you have them on yours, too."

"I do." She smiled but looked away in discomfort. Was he implying that they would be kissing later? Maybe something heavier than kissing? Did he think that her showing up like this meant she was ready for more? She was not.

"I can't stay long," she said, tucking a loose piece of tomato back inside her sandwich. "I just came from the animal hospital and after lunch I'm going to the studio to get some work done. I haven't been there enough. Tom's getting on my case." Tom was a bit annoyed with her. They were supposed to take turns with the less artistic duties of running the studio, but he'd been managing all the sales and administrative tasks lately. She'd been working on her stained glass at the keeper's house in the afternoons, not sure if it was because she wanted to keep an eye on Bobby or she wanted the closeness to him—or both.

Rick swallowed a bite of his sandwich and took a sip of root beer. "So," he said, "how are things going with the little rebel in your house?"

"Better." A smile came to her lips, and he raised his eyebrows in surprise.

She shrugged. "We're just doing better." The feelings she'd experienced a few nights ago in Mackenzie's bedroom were only growing. She'd feared Mackenzie would withdraw from her again once morning came, that she would be embarrassed at how she had reached out to someone she'd previously disdained, but that had not happened.

"Do I detect a change of heart here?" he asked.

She nodded. "I think so. On both our parts."

"I'm glad to hear that, Lacey," he said. "I know it's been hard on you."

"I'm sure I still have some hard times ahead, but we're making progress." She took a bite of her sub. They ate for a moment without conversation, and Lacey grew uncomfortable in the silence. What did she really have in common with this guy, except that he treated her well and she wanted to be treated well? Was that enough?

"You should see the dog Clay's working with," she said. She told him the story of Wolf's transformation from easygoing search-and-rescue dog to unpredictable monster. "I have to say, he scares the daylights out of me. I have to pass the kennel when I walk from the car to the house, and he lunges at the fence to try to get to me."

"Is the kennel secure?" Rick asked.

"Very. I mean, I know he can't get to me, but it freaks me out all the same. And I seem to be the only person at the house he reacts that way to. Clay's thrilled. He says he'll know he's succeeded when the dog no longer wants to attack me."

"Oh, great," Rick said.

"Gina is angry about it." Lacey knew she was blathering, but she felt a need to fill the silence. "She doesn't think we should have a dog like that living so near children, and I think she's right."

Gina and Clay had argued about it over breakfast that morning. It was the first time she'd heard harsh words between the two of them, and it had upset her. "Give me a couple of weeks with him," Clay had said. "It's impossible for him to get out of the kennel, and if I'm ever working with him off-lead, I'll be sure to let you know so that you and Rani are inside."

Gina had finally acquiesced, but Lacey knew she wasn't happy about it. Gina had encouraged Clay to get back into dog training, knowing the passion he felt for it could only do him good, so it seemed fitting that Clay should listen to her when she expressed consternation. Or maybe it was Lacey's own unspoken apprehension about Wolf that was making her want Gina to win the argument. She did not like that dog, no matter how skilled he had once been at search and rescue.

Clay had brought Wolf into the animal hospital that morning to have their father examine him. The second Wolf had spotted Lacey, he'd started growling, baring his teeth, and she was glad she was seated behind the high counter of the reception area. Her hands were shaking, though, as she typed on the computer keyboard. It was rare for her to be fearful of an animal, but it was also rare for an animal to show such hostility toward her. Her sole consolation was that she was not the only person the dog took a disliking to. He had it in for Mike, one of the vet techs, as well, and it was quickly decided that the dog needed to be muzzled before he could be examined.

She did not dare go into the examination room while her father checked the dog over. The examination lasted a long time. Blood was sent to the lab, and Wolf's handsome body was palpated and explored. He appeared to be in good health, her father said. He thought that Clay was probably right, that Wolf had experienced a trauma and needed time and retraining to get past it, but he recommended that the dog have a neurological work-up to be sure there was not something more going on. Clay would have to take Wolf to Norfolk for that, and he could not get an appointment with the specialist for a couple of weeks.

"You haven't mentioned the whole parole thing lately," Rick said, pulling her from her thoughts about the dog. "What did you decide to do about your victim's impact statement?"

She sighed. "You mean, am I going to write it?"

He nodded.

"I really have to," she said. "But I have writer's block or something."

"Let them go forward without yours, then. It sounds like they have plenty of ammunition."

"But everyone's waiting on mine," she said. "The attorney called me yesterday to tell me I could come into her office and speak about...what happened into a tape recorder and her secretary would transcribe it." Lacey had resented the intrusion. The call had made her feel panicky. They were going to get that statement out of her one way or another.

"Lacey." Rick rested his hand on hers, and there was such concern in his face that she felt tears spring to her eyes. "You're putting too much pressure on yourself, do you hear me?" he asked. "You're letting people push you around. Look at all you've had to deal with this summer. Let this one thing go. Wouldn't it be a relief?"

She shut her eyes. Yes, it would be. She wouldn't have to revisit that scene again in her head. She wouldn't have to struggle to write about her mother's wonderful qualities when she knew Annie O'Neill had been two-faced, both saint and sinner.

Rick ran his thumb over the back of her hand, and she did not pull away from the tender physical contact. It was not sexual, not in any way. *This is what I really need,* she thought. *Support and caring.*

"You're the only person who seems to understand how hard it is for me to have that damned statement hanging over my head," she said.

Rick nodded, a sad smile on his face. "What can they do to you if you don't produce it?" he asked. "They're not going to put you in jail for not writing a statement."

"Everyone will be upset with me," she said. She sounded like a little kid, even to her own ears.

"They'll get over it."

"And if Zachary Pointer gets out of prison, they'll blame me." That would be the worst of it, she thought: her family's disappointment in her. She let out a long sigh, shaking off the thoughts as she looked at her watch. "I'd better leave," she said. "I told Tom I'd be there by 1:30."

"You barely touched your sandwich," Rick said.

"I'll take it with me." She wrapped up the sandwich, no longer hungry, and leaned over to kiss him on the lips. He tasted like onions. "Thank you," she said. "I'll talk to you later."

She was more than surprised to find Bobby in the studio when she arrived. He was sitting in her chair, engaged in conversation with Tom, while three women and a young child admired the stained glass and photographs. Tom looked up when she walked through the door.

"Ah, my missing co-worker-slash-daughter," he said. The women looked at Lacey. One of them smiled.

Lacey's gaze rested on Bobby. "Were you waiting for me?" she asked, perplexed as to why he'd be there.

"Well, I'm glad to see you, of course," Bobby said diplomatically, "but I thought I'd just stop in and say hi to Tom."

She frowned, trying to remember if the two of them had ever met before.

"We go to the same AA meeting," Tom said quietly.

"Ah," she said, pleased. Bobby really was in AA, then. The thought of the two men together at a meeting was comforting.

"Go take a break," Lacey said generously to Tom. "I'll take over."

"And I'm heading to Nola's to pick up Mackenzie," Bobby said, standing up. "She called and asked if she could come home early to work with Clay again. I hope that's okay with you?"

"Of course it is," she said. "As long as it's okay with Clay."

She took her seat behind the worktable as the men left the building. The women who'd been strolling through the studio bought two small stained-glass birds and a kaleidoscope, and as Lacey was carefully wrapping the items in tissue paper, she spotted Bobby in the parking lot. He was bent over, leaning into the passenger side window of a small, dark car, talking to a blond woman, and Lacey quickly turned her attention back to her wrapping, unable to watch. She was afraid she might see something she didn't want to see.

35

"YOU WANT TO HEAR SOMETHING REALLY AWE-some?"

Bobby looked up from his work on the belt buckle to see Mackenzie leaning against the doorway of the sunroom, her sneakers tied together and flung over her shoulder. Sasha was at her side, looking up at Mackenzie with big, adoring brown eyes.

"What's so awesome?" he asked, although he could guess it had something to do with a dog.

"Today I get to be Wolf's victim!" she said.

It sounded so funny, he laughed. "All right, Mackenzie!" he said. "You get to be a victim!"

She made a face at him. "You don't get it," she said, walking into the room. She sat down in the chair behind Lacey's worktable. "This is, like, a *turning* point," she said, her hands cutting the air in her typical dramatic fashion. "Clay thinks Wolf is ready to start practicing his search stuff again, so I get to do the hide-in-the-woods thing and Wolf will find me."

Clay had been working with Wolf for a week, and Bobby admired the man's tenacity and skill. He was spending so much time with the dog that Bobby wondered what was happening to his architecture practice, but Clay did not seem concerned. Wolf was not the same dog who had lunged for Lacey that first day. The dog was nearly docile now. He was fatter, too, from all the little chunks of dried liver Clay was using to reward his good behavior. Wolf was even able to remain calm around Lacey, who would bravely walk near him while Clay held the end of the dog's loose leash, just in case. Wolf still went berserk, though, if Lacey walked past his kennel while he was inside it. "That's his territory," Clay had said at the dinner table a few nights ago. "*No one* is to go into that kennel except me. Understood?" He'd looked directly at Mackenzie, who had nodded solemnly.

Wolf and Mackenzie, though, seemed to have a little mutual admiration society going. It was cool to see the dog greet her, his tail going so fast it was a blur. The first time Bobby saw the dog run toward her, though, he'd panicked. He'd been watching from the kitchen window, and he thought that Clay must have lost hold of the leash and that Wolf was on the attack. He'd run to the screen door, yanking it open, but then he saw the joy on Mackenzie's face and the obvious playfulness in Wolf's posture, and relaxed his grip on the doorknob, enormously relieved. The last thing he'd wanted to do was confront that dog. He couldn't help it; he still felt nervous around him.

"Clay said you can come watch if you want to," Mackenzie said now, getting up from her seat.

"I'd like that." He'd hoped to finish the belt buckle in the next hour or so, but this seemed more important.

He walked outside with Mackenzie, a bit shaken to see that Wolf was not on a leash. The dog looked in their direction but didn't budge from his sitting position in front of Clay.

"Clay has him on a stay," Mackenzie explained. "Isn't he

beautiful? He's such a good dog. I can't believe they were thinking of killing him."

"This is a good test," Clay called to them as they neared him and the dog. "He wants to run to you, Mackenzie, but he knows he needs to stay."

"Can I tell him to come to me?" Mackenzie asked.

"No, honey," Clay said. "Let me be the one to release him. You just stand there, tempting him, while I give him another thirty seconds on the stay."

Bobby stood next to Mackenzie, impressed by Wolf's self-control and by the way his steady gaze was locked on Clay. The dog's body quivered with the excitement of having Mackenzie so near and yet so far.

"Okay!" Clay said finally, and Wolf bounded over to Mackenzie, who dropped her sneakers in the sand and ran off with the dog toward the water.

"Man, you have done some amazing work with that animal," Bobby said to Clay as he watched Mackenzie and Wolf play in the shallow water around the lighthouse.

"Well, it wasn't like starting from scratch," Clay said. He had his hands on his hips and his eye on the dog. "He already had all the training inside him. The trauma just knocked it out of him for a while."

"You trust him completely with Mackenzie?"

Clay sighed, shaking his head. "I don't trust him completely with anyone, yet," he said. "He's been great, but who knows what might still be misfiring in that brain of his. And I won't rest easy until after we get that neurological exam next week." He cupped his hands around his mouth. "Mackenzie!" he called. "Bring him back. Let's get to work."

Mackenzie walked back to them, Wolf trotting at her side.

"You ready to hide?" Clay asked her.

"Yup." Mackenzie sat down on the sand and pulled on her

sneakers, looking into the woods. "How far in should I go?" she asked, squinting up at Clay, the sun bright on her face.

"As deep as you feel comfortable," Clay said. "You've got your phone with you in case there's a problem?"

She stood up and nodded, jutting out her hip so that Clay could see the phone fastened to the low waistband of her shorts. She was going to be a seductress, just like her mother, Bobby thought. In another few years, she would be driving the Outer Banks boys crazy.

Clay patted his thigh and whistled, and Wolf trotted over to him. "I'll take him for a walk around the other side of the house for ten minutes or so," he said to Mackenzie. "Then I'll send him after you."

"Okay." Mackenzie ran toward the woods, quickly disappearing into the thick brush. They should be checking this kid for ticks, Bobby thought. He would mention it to Lacey.

He joined Clay and Wolf as they started walking away from the woods and pulled a cigarette from his shirt pocket. "Do you mind?" he asked, and Clay shook his head.

"Not out here," Clay said. "Plenty of fresh air." Wolf took off a few yards ahead of them, following some unseen trail in the sand. "Heel," Clay said, not harshly, not even loudly, and the dog fell into step next to him again.

Around the side of the house, Bobby stopped to light his cigarette, turning his back on the breeze to prevent the match from going out. "I don't want to smoke around Mackenzie," he said, exhaling smoke as they started walking again. He might still have a vice or two, but Mackenzie did not need to know about them. His parents had both smoked—and drank—around him, his father even giving him sips of hard liquor when he was a toddler, thinking it was funny.

Since recognizing Clay a week earlier, he had toyed with the idea of talking to him about the night they met. He thought of asking, "Do you remember meeting me years ago?" But he didn't. What would be the point?

So instead, they talked about Rani's adoption as they slowly circled the house. What an incredible nightmare that had been! He'd known that Clay and Gina had faced a multitude of obstacles when they tried to adopt Rani, but he hadn't understood how close they came to losing the little girl and how close Rani had come to losing her life because she was not able to get the heart surgery she'd needed in India.

"I'm glad it all worked out for you," Bobby said. "Rani's a lucky kid."

Clay did not look directly at him, but he smiled. "So's Mackenzie," he said, and Bobby felt tears burn his eyes at the unexpected compliment.

They returned to the edge of the woods. Wolf stood on the alert, looking from the trees to Clay and back again, apparently waiting for some sort of signal. Clay bent low, saying something to the dog that Bobby couldn't hear, before motioning toward the woods. "Go find!" Clay said.

Wolf took off into the woods, and Clay turned to Bobby as he set out after the dog. "See you in a while," he said. "With victim in tow."

Bobby nodded. "Good luck!" He watched as the woods swallowed the dog and the man, then started walking back to the house.

He was nearly to the porch when he heard the sound of tires on the gravel lane and turned to see Lacey's car pull into the parking lot. Bobby waved at her, then thought of Wolf, loose in the woods, only yards from where Lacey was emerging from her car.

"Lacey, wait!" he called, quickly changing direction from the house to the parking lot. "Don't get out of your car!"

"What?" She couldn't hear him. She was already out of the

car, reaching back inside the driver's seat for something, and an image filled his head: Wolf, streaking out of the woods and knocking Lacey to the ground, his teeth sinking into her jugular.

"Get back in the car!" he called as he got closer. "Wolf is loose!"

At those words, she quickly slipped back into the driver's seat and pulled the door shut after her.

He reached her car and got in on the passenger side, moving a grocery bag off the seat to his lap.

"What do you mean, he's loose?" she asked.

Bobby's heart was pounding all out of proportion to the reality of the situation.

"He's in the woods looking for Mackenzie."

She looked alarmed for a moment.

"She's playing victim," he said, and her face relaxed.

"You scared me there for a second." Then she laughed. "I think you overreacted just a teeny little bit," she said, smiling at him in a way that showed her dimples. "If he's in the woods looking for Mackenzie, he's working. He's not going to suddenly get my scent and come racing out of the woods after me."

He laughed himself, feeling foolish. "I guess you're right," he said. He could see beads of perspiration on her freckled cheeks and forehead. The two of them were more likely to die from the heat in the car than from the attack of a dog.

He opened the car door. "Let's go," he said. "I've got the groceries."

Still shaken, he could think of nothing to say as they walked toward the house. He looked at her from the corner of his eye. She was barefoot, wearing a sundress that fell to her ankles and that, in the way it merely hinted at the body beneath it, was sexier than a bikini might have been on her. He wanted to tell her how beautiful she was. He wanted to say he admired her, that he thought about her when he was in bed at night, that he wished he could make love to her *now,* and do it right this time.

Was she making love to Rick? There was no doubt in his mind that Rick would be far better for her than he could ever be. Money, status and security were all part of that package, not to mention good looks and hair. So he settled for putting an arm around her shoulders on the pretense of protecting her from a dog that was nowhere in sight.

36

"NICE LOCATION," BOBBY SAID, AS HE DROVE THE
VW bus into Alec and Olivia's driveway.

"It is," Lacey agreed. Her father and stepmother's big yellow house was on the sound, half in the sun, half in the shade.
From the driveway, she could see the corner of the broad deck
that took up much of the backyard. "The house I grew up in
was on the sound, too," she said.

"I remember." Bobby smiled at her. She didn't recall him
ever coming to her house, but she supposed he had dropped
her off there at one time or another after a party. She'd often
been too wasted to remember how she'd gotten home.

"I still don't get why I couldn't stay home and do my
e-mail," Mackenzie grumped from the single backseat of the
bus. Bobby had removed the other seat and the old mattress
at some time to make room for his tools and scrimshaw.

Lacey turned to look at her. "It's a beautiful day and I
thought it would be good for you to have a change of scenery," she said. "You've been in the Outer Banks for five weeks
and you haven't even seen Jockey's Ridge yet."

"Imagine that," Mackenzie said. "I haven't seen Jockey's
Ridge and I'm still alive." She'd grown snippier by the mile

as Bobby drove them to Alec and Olivia's, where he would drop them off on his way to an AA meeting. Olivia and Lacey would take the kids to the dunes at Jockey's Ridge, and Bobby would pick Lacey and Mackenzie up later.

"And you like Jack and Maggie," Lacey continued. "Remember what a good time you had bowling with them?"

"It was the highlight of my life," Mackenzie said. She was regressing. *Take the kid out of Kiss River, and she turns back into a little bitch,* Lacey thought. *She's afraid,* she reminded herself. Mackenzie had become secure at Kiss River, tucked away in that safe haven filled with people who cared about her, dogs who loved her, a baby girl who adored her. Out in the world, she was scared again, and if Lacey had learned anything this past month, it was how fear could turn this child into a surly, sullen creature.

Lacey reached back to wrap her hand around Mackenzie's skinny forearm. "It'll be okay," she said gently. "I think you'll have fun."

Mackenzie was not about to be consoled. She drew her arm away and let out a sigh of exasperation.

Bobby gave Lacey a sympathetic wink. "So," he said, opening the driver's side door, "I finally get to meet Olivia and your other siblings."

She thought of telling Bobby that he had met Olivia a couple of times the summer he was seventeen, then thought better of it. She didn't want to remember those awkward meetings herself.

Bobby got out of the bus, and Lacey joined him on the driveway, but Mackenzie made no move to leave the rear seat.

Bobby pulled the door open for her. "You can make up your mind to have a good time or not," he said to the girl. "Your choice."

Mackenzie rolled her eyes at him and stepped out of the

VW, and she lagged behind them as they walked to the front
door of the house.

Maggie was the one to open the door. She grabbed Mackenzie's arm, jumping up and down in her usual energetic,
nine-year-old fashion. "Wait till you see the hang gliders!"
she said. "And you can roll down the dunes so fast you don't
even know what's happening to you."

Mackenzie grunted an unintelligible reply.

Olivia and Jack walked into the living room, Olivia's hand
on her son's shoulder, as though he might have needed some
encouragement to come into the room. He looked every bit
as miserable as Mackenzie did, and Lacey figured he was not
thrilled at the idea of spending his Saturday afternoon with
a couple of girls.

Olivia smiled and reached her hand toward Bobby. "I'm
Olivia Simon," she said, her green eyes warm and welcoming.
"And this is Jack. And I guess you've met Maggie."

Bobby shook Olivia's hand. "Bobby Asher," he said, then
looked down at Jack, an expression of sympathy on his face.
"Not having a good day, huh, Jack?" he asked.

"It's all right," Jack mumbled. He looked at his mother.
"Can I go back upstairs now?" he asked.

"If you take Mackenzie and Maggie with you," Olivia said.

"Mom." Jack used two syllables to say the word as he gave
Olivia a pleading look from behind his glasses.

"Go on." Olivia nudged him.

Stoop shouldered, Jack led the two girls toward the stairs,
but Maggie quickly ran ahead of her brother. "Come on!" she
said to Mackenzie. "We're playing Pandora's Box."

Lacey laughed, watching them leave the room. "Well, at
least one of them is happy about this get-together," she said.

"What's Pandora's Box?" Bobby asked.

"Computer game." Olivia shook her head. "It's gorgeous

out today, and all they want to do is hole up in the study and play games."

"Mackenzie's glued to the computer, too." Lacey liked the sense of commiseration with her stepmother. "When she's not on her cell phone, anyway."

Olivia looked at Bobby. "I hear you've done a good job with your daughter," she said.

"He has," Lacey said. "He—" she looked at him and couldn't stop herself from touching his arm "—I don't know. He just seemed to know from the start what she needed."

"Thanks," he said to her, looking uncomfortable with the accolades. He glanced at his watch. "Well, I have a meeting to get to." He took a step toward the door. "What time should I pick you up?"

"We should be back by four," Olivia said.

"All right." Bobby opened the door and walked outside. "I'll see you then."

For all Mackenzie's sulkiness and all Jack's disdain at spending the afternoon with girls, the three children ran up the dunes with a wild abandon Lacey remembered very well. She used to love playing on the dunes as a kid. She'd especially loved it when her father would bring them up here, illegally, in the middle of the night. It was one of those events that had happened only a few times, but felt in her memory like a tradition.

She and Olivia panted behind the children as they climbed, not even trying to talk until they'd reached the top of the tallest dune. Lacey was disappointed that all her excercise could still leave her this breathless. By the time they'd sat down on the peak, the kids were already rolling down the steep, sandy slope, spinning on their sides, hair flying and sand sticking to their sun-screened bodies.

"How's she doing?" Olivia rested her arms on her knees

and nodded in the direction of the children. Sunglasses covered her green eyes and she wore a baseball cap, the brim putting half her face in shadow. Lacey wished she had thought to bring her own hat.

"Well—" Lacey smiled "—let's just say I have a much better understanding of what it was like for you to deal with me when I was a kid." She could see the deepening lines in Olivia's face and knew she was responsible for putting at least some of them there.

"You were struggling," Olivia said.

"And so's she," Lacey said, pulling a tube of sunblock from the pocket of her shorts. "But she's doing a lot better. She's grumpy today, but that's because she wanted to stay home and e-mail her Phoenix friends."

"Clay said she's been helping him with his dog training."

Lacey smoothed the cream on her face. "He's been great with her," she said. "And she loves it. It's really opened her up."

"It sounds like Bobby's been a help, too."

"Oh, my God, Olivia," Lacey said. "He's been fabulous with her. Can you imagine a guy just stepping up to the plate like that? Taking responsibility for a kid he never even knew about?"

"It's rare," Olivia admitted. The children were climbing up the dunes again, laughing, throwing sand. "So, are you in love with him?" she asked. "Or do you just want to sleep with him?"

Lacey stared at her, wide-eyed. *"What?"*

Olivia laughed. "Sorry. That didn't come out well, did it?" She brushed sand from her bare calves. "It's just that I saw the way you looked at him, like you couldn't get enough of him. And when you talked about him just now, it was obvious how much you respect him."

Lacey let out a long sigh. "I *am* very attracted to him," she admitted, capping the sunblock and returning it to her pocket. She could still feel the weight of Bobby's arm around her shoulders from the day before, when he'd walked her from her car to the house. She couldn't help but wonder if the blond woman would also be at the meeting he was attending this afternoon. Or maybe there was no meeting at all. Maybe he was simply getting together with the woman and didn't want to admit that to Lacey. "I'm attracted to him just like I've been attracted to every other bad boy that ever crossed my path. And I'm doing my very best to resist those feelings. I've been spending more time with Rick Tenley."

"You think Bobby's a bad boy?" Olivia asked.

Lacey shut her eyes behind her sunglasses, unsure of how much to reveal. "Do you remember when I was fourteen and thought I was pregnant and didn't have a clue who the father might be?"

Olivia nodded. "Very well," she said.

"He was one of the candidates."

"Oh." Olivia wrinkled her nose. "Ew."

"Right." She would not tell Olivia about the times she'd met Bobby that summer, one of them in the E.R. when Lacey, Bobby and Jessica had brought in a friend who had overdosed. She didn't want to poison Olivia against him completely.

"Well," Olivia sighed, "that was a long time ago, though. You've changed. He probably has, too."

"Olivia!" Lacey had to laugh. "Why are you pushing me? You know how hard I've tried to clean up my act this past year."

"I know, I know." Olivia waved her hand through the air. "And you've done a good job of it, Lace. But…it's something about the way you looked at him."

"You saw us together for less than a minute."

"I didn't know you were all that taken with Rick," Olivia said.

"He's been incredibly supportive of me. And he makes no demands on me in return."

"But what do you feel for him?"

Lacey picked up a handful of the fine sand and let it slip slowly through her fingers. "Not as much as I wish I did," she admitted.

"You know, it *is* possible to feel physically drawn to a person who is right for you, too," Olivia said. "You seem to think that, just because you had a bit of a rowdy past, you have to settle for stable and boring rather than exciting and attractive."

She couldn't believe she was hearing this advice from Olivia.

"I guess—" Olivia looked pensive "—it's just that he's Mackenzie's father and you are now her…her guardian, and it would be nice if…" She shrugged. "You know."

"I never knew you were such a romantic." Lacey laughed. "Do you know that the advice you're giving me is the exact opposite of the advice Gina gave me? She said I should go for the stable guy and that I'd eventually learn to love him."

Olivia laughed. "Ignore me," she said. "And ignore Gina. Trust your own heart, Lacey. You know what's right for you."

"No," she said, letting the sand sift through her fingers again. "Actually I have no idea."

37

LACEY COULD NOT REMEMBER A NIGHT SO HOT since moving into the keeper's house, and in spite of the sunblock she'd worn while sitting on the dunes with Olivia, her skin felt tender and sore and she could not get comfortable in bed. She heard a door creak open in the hallway and tried to pinpoint the direction the sound had come from. Mackenzie's room?

She got out of bed and opened her own door. In the light from the small lamp they kept burning in the hallway, she could see Mackenzie heading for the stairs.

"Are you all right?" Lacey asked her.

"I can't sleep," Mackenzie said. "It's too hot." She had on plaid boxer-style shorts and a cropped tank top, tight across her barely-there breasts. Her hair was tousled, probably from tossing and turning in bed, and some of it was plastered to her forehead with perspiration. She looked like a skinny little kid who didn't quite know what to do with herself.

"I have an idea," Lacey said, whispering. She didn't want to wake up the others if they had managed to fall asleep. "Let's put on our bathing suits and go for a swim."

"In the dark?" Mackenzie looked dubious. "You're kidding."

"Ssh." Lacey pressed a finger to her lips. "No, I'm not kidding. Wouldn't it feel great?"

"Maybe." Mackenzie still did not look convinced. "But I don't want to go in deep." Other than playing with Rani where the waves washed onto the shore, Mackenzie had not gone into the ocean once since arriving in Kiss River.

"Well, we'll just go in up to our knees, then," Lacey said. "Come on. It'll feel so good."

Mackenzie nodded. "All right."

"Let's get into our bathing suits," Lacey said.

"Okay," Mackenzie said, turning toward her room. "I'll be back in a minute."

Lacey returned to her own room, pulled on her green one-piece bathing suit, took two beach towels from her closet, and met Mackenzie in the hallway. They tiptoed down the stairs, but once they'd reached the first story, it became clear that they were not the only members of the house awake in the middle of the night: the light was on in the sunroom.

"It looks like Bobby's still working," Lacey said. She knew he'd spent the afternoon photographing the finished belt buckle before mailing it to the woman who had commissioned the piece.

"Let's ask him to go with us," Mackenzie said.

They walked into the sunroom, where Bobby was working on a drawing for his next piece of scrimshaw. He looked up from the table.

"Looks like you guys can't sleep, either," he said.

"We're going swimming," Mackenzie announced. "Want to come?"

"That sounds like a damn good idea." Bobby leaned back

in his chair. He rubbed his eyes as he turned out the halogen lamp on the worktable. "I'll change and join you out there."

The night was still and breathless when Lacey and Mackenzie stepped onto the porch. "Ssh," Lacey said as they started walking toward the beach. "Let's not wake up Wolf." When Lacey had walked past the dog's kennel that morning, Wolf had literally jumped onto the chain-link fencing, hanging there for a minute, all four paws somehow clutching the wire mesh. She'd stopped, frozen in her tracks, afraid he was going to actually climb over the fence to get at her. The thought of him barking and snarling at her in the darkness, when she couldn't see well enough to know that he was safe inside the enclosure, was not reassuring.

Passing the lighthouse, she could see that the ocean was as calm as the sound tonight, as if the heat had sapped its energy as well as theirs, and the quarter-moon was reflected intact in the water. There was no rush of waves to the shore, but instead, the sea gently lapped against the sand. If Mackenzie was ever to get up the courage to go into the ocean, tonight should be the night.

"Look at this, Mackenzie," she said, dropping their towels to the sand. "Have you ever seen it more beautiful?"

"It is pretty cool-looking," Mackenzie admitted as she headed for the shallow water. She marched around in a circle, kicking up sprays of seawater with her feet. "Oh, this feels so good!" she said.

Lacey walked past her until she was in the water up to her thighs. She turned around to look at Mackenzie. "Let's go in deeper," she said. "It's so calm."

Mackenzie sat down on the wet sand, letting the water lap at her legs. "I'm all right here," she said. "And *you've* got your back to the ocean. You're not supposed to do that."

"That's true," Lacey said. "But there are practically no waves tonight, so I don't think it's a problem."

She spotted Bobby walking toward the beach, shirtless, dressed in baggy shorts and carrying a towel. He looked good, and she was so pleased to have him joining them that it scared her.

"How did you like the dunes today?" she asked Mackenzie, struggling to return her attention to the girl. Mackenzie's mood had improved considerably after the visit to Jockey's Ridge.

"Awesome," Mackenzie admitted.

"How's the water?" Bobby called. He was sloshing through the ankle-deep pool of salt water surrounding the lighthouse. Mackenzie remained seated, but she twisted her spine to be able to look at him.

"Awesome!" she repeated.

"I've had baths in water colder than this." Bobby had reached the shore where Mackenzie was sitting. He tapped the top of her head. "Come on, Mack," he said, walking past her. "Let's really get wet."

He was headed toward Lacey, grinning his cockeyed grin. *Oh, God.* She had seen him in at least five different T-shirts, but she had never seen him bare chested before—at least, not since she was fourteen. He was slender, but his pectoral muscles were well-defined, and the line of hair running from his navel to where it disappeared beneath his shorts set up a longing in her. She wanted to run her finger down that trail of hair. She wanted to slip her hand beneath the waistband of his shorts. She'd fought those feelings this past year. Fought them hard every time she saw a man who might have the ability to elicit them. Now they were bubbling up inside of her like steam. *He's your test,* she reminded herself, but even as that thought entered her mind, she knew this was one test she was going to fail.

"Well, I don't know about the two of you, but I'm going to cool off," he said, then he dove into the water behind Lacey. Surfacing, he turned to look back at the two of them. "It's beautiful out here," he said. "Come on, you guys."

Lacey looked at Mackenzie. "You willing?" she asked.

Mackenzie shook her head, getting to her feet. "I'm, like, totally cooled off now," she said. "I'm going back to bed."

"Are you sure?" Lacey asked, and Mackenzie nodded. Lacey turned to wave to Bobby, who was now treading the deeper water a distance behind her. "I'm going to walk Mackenzie up to the house," she called.

"You come back, all right?" Bobby asked, and even in the faint moonlight, she could see the crooked grin.

She walked Mackenzie toward the house. Wolf heard them, and let out a few barks that she hoped would not awaken Clay or Gina or Rani. At the back door they used their towels to wipe sand from their feet.

"You don't have to come in with me," Mackenzie said.

"I need to use the bathroom before I go back out," Lacey said, but it was a lie. Her heart was pounding hard against her rib cage as she walked up the stairs next to Mackenzie. At the door to her room, she put her arm around the girl and kissed her temple. "Good night, honey," she whispered. "Hope you can sleep now."

In her room, Lacey shut the door behind her and leaned against it, eyes closed. *What are you doing?* she asked herself. *What the hell are you doing?*

She could not let herself think too much for too long. Opening her eyes, she walked over to her closet and pulled down a small overnight case from the top shelf. Inside the case, she found what she was looking for: a box of condoms.

Her fingers shook as she pulled one from the box. It was too dark to see the expiration date, and it had been a year since she'd touched this box, but right now, she didn't give a damn if it had expired or not. She wrapped the condom in her towel and left her bedroom.

On the beach, she dropped the towel on the sand, and walked into the water. Bobby was floating on his back, but he stood up in waist-deep water as she neared him. She was walking so quickly that she left a wake behind her, and as if he knew what she had in mind, he took a step toward her, opening his arms, reaching for her, pulling her against him.

"God." He breathed into her hair, and she felt his hand against the back of her head. "You look so sexy in that bathing suit."

Drawing her head away from him, she let herself look directly into his eyes for what seemed like the first time since his arrival, letting herself feel the temptation she'd been running from for the past few weeks. He ran his fingertip over her lower lip, and she turned her head slightly to let his finger slip into her mouth. It tasted like salt, and all she could think about was having him touch her body with that salty finger, having him run it over her nipples and slip it deep inside her. He drew his finger from between her lips and tilted his head to kiss her. The kiss reached someplace deep in her belly, and it flowered there into something huge and hungry, making her groan. She hung on to him to keep from being swept away by the gentle current as they kissed again, and she felt her body shaking as if she was cold.

He rubbed his hands up and down her arms. "Goose bumps," he said. "Are you chilly?"

She shook her head. "I'm anything but chilly," she said. They gazed at each other, and she saw the desire in his eyes. She lowered her hand from his shoulder, running the back of her fingers down his body, from his breastbone to the place where that line of hair disappeared beneath his shorts, and she heard him suck in his breath. Moving his hands to her hips, he pulled her gently against him so that she could feel his erection.

Letting go of him, she smiled as she lowered the straps of her bathing suit. He watched as she lowered herself into the water up to her shoulders, and as she slipped out of the suit, she felt the cool water against the heat of her body. She released her grasp on the suit, letting the sea carry it away, not caring if she lost it, and stood up again. Bobby let out his breath, reaching up with one hand to touch her breast. Shutting her eyes, she felt him circle the areola with the tip of his finger, over and over again, teasing her, before he leaned over to draw her nipple into his mouth.

She slipped her fingers under the waistband of his bathing suit. "Give me more," she said. She used the buoyancy of the water to wrap her legs around him, pressing her body hard against his erection.

"*Jesus,* Lacey." He cupped his hands beneath her thighs, helping to hold her up, and she felt his fingers inching toward that place she was longing for him to touch. Not here, though. Not right now.

"I have a condom on the beach," she said, and she leaned her head back to watch his expression turn from lustful to amused.

"You conniving little *hussy,*" he said, grinning.

The word hurt; she couldn't help it. Maybe because it felt too close to the truth. "Don't call me that, okay?" she asked him. She knew he was only teasing her, but that word had been used to describe her more times than she cared to remember.

He must have heard the pain in her voice, because a worried crease appeared between his eyebrows.

"I'm sorry," he said. He let go of her thighs, and she lowered her feet to the sand.

"It's all right." She smiled at him and took his hand. "Let's go."

They had made love on the beach twelve years earlier, but it might as well have been a lifetime ago. Lacey lay in his arms afterward, in the darkness, her legs twisted around his, her head on his chest and her heart heavy with shame. She was crying, very quietly, so that Bobby wouldn't know. Crying for the confused fourteen-year-old she'd once been. Had that night with him been the start of everything? The beginning of her downfall? That little girl had had no idea what she was doing or why she was doing it. All she knew was that she needed to be held. And Bobby had barely held her at all back then, just used her and left her. And even though he was holding her now, it wasn't enough to erase the pain she felt inside. She was still that little girl, she thought. She might be a better sexual partner than she had been back then, but she still had no idea what she was doing or why.

"Are you all right?" he asked her.

She did not want to have to explain what was moving her to tears, so she made her voice strong as she answered him. "I'm fine," she said.

A moment passed before he spoke again. "No, you're not," he said, rubbing her back.

She shut her eyes. All she wanted was to be inside the keeper's house, upstairs in her bed, asleep. She wanted to walk away from him, like she had from all the others, and yet she knew it would not be so easy this time.

"Come on," he said, gently giving her shoulders a squeeze. "Spill it."

She breathed in the scent of the sea from his skin. "Too hard," she said, her voice so muffled she doubted he could hear her. "It's too hard for me to explain."

"Is it Rick?"

"No," she said quickly. "No. Rick and I don't have that kind of relationship. At least, not yet."

"What is it then?"

She could feel him stroking her hair, playing with it. "It's my mother," she said, and his hand suddenly stopped moving.

"I don't get it," he said.

Lacey licked her lips. "A year ago, I found out that my mother had been unfaithful to my father."

"With Tom," Bobby said.

"Yes, with Tom," she said, "but with many, many, *many* other men as well." She lifted her head to look at him. "Tom doesn't know any of this," she said. "Please don't say—"

He pressed his fingers to her lips. "I won't," he said. "How did you find this out about your mother?"

"My father told me. He hadn't known about it, either, until Mary Poor, the old lighthouse keeper who used to live here, told him."

"How on earth did *she* know?"

"Because this is where my mother brought her lovers," Lacey said. "She and Mary had some sort of…I don't know. Some deal or something. Mary would let my mother bring men here. She cheated on my father over and over and over again. She was…she was a *slut*. There's no other word for it. That's why I can't get that victim's impact statement written. Every time I try to write about how terrible it was that my family lost a wife and mother, I think about what a lying, cheating, two-faced tramp she was." She winced as the words left her mouth. They felt blasphemous.

"Why didn't she ask your father for a divorce if she wanted to be with other men?"

"You're being logical, and my mother was anything but," she said. "She was an incredibly complicated person. I always *knew* she was complicated, but until a year ago, I had no idea how much. She loved my dad. I believe she truly did, with all her heart. But something drove her to have all these other guys." She squeezed her eyes closed more tightly. "And the scary thing is," she said, "I seem to have inherited the...the slut gene."

He laughed, and she could hardly blame him. "I don't think that's possible," he said.

She lifted her head to look at him. "I know it sounds ludicrous," she said, "but Bobby, I was repeating the pattern and I didn't even know that she'd been like that."

"What do you mean, you were repeating the pattern?"

She sat up and reached for her beach towel, wrapping it around her shoulders in spite of the fact that she was still very warm. She had a sudden need to cover herself from his eyes. "Until a year ago, I had one lover after another with no steady relationship," she said. "I avoided anyone who wanted to get closer. I avoided anything deep. It was so bad that my family was worried about me and I know some people—maybe a lot of people—talked about me. After I found out about my mother last summer, I made a pact with myself that I'd stop."

"Did you see a counselor?" He was looking at her, but seemed to know better than to touch her.

"Yes."

"Did she say you were a sex addict?"

"She said I didn't fit the criteria."

"Were you able to stop?" He was asking a lot of questions, but she thought she owed him the answers.

"Yes," she said. "Until tonight."

He smiled at her. "I contend that tonight is different, though," he said. "Or am I just kidding myself?"

She shook her head. "I'm sorry, Bobby," she said. "I just don't know. All I know is that I wanted you to make love to me. But it's not as simple as it was with all the other guys, because you're Mackenzie's father. I have too many other feelings for you. They complicate things."

"That's the way it's supposed to be, Lace," he said, reaching up to run his hand down her arm. "It's not supposed to be just about sex."

"You're the type I've always been drawn to," she said. "The wild sort of guy. I can spot a bad boy across a room."

"I'm really not a bad boy," he said. "Maybe once upon a time, but not now. And I'm not interested in only having sex with you."

She sighed and dropped her head, feeling defeated. "I think I need to revisit my therapist," she said.

"Not a bad idea."

Resting her cheek on her knees, she studied his face. The whites of his eyes looked luminous in the darkness. "Do you think I'm a sex addict?" she asked.

"I don't know," he said. "Are you into porn?"

"Ugh. No. Not at all."

"Are you preoccupied with sexual fantasies?"

She shook her head, amazed she was sitting here, having this conversation with him.

"Do you always feel as bad after sex as you're feeling right now?" There was a small, sad smile on his lips.

"I didn't used to," she said. "But tonight I feel...disappointed in myself. Weak."

With a sigh, Bobby sat up and looked out to sea. There was a light in the distance, a ship out there, traveling through the dark night. "I don't think you're the classic sex addict," he said, turning to look at her. "But I do think you have some things to work out."

She nodded. "That's why I've been hanging around with Rick. I'm not at all attracted to him."

Bobby laughed. "You're beautiful," he said, "but I'm afraid one of your beautiful screws is loose."

She nodded. "I know," she admitted. "But it's like…" She watched the light make its way slowly along the horizon as she struggled to gather her thoughts. "It's like you're the equivalent of my mother's lovers, and Rick is the equivalent of my father."

He said nothing, and she knew she had spoken too freely. She'd hurt him.

"I'm sorry," she said. "That sounded awful."

"It's okay," he said.

"I'm afraid of you," she admitted. "I mean, I'm afraid of how I feel around you. Of losing control, like I did tonight. I'm not afraid of Rick."

"He seems very safe." Bobby acknowledged the truth.

"I think he could be good for me," she said.

"You make him sound like cod liver oil," he said, "and when's the last time you had a swig of *that* stuff?"

"Bobby, I'm really sorry," she said again. "I feel like I used you tonight. Like I took advantage of you."

He smiled at that, then sobered. "I was going to invite you to take advantage of me any time you like, but after all you just told me, I know that's not what you need to hear."

He stood up, and she turned away as he pulled on his shorts. She looked toward the dark shoreline, wondering what had become of her own bathing suit.

"Come on." He held his hand out to her.

She got to her feet, rearranging the towel around herself before taking his hand and walking with him toward the house.

"Will we be okay?" she asked as they neared the porch. "You and me? I mean, we have to be able to get along all right, for Mackenzie's sake."

"Of course we'll be okay, Lacey," he said. "Though if you expect me to forget that tonight happened…" He shook his head. "I can't do that."

She nodded, knowing she could never ask that of him. She didn't even want to, because despite the pain it had caused her, despite her shame and disappointment, she didn't want to forget it, either.

38

FAYE PARKED THE RENTAL CAR IN FRONT OF A beautiful old Victorian-style house a few blocks from the Princeton campus. The street was lined with trees that hung so low they formed a leafy green tunnel over her head as she got out of the car, and the air was thick with the sound of cicadas. She gazed at the house. It had been carefully restored, she thought, painted a soft blue color with maroon trim, and a turret rose from the right-hand side of the second story. A porch ran the entire length of the house and curved around the side, and a swing hung on chains from the porch's high ceiling. If this was truly Freddy's house, he was doing very well for himself. And he must be married. A single man would not live in a huge house like this one. Did she have grandchildren? Faye could not see the backyard, but she imagined a swing set back there, or a tasteful wooden playground, or maybe a playhouse in keeping with the style of the main house. She'd been speaking to her son in her mind for the entire trip from San Diego to Princeton, and she was still speaking to him now: *Please, Freddy, no matter what's gone on between you and me, please let me be a part of my grandchildren's lives.*

Maybe, though, she thought suddenly, this was some sort

of student house, so close to the University. Maybe Freddy was in graduate school and lived with a bunch of other guys.

There was only one way to find out. She pressed her damp palms together, took in a breath as if she were about to jump off a high dive, and started up the slate sidewalk.

There was no doorbell, and she used a huge brass knocker shaped like the house itself. She waited nearly a minute, and was about to knock a second time when a young man—who looked nothing like Freddy—opened the door. Her guess that the house was being used by students was probably correct, and she had to quickly let go of her fantasy about grandchildren.

"Can I help you?" the man asked. He was about her height and somewhat overweight, and his smile was warm. He lifted his eyebrows, waiting for her to speak.

"I'm looking for Fred Pointer," she said.

"Oh, I'm sorry, but he's out of town for a while." The man tilted his head to the side, a look of frank curiosity on his round face. "Can I give him a message?"

"Is this where he lives?" She peered behind him, trying to see what the house looked like on the inside, and had a terrible thought: Maybe Freddy had seen her arrival from one of the upstairs windows and told his friend not to let her in.

The man nodded. "Are you from the university?" he asked.

"I'm his mother," she said, returning her gaze to him.

His jaw dropped open, but the smile never left his eyes. "Mrs. Pointer?"

"I go by Collier now," she said. "Faye Collier."

The man shook his head. "I absolutely cannot believe you're here." He stepped back from the door. "Please come in."

His response both perplexed and pleased her. "Thank you," she said as she walked into the house. The floor of the foyer was marble and the walls were painted a pale gold, but she knew that the house had not been completely restored to its former glory because welcome, cool air surrounded her. She could see into the living room, which was richly furnished with antiques, or at least, with reproductions. A baby grand piano sat in one corner. The decor did not fit any student housing she could imagine.

"My name's Christian," the man said. "Come in and have a seat." He led her into the living room, and she sat down on a red camelback sofa. In her shorts and sandals, she felt too casually dressed for the room.

"Is this Fred's house?" she asked. "I mean, does he just rent a room here, or—"

"It's his house." Christian took a seat at the other end of the sofa. "His and mine."

"Oh," she said, still struggling to make sense of the situation. "You two bought it to fix up and sell, or…" She stopped talking, suddenly understanding, and she could not seem to say another word.

"He's my partner," Christian said, an endearing mix of joy and apology in his face that made her feel an instant tenderness toward him.

She pressed her fingers to her mouth, letting the news sink in, and Christian leaned forward to study her face. "Are you okay?" he asked.

She was able to smile. "I just…I never had a clue," she said. "He was…" She'd been going to say that he'd been interested in girls as a teenager, but did she know that to be the truth? Or had he had feelings for other boys all along and had never felt able to express them to her? "I thought he liked girls when he was younger," she said.

"Well," Christian said, "technically, he's bi."

"Bi? Oh, bisexual." She shook her head, smoothing a trembling hand over her short hair. "This is a lot to take in," she said, trying to laugh.

Christian looked amused by her reaction. "Can I get you something to drink while you absorb the shock?" He started to get to his feet and she noticed his hands.

"You're wearing a wedding ring," she said.

He sat down again. "We have a civil union."

She was not sure what that meant, but she was certain it reflected a deep level of commitment between her son and this likable man. Although she had never expected to learn that Freddy was gay, the thought of him being able to commit to another person in a loving relationship pleased her. She had worried that she and Zachary might have ruined him.

"How long have you been together?" she asked.

"Five years."

A realization suddenly struck her, and she laughed. "I guess I'm your mother-in-law," she said.

"You can be," he said, but for the first time his expression grew serious. "First, though, you have to be…Fred's mother."

She felt mildly chastened and feared she deserved it. "Does he still hate me?" she asked quietly.

"I don't think he ever did," Christian said. "He just felt that you turned against his father and he wasn't able to do that."

Except for her conversations with Jim, Faye had wiped Zachary from her mind, but now she had an image of him playing catch with Freddy on the beach, fishing with him from the pier near their trailer park. Zach had been a good man at one time.

"Is he still in touch with his father?" she asked.

"Often."

"My God." She shook her head. She never even thought of Zachary in the present tense, as if he still existed.

"Listen." Christian got to his feet. "Would you like to see some pictures of Fred?"

She nodded. "Oh, yes!"

He left the room for a moment, returning with a photograph album, and he sat down close to her on the sofa.

"These are a few years old," he said apologetically as he opened the cover. "They're from our civil union ceremony."

An engraved invitation was on the first page. "This is our invitation," he said. "A friend designed it for us."

She looked at the names: Christian Tenley and Rick Pointer.

"Rick?" she asked, confused.

"He goes by Rick," Christian explained. "You know, short for Frederick. You're the first person I've ever heard call him Fred."

"Oh," she said, remembering that Freddy had told people to call him "Rick" as long ago as high school. "He never liked the name Fred."

They paged through the album. "My God, he's handsome," Faye said, and Christian laughed.

"You don't need to tell *me* that," he said.

She came to the picture she and Jim had found on the Internet: three men standing in front of the Princeton chapel. She recognized one of the men as Christian.

"Are the two of you graduate students at Princeton?" she asked.

Christian laughed. "We were at one time," he said. "But now we teach there. I teach biology, and he teaches law."

"Law!" She shook her head. She wondered if she'd been holding him back in some way, that he'd needed to escape from her to carve out his own path. "He's accomplished so much," she said with a sigh. "He didn't really need me in his life, did he?"

"Yes, he did," Christian said. "And he still does."

She turned one page of the album, then another. Freddy was smiling in every single picture. "He's happy, isn't he," she said. It was a statement rather than a question.

"Yes, except for..." Christian's voice trailed off.

"Except for what?"

Christian rested his hands on the photograph album. "He wants his father out of prison," he said. "Right now, this summer, he's on sabbatical in North Carolina, working on a book about the parole process, which is inspired, of course, by his father, who's up for parole."

"I didn't know that." Shouldn't someone have told her? She guessed she would have been contacted if she'd been easier to find. "What are the chances that Zachary—that Fred's father—will get out?" she asked.

"I don't know," he said. "All I know is that he *should* be out. He doesn't belong in prison."

"He *killed* someone," she argued.

"He's completely rehabilitated," Christian said with such conviction that she decided she would say no more.

She looked down at the album again, at Freddy's handsome smile. "When is he coming back to Princeton?" she asked.

"He comes home every other week or so," he said. "But he's staying down there at least for the summer."

"I want to see him," she said. "I'll go to North Carolina." The thought of setting foot in the state she thought she had left in her past was not pleasant, but right now, she didn't care.

"He will be so *happy* to see you, Faye," he said, using her name for the first time. "He's always regretted the way things ended between the two of you."

"Me, too," she said.

"Shall we call him and tell him you're coming?" Christian asked.

She still felt afraid to speak with him on the phone. "Let's not," she said. "Now that I know he'll want to see me, I'd rather surprise him, okay?"

"Sure." He nodded.

"Can you give me directions?" She was already reaching into her purse for her keys. She couldn't wait to call Jim to tell him everything she'd learned about her son.

"It's a long drive," Christian said. "Why don't you stay here tonight and head down tomorrow?"

She shook her head. "Now that I know where he is," she said, "I can't wait another minute to see him."

39

"HOW ABOUT PIZZA TONIGHT?" RICK ASKED.

They were floating on rafts on the water behind his cottage, as they did every once in a while. They lay on their stomachs, covered in insect repellent because it was dusk and the mosquitoes were quite literally out for blood. Lacey rested her chin on her hands so she could look at him.

"Pizza would be great," she said. "Do they deliver to your cottage?"

"They tried once, but the guy got so lost, the pizza was ice-cold by the time he found me." His cheek was against the raft, the sound of his voice muffled. "It's easier for me to just go pick it up. So as soon as we go back in the house, I'll do that."

Lacey's feet hung off the end of the raft and she kicked them gently in the water, thinking through all she wanted to say to him. That morning she'd called Judith, her old therapist, from the privacy of her bedroom. Judith had had no appointment time available, but she'd spent a good half hour with her on the phone, and Lacey had felt unleashed as she poured out everything that had happened during the past couple of months. Finally, she told her about Bobby and the night before.

"Oh, Lacey," Judith had said, "how hard that must have been for you."

Tears had sprung to Lacey's eyes. Judith was the one person who never seemed to judge her.

"He's the personification of your old self-destructive pattern," Judith said. "He's the one who started that pattern for you, back when you were fourteen, so how could you not be drawn into it again? I wish you'd come in the minute he showed up at Kiss River."

"I thought I could handle it," Lacey said.

"And you've done remarkably well," Judith commended her. "You need to give yourself a lot of credit. *Yes,* you slept with him. *Yes,* you got sucked in. But you realized what you were doing and told him it wouldn't happen again. And you called me first thing this morning for help, so let's focus on what you're doing right."

"I feel like he was my test and I failed it."

"It was more like a pop quiz," Judith said. "With all you had going on this summer, you never had a chance to study for it."

Lacey laughed, but she still had tears in her eyes.

"I have a group I'd like you to consider joining," Judith said. "It's for women like you, who've...you know, had difficult histories, maybe some self-esteem issues."

Lacey wrinkled her nose. She didn't think she could take on one more thing. "Can I get back to you on it?" she asked.

"Of course. And Lacey, the other guy you told me about?"

"Rick?"

"He sounds like he's been good for you. Like he cares about you," Judith said. "Nurture that."

So she'd driven to Rick's cottage with a plan in mind: she was going to come clean with him tonight. She'd tell him the truth about why she'd been so reluctant to get close, about her history with bad boys and her desire to have a fresh start with him. If only she would open herself up to the possibility, she could be attracted to him. She'd tell him she truly wanted someone more like him, with his intelligence and education and the stability and security he offered. Right now, when they were floating out here, relaxed and at ease with each other, seemed like the right time to talk.

"Let's not go back to the house yet," she said. "I want to talk to you."

He lifted his head from the raft to look at her. "You sound serious," he said.

"I want to explain why I've been so...cold with you. Physically I mean."

"You don't owe me any explanation," he said. "You just have a different comfort zone than I do when it comes to timing, and you—"

"Rick, *please*," she said. "This is hard enough. I want to tell you. Please let me."

He tugged her raft toward him to put his hand on the back of her neck, giving the muscles an affectionate squeeze. He was so sweet. "Okay," he said. "Go ahead." Withdrawing his arm, he clasped his hands together beneath his chin and gave her his full attention.

She would offer him the abbreviated version. She didn't want to tell him the extent to which she'd slept with men she barely knew, and she did not want to talk about her mother.

"I've always been attracted to guys who aren't very good for me," she said. "You know the ones. A little rough around the edges."

Rick nodded.

"What would happen was..." She pretended to swat a mosquito on her shoulder, trying to gather her words. "What would happen was that I would end up sleeping with them and that would be it."

He frowned. "What do you mean, that would be it?"

"I mean, there would be no real relationship. Just sex."

"Lacey." He took in a breath and blew it out again. "You don't need to tell me this. I really wish you wouldn't." His reaction surprised her. For the past month and a half, he'd listened to every thought that had come into her head. But they'd never talked about sex before. Maybe that was what was making him uncomfortable.

"You're very different from those guys I used to be attracted to," she continued.

"How so?"

"You're...well, you're very conservative," she said, hoping that didn't sound like an insult. "You don't have a single tattoo that I know of."

He smiled. "That's true."

"You've probably never done drugs in your life."

"Marijuana in my teens," he said. "And I must confess to inhaling."

"You have no pierced body parts."

He tilted his head to look at her. "The kind of guy you're attracted to sounds suspiciously like Bobby," he said.

She lowered her gaze from his, feeling the color rise to her cheeks. "It is," she admitted. "And he's been wonderful with Mackenzie, I can't deny that, but—" she shook her head "—I don't completely trust him. I don't trust guys like him. Leopards don't change their stripes."

"Leopards are spotted," he said.

"Don't make this difficult," she pleaded.

He reached out to pry her hand loose from beneath her chin and held it in the water. "You don't have to tell me all this, Lacey," he said. "It's your past."

"It was last night." She winced. Last night was not supposed to be part of this conversation.

"What do you mean?" he asked.

"I mean that I had sex with Bobby last night," she said.

He was quiet for a moment as he absorbed her words. She
waited for him to let go of her hand, but he didn't.

"It was a mistake," she said. "And it's a mistake I don't want
to make again."

"And it was last night," he said, nodding. "And last night
is your past." She smiled. "You're so amazing. You're so toler-
ant of me. So patient. You listen to everything I say. I want...
what I want is to feel..."

"You're not attracted to me because I'm too squeaky clean,"
he said, helping her out.

"And I want that to change," she said. "Not your squeaky
cleanness," she added quickly. "What I want is to *want* you."

"I don't think that's something you can make happen."

"*I* do," she insisted. She needed it to be something she
could make happen.

He smiled at the passion in her voice. "I still think we
should take it slowly," he said. "You regret sleeping with
Bobby last night. I don't want you to regret sleeping with
me tonight."

"Not tonight," she said, "but maybe soon. I just needed to
be honest with you about my feelings. About why I've been
holding back, so we're starting over with honesty. But now I
want to move forward. Okay?"

He pulled her hand deep under the water so that their rafts
were drawn together, and he kissed her. "Okay," he said.
"Now let's go inside and I'll get the pizza."

They paddled toward shore and didn't get off their rafts
until they'd reached the beach to avoid having their legs
grasped by the long water grasses. Something was not quite

right. It might have been her imagination, but she thought she felt a chill from him, despite that kiss. She was not certain how to make things better, since it was obvious that he'd wanted to end the conversation, and she needed to respect that. After all, she'd just told him that she'd slept with someone else, someone she was attracted to in a way she was not attracted to him. She could hardly expect him to welcome that news.

She followed him onto the small deck behind his cottage, where they dried off with the beach towels they'd hung over the railing. He was quiet, the silence uncomfortable and tense, but it occurred to her that there was one topic she could always get him to talk about.

"Could we work on my victim's impact statement after we eat tonight?" she asked, as they walked into the cottage. He was three steps ahead of her and he turned around.

"I thought you weren't going to write one," he said.

"I decided I need to."

"No," he said, "you don't." He put his hands on his hips and there was something in his eyes that she'd never seen there before: annoyance.

She squeezed the wet ends of her hair with her towel. "I don't blame you for being fed up with me," she said. "I know I've been going back and forth on this. But I *do* need to write it, Rick." The attorney had called her twice that afternoon, and it was clear she could not get out of it. She had to do it, and she couldn't seem to do it alone.

"You don't," he said again. He pulled his T-shirt from the back of one of the kitchen chairs and pulled it on over his head. "*Look* at you, Lacey," he said, nearly punching his arms through the sleeves as he put on the shirt. "You're in… you're in *distress*. And this whole victim's statement thing is a big part of it. You've put so much energy into hating Zach-ary Pointer that it's eating you up."

She shook her head. "It's not that I hate him," she said. "It's that he doesn't deserve—"

"I sympathize with your past," he said, interrupting her. "With the loss of your mother. With your issues with men. I sympathize with all you've gone through this summer with Mackenzie. But I'm having trouble sympathizing with you over this. By all accounts, the man's rehabilitated." He was nearly shouting now, his voice so loud the little cottage couldn't contain it, and she was glad he had no neighbors to overhear them. "And it's very obvious," he continued, "to *me* at least, that having to write this damn thing is taking a toll on you. So, I just don't get why you're putting yourself through this."

She didn't know what to say. She had never heard him raise his voice before. He was more than annoyed with her; he was *angry*. She'd thought it was safe to talk to him, that he was so generous a listener he would listen to her into the next mil-lennium, and she knew that that had been a very unfair as-sumption. She'd used him as her listening post. She'd used him all summer long.

"I think you're angry with me because of Bobby," she said. "And I understand that. I would be, too. I shouldn't have told you about last night."

"Whether you told me or not, it still happened, right?" he asked as he strode to the door. "I'm going to get the pizza."

She watched him leave, the screen door slamming shut behind him, and she bit her lip. If only she could wind back the entire evening—and the night before, while she was at it. Making love to Bobby had been wrong—for her, for Bobby, for Mackenzie. She thought of the woman she'd seen him with. The drug history. The alcoholism. The ridiculously ancient VW bus. The income that was probably punier than her own.

And yet, she found the regret very hard to hold on to.

40

LACEY CHANGED OUT OF HER WET BATHING
suit in the cottage bedroom that had, for a very short time,
belonged to Bobby. She thought she could still smell him in
there, that funny blend of sweet shampoo and pungent tobacco, but it was probably her imagination. She lay down on
the bed on top of a thin and faded bedspread that she feared
had covered the sweaty, sandy bodies of too many renters over
too many years. She hoped Rick would have cooled off by
the time he returned with the pizza. Right now, as she replayed their conversation in her mind, the last thing she felt
like doing was eating. She was an idiot. You don't tell Guy
Number Two that you just slept with Guy Number One. She
had wanted to clean the slate with Rick for a new beginning.
That had probably been unfair. She had thought only of her
needs, not his.

She must have dozed off, because the sound of knocking
seemed to be coming to her in a dream. The sound came
again, waking her up, and she felt the slightest twinge of fear
at being alone in an unlocked cottage in the middle of the
woods. Evening had turned to nighttime while she'd been
asleep, and the cottage was as dark as the outdoors.

A woman's voice called from the deck, "Hello? Fred?"

Getting off the bed, Lacey padded out of the bedroom and across the sandy linoleum floor of the dark living room. She could see a woman standing on the other side of the screen door, illuminated by the deck light, her short hair a golden color.

"Hi," Lacey said, as she neared the door. She flipped on the light switch in the kitchen so she wouldn't be a disembodied voice as she spoke to the woman. "I think you must have the wrong cottage," she said through the screen. "There's no Fred here."

The woman looked at a sheet of paper in her hand, holding it under the light. "You must be right," she said, "but I'm so turned around. It took me ages to find this place, and—"

Lacey pushed the door open. "Come in," she said. "Maybe I can help you figure out where you need to go."

The woman offered her a look of gratitude as she walked into the cottage. She appeared to be in her late forties, probably pretty under other circumstances, but right now she had that dazed, puffy-eyed look of someone who was completely lost and tired of trying to find her way.

Lacey switched on the table lamp in the living room and motioned to the woman to sit down on the old couch. "Have a seat," she said.

"Here are the directions I have." The woman held out the sheet of paper, covered with lines of neat handwriting and a hand-drawn map, complete with squiggly lines that served as waves in the sound and tiny trees dotting the woods. Lacey sat down on the end of the couch closest to the light and studied it.

"Well, it certainly looks like this is the right cottage. But you know what?" It suddenly dawned on her. "The owner is away for the summer, and I don't know his name. Maybe that's who you're looking for?"

The woman frowned. "I don't think so. I'm looking for my son, Fred Pointer."

Lacey shook her head. "I don't know—" The name suddenly sunk in, and she felt an icy chill up her spine. "Pointer?" she asked.

The woman nodded. "Do you know him? Oh, I forgot! He goes by Rick, now. I've always called him Fred, though."

Lacey pressed her hand to her throat, suddenly nauseous, wondering if she was going to throw up. The woman was beginning to look familiar to her. She could picture her face across the serving table at the women's shelter as she ladled green beans onto her plate.

She stood up. "Oh, my God."

"Are you all right?" The woman looked alarmed.

"He's been *using* me," Lacey said.

You don't need to write that victim's impact statement, Lacey. Let them go ahead without yours.

"Are you talking about Fred?" the woman asked. "About Rick?"

She couldn't answer. She felt afraid, her head spinning, as she tried to sort one thought from another.

The woman got to her feet. "You'd better sit down," she said, taking Lacey's arm. "I don't know what's got you so upset, but you look like you might pass out."

The woman nearly had to bend Lacey into a sitting position on the couch. She felt as rigid as a stick.

"I've upset you, and I'm very sorry," the woman said, sitting close to her.

Lacey turned her face to hers. "Do you recognize me?" she asked.

The woman shook her head. "I...you do remind me of

someone," she said. "But I'm afraid that woman died a long time ago."

"My mother," Lacey said. "Annie O'Neill."

It was the woman's turn to blanch, her mouth open in disbelief. "Oh, honey," she said, touching Lacey's arm. "Oh, my God. You were there, too. I remember. And I've thought of you so often. But…" She looked around the room, helplessly. "I don't understand what's going on. Why would you be here with Fred? Is it just a…coincidence?"

"Oh, no." Lacey stood up again, anger replacing the shock and nausea. She remembered the book he'd given her about forgiveness. She remembered the flowers. She remembered how he'd steer every conversation to the topic of Zachary Pointer's parole. "*Damn* him!" She picked up an empty mug from the coffee table and threw it at the wall with such force that the woman recoiled. "He's been using me all summer." She raked her hair away from her face with her fingers as she let the reality of the situation sink in. She looked at the visitor. "Are you in on this?" she asked.

"What do you mean?"

"Your husband is up for parole," Lacey said.

"My ex-husband." The woman nodded. "I learned that just today."

Lacey sat down on a lumpy old chair near the window. "Well, here's what happened," she said. "Your son showed up in my art studio one day. He never said a word about Zachary Pointer being his father. He told me his name was Rick Tenley and—"

"That's his partner's name. Christian Tenley."

Lacey stared at her. "His law partner?"

The woman shook her head. "His…his significant other."

Lacey was incredulous. "He's *gay?*"

The woman nodded, and in spite of her rage, Lacey could not stop a laugh. "Well, *that* explains a few things," she said.

"So…" The woman prompted her. "Was it just a coincidence he came to your studio?"

"No way," Lacey said. "He knew what he was doing. He started… courting me. Sending me flowers. Asking me out. And when he got close enough—not that we had sex," she added quickly. "You can tell this Christian guy that Rick's been faithful to him, if to nobody else." She thought back to their conversation that evening. It all made sense now: He had not been angry about her sleeping with Bobby. His rage had to do with her decision to write the victim's statement. "When he got close enough to me," she repeated, "I told him about my mother's death and that my family was going to fight her killer's parole. He started talking about the whole parole thing, telling me how I shouldn't fight it, how I should learn to forgive your…husband, or whatever he is to you now. I was so touched that he took such an interest in me. He was such a good listener. God, he really sucked me in!" She looked at the table in the corner, where a stack of papers rested next to his computer. "He told me he was staying here in his friend's cottage so he could have some peace and quiet to write, that he was working on a book about tax law."

"I believe he *is* working on a book," the woman said quietly, "but Christian told me it has something to do with parole."

Lacey got to her feet and walked the two steps to the table in the corner. Lifting a few of the sheets from the top of the pile of paper, she scanned them quickly. The word "parole" was everywhere on the pages. "Bastard!" She lifted the entire stack of papers in her hands and tossed them into the air, letting them fall into disorderly layers on the floor. She felt wildly out of control. She wanted to destroy something.

The woman was leaning forward, watching Lacey's tirade, with her fist pressed hard against her mouth and a deep crease between her eyebrows. Suddenly, she lowered her hand to her knees and sat up straight.

"What's your name?" she asked.

"Lacey O'Neill."

"I'm Faye Collier," the woman said. "I took back my maiden name when I divorced Zachary, and I've been estranged from my son since he was a teenager. I've had no contact with him, and I came here to try to reconnect with him. I live in California now, but I was able to find out that Fred lives in Princeton, so I—"

"Princeton?" Lacey stood riveted to the floor in the sea of papers. "He told me he lived in Chapel Hill and taught law at Duke."

"He *does* teach law," Faye said, "but it's at Princeton. I went to the address I had for him there and met Christian, who told me I could find Fred here. He doesn't know I was coming. We haven't talked in ten years, Lacey, so I don't even know him anymore. But even though I don't..." The woman blinked back tears, and Lacey could see the pain in her eyes. "Even though I don't know him, I feel like I need to apologize to you for what he's done."

Her voice was calming. Lacey sat down on the couch again, sideways, drawing her feet up and wrapping her arms around her legs.

"You're not the one who owes me an apology," she said.

They both turned at the sound of the screen door creaking open, and Rick walked into the room carrying a pizza box. It took him a moment to recognize his mother, but when he did, Lacey saw all color leave his face, and the box fell to the floor with a thud.

"Mom?"

No matter what Faye had just learned about her son, it was apparent that it didn't matter. She rose from the couch in a rush, moving toward Rick, motherhood transcending all else. And despite the fact that Rick had to know the jig was up, he opened his arms wide for her. They embraced with an intensity that Lacey couldn't watch. She rested her head on her knees, feeling intrusive, and it was a full minute before the two of them finally let go of each other.

"How did you find me?" he asked.

"Christian," Faye said.

They were both quiet for a moment, then Rick seemed to notice her. "Lacey," he said.

She lifted her head and saw that he was crying, his face red.

"I'm truly sorry," he said.

She shook her head slowly, without speaking, filled at that moment with more pity than anger.

"I lost it," he said. "I'm sorry. I just want my father to be free. He was crazy when he shot your mother. Crazy and needed help, not prison. I need to get him out. I—"

"What you need right now is time with your mother," Lacey said abruptly, standing up. "And what I need to do is go home and write my victim's impact statement. And you can bet it's going to be a good one."

She marched past the two of them, deliberately stepping on the loose pages of his book about parole, and let the screen door slam behind her as she left the cottage. She'd forgotten to get her bathing suit from the spare bedroom—the second bathing suit she had lost in as many days—but she didn't care.

It wasn't until she was sitting in her car in the dark wooded driveway that she started to cry. The windows were down, the song of the cicadas blaring in her ears, and she didn't reach for the ignition or even bother to wipe the tears from her face for a long time. She'd been taken advantage of sexually by men, too many times to count. But Rick—the one man she'd never imagined would hurt her—had used her in a way that cut right to the core.

41

NEVER, NEVER CUT GLASS WHEN YOU'RE UPSET.

Tom had told her that a dozen times and yet Lacey needed to lose herself in something, and working on a stained glass project had always been her release. But she was making a shambles of things in the sunroom. She cut pieces too big or too small. She cracked one of the most expensive pieces of glass she owned, and got a sliver of glass caught in her forearm where she rested it on the table.

She'd hoped that the work might drive the previous night's incident at Rick's cottage from her mind, but that did not seem possible. When she'd arrived home the night before, she'd found Gina, Clay and Bobby in the living room, watching a movie on the VCR, and for once she was glad that Mackenzie preferred the company of her computer to that of the adults in the house, because she'd needed to fall apart and didn't want to do it in front of her.

She'd been calmer than she'd expected to be, sitting on the sofa as she simply told them the facts, trying not to embellish them with her emotions. Clay, though, was livid.

"He hung around this house like he thought he belonged here, manipulating all of us," he'd said. He was on his feet, pacing, the way their father did when he was upset over something. "Give me the directions to his cottage, Lacey," he said. "I'm going over there."

It took both her and Gina to calm him down. "He's with his mother right now," Lacey said. "It's not the time."

"Did he sleep with you?" Clay asked with such righteous fury that she loved him for it. Especially since he'd asked if Rick had slept with her rather than the question that would be, to her ears, at least, more accusatory: "Did you sleep with him?" She assured him that she had not. She didn't bother to tell them that he was gay.

Bobby said very little while she spoke, and she avoided his eyes as much as she could, afraid that something in her face might give away their altered relationship to Gina and Clay.

Later, when she was alone in the kitchen pouring herself a glass of lemonade, Bobby came into the room and put his arms around her. She waited for him to mock her, however gently. After all, she'd told him that she was afraid of him, but not of Rick. That she thought Rick would be good for her. Bobby would be perfectly justified in taunting her with her words. But he said nothing of the sort.

"I'm sorry" was all he said, before squeezing her shoulders and leaving the room, and she had the feeling that he meant it from his soul.

She stopped in Mackenzie's room on her way to bed to tell her good-night, then climbed into her own bed with her notepad. She'd planned to pour her fury into the victim's impact statement, only to find that the words still eluded her. If she couldn't write the statement when she had her anger to propel her, she was never going to be able to write it. She gave up after ten minutes, then tried to sleep, but the evening at Rick's played over and over in her mind. Finally, she got up and knocked on Bobby's door. He was still awake, and when he opened his door his expression was one of frank curiosity at finding her there.

"I was wondering if you had anything to help me sleep?" she asked, speaking quickly to prevent him from thinking she might be there for something more.

He shook his head. "Sorry, Lace," he said. "The only drug I take these days is aspirin."

She'd nodded and took a step out of his room.

"Lacey?"

She turned to look at him.

"Do you want to talk?"

She shook her head. "Thanks," she said. "Not now." Talking to Bobby, in his room, in the middle of the night, when she was feeling so fragile, could only lead to trouble. Plus, she felt a strong need to be by herself. She was the only person she knew she could trust—and, occasionally, even she was suspect.

Lacey finally managed to score a piece of glass cleanly and was congratulating herself when she heard the screen door creak open and closed. In a moment, Mackenzie was in the doorway of the sunroom, Sasha next to her. Lacey knew she'd been outside, walking around the perimeter of the house with the dog, trying to find the best reception for her cell phone. It was not working well inside the house today.

"Did you get your phone to work?" Lacey asked, slipping her safety glasses from her face to the top of her head.

Mackenzie nodded. "I talked to everyone," she said.

"That must have felt good."

Mackenzie sat down at the second worktable in the chair Bobby usually used and began to swivel it back and forth. "I think they're all forgetting about me," she said.

"No," Lacey said with sympathy. Sasha walked over to her chair and she ran her hand over the dog's shiny black fur.

"They might be getting involved in activities you're not a part of, but they're never going to forget about you."

Mackenzie sighed.

"You're missing them, huh?" Lacey asked.

"That's the weird thing," she said. "I feel like I *should* be missing them, but I don't so much anymore." Mackenzie ran her fingertip over a small piece of ivory lying on the worktable. "Like, I talked to Sherry about Wolf and everything, but she doesn't even like dogs, so she wasn't really interested. And all Marissa talks about is this boy I don't even know at her swim club, and she doesn't get why I'd want to hide in the woods waiting for a dog to find me. And the most annoying part is she keeps saying 'tight.'"

"Tight?"

"Yeah, it's like this new word that's supposed to be cool or something. The boy she likes is *tight*. She thinks the new store at the mall is *tight*. Doesn't that sound stupid?"

Lacey had to laugh, the warmth she felt for Mackenzie pushing the venom from her heart. "You are so cute, you know that?" she asked.

Mackenzie nodded, smiling herself. "Yeah," she said. She peered out the windows, then leaned forward, her elbows resting on the worktable as she pressed her cheek against the glass. "You can't see the kennel from here," she said.

"No."

"Do you know when Clay's coming home?" Mackenzie sat down again.

Lacey shook her head. "I don't know." As they often did on the weekends, Gina and Clay had taken Rani to Shorty's Grill to entertain Henry and Walter and the other regulars. She wasn't sure where Bobby was, but she guessed he was at a meeting. "Were you supposed to do some training with Clay today?"

"No, but Wolf's bone is stuck behind his doghouse and he's going crazy trying to get it out," Mackenzie said. "I went over to the kennel when I was out there and he was, like, *crying* trying to get at it. I felt so bad for him."

"He'll be okay," Lacey said. She gave Sasha a dismissive pat on the head, and, with a heavy sigh, the dog lay down next to her worktable.

"Don't you think I could go in and get it for him?" Mackenzie asked. "He loves me."

"Clay said no one should go into his kennel except him."

"That was a while ago, though," Mackenzie protested. "Wolf *loves* me now."

"Yes, he does." Lacey smiled. "But you know what Clay said."

"Well," Mackenzie stood up. "Maybe I can use a stick or something to reach through the fence and try to get the bone unstuck for him."

"That's a good idea," Lacey said. "Just be careful."

The phone rang the moment Mackenzie left the room, and Lacey checked the caller ID display: Rick, for the third time that morning. She was not ready to talk to him, and was not sure she ever would be. She lowered her glasses over her eyes and thought once more about the statement she needed to write. What if she simply avoided any discussion of her mother's character? All the other statements would be addressing how wonderful and generous Saint Anne had been. But none of them could describe her murder with the sort of detail Lacey could provide. It seemed like a brilliant idea and she wondered why she hadn't thought of it before. She would write the facts about what had happened that evening in the battered women's shelter. She didn't need to pass judgment on her mother's morality.

She was setting her glass cutter to a piece of cobalt glass

when she heard a scream that made Sasha spring to his feet. *Mackenzie.* Releasing the glass cutter, she jumped out of her chair and ran from the room, tearing off her glasses and dropping them to the floor. The screams were unceasing. She pictured Wolf, having somehow climbed over the six-foot-high kennel fence, chasing Mackenzie around the yard. But that was not the scene that greeted her when she pushed open the screen door and ran onto the porch.

Mackenzie was lying on the ground inside the kennel, the German shepherd standing above her, snarling and growling and tearing at her clothing or—God forbid—her flesh. From this distance, Lacey could not tell which. The dog shook his head as though he was trying to kill whatever prey he had caught in his mouth. Mackenzie's screams pierced the air, and Lacey heard the terror in them.

"I'm coming!" Lacey called as she jumped off the porch and raced toward the kennel, sand flying behind her. Sasha was far ahead of her, barking and growling himself. Lacey waved her arms in the air. "Get off her! Get off her!" she screamed. She could see blood on Mackenzie's leg, blood on the sand. *God, please let her be all right!*

She reached the kennel and pounded her fists against the fence. "Get away from her!" But the dog might have been deaf for all the attention he paid her. Lacey watched him take a mouthful of Mackenzie's long hair and lift her head a few inches from the ground, dragging her over the sand while the girl tried to beat him away with her fists. He was going to kill her, Lacey thought, but she wasn't going to let that happen.

She pulled open the wire door of the enclosure and ran inside, heading toward the opposite end of the kennel, knowing that Wolf would turn on her in a heartbeat. Sasha followed her in, but gentle dog that he was, he only stood by helplessly, barking in distress. Sure enough Wolf let go of Mackenzie's hair and turned to glare at Lacey, his lips curled up, every inch of his body letting her know that she was his next victim. "Get out, Mackenzie!" she called as the girl struggled to her knees. "Get out!"

Blood dripping down her leg, Mackenzie half hobbled, half crawled, toward the exit. Mackenzie forgotten, Wolf ran toward Lacey, his teeth huge, sharp daggers in his mouth, and although she raised her arms high above her head, trying to appear to be bigger than she was, and although she shouted and screamed in an attempt to frighten him away from her, he didn't hesitate. She pressed her back against the chain-link fence and watched him open his jaws wide as he dived for her thigh. Excruciating pain shot through her leg as the dog dug his teeth deep into her muscle and dragged her to the ground, and her only prayer was that someone would arrive soon to help Mackenzie, because she would not be able to do it herself. She was going to die.

42

SOMEONE WAS HOLDING HER HAND. WHISPERING her name. Lacey struggled to lift her eyelids, then quickly let them fall shut again. The light in the room was too bright.

"That's it, Lacey," a male voice said. "Come on out of it."

She forced her eyes open and saw Tom, his wiry blond ponytail hanging over his shoulder, his face close to hers, and she thought she must be lying on the floor of the studio she shared with him.

He smiled. "You're back, sugar," he said. There were tears in his eyes. She felt his hand on her head, smoothing her hair.

Then she remembered Wolf's mouth coming at her. She couldn't see the dog's face at all; he was one gigantic cavern filled with teeth, and the memory made her wince. She heard a whimper and it took her a few seconds to realize that she was the person producing it.

"Is this...studio?" she whispered to Tom.

"The studio? Oh, no, baby. No." He smoothed his big rough hand over her temple and onto her hair again. She'd known Tom was her father for more than a decade, but she had never felt his fatherliness more than at that moment, when he was stroking her hair and blinking back tears. "You're in the hospital, honey," he said. "That dog gave you a couple of bites."

It had been more than a couple, she was certain of that. Her body ached and burned. It felt as though someone was twisting a vise around her limbs tight enough to break the skin. "Pain," she whispered.

He nodded. "I'll call the nurse." He started to stand up, but she reached out to grab him, catching the shoulder of his T-shirt in her right hand.

"Don't go," she said, frightened. Her head was so foggy. If he left, she was afraid she would slip back into the strange dark world from which she'd just emerged.

"Okay," he said, sitting down again.

She remembered Mackenzie, remembered the blood on the sand.

"Mackenzie?" she asked. She felt unable to produce more than one or two words at a time.

"You saved her life." Tom grinned. "Baby, you were so brave. I always knew you were a remarkable kid, but I didn't know you had that in you. I couldn't have done it."

Not even for me? she wanted to ask him, but it was too many words, and she knew the answer, anyway. He would have done it. He would do anything for her.

"There was blood...sand." She struggled to get the words out, to make her mind and her mouth work together. "Mackenzie."

"She got a good bite on her leg," Tom said, "and a few bruises. But she didn't even have to spend the night in the hospital."

"Do I?" she asked, and he grinned at her again.

"You've already been here a couple of days, sugar," he said. "We've all been taking turns sitting with you—Alec and

Olivia and Gina and Clay and Bobby—and I'm the lucky one who gets to be here when you wake up."

"Couple days?" she asked. How had she lost a couple of days?

"They think you must have hit your head on a corner of the doghouse or something," Tom said. "Knocked yourself out. Which maybe was for the best, Lacey, so you didn't have to know what that frigging dog was doing to you."

That explained the knifelike pain in the back of her head.

"He didn't kill me," she said, amazed and a little euphoric.

"He would have if Bobby hadn't gotten home when he did," Tom said.

"How many bites...really?" she asked.

Tom looked hesitant, then obviously decided on the truth. "Nine," he said. "Nine really good ones, and a few less serious."

"My legs?" Her legs were on fire, and Tom nodded.

"Your legs. Your butt. Your left arm. But your beautiful face is just fine."

"Put the dog down?" she asked.

"It's already been done," Tom said bluntly. "They did an autopsy. The dog had some...I don't know...some kind of epilepsy or something. Your dad's kicking himself for not pulling strings to get him that neurological exam sooner. They might have been able to help him, then."

She shut her eyes at that news. "Poor dog," she said.

"You know what?" It was clear that Tom wanted to change the subject.

She looked at him, too tired to ask "What?"

"I think Bobby has a thing for you," he said. "A big thing. He's practically been living here since they brought you in."

She tried to smile, but was not sure she succeeded.

"Is it mutual?" Tom asked.

"I'm…" She licked her lips. They were very dry. "I'm fighting it," she said.

"Why, sugar?"

"Lot of reasons," she said. She wanted to tell him about Bobby handing a wad of bills to the skinny blonde in the parking lot, but knew she could not possibly string all those words together.

"Hey." The voice came from somewhere else in the room, and Lacey turned her head to see her father standing in the doorway, a smile on his face.

"Hey, Alec," Tom said, standing up and taking a few steps away from the bed to make room for the man who was, in all ways but one, her father.

Her father leaned over to kiss her cheek. "I am so glad to see you awake," he said. "You had all of us pretty shaken up."

Tom rested his hand on Alec's shoulder. "I'll take off now," he said, and Lacey was quite certain he didn't want to go, but felt he needed to give her some time alone with her father.

"I'm glad you were here," her father said to Tom, and the two men shook hands.

"Bye, Tom," she said, touched by the careful cordiality between the two of them. She knew how hard the last decade had been for them both, how they had each struggled with their own demons, doing their best not to put her in the middle. And she knew that each man's love for her mother had been pure, even if Annie's love for them had been tainted by her lies.

Her father didn't immediately sit down in the chair Tom had vacated. Instead, he lifted the covers from her legs and checked her bandages, then did the same to her left arm. She shut her eyes, not yet ready to see her body.

"You're going to have some scars, honey, but the docs don't think you'll loose any functioning, and that's great news. You were very lucky. The one bite came too close for comfort to your femoral artery. Speaking of which, how's the pain?"

"Sucks," she said, and he smiled.

He touched the bag hanging on the pole next to her bed, studying whatever it said on the label. "I'll go talk to the nurse and see what she can do for you," he said.

"Not yet." She was afraid the drugs would knock her out, and she wasn't yet ready to slip away again. If she was in pain, at least she knew she was alive.

"Tom said you put Wolf down," she said.

Alec shook his head, finally sitting down in the chair next to her bed. "I didn't have to," he said. "Bobby took care of that."

"What do you mean?"

"Tom didn't tell you?"

She struggled to remember the conversation with Tom, but it was already muddy in her mind. "Tell me what?" she asked.

"Bobby pulled into the Kiss River parking lot while Wolf was attacking you," her father said. "He ran into the kennel, grabbed the dog by the collar, lifted him up, and threw him against the doghouse. The dog's neck was broken. He died instantly."

"Oh, my God." Lacey covered her mouth with her hand. "I'd be dead if he didn't get there when he did."

"I don't want to think about it," her father said, "but I admit I'm pretty grateful to him. *You're* the local hero, though. You saved Mackenzie's life, running into the kennel like you did. There's no doubt about that."

"It's the kind of thing Mom would have done, huh," she said.

He leaned away from the bed, folding his arms across his chest. "Your Mom wasn't either all good or all evil, Lacey," he said. "You've tried to get rid of her good qualities along with the bad. Ever since the day she died, you've scrutinized every move you made to see how it compared to what your mother would have done. First, you tried to be Saint Lacey. Then when you found out about...her indiscretions, you tried to be as unlike her as you could be."

"I know," she whispered.

Her father leaned forward, his faded blue eyes filled with love for her. "This is your second chance, Lace," he said. "Forget about what your mother would or wouldn't have done in a given situation. All anyone wants from you is to just be Lacey."

43

THE DRUGS HAD HER FLOATING IN AND OUT OF consciousness, and the in-between stage was filled with nightmare images of Wolf and a variety of nonsensical hallucinations. Late that night, when the lights were low in her hospital room and the pain had shifted from viselike to a grueling, fiery ache, she thought she saw a nun sitting in the chair next to her bed. Through her half-opened eyes, she could see white and black cloth, wavy and out of focus.

"Hello, beautiful."

She knew the voice, and it did not belong to a nun.

"Bobby?"

"You recognized me even in these duds?" he asked with a laugh.

Opening her eyes wider and struggling to clear her head, she saw that he was wearing a tuxedo. Black tie, red cummerbund.

"What are you—" She tried to raise her head, but winced at the pain. "Where are you going? Why are you dressed up?"

"I rented it," he said. "Do you know how hard it is to rent a tux in the Outer Banks in August?"

She wondered if she was hallucinating the entire conversation. "I don't get it," she said.

"I wanted to see if you'd like me any better if I looked straight-arrow. You know, if I lose the bad boy image." He turned his head to the side and pointed to his earlobe. "See?" he said. "I even took my earring out."

She laughed, her first laugh all day, and it hurt all the way to her toes. "Can you...you know..." She made a circling motion with her hand, but could not think of the word. "Could you wind up my bed so I can see you better?"

He moved to the end of her bed and turned the crank until she was nearly in a sitting position. He looked at her. "You okay?"

"Now turn on the light," she said, shifting a bit on the bed. Sitting up made her very aware that Wolf had made mincemeat of her buttocks. "It's too dark in here," she added. "I thought you were a nun."

He laughed as he turned on the light, then he stood next to the bed so she could get a good look at him. His hands were on his hips, the cockeyed grin on his face. He was gorgeous in his jeans and tattoo and earring, and he was just as gorgeous now. She smiled. "You could wear a wedding gown and you'd still look like a bad boy," she said.

"Well, *that's* a repellent image," he said. "Are you saying I went to all this trouble for nothing?"

"It was sweet of you," she said.

His expression sobered. "How're you feeling, Lace?" he asked.

She hesitated, trying to find both a comfortable position on the bed as well as the words she needed to say what she was thinking.

"Something's bothering me," she said.

"Want me to get the nurse?"

"No, that's not what I mean." She looked him squarely in the eye. "I saw you with that woman a few times," she said, "and I…I just need to know…you gave her…" She winced as a fresh wave of pain coursed through her head.

He sat down in the chair next to her bed. "I think your pain meds might be doing something to your brain," he said.

"Please don't do that," she pleaded. "Don't pretend that you don't know what I'm talking about."

"Lacey…help me out, okay? What did you see me give her?"

"Shh!" she whispered. He was talking too loud, his voice a jackhammer in her head.

"Babe." He rested his palm against her forehead. "I told you. That woman is just a friend."

"What's her name?"

She saw the hesitancy in his face as he leaned forward, resting his elbows on his knees. He had a five-o'clock shadow, and she could see the red veins in his eyes and knew that he had had a rough couple of days himself.

"I…" he began, then stopped. "I'll tell you, Lace. It's only fair that I do, but you have to keep this between us, all right?"

She said nothing, hoping he was not going to hand her another cock-and-bull story.

"Her name is Elise," he said. "She's my cousin."

"Your *cousin?*"

He nodded. "Years ago, I got her hooked on crack and booze," he continued. "She discovered heroin all on her own. She started turning tricks to feed her habit. She got in with some bad people—some *really* bad people. I was helping her get clean, but her pimp and her dealers were after her and they were not small-time players. She was in serious danger. So I hid her with some friends, because I knew my house would be one of the first places they looked for her. When you called and I decided to come here, it seemed perfect. She had old friends here, in Kitty Hawk. So she's been staying with them, but I have to keep in close touch with her because she's still… fragile. She could slip any minute. Worse, those guys could find her. I don't know what they'd do to her if they did."

She wasn't sure if the relief she felt was from his explanation or from the drugs, but for the second time that day, that odd sense of euphoria came over her.

"Do you believe me?" he asked.

She nodded. "Yes," she said, and she meant it.

He lowered the metal railing on the side of her bed and took her hand, holding it in both of his. "I don't think I've ever been as scared or as furious as I was when I saw that dog tearing into you," he said. "You weren't moving. I thought you were dead, Lace."

"Dad told me you killed the dog," she said.

"I did, and I have no regrets about it," he said. "Does that bother you?"

Under other circumstances, it would have bothered her a great deal. But not this dog. Not now. "No," she said.

"Mackenzie needs to see you," he said. "She's pretty sore, still, and I persuaded her to wait until tomorrow, but she's terrified you might die, and no matter how many times I tell her you're going to be all right, she doesn't believe it."

"Oh." Lacey frowned, knowing how empty those words must sound to Mackenzie. "People told her that her mother was going to be all right, too," she said.

Bobby pressed her hand between his. "Do you remember," he said, "when I first got here, you and I had a talk about relationships, and you said that you had a romantic notion that you could find someone you'd love so much you'd lay down your life for that person?"

She nodded.

"I was thinking about that the past few days." He smiled. "I'm willing to bet you never expected that someone to come in the form of a child."

Her eyes filled with tears. "No," she said. "I didn't."

He stood up and leaned over to kiss her forehead. "Get some sleep, babe," he said. He moved to the end of the bed to crank the mattress flat again. "I'll be back in the morning."

He walked toward the door, in his tuxedo and his shiny black shoes, and the whole getup touched someplace deep in her heart.

"Bobby?" she said softly.

He turned around to look at her.

"I would have done the same for you," she said.

Sometime the next day, the tall, slender blond woman herself appeared in Lacey's hospital room. She sat down in the chair next to the bed, and for a groggy moment, Lacey thought she was a vision.

"I'm Elise," the woman said. "I'm sorry you got so chewed up by that dog."

This close, Lacey could see the woman's hollow-eyed look. Her hair was bleached and frayed, like the bristles of a broom. Her tank top fell too low, and her ribs were clearly visible beneath the skin of her chest.

"Thank you." Lacey was not certain what else to say. The pain was even worse than it had been the day before.

"Bobby asked me to come see you," Elise said. Her voice was husky from too many cigarettes. "You know. Explain who I am and all."

"His cousin," Lacey said.

Elise nodded.

"He said he got you hooked," Lacey said.

Elise smiled and Lacey saw the prettiness hiding inside

the haggard face. "He blames himself, but I would've gotten hooked all on my own. I didn't really need his help."

"He said you've gotten straightened out, though," Lacey said. Her mouth was dry and it hurt to swallow. "That's good."

Elise let out a sound, half laugh, half snort. "I'm straight now," she said, "but sometimes I think it would be easier just to go back. I'd get beat up for sure, but then I could get high again." She looked dreamy, her expression one of longing, and only then did Lacey notice the tracks on her skinny arms. "Bobby thinks my life was shit," Elise continued, "but it wasn't all that bad."

Lacey wanted to tell the woman she was doing the right thing by getting away from a life on the streets, but the words would require more strength than she had. Instead, she put her energy into shifting in the bed, struggling to find a position that might relieve some of the pain in her legs.

"He's in love with you, in case you don't know it," Elise said. "I mean, every time I talk to him, it's like, 'You doing okay, Elise? You clean? Do you need anything?' and then he goes off on you."

Lacey tried to smile. "Thank you for telling me that," she said. "And for coming here."

Elise stood up, then looked down at Lacey, studying her hard for a moment. "You're in a shitload of pain, aren't you," she said.

Lacey was barely able to nod.

"They'll give you more if you ask for it." Elise nodded toward the I.V. pole from which bags of liquid were slowly emptying into Lacey's veins. "Enjoy them while you can get them," Elise said. "I'd trade places with you right now in a heartbeat."

44

RICK SENT AN ENORMOUS ARRANGEMENT OF flowers to the hospital. He was good with flowers. Ordinarily, they could mend any problem. In this case, though, he knew they would not be enough. Still, he sent them. Even if Lacey had not been hurt by that dog, he would have sent them to her, maybe every day for the rest of her life. He owed that to her, and more.

It was Clay who told him what had happened. Rick had called the keeper's house for the fourth or fifth time, hoping Lacey would finally pick up the phone and let him apologize, but it was Clay who answered and who chewed him out. Clay told him about Lacey being attacked by the dog, and even though Rick could not possibly be responsible for that horrific event, he felt guilty about it.

"She's really a fine person," he told Clay. "She didn't deserve that. And she didn't deserve what I did to her, either."

"I hope your father stays in prison for the rest of his life," Clay said, and hung up on him.

Rick didn't give up. He called again two days later, wishing that Gina would be the one to answer the phone, but once again, he got Clay on the line. He asked if he could visit

Lacey in the hospital and Clay told him that he was the last person Lacey wanted to see. Again, Clay hung up on him, slamming the phone down so hard, Rick's ear hurt for minutes afterward.

"She won't see me," he'd told his mother after getting off the phone. It was the fourth day of her visit with him.

"You can't possibly blame her," his mother had said. "You hurt that entire family by trying to save your own."

He shook his head. "I feel terrible for Lacey," he said. "At first she really had no romantic interest in me, and that made it so easy. I didn't want to…you know, I wasn't really sure what I was going to do if she wanted more from me. But that last night, she was starting to talk serious and…I guess it's best the truth came out. Just not best for Dad."

There were so many other ways, better ways, he could have handled his desire to get his father released. Sometimes, he realized, when you were caught up in your emotions, you could do really insane things, and that's what he'd done with Lacey. When he'd learned that his father was up for parole, he knew Annie O'Neill's family would be asked to write victim's statements, and that Lacey's would be most important. He remembered her from that horrible Christmas Eve in the battered women's shelter. He knew she had been close to him in age and he thought that he could meet her, befriend her without revealing his identity and influence her through seduction. Women had always been attracted to him, despite his disinterest in them. He was ordinarily an honest man, but the deceit seemed worth it in this case. Lacey, though, had turned out to be a different sort of person than he'd anticipated. He could have appealed to her sense of justice, but he didn't know that going in, and by the time he realized how good she was, how fair-minded, it was too late. He was already well into the game.

Now, though, he feared his plan had backfired. Her statement would be fueled by her anger at him. He'd hurt his father more than he'd helped him.

The only good thing about the week was having his mother with him. What a way to start things off, though, with her learning that her son was a conniving, manipulative scam artist. They'd talked all night long after Lacey left, never mentioning his father, both of them carefully avoiding the topic. Instead, they caught up on each other's lives. He was impressed by her: she'd made a name for herself, writing an acclaimed book on pain control. She'd gotten a good education, and she was beautiful. His father had held her back, he thought. Not intentionally. Not in any mean-spirited way. But his father had wanted to live in Manteo, and there had been little opportunity for her to blossom there. He didn't like thinking about the fact that she had done better without her husband than she had with him, but it was probably the truth.

His father had been a simple man, content to sell boogie boards in a shop that catered to tourists, to live in a little village where he knew most of the natives by name and where the simplicity of his life had enabled him to keep his mental illness in check. Rick had always felt that his and his mother's escape to the shelter had thrown his father's carefully maintained stability out of balance, and he'd suffered a meltdown.

He'd been a loving father. He'd never said those words, "I love you," to Rick, although he said them all the time now. But it didn't matter. His father had taken him on fishing expeditions and never missed a Little League game, and Rick had known how much he was treasured.

He told his mother about getting his law degree and how much he enjoyed teaching. He told her he'd known he was gay from the time he was in elementary school. And he told her about Christian.

"Did he know what you were truly doing here?" she asked.

"No," he said, once again tapping into his overabundant supply of guilt. "He would have talked me out of it. He'd tell me I was acting irrationally, and I already knew that. I didn't want to hear him reinforce it."

Whatever his mother's feelings about his behavior toward Lacey, that first night she'd been careful to keep them to herself, as if she knew they needed to avoid potentially combustible topics as they got to know each other again.

It wasn't until their second evening together, when they were preparing dinner in the tiny kitchen of his cottage, that they began to work their way into the difficult topic of his father.

"What is he like?" she asked without even identifying who she was talking about, but he didn't need to ask her for clarification.

He was washing lettuce in the sink, and he kept his eyes on the task. "He's contrite," he said. "He's been contrite for many years. He was sick, Mom." He looked over to where she was chopping onions for the chili. "If he could have changed what happened, he would have. He'd give up his own life to change it."

She said nothing, the chopping and the running water the only sounds in the kitchen.

"I think he needed to live in Manteo," he said. "He knew he wasn't well. He told me once that when he had any change of routine, or when he traveled anywhere, even to Elizabeth City, he started feeling scared and out of control."

"I didn't know that," she said. "I mean, I knew it was hard to get him out of Manteo, but I just thought he was being stubborn."

He waited a moment before he spoke again. "Would you like to see him?" he asked.

"No," she said quickly. "Whether he's really changed for the better or not is no longer my business. He's a part of my past, Fred." Her hands stopped chopping the onions and she looked at him. "I know he's your present, though. And your future. I understand that, but I don't want or need any part of him."

He nodded, disappointed but not surprised. If she saw his father, she would know how dramatically he had changed. But it was too much to ask of her, just as it had been too much to ask of Lacey to try to forgive the man who had wreaked such havoc on her life.

"Are you still angry with me for going to the shelter that night?" his mother asked.

Rick shook the lettuce leaves dry and began tearing them into pieces over the salad bowl. "I know you thought you had to," he said. "I know you had information from the neighbors that led you to believe we were in real danger. I just don't think he would have flipped out the way he did if we hadn't left."

His mother scraped the chopped onions from the cutting board into the pot on the stove. "I guess that's something we'll never know," she said.

By the time he drove his mother to the airport in Norfolk, he felt nearly at peace. He may have harmed his father's chances at parole, and he was certain he would never be given the opportunity to truly apologize to Lacey, but there was one thing of which he was certain: he was never going to lose his mother again. Nothing he did would ever drive her away.

45

"SO," BOBBY SAID AS MACKENZIE CLIMBED INTO his VW bus in front of the school, "how was it?"

"Awesome!" Mackenzie said, hugging her backpack to her chest. She had a glow in her eyes he hadn't seen before. She waved to a couple of girls, dressed as inappropriately as she was in their too-low shorts and too-high tops, and the girls waved back at her. One of them shouted to Mackenzie, "Call me!"

"Looks like you made some friends," he said as he pulled away from the curb.

"Could I ask them over?" She was still waving to the girls, her neck craned to look back at them. "They want to see the keeper's house."

"Sure," he said with a smile. Suddenly the keeper's house was an asset rather than a liability.

"They have the cutest boys here," she said. "And I heard one of them talking to another one about me. He said, 'That new girl is hot.'"

Oh, God, Bobby thought. It was starting already. Lacey would have to have the sex talk with her, and probably very soon.

"And I remembered not to say anything about how much

better Phoenix is," she said. "But people asked me about it. And there's another girl who used to live there."

"How are your classes?" he asked.

"Awesome," she said. "The teachers are really nice. Except one, who's a total loser." She wrinkled her nose.

"There's always got to be one of those," he said. "It's a requirement."

She reached for her cell phone, then remembered it was not attached to her waistband and let out a dramatic groan. "I can't *stand* that they won't let us have cell phones in school," she said.

"It makes sense, though, don't you think?"

"But what if there's, like, a disaster or something and I needed to call you or Lacey?"

He smiled, guessing this was the argument the kids were using to get the authorities to change the rule. "I suppose it would be like in the old days," he said. "We'd just have to sit around and worry about you until we found out you were safe."

"Half the boys have earrings," she said, then she looked at her watch. "Clay's got a new dog coming at four. It's an eight-month-old Border collie. I can't wait to meet her."

From boys to dogs, all in one breath. Eleven-year-old girls were complex little creatures.

"Do you have homework?" he asked, amazed to hear the parental words coming out of his mouth. He glanced at her bulging backpack. "That backpack looks pretty full."

"I have a little," she said. "I'll do it after dinner, okay? First I want to see Lacey and tell her everything about today. Then I'll meet the dog. Then we'll eat. Then I'll do some homework. Then I'll read Rani a bedtime story. Then I'll do some more homework."

She looked so pleased with herself that he wanted to stop the car and pull her over for a hug.

"And when are you going to fit in all the phone calls you have to make?" he teased her.

She rolled her eyes at him. "You are, like, getting to be such a dad, with lame dad humor and everything."

He wondered how she knew about "dad humor," having never had a dad before.

"You don't have to drive me tomorrow," she said. "Everyone takes the bus. It's cool." She'd insisted he drive her that morning, anxious about taking the school bus, uncomfortable in her newness.

She chattered nearly nonstop all the way to Kiss River, and when he pulled into the parking lot, she hopped out of the VW and ran toward the house, backpack swinging from her shoulder. He knew she was anxious to tell Lacey about her day.

He moved more slowly than she did, reaching into the backseat for the two bags of groceries he'd picked up on his way to the school. He walked past the blessedly empty kennel, wondering if he would ever be able to pass it without remembering the previous week, when he'd come home to the bleeding child he adored and the nearly dead woman he loved. He would never forget all the blood on the sand, or the feeling of strength in his muscles as he lifted Wolf into the air, or the sound of the dog's neck cracking as it hit the doghouse. The best he could hope for would be to be able to pass the kennel without feeling sick to his stomach. That would be progress.

Inside the house, he found Mackenzie in the living room with Lacey, who was relaxing in the recliner they'd bought so that she could keep her bandaged legs elevated. She'd had surgery two days earlier and might need another some time in the future, but she was recovering very well, by all accounts.

He put away the groceries in the kitchen, listening to Mackenzie recount to Lacey all the news she'd just told him. Lacey was better at that sort of conversation than he had been. She asked Mackenzie a lot of questions and made sounds of appreciation and wonder at her answers, as though Mackenzie was the most interesting and amazing child on earth.

Once Mackenzie had gone upstairs to her room, Bobby brought Lacey a glass of lemonade and sat on the sofa. "Looks like the first day of school was a success," he said.

"Better than expected." Lacey nodded.

She was so pale. He knew she was still in a good deal of pain that the medication could not control. Or rather, she would not take the amount of medication needed to control it because it put her to sleep, and she seemed to want to be awake all the time, as though she might miss something important if she was not.

They were pampering her, waiting on her hand and foot, and she deserved it. There was a lot of guilt in this house. Clay was filled with it for having Wolf there in the first place, and Bobby knew that Mackenzie had cried herself to sleep at least two or three nights for having gone into the kennel when she'd been warned not to. But Lacey seemed to bear no grudges. "I am so *happy* to be alive," she said, so frequently and with such fervor that he thought the meds might be frying her brain just a little.

"You're going to need to talk to her about sex soon," Bobby said now.

"Already?"

"The boys are cute, they wear earrings, they think she's hot."

Lacey let out a giggle.

"I think she's taken the school by storm," he said.

She smiled at him. "You look like you're feeling some fatherly pride."

He nodded. "I'm proud of her," he said slowly. "And I love her. But she's not my daughter, Lace." He shook his head. "I wish she were, but she's not."

She raised her head a few inches from the back of the recliner. "Why do you still think that?" she asked.

It was time to tell her. There was no point in keeping the truth to himself any longer.

"Look at her eyes," he said, "then look at mine."

She frowned. "You both have blue eyes," she said.

"Then—" he felt his heart start to race "—look at your brother's."

46

LACEY STARTED TO TELL BOBBY THAT HE WAS being ridiculous. Clay could not possibly be Mackenzie's father. But before she even opened her mouth to speak, the evidence began to pile up in her mind. It wasn't just Mackenzie's eyes, although she certainly did have those translucent blue eyes that belonged to both her brother and father, while Bobby's were a deeper blue, and Jessica's had bordered on green. It was also the lanky body that was an O'Neill trait and that neither Jessica nor Bobby possessed. It was the shape of her teeth and the arch of her eyebrows. Still, it seemed an outrageous idea.

"Clay would never have slept with Jessica," Lacey said. "He couldn't stand her—or me, for that matter. We were nothing more than little annoyances to him that summer. And he had a girlfriend. Terri. The woman he married when they got out of college."

Bobby gnawed on his lip, looking unsure if he should say any more.

"What makes you think he is?" Lacey prodded.

Bobby leaned toward her, resting his elbows on his knees. "When I first saw Clay here at the keeper's house, he looked familiar to me, but I couldn't place him. I just figured that I must have met him somewhere that summer, since you and I were hanging around together all the time. But a few weeks ago, Mackenzie and I were out in the yard talking to...to Wolf's owner and Clay. Wolf had just arrived." He looked apologetic for mentioning the dog's name. "The sun was really bright, and at one point Clay turned around to look up at the house and the sunlight was in his eyes and they looked so..."

"Oh, I know what you mean," Lacey said. He didn't need to finish the sentence. "It's like you can see clear through them when the sun hits them."

"Exactly," Bobby said. "They're unusual, right? And I remembered seeing them once before."

"Where?"

"One of those parties we went to that summer. You remember what those parties were like, don't you?"

She nodded. Drugs, sex and rock and roll, with very little emphasis on the music. She'd had a love-hate relationship with those parties. The easy sex she gave away, along with the huge quantities of alcohol she'd consumed, had tortured her conscience. And sometimes her brother would be there. He'd yell at her, tell her she and Jessica didn't belong at the older kids' parties, and how right he'd been about that. But she'd tell him to leave her alone. She'd hated it when he was around, because she would need to be secretive about what she was doing to prevent him from telling their father what she was up to.

"Jessica was in one of the bedrooms," Bobby continued. "We'd had a fight or something, I don't remember, but we had chilled on seeing each other for a while. It was killing me, because I knew she was in there with someone else."

Lacey's hand was wrapped so tightly around her glass of

lemonade that her fingers hurt. She was afraid to think about where this story was going.

"The house was pretty dark, but there was this light on in the living room," Bobby said. "When I heard the door open to the bedroom, I kind of was…I don't remember, exactly, but I was hanging out around there, trying to look cool, but really wanting to see who she'd been with. The guy came out, and the light in the living room shone right in his eyes. He blinked, it was so bright, but right before he blinked I saw how strange they were. He looked right at me, although I don't think he knew Jessica was my girlfriend."

Her hand over her mouth, Lacey felt momentarily numb, her physical pain forgotten. "Are you sure it was Clay?" She was whispering.

He nodded. "I'm ninety-eight percent certain," he said.

Lacey let out her breath, resting her head against the back of the chair. Could Clay truly have slept with Jessica? It seemed unbelievable. Jessica had been barely fifteen and he'd been seventeen. In retrospect, the age difference did not seem that great, but at the time, it had seemed insurmountable. And what about Terri? She couldn't picture Clay cheating on her. Back in those days, she'd thought of her brother as straitlaced, a bit of a moralistic stuffed shirt. Maybe she'd been wrong.

"If he *did* actually sleep with her…" Lacey's mind was racing. "Do you think he might suspect that Mackenzie is his?"

"I don't think he has a clue," Bobby said. "Jessica let everyone believe Mackenzie was mine right from the start, so the thought probably never entered his mind. But I believe that's why Jessica was so adamant that Mackenzie go to *you*." He sat up straight, his hands cutting the air to make a point. "She *knew* Mackenzie was an O'Neill. If she died, she wanted Mackenzie to be part of your family—part of *Clay's* family. And that was the only way she thought she could do it."

"That would also explain why she refused to tell you that you were Mackenzie's father." Lacey was thinking out loud. It all was beginning to make terrible sense.

"And why she couldn't tell you the truth, Lace," Bobby said. "She couldn't tell you she'd slept with your brother."

"Oh, my God," Lacey said, struggling to take it all in. "And he's gotten so close to her these past few weeks."

"I've been glad about that," Bobby said. "They really care about each other."

"I think we need to talk to him," she said.

Bobby looked surprised. "Are you up for that?" he asked. "Do you want to wait until you're feeling better?"

"I'm not going to be able to relax until I talk to him about it," she said. "Not in an accusatory way, though," she added quickly, "because, who knows, we could still be wrong. But I think he needs to know what we're thinking." She shut her eyes with a sudden realization. "Oh, Bobby," she said, "if she's Clay's, then I've dragged you into something that had nothing to do with you."

He smiled, leaning forward again to take her hand. "Do you think for one minute that I regret that?" he asked.

47

THEY MADE A DECISION TO WAIT A FEW DAYS before talking to Clay about their suspicions, so they would have a chance to think through what they would say. They also needed to find a time when neither Gina nor Mackenzie would be around. The best-laid plans, though, sometimes went awry. That same evening, Gina took Rani to visit Henry and Mackenzie was upstairs doing her homework when Clay came into the living room, flipped on the TV to a news station and sat down on the sofa.

He turned to Lacey and Bobby. "How are you two doing?" he asked, conversationally, and she and Bobby looked at each other. Lacey knew they were both wondering the same thing: should they seize the opportunity or not? Lacey made the decision for them both, and she hoped Bobby didn't mind.

"There's something we want to talk to you about," she said.

Clay looked concerned by the serious tone in her voice. "Are you worried about Mackenzie working with the dogs during the school year?" he asked.

Lacey shook her head. "Heavier than that," she said, and Clay used the remote control to click off the TV.

"Let's leave the TV on," Bobby suggested, looking at Lacey for confirmation. "We could use the background noise."

She understood. He was worried Mackenzie might be able to hear them.

Clay clicked on the set again. The newscaster was talking about the first day of school in North Carolina, using footage of weepy kindergartners in their new classrooms as they were being deserted by their mothers.

"So," Clay said, "what's going on?"

Lacey would have liked Bobby to tell him, but she thought it would be better coming from her, so she jumped in quickly. "Bobby and I think there's a possibility that you're Mackenzie's father."

She watched all color leave her brother's face, and she waited for him to protest, but he surprised her.

"I wondered," he said quietly. "She has my eyes."

Lacey felt torn between astonishment and relief. He already knew. She was not going to have to go into the details of Bobby seeing him leave the bedroom at that long-ago party.

Clay looked at Bobby. "You're the more logical candidate," he said. "You were with Jessica all summer long. I was just with her once."

"I'm the proud owner of extremely lethargic sperm," Bobby said. "I've never been able to impregnate anyone even when I was trying to. I love Mackenzie, but I've had my doubts that she was mine from the start."

The color was returning to Clay's face and now coins of hot pink were on his cheeks. He turned to Lacey. "Did Jessica ever tell you that we'd…hooked up?" he asked.

She shook her head. She wanted details. She wanted to know what had gotten into him that he would bed her fifteen-year-old friend. But what had happened twelve years ago didn't matter now. It truly didn't. What mattered at this moment was the probable result of that night: Mackenzie.

"No, she didn't," she said, "but I'm pretty sure that's why she wanted to leave Mackenzie with me. It was as close as she could get to leaving her with you."

Clay fiddled with the remote where it rested on the arm of the sofa, and Lacey noticed the faint tremor in his fingers.

"Mackenzie's a great kid," he said. "I don't care if she's my daughter or Bobby's, she's part of our family."

"I think we'd better have a DNA test done," Bobby said, resting his elbows on his knees and looking from Clay to Lacey. "I know we both care about her, but I think we need to know one way or another for sure."

Clay nodded. "And if it turns out to be me, what do we tell her?"

For the first time, Lacey understood why her father had waited until she was sixteen to tell her that Tom was her biological father. She could not have coped with that news at fourteen. "We tell her the truth," Lacey said, "but not now. She's been through too much these past few months." She turned her head against the back of the recliner so that she was looking squarely at Bobby. "That is, if you can handle playing the role of dad a while longer."

"I could handle it till the day I die," Bobby said.

48

"I MISSED THESE COOL SUMMER EVENINGS WHILE I was in North Carolina," Faye said. She and Jim were sitting in his hot tub across from one another, the bubbles warm around their shoulders and the heavy, dark coastal clouds so low in the sky they seemed to be suspended directly above Jim's house. "I'd forgotten how miserably hot it could be there."

"Fred's cottage didn't have air-conditioning?" Jim asked.

Faye laughed. "I'm amazed his cottage had running water," she said. "And the bugs! I'm still scratching mosquito bites."

She'd stayed with Fred for five days. Good days, for the most part, as she got to know the stranger who was her son. In the day and a half since her return to San Diego, it seemed all she had talked about was Fred, analyzing her son and her visit, and Jim had not complained once. He knew she couldn't help herself. And she was still at it.

"It's so strange, Jim," she said. "If I'd met Fred in Princeton, with his wonderful life, his excellent career, his law degree, his beautiful house, I would have been so awestruck at how perfectly he'd turned out. Instead I met him in the middle of a lie. I saw him at his worst. I'm worried he may have inherited some of his father's psychological problems."

"Did you talk to him about that?" Jim asked.

She shook her head. "I will at some point, but we just needed to get to know each other again first."

Jim ran his foot up her shin beneath the bubbling water. "And now, *I'd* like to get to know you again," he said.

"Later." She smiled. "I promise."

"You're on a roll, aren't you?" he said, giving up. "One thing that drew me to you was your tenacity, so I guess I can't complain about it now."

"Thanks," she said. "For not complaining. For listening to me go on and on."

"Go ahead," he said. "What else is on your mind?"

"You know how I told you that every young male patient who came into the pain program would make me think of Fred?" she asked.

"Uh-huh."

"Well, we got a new patient today. An eighteen-year-old boy. Young man."

"Ah," Jim said. "And he reminded you of Fred."

"That's the funny thing." She ran her hands through the water. It felt soft against her fingers. "I didn't think of him at all. I think that spell must be broken now that I've seen Fred in the flesh again. Instead, I was thinking about that young woman, Lacey O'Neill."

"What made you think of her?" Jim asked.

"The new patient was bitten on his shoulder by a dog a year ago. He's healed fairly well, but the bite left him with severe chronic pain. Isn't that ironic?" She raised her eyebrows to Jim. "I don't think I've had a single dog bite in the program and then, suddenly, he appears."

Jim hummed the *Twilight Zone* music.

"So, it made me wonder how Lacey's doing with her re- covery, from both the dog attack and from Fred's...misuse of her." She thought of Lacey often, unable to forget the rage in her face the night she'd stormed out of Fred's cottage. Faye knew a lot about rage. Her program was filled with pa- tients whose anger fed their pain. Anger at an illness. Anger at the driver of the other car who gave them their back in- jury. Anger at God for making them suffer. Anger that only served to prolong their pain. One of the parts of the program she'd designed—one facet most resented by her patients until they truly understood its purpose—was to learn to let go of that anger.

"I don't really know her," Faye said about Lacey. "I may just be thinking about how I'd feel in her situation. But she was so furious when she left Fred's that day, that—"

"I don't blame her," Jim interrupted.

"No, I certainly don't, either," Faye said. "But she was ready to pour her anger into testifying about her mother's murder in order to keep Zach in prison forever. To write something truly scathing to the parole board. And then she was attacked by that dog, and—"

"What are you trying to say, honey?" Jim moved across the hot tub to sit next to her, his arm around her shoulders. "You think Zach should get out on parole?"

She shook her head. She wasn't speaking clearly, because her thoughts were not yet well formed.

"It's not that I want Zach to get out," she said. "It's that I want Lacey to be *well*. She's suffered too much in too many ways at the hands of my family, and I can't believe my son added to that suffering the way he did. Her rage is well founded, just as it is in all the patients I work with, but it can only harm her in the end."

"You know what I've figured out about you, Faye?" Jim asked.

"What's that?"

He touched her temple, making a little circular motion with his fingertip. "You're the sort of person who can't rest easy until you've taken action on whatever's spinning around in your brain," he said.

He was right. That was why she'd been able to transform the chronic pain program from a simple idea into a reality. It was why she'd gone to see her son. And she knew right then that it was why she would call Lacey O'Neill.

49

"HOW DO YOU THINK IT'S GOING IN THERE?" Bobby was sitting on Lacey's bed the night after their conversation with Clay, gently massaging vitamin E oil onto the developing scars on her legs. They knew that Clay was talking to Gina in their bedroom, telling her that Mackenzie might possibly be his daughter.

"I think Clay is lucky that Gina is madly in love with him, and they'll be okay," she said, wincing at the pain he was causing her. She knew it was important to massage the scars to prevent adhesions from forming, but that knowledge didn't stop the procedure from hurting. She was lying on her back in her panties and T-shirt, well aware that her chewed-up legs looked anything but sexy these days. She suddenly chuckled. "This is so romantic, isn't it?" she said. "Having you massage my revolting legs?"

"I think it's very romantic, actually," he said. "And it could be even more so if you'd let me massage the rest of you, too." He shifted on the bed so he could lift the hem of her shirt up a few inches. He ran his slick hand over the skin of her stomach, from the bottom of her ribs to the top of her panties, and it felt wonderful to have him stroke her there, one of the few places on her body where touch could give her pleasure instead of pain. Bobby had been so good to her since the attack, but he hadn't kissed her until tonight, as if fearing she was too fragile to be touched.

"Lacey!" he said suddenly, and her eyelids flew open at what sounded like alarm in his voice.

"What?"

"You devil!" he said. "You have a pierced belly button."

She laughed, glancing down at the tiny tiger's eye protruding from the skin above her navel. "Surprise," she said.

"And here you were giving me a hard time about my earring."

She reached up and touched the gold hoop. "I love your earring," she said. *And I love you,* she wanted to say, but she and Bobby were not quite there yet. Not quite ready for those words. One day they would be, though. She knew that, and she could wait.

Her phone rang, and Bobby lifted the receiver from the cradle and handed it to her.

"Hello," she said, closing her eyes again as he continued to rub her stomach.

"Is this Lacey?" a woman asked.

"Yes."

"Lacey, this is Faye Collier. Fred—Rick's—mother."

Why was Rick's mother calling her? Her memory of the woman was vague with all that had happened since their meeting at the cottage. Her memory of Rick himself was growing vaguer by the day, and for that she was grateful. If anything good had come from the past two weeks, it was that she had learned which of the two men in her life was by far the best.

"Why are you calling?" Lacey asked, hoping she did not sound rude.

"I just wanted to see how you are," Faye said. "I think about you every day and hope that you're healing well. Are you having much pain?"

"Define 'much,'" Lacey said, annoyed by the question as well as by the call, but then she knew she truly *was* sounding rude. "I'm sorry," she said. "I've just about gotten Rick out of my mind, and I'm not sure why you're calling me. And yes, I have a lot of pain."

Bobby looked concerned. "Who is it?" he whispered, and she mouthed the words "Rick's mother."

There was a long pause on Faye's end of the line. "I'm not calling to defend Rick," Faye said. "What he did was inexcusable. I know you've suffered so much because of my family, and *that's* why I'm calling. Just to see how you are. I guess I need to know you're okay."

It was Lacey's turn to hesitate. She found sharp, ugly responses coming into her head, but nothing that had happened to her was this woman's fault.

"I'm all right," she said. "My doctor says I'm healing well. It's just going to take a long time."

"What pain meds are you on?" Faye asked.

Lacey ran down the list of medications she was taking.

"Good," Faye said. "I don't mean to be nosy, but I'm the head of a chronic pain program in a hospital in San Diego, so I know something about what works and what doesn't. How much are you taking of each of them?"

"I try to take as little as I can get away with," Lacey said. "I don't like to be so dependent on drugs."

"It's important to stay on top of the pain, Lacey," Faye said. "Don't wait until it's got you in its grip. We used to tell people to tough it out—which I think is what you're trying to do—but that only makes it worse. That causes you to tense up and makes the pain harder to treat in the long run."

Her own doctor had said the very same thing, and she'd ignored him, but maybe they both knew a bit more about this than she did. "All right," she conceded. "I'll try to be better about it."

"How are you doing with your anger?"

Now Lacey was really getting irritated, so much so that she had to put her hand over Bobby's because even his touch was starting to chafe.

"I don't know what you mean," she said.

"When you left Fred's cottage, you were understandably furious. You said you'd write a scathing victim's statement, or whatever it's called. I was just wondering—"

"I haven't been able to write it," she said. "I got sidetracked by a hundred-pound dog. But I will."

Faye hesitated, then spoke again. "I don't know Zach anymore," she said, sounding suddenly very tired. "I do know at one time he was a good man. I know he had some sort of terrible breakdown. I don't know if he should get out of prison or not. I don't have, or want to have, any say in that. But I think it's important that you don't base the statement that you write about Zachary on your anger toward Fred. Toward Rick. That's not fair."

"Faye…" Lacey felt her anger mounting. "I frankly don't care about being fair to your ex-husband."

"I'm not thinking about *him*," Faye said. "I'm thinking about *you*."

"What do you mean?"

"I mean that that anger you're holding on to…that sense of revenge…it's like swallowing poison and expecting someone else to die. Do you understand what I'm saying?"

"I understand it. I just don't get why you're saying it, though."

"Because you're the one that poison will ultimately hurt,

Lacey. You need peace of mind to be able to heal, both physically and emotionally."

"You sound like Rick," Lacey said. "Forgive and forget."

"No, never forget," Faye said quickly. "Rick had an ulterior motive. You know that. You should never forget what happened."

"Faye…I'm sorry, but I'm really tired," Lacey said. "I'm going to hang up now."

"Wait a second," the woman said hurriedly. "I didn't see Zachary while I was there. I couldn't bring myself to do it, so I frankly have no idea if Fred's assessment of him as rehabilitated is accurate. But I think that may be a piece of information you need to have to be able to write your statement. Don't base your testimony on your anger, Lacey. Base it on reality. Whatever you write, make sure you're doing it for the right reasons."

Lacey pled exhaustion once more, then handed the phone to Bobby, who rested it back in its cradle.

"What was that all about?" he asked.

Lacey looked at him. "Do you think it's possible for someone to truly be rehabilitated?" she asked.

Bobby grinned at her. "Hey, babe," he said. "Just look at me."

The following morning, Lacey walked into the kitchen to find herself alone with Gina and Rani. She searched her sister-in-law's face for some clue to her emotional state after learning that Clay might be Mackenzie's father, but Gina only smiled at her as she set a bowl of cereal on the tray of Rani's high chair.

"How are you this morning?" Gina asked her.

"Good," Lacey said, taking a seat at the table. "Much better, actually." For the first time, she did not feel as though every molecule in her body had been shredded and pasted back together. Maybe she was just getting better, or maybe it was that she'd listened to Faye's advice and taken her medication both the night before and this morning instead of waiting for the pain to hit her first. Or maybe it was that Bobby had spent the entire night in her bed, lying next to her, just keeping her company with no demands or expectations of anything more.

"Clay's already left for work?" Lacey asked.

"Uh-huh." Gina poured coffee into a mug and handed it to her. "And Bobby's driving Mackenzie to the bus stop." And, Lacey knew, visiting Elise after he dropped Mackenzie off. Elise had fallen down on her promise to keep in touch with him, and he was worried about her.

"I go swimming today!" Rani said.

"You are?" Lacey said. "Are you getting to be a good swimmer?"

Rani nodded, plucking a piece of banana from the top of her cereal and stuffing it into her mouth.

"She's doing great," Gina said. "You love the water, don't you, Rani?"

Rani nodded again, the banana making speech impossible.

"I guess the real question is, how are *you* this morning?" Lacey asked Gina.

Gina sat down next to Rani's high chair. She lowered her eyes to her own coffee mug, running the tip of her finger over the handle.

"I feel sorry for Clay," she said, lifting her gaze to meet Lacey's. "All his mistakes are coming back to haunt him."

Lacey nodded. She knew how upset with himself Clay was for bringing Wolf into their lives against Gina's wishes. And now he had to face his long-ago indiscretion with Jessica Dillard, as well.

"Were you shocked?" Lacey asked.

Gina smiled, and there was something secretive about it. It was a moment before she spoke.

"He'd already told me about Jessica," she said. "When she died, he was more upset than he let on to you, because he knew her a little better than you thought he did. Not that they had any sort of real relationship, but I think...as an adult, he looked back and saw how he'd used her. So the night after she died, he told me what he'd done—that he'd slept with her at a party when he was seventeen, that she was a sweet kid who was screwed up, and that he took advantage of that fact. In other words, he let me know that he'd been a jerk, in case I couldn't figure it out on my own from what he was telling me."

"I'm glad you two have that kind of relationship," Lacey said, surprised that her brother had so openly confided in Gina.

"Me, too," Gina said.

"Me, too!" Rani added, and Lacey and Gina laughed.

"Drink your juice, Rani," Gina said, pushing the cup a little closer to the cereal bowl on Rani's tray. Gina looked at Lacey. "Do you know that Clay and your dad are meeting with the lawyer again today?" she asked. "They're going to go forward without a statement from you, so you don't need to have that hanging over your head anymore."

"Oh," Lacey said, wondering why she felt no relief at that news.

"It must give you some peace of mind," Gina continued. "I know how that's been driving you crazy."

"I think I figured something out," Lacey said. She took a long drink of her coffee before continuing. "I haven't been able to write it because I've been focusing on my mother and my family, not on the killer," she said. "My mother's already gone. My family's healing. But Zachary Pointer's the one who'll stay in or out of prison based on what we say. He's the one the statement should really be about."

Gina looked confused. "What are you saying, Lace?" she asked.

"That I still want to write my statement," she said, standing up, the coffee mug in her hand, "but there's something else I have to do first."

50

SHE'D EXPECTED TO HAVE TO TALK TO ZACHARY Pointer through a wall of Plexiglas, like they did in the movies, but when she arrived in the section of the prison where he was incarcerated, she was led directly to the chaplain's office.

"Reverend McConnell's not here today," said the uniformed guard, his hand on the office door, "but he said Mr. Pointer and you could meet in here. Zach's already inside."

Lacey felt unexpected fear rise up inside her. Being alone in a room with her mother's murderer suddenly seemed comparable to being trapped in a kennel with a vicious dog. Surely, though, they wouldn't let her meet with him if they had any doubts about her safety. Still, she hesitated before stepping inside the office.

"Go ahead in," the guard said. "Just stop by the front to sign out when you leave."

She opened the door and walked into a small, bare-walled waiting room containing five chairs upholstered in turquoise vinyl. Behind her, the guard closed the door and it felt as though he took all of the air in the room with him.

"Hello?" Lacey called.

She heard the sound of a chair scraping against the floor,

and in a minute the man she had long despised stood in the doorway between the two rooms, wearing blue prison garb. She took an involuntary step backwards, but it was *his* face that turned ashen and held a look of fear.

"Annie?" he asked.

Lacey couldn't speak. Why would he call her Annie? He hadn't known her mother as anything other than an obstacle in his path as he tried to kill his wife. She pictured him at the battered women's shelter, filling the doorway in his soaking-wet green peacoat. She remembered him pointing the gun, yelling "Whore!" and "Slut!" and she knew all at once it had not been Faye Collier that those words had been meant for.

"You were one of them," she said with a calmness that belied the turmoil inside her. "You were one of my mother's lovers."

He seemed to shrink inside his blue uniform. His face bore deep lines and crevices that seemed to multiply at her words.

"You're her daughter," he said. "Lacey, is it?"

Her back was pressed against the door to the room, more for support than anything else. She was beginning to feel dizzy. "Was it actually my mother you meant to kill when you broke into the shelter?" she asked. "Was that who you were really after?"

He licked his lips, looking away from her for a moment, and she could see that he was trying to decide how to proceed. Finally, he motioned toward the interior office. "Come inside and we can talk," he said.

"I'll sit right here." She lowered herself to the chair closest to the door. The vinyl made a sound like air being let out of a tire as she sat down on it.

He took a seat on the other side of the small room, and Lacey studied him. She would not have recognized him in a lineup. His dark hair had turned completely white during the past twelve years, and he *was* smaller, or maybe it was just the fact that he was not wearing a heavy coat or carrying a gun that made him seem diminished in size.

"I hadn't expected…" He looked down at his hands as though he was not certain what to say. "They told me you were coming." He smiled at her and she had to look away. The smile was too unexpectedly warm, and she did not want to be seduced by it. "I figured we'd have a little talk and I would tell you how sorry I was that your mother tried to protect my wife. But I realize now that the truth must be written all over my face."

She couldn't breathe. The light-headedness made her want to lean over and hang her head between her knees. Did she want to sit here and have him tell her things that were guaranteed to distress her even further, or should she simply tell him she'd made a mistake in coming and run from the room?

"I'm sorry," he said. "I don't want to say anything bad about your mother."

"Tell me," she said. She had come this far. If she didn't have this conversation with him now, not knowing what he had to say would always haunt her. "I already know she was… unfaithful to my father."

He stared at her, licking his lips again. "I met her in the little shop I used to work in," he said. "A little sundries store in Kill Devil Hills, over by…well, it doesn't matter. I'm not even sure if it's still there. She came in one time to buy a pair of sandals she saw in our window, and we started talking. She started coming in then, almost every day, just to talk, and to make a long story short, I fell in love with her. I had a bipolar disorder, although I didn't know that at the time. I just knew that I'd go on these jags of having loads of energy and feeling like the world was a pretty terrific place to be, and then, without warning, I'd plummet. Drop lower than low.

But I could always manage to hide what was going on inside of me—to stay in control of it—as long as my life was on an even keel." He looked down at his hands. They were folded in his lap, and he was rubbing one of the thumbs over the other. "I was in a manic phase when I met your mother," he said. "A long one. And at first it was great."

"Did she take you to the keeper's house?"

He looked surprised. "You know about that?" he asked. She nodded.

"Yes, that's where we'd meet." He looked apologetic. "I don't like talking to you about this."

"Go on." She was picturing her father at the animal hospital, working hard as he always did, making money to support his family, while his wife was taking men to the keeper's house without a thought to how she was hurting her family.

"I didn't feel right about what I was doing," he said, "but I was so driven. It's hard to explain the effect she had on me."

"She had it on a lot of men," she said, wanting to take some of the wind out of his sails.

"Yes, I know that," he said. "Not at the time, though. I thought we were so much in love that it somehow legitimized the infidelity. I convinced myself that it was all right." He studied his hands again, the movement of his thumbs the only clue that he was nervous. "But as I said, I didn't do well under stress and my mood started to go south. I wasn't much fun for her anymore, I guess, and she wanted to end the affair. I couldn't bear the thought of being without her, and I was so...so ill at the time, that I threatened to kill both her and myself if she left me. If I couldn't have her, I didn't want anyone else to have her, either. I was selfish and crazy and self-absorbed," he said. "I think what happened was that Annie— your mother—became afraid that I might hurt my wife and son, so she made up some cock-and-bull story about getting a call from one of my friends or a neighbor or someone and got them into the battered women's shelter where she worked. Of course, I knew where the place was because she'd told me all about it back when things were good between us. When I went there, Lacey, I was out of my mind. I intended to kill all three of them and then myself, but you're right, that first bullet was meant for your mother."

"And she knew it," Lacey said. "She had to know that if she stepped in front of your wife, you were going to kill her."

He drew in a long breath. "I believe—and will believe to my dying day—that she thought that if I shot her first, I would never get around to killing my wife and son. That they'd be able to escape before I could get to them. Everybody said she was trying to save their lives by stepping in front of Faye— my wife—and they were right. They just didn't know what Annie knew—that I was there to kill her as well as them, one way or another. Once I shot her, it was like something snapped in me and I realized what an insane thing I was doing. That's why I didn't hurt anyone else." He lifted his head to look at her and there were tears in his eyes. "Oh, Lacey," he said. "I'm so sorry. The truth is, I've grown in here. I'm not just a healthier person, I'm a better person, and this place…" He waved his hand through the air. "The doctors and the chaplain…I don't know what would have become of me if I hadn't landed in here. But I would give anything…*anything* if I could bring your mother back and erase everything that happened between us and return her whole and unharmed to you and your family."

She did not want to believe him or to trust his sincerity. He was, after all, Rick's father. But there was something in his eyes that convinced her he was telling the truth, that he was done with lies.

"It took a long time," he said, "with a lot of shrinks trying me on a lot of different medications, but finally, they hit the right one. That was when I truly realized what I'd done. That I'd taken a life. That I'd ruined many other lives. I wanted to die. I tried to kill myself, but they make that hard to do in prison." He offered her a rueful smile. "It was the Reverend McConnell who got me through it all. You probably don't need to hear that," he said. "That I got through it. Your mother's story ended, and mine continued. I know how unfair that must seem to you."

"What will you do if you get out on parole?" she asked.

"I want to enter the seminary," he said, then smiled his apology again. "Does that sound like a line to you?"

She looked away. It would have sounded like a line if she hadn't heard about it from his son first. "I'm not sure," she said.

"I'd like to be a prison chaplain," he said. "And if I don't get out, it truly doesn't matter, because I've been able to work here. Maybe I have even more credibility on the inside than I would on the outside. There are a lot of people in here in need of spiritual guidance. My son wants me out so badly. He thinks I can only do what I want to do if I'm released. He doesn't get it."

"Get what?"

"That I'm every bit as free in here as I would be out there," he said. "I'll have peace in my heart no matter where I am." He leaned forward, his elbows on his knees. "And what about you, Lacey?" he asked. "How is your heart these days?"

Lacey couldn't hold it together any longer. Lowering her head, she started to cry.

51

Victim's Impact Statement
by Lacey O'Neill

PEOPLE CALLED MY MOTHER SAINT ANNE. SHE was probably better loved and better known in the area than anyone else. She loved animals and children and nature. She was generous in the extreme to her friends and neighbors, treasured everyone she met, and she tried to help make the world a better place in an enormous variety of ways, most of which you have probably heard about in the other statements you've received.

What you haven't heard about is that my mother knew how to forgive. I don't think she held a grudge against a soul. If I put someone down, she would come to their defense. She had the gentlest way of confronting people who had done something wrong. Once I saw her stop a teenaged boy on the street after hearing him utter a racial slur. She didn't yell at him, but instead gave him a little, soft-spoken lecture on the way that fear and ignorance can make us hate other people. When she saw a mother yell at her young child one time, she talked to the mother about how hard it could be to have demanding little children, and she gave the woman her phone number to call her the next time she lost her temper at her son. Another time, I saw her confront a boy who dropped a candy-bar wrapper on the sidewalk. Instead of giving him a piece of her mind, she told him about the elderly man who owned the store on that part of the sidewalk, and how he came out of the store every evening to sweep the sidewalk clean.

I'm not writing this to tell you more stories about my mother being a saint, because she wasn't one. She was just a human being who did her best to understand why other people made mistakes, and she forgave them.

If I could talk to my mother right now and ask her how she felt about Zachary Pointer getting out on parole, I know what she would say. She would tell me he was human, that he had been hurting when he killed her. She'd say that he had paid for his crime, and that he had redeemed himself. She would tell me that, as long as he is no longer dangerous to anyone, he should be set free to become a productive member of society.

So, I am writing to suggest that Mr. Pointer be released from prison on parole. Please give him the chance to continue the good deeds that my mother is no longer capable of doing.

Epilogue

AT TEN O'CLOCK ON CHRISTMAS EVE, LACEY and Bobby, Clay and Gina and Mackenzie stood in the kitchen of the keeper's house and bade farewell to their guests. It had been a wonderful, even an amazing evening. There had been fifteen of them for the buffet dinner, all of them in one way or another family, from Nola Dillard to Tom Nestor to Paul Macelli, who was Olivia's first husband and Jack's father, down visiting from Washington, DC. Nothing could have pleased Lacey more than to have that diverse group of people together and see everyone get along. Rani provided the bulk of the entertainment, simply by being a two-and-a-half-year-old adorable peanut of a child, and Jack, Maggie and Mackenzie had been coerced into singing carols with everyone else before scooting upstairs to hang out on Mackenzie's computer.

The only person missing from the holiday celebration was Bobby's cousin, Elise. Around Halloween Elise had disappeared. The friends she'd been staying with told Bobby that she simply didn't come home one night. Bobby feared that her contacts in Richmond had found her and dragged her back up there—or worse—but Lacey thought that Elise might have returned to her old life of her own volition. Either way, if

Elise's disappearance was a mystery that could be solved, she planned to help Bobby solve it.

This was the first year that Lacey had agreed to have a real tree for Christmas. After her mother's death in the battered women's shelter, where the scent of pine had filled the rooms, she'd been unable even to pass a Christmas tree lot without feeling sick to her stomach. But Mackenzie had pleaded for a real tree. She and her mother had never had one in Arizona, she'd said, and Lacey felt ready to give it a try. Once the tree was up and the scent was strong in the living room of the keeper's house, she discovered that she actually liked the smell. It was so fresh and welcoming. She would miss it when it was time to take the tree down.

In the opposite corner of the living room stood an enormous poinsettia, a gift from Rick that had arrived the week before Christmas. He was always sending flowers, using any occasion he could as an excuse for the gifts. Lacey had written to him, extending her forgiveness, and he'd written back to thank her, but still the plants and flowers came. Maybe they would come for the rest of her life.

In two weeks, she would be leaving the keeper's house forever. In the late spring, it would open as a museum. She would be one of the docents, but it would not be the same. The history *she* knew of the house was not the history the tourists would be paying money to hear. She could not tell them how her parents had met on the beach by the lighthouse. She couldn't tell them how the old lighthouse keeper, Mary Poor, had allowed her mother to use the keeper's house for her illicit trysts, or how her mother's ashes had been tossed into the ocean from the nearby pier after her murder. She couldn't tell them how the lighthouse had become her father's obsession, how he probably had thousands of pictures of it still stored in boxes somewhere in his house. And she could not tell them how she had lived in the house for two years herself, turning it into her safe haven as she tried to put the pieces of her life back together.

With all the guests gone, the residents of the house began cleaning up, stuffing used wrapping paper into garbage bags and picking up plates and glasses from all over the house and bringing them into the kitchen.

"Will we *finally* have a dishwasher in the new house?" Mackenzie asked, as she dried plate after plate that Lacey was washing.

"Yes, we will," Lacey said.

"And Clay and I will have one, too," Gina said. "How about you, Bobby?"

"No dishwasher for me," he said. "Except when Mackenzie comes over."

It took Mackenzie a second to get it, but then she groaned. "You're so full of dad humor tonight," she said.

Lacey smiled at Bobby across the top of Mackenzie's head. There are and always will be secrets in this family, she thought. Perhaps there were even secrets she was not privy to, but there were definitely two that she knew about. No one other than Clay, Bobby, Gina and herself knew that Clay was Mackenzie's father. The DNA test had proven it unequivocally, and as elated as Clay had been by that news, Bobby had been equally saddened. Mackenzie was as close to one man as she was the other, though, and Lacey planned to do her best to keep things that way. One day they would tell Mackenzie the truth, and by that time, Lacey prayed the girl would be so attached to both her fathers that the fact of her conception would not erase the endearment she felt to either of them.

One final secret would remain forever between two people only: Zachary Pointer and herself. There was nothing to be gained by revealing his relationship to her mother. Nothing but hurt, all the way around.

Zachary had called her around nine o'clock that evening, when the gifts had all been opened and everyone was full and content. She took the call in the sunroom, away from the chaos of the living room.

"I wanted to thank you for the kaleidoscope," he said. "It's amazing."

"You're welcome." It was good to hear his voice. He sounded strong.

"I've been thinking about you and praying for you all day," he said. "I know Christmas Eve must be hard for you." They both knew he was thinking of the long-ago Christmas Eve that had so irrevocably altered both their lives.

"Your prayers worked," she said. "This is the best Christmas Eve I've had in a long time."

"Have you and Mackenzie found a place to live yet?" he asked.

"We found a perfect little house to rent," she said. "And she'll be able to stay in the same school, which is the most important thing."

"Wonderful. And Bobby?"

"He'll be right next door to us." She laughed. "Literally."

Their houses were identical. Tiny, a little too old, but affordable, the only difference being that the house Lacey would be renting did, indeed, have a dishwasher, while Bobby's did not. "And Clay and Gina are in the process of buying a house in Pine Island," she added.

"Excellent," he said.

"And how about you, Zachary?" she asked. "When do you start at the seminary?"

"January fifth," he said. "It will be a wonderful beginning to a new year. To a new life. Thank you, Lacey."

"You're very welcome."

There was a brief moment of silence on the line.

"Are you ready to leave Kiss River?" he asked.

"It's going to be hard," she admitted. "It's been my refuge while I learned how to avoid following in my mother's footsteps."

"You're still angry at her," he said.

"Not really," she said, but she knew it was a lie, and so did he.

"If you could forgive me, you can surely forgive your mother, Lacey," Zachary said.

"You were mentally ill," Lacey was quick to answer.

"So was she, honey," he said. "So was she."

The conversation in the kitchen swirled around her, now, as the dishes were washed and dried and put away, but Lacey barely heard it. With the revelers gone and the five of them packed into the warm room, she suddenly felt the loss of the house to her bones. She took a step away from the sink, although it was still full of dishes with more waiting to be washed, and dried her hands on a paper towel.

"I want to go out to the lighthouse," she said.

"What?" Clay sounded incredulous. "You'll freeze your butt off up there."

"I'll get my jacket," Bobby said, but she rested her hand on his arm.

"I want to go alone, okay?" she asked.

He understood. "Of course," he said.

She walked to the hall closet and retrieved her down jacket and her gloves, then pulled her thigh-high waders on over her slacks. It had grown quiet in the kitchen, the only sound the rattling of dishes in the sink where Bobby had taken over her job.

"I won't be long," she said, walking back through the

kitchen toward the door. She was stepping onto the porch when she heard Mackenzie ask in a near whisper, "What's the matter with Lacey?" and Bobby's answer, "Sometimes people just need time alone."

Clay had been right; it was very cold outside. She pulled her knit hat from the pocket of her jacket and put it on, tugging it low over her ears. She pressed her body into the wind as she walked in the direction of the ocean. In a few weeks a fence would be built around the lighthouse, one that would allow the water to pass through it but would keep the tourists out. She had plotted a way to get up in the lighthouse after the fence was built, but then she learned that a padlocked door would block the entrance and she'd been foiled. It was time to give up her attachment to the tower.

The ocean was ferocious, the water nearly reaching the top of her waders as she walked through it to get to the steps. Inside, the octagonal room was cold, the sound of the sea muted by the thick brick walls, and she began to climb. When she rose out of the tower onto the exposed steps at the top, the wind nearly knocked her over, and she held tight to the railing as she turned around to sit down.

God, it was dark! The wind carried with it tiny, sharp ice crystals, which bit into her cheeks. Yet the sky was filled with stars. Sometimes she had to remind herself that the stars existed in the winter as well as the summer. It was easy to forget when all the time you spent outside was rushing from the car to the house.

She tilted her head back to look at the dome of stars above her, and suddenly felt, more deeply than she ever had before, her mother's presence. The feeling was so strong it frightened her, and she thought of descending the stairs and returning to the warm house. But something kept her there, clutching the railing with her gloved hands, her face lifted up to the sky.

"I have to leave here soon, Mom," she said out loud, but she couldn't even hear her own words, the wind stole them from her so quickly. It was not so quick to steal her tears, though. She felt afraid, as though leaving Kiss River meant that she would also be leaving her mother behind. That's what she'd been trying to do all year, yet now she realized how impossible a task that was. "I want you with me forever," she said to the sky. "Just, please—" she began to smile "—leave the crazy parts of you behind, okay?"

She wiped the back of her gloved hand across her wet face and stood up. Taking one step down, she stopped and looked up at the sky again.

"Bye, Mom," she said, watching the tiny diamond lights flicker high above her. "I love you."

★ ★ ★ ★ ★

Acknowledgements

So many people helped me with my research as I wrote *Her Mother's Shadow*. For their various contributions, I would like to thank Rodney Cash, Kimberly Certa, Steve Cook, Paul Holland and my friends at ASA, who are always ready with an answer to my questions, no matter how esoteric those questions may be.

I am grateful to fellow authors Emilie Richards and Patricia McLinn for their brainstorming skills. The inspiration to make Bobby Asher a scrimshaw artist came from my favourite scrimshander, Cathy Guss, whose stunning craftsmanship I discovered a number of years ago.

Special thanks goes once again to Sharon Van Epps, for sharing with me her experiences as she attempts to adopt a child from India. As I write this, Sharon is still engaged in that struggle and it's my fervent hope that her story has a happy ending.

Betsy Reitz earns a mention in these acknowledgements for winning the essay contest on my website. Betsy's love of the *Keeper of the Light* trilogy was evident in her essay. It's readers like Betsy who make writing worthwhile.

As always, I'd like to thank my agent, Ginger Barber, and my editor, Amy Moore-Benson. I am so lucky to be able to work with both of them.

I would love to hear your thoughts about *Her Mother's Shadow*. Please visit my website at www.dianechamberlain.com.

Turn the page for an exclusive preview of

THE COURAGE TREE

the compelling novel from
Diane Chamberlain available soon!

The Courage Tree

The guest cottage seemed stuffy, its four small rooms over-flowing with sunlight. At two-thirty, Janine turned off the air-conditioning and opened all the windows, starting in her bedroom and Sophie's room, then the kitchen and finally the living room. Although it became instantly warmer in the cottage, the air was arid, a remarkable phenomenon for June in northern Virginia, and the faint breeze carried the scent of magnolia and lavender into the rooms.

Janine sat sideways on the sofa in the living room, her back against the overstuffed arm, bare feet up on the cushions, gazing out the window at Ayr Creek's gardens. In fifteen minutes she could leave, she told herself. That would make her early, but there was no way she could wait here any longer.

The view of the gardens was spectacular from this window. Bands of red and violet, yellow and pink dipped and swirled over more than two acres of rolling landscape before losing themselves in the deep woods between the cottage and the mansion. The nineteenth century, yellow frame, black-shuttered mansion could barely be seen at this time of year due to the lush growth on the trees, allowing Janine to imagine that she was master of her own life and not living on her parents' property. Not that Ayr Creek truly belonged to her parents, who were little more than caretakers. The house was owned by the Ayr Creek Foundation, which was operated by the descendants of the estate's original owner, Angus Campbell. The Foundation had deeded enough money to the county to keep the garden and a few of the mansion's rooms open to the public on weekends. And through some quiet arrangement, Janine's mother, Donna Campbell Snyder, had been given the right to live in the mansion until her death, although she did not otherwise have a cent of her family's fortune. This, Janine had always thought, was the source of her mother's bitterness.

Nevertheless, Donna and Frank Snyder adored the Ayr Creek estate. Retired history teachers, they relished the task of over-seeing the upkeep of the house and gardens. And they willingly allowed Janine and her daughter, Sophie, to live rent-free in the "guest cottage," a euphemism designed to masquerade the true history of the diminutive structure: it had once been home to Ayr Creek's slaves.

There was a tear in the window screen. Just a small one, and if Janine closed one eye and leaned nearer to the screen, she could see one perfect, blue-blossomed hydrangea captured in the opening. If she leaned a little farther to the left, she could see the roses Lucas had planted near the wishing well. She should get up and repair the hole instead of playing games with it, she thought briefly, but shifted positions on the sofa and returned her attention to the gardens instead.

This restlessness, this stuffy, claustrophobic feeling, had been with her all weekend and she knew it was of her own creation. She had not drawn a full breath of air since Friday evening, when she'd watched her daughter ride away in the van with the rest of her Brownie troop. Sophie had grinned and giggled with her friends, looking for all the world like a perfectly healthy eight-year-old girl—except, perhaps, for the pallor and the delicate, willowy, white arms and legs. Janine had waved after the van until she could no longer make out Sophie's red hair against the tinted window. Then she offered a quick smile to the two other mothers in the parking lot of Meadowlark Gardens and got into her car quickly, hoping that the worry hadn't shown in her face. There hadn't been a day in the last five years that she had not worried.

She'd planned to use this weekend alone to clean the cottage from top to bottom, but she'd gotten little done. She'd spent time on Saturday with her mother in the mansion, helping her research historically accurate wallpaper patterns on the Internet for one of the mansion's bedrooms, and listening to her complain yet again about Lucas, the horticulturist in charge of the gardens. Janine knew, though, that she and her mother were both preoccupied with thoughts of Sophie. Was she all right? Eight years old seemed far too young to be spending the weekend at a Girl Scout camp nearly two hours away, even to Janine, and she knew her mother was furious with her for allowing Sophie to go. Sitting in the office, which was part of the mansion's twentieth-century addition, Janine had tried to concentrate on the computer monitor while her mother leaned over her shoulder.

"It's hot out and she'll drink too much water," her mother said. "She'll forget to take her pills. She'll eat the wrong things. You know how kids are."

"She'll be fine, Mom," Janine had said through gritted teeth, although she couldn't help but share her mother's concerns. If Sophie came back from this trip sicker than when she went, the criticism from her parents would never end. Joe would be furious, as well. He had called last night, wanting to know if he could come over to see Sophie after she got home tonight, and Janine knew he was feeling what she did: the deep love and concern for the child they both treasured. Like Janine's mother, Joe had expressed strong disapproval over Sophie's going on this trip. One of many things Joe was angry with her about. Joe's anger was hard for Janine to ignore, because she knew it came from a place of caring, not only about Sophie, but about herself, as well. Even in the ugliest moments of their separation and divorce, she'd been aware that Joe still loved her.

At two-forty-five, Janine left the cottage and got into her car. She drove down the long gravel driveway, banked on both sides by boxwood as old as the estate itself, and looked toward the mansion as she passed it. Her parents would be inside, waiting anxiously for her to bring their granddaughter home. She hoped she'd have some time alone with Sophie before she had to share her with them and Joe.

Meadowlark Gardens was less than half a mile from the Ayr Creek estate, and the parking lot of the public gardens was as full as she'd ever seen it. As Janine turned into the lot from Beulah Road, people dressed in wedding regalia spilled out of one of the brick buildings, probably getting ready to pose for pictures. In the distance, Janine could see another wedding taking place in the gazebo by the pond. A beautiful day for a wedding, she thought, as she drove toward the southeastern corner of the lot, where she was to meet the returning Brownie troop, but her mind quickly slipped back to her daughter. Suddenly, all she could think about was scooping Sophie into her arms. She pressed her foot harder on the gas pedal, cruising far too fast through the lot, and parked her car near the corner.

Although Janine was early, one other mother was already there, leaning against a station wagon, reading a paperback. Janine knew the woman, whose name was Suzanne, vaguely. She was pretty, a bit older than most mothers of children Sophie's age, and it was hard to tell if her chin-length hair was a pale blond or actually gray. Janine smiled as she walked toward her.

"They certainly had great weather, didn't they?" Suzanne asked, shading her eyes from the sun.

"They did." Janine joined her in leaning against the car. "I'm glad it wasn't too humid."

Suzanne tossed her paperback through the open window of her car. "Oh, that wouldn't have bothered them," she said with a wave of her hand. "Kids don't care whether it's humid or not."

Sophie would have cared, Janine thought, but she kept the words to herself. She tried unsuccessfully to remember what Suzanne's daughter looked like. In truth, she'd paid little attention to the other girls in Sophie's troop. It was so rare that Sophie could take part in any of their activities that Janine had had no opportunity to get to know any of them or their mothers. She looked at Suzanne. "Has your daughter..." she began. "I'm sorry, I don't remember her name."

"Emily."

"Has Emily been on one of these camp-outs before?" Janine asked.

"Yes, she has," Suzanne said. "But none this far away. And I know this is a real first for Sophie, isn't it?"

"Yes." She felt somehow touched that Suzanne knew Sophie's name. But, then, the other mothers probably talked about her.

"It's wonderful she could go," Suzanne said. "I guess she's feeling better, huh?"

"Much better," Janine admitted. So much better it was scary.

"I heard she's receiving some sort of experimental treatment."

"Yes." Janine nodded, then hesitated a moment before adding, "She's in a study of an alternative medicine. She's only been in the study a couple of months, but she's had some dramatic improvement. I'm just praying it will last." It was hard for Janine to give words to Sophie's improvement, to actually hear herself say those words out loud. She lived in terror that it might not last. Since being in the study, Sophie had not only remained out of the hospital, but had finally learned to ride a bike, had eaten almost anything she wanted, and had even attended the last of week of school. For most of the year, she'd been tutored at home or in the hospital, and last year had been equally as bad. Most indicative of Sophie's improvement, though, was the fact that she no longer needed to spend every night attached to her dialysis machine. For the last couple of weeks, she'd required treatments only two nights a week. That had given her the freedom to do something she'd never before been able to do: spend the night away from home with her friends.

Sophie's astonishing improvement seemed miraculous, although Dr. Schaefer, the researcher behind the study, had warned Janine that her daughter still had a long road ahead of her. She would need to receive twice-weekly intravenous infusions of Herbalina, the name he had given his herbal remedy to make it more appealing to the pediatric population of the study, for at least another year. Despite the ground Sophie had gained, her own nephrologist, the doctor she'd been seeing for the past three years, scoffed at the study, as did every other specialist with whom Janine had spoken. They'd pleaded with Janine to enroll Sophie in a different, more conventional study of yet another experimental drug, but Sophie had already participated in several of those studies, and Janine could no longer bear to see her daughter suffer the side effects of the toxic drugs they gave her. With Herbalina, Sophie had only gotten better. No rashes. No cramps. No bloating. No sleepiness.

The positive results were merely a temporary reduction in symptoms, Sophie's regular doctor and his colleagues had argued. Beneath the surface, the disease still raged. They claimed Schaefer offered false hope to the hopeless, but stopped just short of calling the small, wiry, soft-spoken doctor a charlatan. Janine could easily see the situation from their perspective. After all, the medical profession had been grappling with Sophie's form of kidney disease for decades, searching for a way to turn the tide of its destruction. Then along comes some alternative medicine doctor, with his combination of tree bark and herbs, and he thinks he can do what no one else has been able to do: cure the incurable. Sophie's regular doctor said Schaefer's treatment was nothing more than a Band-Aid, and it terrified Janine that he might be right. She was just getting her daughter back. She could not bear to lose her again.

"Where are the other parents?" Janine looked behind her toward the parking lot entrance. It was nearly three.

"Oh, I think it's just you and me. I'm going to drive a couple of the girls home. Gloria and Alison will take the rest, but we figured you'd probably be anxious to be with Sophie, so we didn't think to ask if you wanted one of us to give her a ride."

"You're right," she said. "I can't wait to see how she made out."

"She looked so excited when she got into the van Friday evening," Suzanne said.

"She was." Janine was glad she was wearing sunglasses, because her eyes suddenly burned with tears. *Her baby girl.* How rare it was to have seen such unfettered joy in Sophie's face rather than the usual lines of pain and fear. The sort of fear no child should have to endure.

"She's so cute," Suzanne said. "Where'd she get that red hair?"

"It's a combination of mine and her dad's, I guess," she said, touching her hand to her own strawberry-blond hair. Joe's hair was dark, his eyes blue, like Sophie's.

"It's her kidneys that are the problem, right?" Suzanne probed.

"Yes." Janine didn't mind the questions. The only time she was bothered by them was when they were asked in front of her daughter, as though Sophie were deaf and blind as well as very, very ill.

"Would a transplant help?"

"She already has one of mine." Janine smiled ruefully. "Her body rejected it." Joe had offered one of his, as well, but he was not a good match. And now, Sophie was beyond being helped by a transplant.

"Oh, I'm so sorry," Suzanne said kindly. "She seems to handle everything very well, though. I was so surprised when I met her, because she's so tiny. I thought she was about six. But then this eight-year-old voice comes out of her, with a ten-year-old vocabulary. It's such a surprise."

Janine smiled. "Kids with kidney disease tend to be small."

"What a lot you must have been through with her," Suzanne said. "And to think of how much I worry when Emily has the sniffles. I really admire you."

Janine didn't feel admirable. She was coping the only way a desperate mother could—searching for solutions, doing all she could to make Sophie's time on earth as happy and carefree as possible…and crying only when she was alone at night.

"Emily told me you're a helicopter pilot," Suzanne said.

"Oh." Janine was surprised. "I was, a long time ago. Before Sophie got sick." She had learned to fly a helicopter in the army and had flown for an aircraft leasing company after getting out of the reserves. Was Sophie telling people she still flew? Maybe it embarrassed her that Janine had turned from an adventurous pilot into a stay-at-home mom. But with a chronically ill child, she could imagine no other course of action.

"Emily has a secret hope that, when the girls in the troop get a little older, you might give them flying lessons."

She had thought of that herself, in those rare, optimistic moments when she could picture Sophie reaching her teenage years. "Maybe one day," she said. "That would be fun." She turned to look at the parking lot entrance again.

"You must worry about Sophie when she's away," Suzanne said suddenly, and Janine knew that the worry was evident in her eyes, or maybe in the way she was knotting and unknotting her hands.

"Well," she said, "this is new to me. Sophie's never been away from home without me or her father by her side." She'd also never been so far from emergency care, which was why Joe had said the trip was out of the question. But Sophie had begged to go. There was so little she ever asked for, and so little Janine could do for her. She said yes, after getting permission from Dr. Schaefer, who even called Joe to assure him that Sophie would be fine, as long as she watched her fluid intake and was home for dialysis on Sunday night and back at Schaefer's office for Herbalina on Monday. Joe, who lost his temper too easily and too often, had hung up on him.

Like Sophie's regular doctors, Joe thought Schaefer's study was a sham, and he had argued with Janine about making Sophie into a guinea pig. Although Janine and Joe had been divorced since Sophie was five, they usually were in agreement on how to handle their daughter's treatment. This study had driven a wedge between them and was unraveling the already frayed edges of Janine's relationship with her parents, as well. They hadn't wanted Sophie to take part in such an unconventional treatment, either. It wasn't like Janine to stand up to any disapproval from Joe or her parents, at least not in recent years. But Sophie was terminally ill. Even dialysis was failing her, and she'd been given mere months to live. There was little to lose.

"I don't think you need to worry," Suzanne said. "Gloria seems like a very caring and responsible leader."

"I wonder about Alison, though," Janine said. Alison was the younger of the two troop leaders. Only twenty-five and single, Alison had no children of her own. She'd been a volunteer leader in Sophie's troop for the past two years, and all the girls loved her. She was fun-loving, comical and had a spirit of adventure that the girls adored and the parents feared. Alison had made a few errors in judgment over the past couple of years. Very minor. Nothing life-threatening. But then, she hadn't had a child as frail and needy as Sophie under her care before.

"Oh, I think Alison's super," Suzanne said. "How many young women do you know who are childless themselves but still volunteer to work with kids? And the girls love her. She's a good role model for them."

Janine felt mildly chastened and wished she had thought before she'd spoken.

She was about to apologize, when she spotted a white van pulling into the parking lot.

"Is that them?" she asked.

"Looks like it," Suzanne said.

The van was heading toward them, and Janine waved.

Stepping away from Suzanne's station wagon, she wished she could make out the faces behind the van's tinted windows. *Patience*, she told herself. If she charged the van, or God forbid, started crying when she saw Sophie, she would only embarrass her.

The van came to a stop next to the station wagon, and Gloria stepped out of the driver's side, giving them a quick wave as she walked around the front of the car to slide open the side door. Five grimy, tired little Brownies began tumbling out. Suzanne stepped forward to give her daughter, Emily, a hug, and Janine looked past them, watching for a sixth girl to emerge. She walked toward the van, trying to see through the dark windows, but there appeared to be no movement inside.

"Janine," Gloria said. "How come you're still here?"

"I'm waiting for Sophie," Janine said, confused. "Isn't she with you?"

"Didn't Alison get here yet?" Gloria asked.

Janine frowned. Alison? Gloria had let Sophie ride with *Alison*?

"No." She tried to keep her voice calm. "I've been here since ten of. I haven't seen her."

"That's strange," Gloria said, reaching into the van to pull out one of the girls' knapsacks. "Sophie and Holly wanted to ride with Alison," she said, "and they had a good ten-minutes' head start on us."

Suzanne must have caught Janine's look of panic. "Maybe Alison drove Sophie straight home?" she suggested.

"She knew she was supposed to come here first," Gloria said, reaching for another knapsack.

"But maybe Sophie or Holly persuaded her to take them straight home," Suzanne said.

Gloria shook her head. "She knew Janine would be waiting here for Sophie."

Janine turned her head between the women as if following a Ping-Pong game. "I'll call home," she said, heading for her car. "I'll see if they showed up there."

Her hands shook as she opened her car door and reached inside for her cell phone. She dialed the number for the mansion, and her mother answered.

"I'm at Meadowlark Gardens, Mom, waiting for Sophie to get back, and I just wanted to check to see if her troop leader might have dropped her off there."

"I haven't seen her," her mother said. "Could she be in the cottage?"

"Possibly." Although if Sophie had been dropped off at the cottage and found that Janine wasn't there, she probably would have walked up the driveway to the mansion. "Could you check, please?"

Janine heard some movement of the phone. "Frank?" her mother called, her voice obviously directed away from the receiver. Janine pictured her father sitting in the leather recliner in the Ayr Creek library, his favorite perch, either reading or working on his laptop. "Go over to the cottage and see if Sophie's inside. She might have been dropped off there."

"Thanks, Mom," Janine said, once her mother was back on the phone.

"Why would they bring her home if they were supposed to meet you at Meadowlark Gardens?"

Janine tensed. *Here we go,* she thought. "There might have been a misunderstanding," she said.

"Well, if they could get something as simple as that wrong, what else could they get wrong?"

"Mom, please."

"She's only eight years old, and a very fragile little girl," her mother said. "I wouldn't have sent you off to camp when you were eight, and you were healthy as a horse."

It was true that her parents had never sent her to camp. She'd had to create her own adventures, and create them she did.

"I think this was a terrific experience for Sophie," Janine said, although she'd argued about this with her mother and father and Joe so much over the past few weeks that she knew anything she said now was pointless.

Janine heard her father's voice in the background, but she couldn't make out what he was saying.

"She's not there," her mother said into the phone.

"All right. Please call me on my cell phone if she shows up there instead of here, okay?"

"How late is she?"

"Not really late at all, Mom. I was just checking in case they took her home. I've got to go now." She hung up and walked back to the van, where Gloria and Suzanne were talking. Emily leaned tiredly against her mother, and Janine felt a pang of envy witnessing the simple, uncomplicated warmth between them. She wanted Sophie here with her, *now.*

Gloria and Suzanne were looking toward the entrance to the parking lot. Janine followed their gaze, but there were few cars pulling into the lot this late in the day.

"What color is Alison's car?" she asked.

"Blue Honda," Gloria said. "Sophie's not at home?"

Janine shook her head.

"They probably took a bathroom break," Suzanne suggested.

"We had to take three of them," Emily groaned. "Tiffany had to pee twice."

"Shh," said her mother.

Janine turned to look toward the far corner of the parking lot, searching for a blue Honda. Maybe Alison had her southeast and northeast confused, but this was the same spot from which the troop had taken off. Besides, she surely would have noticed the van by now.

"I'm sure they'll be here any minute." Gloria touched her arm. "They probably got stuck in a traffic jam."

"You would have gotten stuck in it, too, then," Janine said. "Does Alison have a cell phone with her?" Her voice sounded remarkably calm despite the fact that she was furious with Gloria for allowing Sophie to ride with the young troop leader.

"*Yes*, she does." Gloria sounded relieved at that realization. "I have her number in the van. Hold on." She walked quickly toward her van, stopping only a second to talk to her daughter.

"Sophie's just fine," Suzanne said in a reassuring voice.

Janine tried to nod, but her neck felt as if it were made of wood.

Diane Chamberlain

GETS TO THE **HEART** OF THE STORY

THE LOST DAUGHTER

By telling the truth she'll lose her daughter. By living a lie, she'll lose herself.

THE BAY AT MIDNIGHT

All children make mistakes. But some mistakes are deadly.

BEFORE THE STORM

Your little boy has been accused of murder. Would you stop at nothing to protect him?

SECRETS SHE LEFT BEHIND

She almost killed her brother. Her punishment is just beginning.

Diane Chamberlain

GETS TO THE HEART OF THE STORY

BREAKING THE SILENCE
Your husband commits suicide.
Your daughter won't speak.
Do you want to know the truth?

THE LIES WE TOLD
How far would you go to
protect your sister?

THE MIDWIFE'S CONFESSION
Only you know a terrible truth.
Can you keep a secret?

THE SHADOW WIFE
You're pregnant by your best
friend's husband. Can you
live with the guilt?

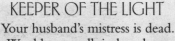

Diane Chamberlain

GETS TO THE HEART OF THE STORY

KEEPER OF THE LIGHT
Your husband's mistress is dead.
Would you walk in her shoes
to get him back?

THE GOOD FATHER
Would you abandon your little
daughter to give her a better life?

KISS RIVER
What would you risk to hold
your child again?

HER MOTHER'S SHADOW
Two lives rest on Lacey's choices.
Two lives only she can save.

M_CHAMB_LIST4c

*'I don't know how to tell
you what I did...'*

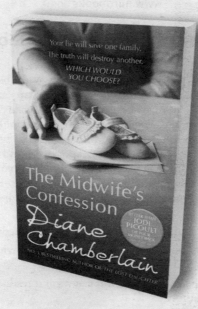

One tragic moment
Four lives changed forever
Only you know
Can you keep a secret?

'Essential reading for Jodi Picoult fans'
—*Daily Mail*